D1330806

RECKLESS SLEEP

RECKLESS
SLEEP

Roger Levy

VICTOR GOLLANCZ
LONDON

The right of Roger Levy to be identified as the author
of this work has been asserted by him in accordance with
the Copyright, Designs and Patents Act 1988.

First published in Great Britain in 2000 by
Victor Gollancz
An imprint of Orion Books Ltd
Orion House, 5 Upper St Martin's Lane,
London WC2H 9EA

To receive information on the Millennium list, e-mail us at:
smy@orionbooks.co.uk

A CIP catalogue record for this book
is available from the British Library

Typeset at The Spartan Press Ltd,
Lymington, Hants

Printed in Great Britain by
Clays Ltd, St Ives plc

In bright memory of my parents
And for Tina, and Alex and Georgia.

Acknowledgements

Above all the Azzurri writers – Simon Campbell, Susan Clegg, Nick Doughty, Beverly Johnson, Steve Mullins, Sam Patterson, Joanna Pocock, Mike Roberts, David Simons, Mike Stewart, Elise Valmorbida. Also Tina, without whom it would never have been finished, Simon Wooden, Antony Harwood and Simon Spanton. Thanks.

PROLOGUE

The two men stood outside for two minutes buzzing the door alarm, their fat guns raised and ready, only slowly relaxing as the time passed. After that they packed the guns away.

It took them the next hour to break in. They could have done it in a fingerclick, but they took an hour.

They removed the security mechanism like archaeologists, stroking away the steel and qualcrete casing with cutters barely smouldering, then they dissected it in the corridor without a glance through the hard-edged access hole. They reassembled the mechanism carefully and dropped it into a clear plastic bag, sealed the bag and slid it into a soft black nylon holdall.

'Locked from inside,' the older man noted finally, flicking a long lick of blond hair from his eyes. 'No tampering.' He took a small camera from the holdall and activated it. An amber light quivered above the bull's-eye lens. In his other hand he was working a wad of red jelly.

His partner rolled a sleeve up to his shoulder. 'Yeah. What a surprise.' On his biceps was a faded blue tattoo of a naked fox-headed woman straddling a man with a wolf's head. He stretched his arm through the door. The tattoo was nearly gone before his fingers reached the other side. He felt around, the fox-woman bucking as his biceps worked. After a moment he grunted and leaned against the door. The door swung heavily in.

'Wait, Maxie,' said the man with the camera. He stood in the doorway and panned the camera evenly around the room, not pausing at the corpse in the chair in the centre of the room, then he slapped the sticky jelly high on the wall by the door. The jelly sagged fractionally and he kneaded it some more with the heel of his hand to stiffen it before easing

1

the camera into place. He thumbed the focus button and stepped back. The lens turned several times then settled. The amber light blinked off.

'You smell something?' Maxie said, walking past the corpse to the window.

'Nothing. You always say that. You know I got no sense of smell.'

Maxie stared squinting for a moment at the setting, a blinding noon view over a long beach of shining white sand, and in the distance a dark rocky outcrop squatting in the deep blue sea, then he touched the command sensor on the sill. He rested his forehead against the soft clear glass and glanced down. Five floors below him the rucked concrete was barely visible, almost lost in swirling grey dust. He opaqued the window quickly with a shudder and turned around.

'Shit, Bly, this makes me nervous,' he said.

His companion was following the wall left of the door. Maxie started right of it. His wall led him into a small windowless kitchen. He gagged at the smell in there and pulled a plastic respirator from his hip pocket, slapping it over his nose and gulping air. He looked at the ExAir vent. It was thick with grease and dirt. It had never been removed. It looked like it had never been cleaned. He counted seven knives and six forks and a few chipped plates beached in a bowl of congealed, cloudy fat, then he turned and opened the refrigerator. The freezer compartment was stuffed with ice trays. Maxie closed it, checked the cupboards and finally confronted the trash bin.

The trash hadn't been cleared for days. He rolled on a pair of surgical gloves and began to sift through it.

He met Bly half an hour later at the window. Bly had set it to LoGlo, and the soft yellow luminescence honeyed his cheeks.

'Anything?' asked Bly.

Maxie nodded. 'Yeah. He liked chocolate Weeties, and I guess he liked them on the rocks. But he must have ate them with a fork, 'cause there's no milk and there ain't a single spoon in the kitchen. You?'

'Zip. No way out of the bathroom. Never cleaned his toilet. Filthy bastard. Didn't even have a toothbrush in there.' He made a face. 'People's lives, Maxie. Shit.'

They both looked at the dead man sprawled in the chair. His head was tipped so far back that his Adam's apple was pushed out like a knuckle and his open eyes stared at the cracks in the dusty plaster ceiling.

Maxie reached out and touched his left eyelid, closing it into a wink.

Water dribbled from the dead lips at the faint touch, and Maxie drew back with a start. The corpse was like a bucket filled to the brim.

Bly said, 'Well, he observed inner cleanliness.'

Maxie glanced towards the window. 'Very funny. Shit, Bly, I don't like this. It gives me the shivers.'

'It's a body,' Bly said. 'It's just a forensic take-out. Not the first and, the way things are going, not the last. Maybe not even the weirdest. It's a body. Lighten up.'

'I don't mean the fucking body, I mean the fucking height. Five floors. It ain't natural. What if there's a tremor?'

'Then you're nearer to heaven than to hell, Maxie. And this block's quake-stable, and there's nothing forecast here today. So let's get on with it, huh?'

Bly took the body's temperature and compared it to the room's ambient temperature, and spent a minute with an addpad. Then Maxie found the heating console.

'Hey, Bly. Thermostat was automatically reset two hours ago. It was seven degrees cooler till then. What difference does that make?'

Bly shrugged. He pocketed the addpad. 'Don't bother. I'll make a note. All this water screws everything anyway. It sure isn't spit. Christ knows what temperature it started out at.'

'So how the fuck do we get a time of death, Bly?' said Maxie.

Bly stood back and surveyed the body. Then he walked slowly around it. The clothes were dry, apart from a fresh damp streak down the man's maroon shirt where the water had overflowed at their touch.

'I remember reading these murder stories,' said Bly. He knelt down by the corpse's feet and pressed his palms to the pale green carpet beneath the chair. It was bone dry. 'Locked room mysteries, they called them,' he said.

Maxie grunted.

Bly stood up. 'The pacifists think at first it's suicide or an accident. Murder seems impossible.' He walked once more around the body. 'I had an idea for one, a while back.'

Maxie grunted again. Bly didn't say anything, so Maxie said, 'Yeah?'

'Picture it, Maxie. Man in an empty room, dead of a heart attack. Slumped against a door which is bolted from the inside, like he'd tried to get out but not quite made it. To get in, to get at the body, they have to bust down the door, then shove the body back out of the way.'

3

Maxie rubbed his chin, his fingers rasping against the stubble.

'I wish you wouldn't do that,' said Bly. 'You know I hate that. Are you interested or not?'

'Any windows in the room? Ventilator shafts and shit?'

'Uh-uh. Forgot that. Like here, you can forget beta-access.'

The tattooed man sighed. 'This one – these ones – aren't like your story, though. Are they?'

'How do you mean?'

'Well, this one, for instance.' Maxie made a gesture at the corpse. 'Sitting in his chair in the middle of his room, drowned. Hardly an attempt to make it look like suicide. So how was it done?'

'Jesus! I don't know.'

'Hosepipe. That'd do it. Feed it down his throat, turn the tap. Glug glug.'

'You think so, Maxie?' The blond man prodded the corpse's chest. More water washed from its mouth. He drew his finger across the cold chin and wiped it over Maxie's lips before Maxie could recoil.

Maxie spat. 'Shit. Now *that's* good.' He spat again and rubbed his sleeve across his mouth. He looked at the corpse with respect. 'Seawater.'

'Right. Whoever killed this one's a clever bastard. "I killed him," he's saying. "But how did I do it?" Just like these detective books, see. The writer's fucking with the reader, like the murderer's fucking with the detective.'

'Okay, Bly, I get it. Stop fucking with me. So how? In your story.'

'I've got it,' Bly said suddenly. 'Rough time of death, at least.' He pointed a finger across the room. 'The chair was originally over there – see the space? Assume it was moved out here just prior to death, though Christ knows why. We weigh wetboy and the chair, then calculate TOD from crush damage to the carpet and fibre recovery time. Good, huh?'

Maxie cracked his knuckles. 'Bly . . .'

Bly held up a hand to Maxie, listening. His eyes unfocussed for a moment and he spoke under his breath for a while, then nodded. He said to Maxie, 'There's supposed to be a book somewhere, we're to take it back. Some sort of journal, diary maybe. Handwritten. You seen anything?'

Maxie shook his head.

'Concealed, perhaps. If it's here we'll find it. And when we're done here we're to drop wetboy off for a real swim.'

Maxie wasn't listening. 'Blowpipe dart puffed through the keyhole,' he said triumphantly.

Bly gave him a blank look.

'Your dead guy in the locked room. Poisoned dart.'

'Ah. Very good, Maxie. But no keyhole.'

Maxie glanced away at the body. 'Okay, I give up,' he said sourly. Slumped in the chair, the wide-eyed dead man seemed to have tossed his head back in a gesture of exasperation. Maxie muttered, 'I know how you feel, pal.'

Bly grinned at him. 'Tiny holes drilled through the door and the frame, from the outside. Then wires pushed through and connected to both parts of the bolt, and outside to a portable power source. The guy inside wasn't trying to get out at all, see. Poor pitiful fuck thought he was locking himself inside. Slides the bolt home, makes the circuit and, yippety-zip, he's in California.'

Maxie thought about it. 'Okay, powerhead. So who sent this guy to California? King fucking Neptune?'

ONE

Jon didn't much like working out of London, and he definitely didn't like flying. He could have done without the display on the screen that had just told him, 'Velocity two hundred and ten kph, altitude fifteen hundred and seven metres. Approaching Maidenhead.' The copter pilot kept turning round and nodding vigorously, which was just about as much communication as the guy could manage with the opaque black headset on and the engine roar deafening them both. Even that was more than Jon needed right now.

While the pilot had been doing his preflight checks Jon had spent half a minute keying in the message that he'd failed to send every morning for three years. All last night he'd reworded it in his head, thinking things had changed now. And there they were as usual, those same two lines of inert text.

He left the message at the top of the screen, still unsent, as the machine tilted woozily into the air, and then he spent the first ten minutes of the flight checking the morning's recons of the target.

If it hadn't spread during the intervening hours, it was a kilometre end to end, pretty much a straight-line rupture. Fifteen metres wide, max. It wasn't a spectacular rift, just one of the minor tectonic stress fractures Seismic was recording every few months now. And there had been ten minutes' warning, too, and they'd got the location to within three square kilometres. It was getting better all the time. But then Seismic was getting the practice.

The pilot jerked round and nodded at him again. Jon shut the recon display down and stared at the words some more, then, without thinking, he made the mistake of glancing out of the window.

He took it in like a snapshot. The sky was unusually clear, which was probably the source of the pilot's enthusiasm. The jumble of London was behind them and distantly picked out beneath the copter were the calm fields of the countryside.

Then he squeezed his eyes closed and pulled his head away. Against the tight blackness of his eyelids the sunlit river shone like a seam of fading chrome.

He opened his eyes and fixed on the lines of words again. His finger hovered over the send button, but instead he screened up the copter's ventral camera display. He nined the colours and nilled the shadows so that the landscape they were crossing became a comfortably garish two-dimensional cartoon.

The road patterns stood out in ash-grey, and Jon studied them with vague interest. They looked like they had meant something once and were now indecipherable. Motorways arrowed over the land like the skewed axes of forgotten charts. Minor roads were curves plotted between clumps of houses, and irregularly slashed across the whole thing were the dark impatient scores of geo-rifts. It was as if the calculations had been flawed and the printout jabbed and ripped in irritation.

After a while the outskirts of Maidenhead slowly took over the screen and the details began to swell as the copter started its descent. Jon checked his harness, running his fingers over the rough canvas webbing. Without looking round, the pilot made a sharp movement with his hand, up and down. There was a swift swelling blur of streets on the screen, then quakeside wreckage loomed close and stabilised. A figurine carved of rusty red stone abruptly centred in the camera's field. It seemed inexplicable, a dragon with serpentine neck and coiled tail. Jon squinted at it, assuming the screen had gone to some standby display, then he sprang the harness and felt a blast of warm wind as the door slid wide for him. He looked down at the wavering ground and reached quickly back to the screen. He punched his thumb on to a key and over the dragon the screen winked 'Sending' twice in pale green, and then in white, 'Message sent.'

Jon lowered his toolbag down before dropping the final metre to the ground. He crouched low in the debris, keeping his head down until the copter's airwash had receded. Then he stood up, catching something with the toe of his boot. He glanced down and saw the red dragon there. It was the size of his fist, just the rooftop ornament of some quaked house. He stepped over it.

This was the edge of the town. It was semi-urban, less densely built than

London. Fewer buildings had been quake-proofed here, so there was a lot of structural damage. The cleaned-up recon display had shown none of that.

Jon looked across the rift, searching for Dekk and not yet finding him. On the far side a road approaching the rift through the uneven debris of buildings ended abruptly, its thin veneer of tarmac slumped over the rim. Beneath it was a quake-resistant ten-metre sheet of visgel. At least they had that. The quake had stretched the visgel way beyond its specifications and then snapped it like bubblegum, and the exposed layer was gradually tonguing out. Severed electricity cables curled down, and water and sewage streamed from cracked piping like drool. Beneath this, mud and weeping rock descended maybe twenty metres. Jon could have been examining a cross-section of the world. There wasn't too much more to see, peering down through the dust of whatever had plunged into the fault and the vapour of heat rising up from it.

Jon looked around at the wreckage. He lifted up his sack and then dropped it again. This was the widest stretch of the fault. Lengthwise, it looked like it extended further than on the recon chart. He searched the far side for Dekk again, still not seeing him.

He'd need more cable. He had enough in the sack to sew across ten or twelve times, which looked like taking him no more than two thirds of the way along the rift. And that was before he started cross-lacing. Dekk's crab wouldn't be any help across it, the gap was too great for its arms to span. So Jon would lace and web it, then they could leave it to the Cleanup and Carpet team to lay down expansion foam and hardcore to level it off for rebuild. But he'd need more cable first.

'That's a three,' said Dekk's voice flatly in Jon's ear, as if Dekk were reading his mind. He still couldn't see him. 'That ain't no way a two. That's a twenty-em jump, and my rig won't stretch to that.' Dekk's nasal whine made the earpiece buzz. 'An' I'm registering a secondary hairline over here. I'll fix that, then it's over to you, web man.'

Jon caught a small movement across the rift. He brought the long glasses up to his eyes. That wasn't Dekk. Usually there was nothing so soon after a tremor. Dogs and cats were often better predictors than Seismic, and they fled well before the ground cracked, or else they froze for days afterwards. So nothing should have been moving over there except for Dekk.

He shifted his gaze. Now he could see Dekk on the far side, standing well back from the edge. He was dwarfed by the bright yellow steel webbing-crab the spider team used for hairlines and smaller faults.

'Uh-uh,' Jon said into the throat mike, shaking his head. He pointed at what remained of a two-storey building forward from Dekk, right on the rim, Dekk's side. It was pre-quake, Edwardian probably, part of a long straight terrace. The terrace had been obliquely interrupted by the fault, and the house to its left had fallen in, while those to its right had collapsed. Much of the standing building had caved away into the fissure but the greater part was still just about standing in the way they sometimes did, like it was in a daze, punch-drunk or something. It was what happened when wave theory washed up against chaos theory. There were always tiny nodes of brief stability. The building over there was a textbook case. Rooms were left gaping and an exposed stubby rise of stairs led nowhere any more. At the point of the roof's gable a small red dragon gazed over the rift.

'Top room,' Jon said. 'Rear right corner. There's a cot.'

Dekk took up his mags and focussed them on the shattered building. He clambered up on the back of the crab to see better, then sat astride one of the front pincers and had it lift him high.

'I see it. An' it's empty.' He let the mags fall on their neck loop and swept his gaze left and right along the rupture. 'We'd better get right along now and stitch this trench. C&C'll be along soon.'

'You can't see from there, Dekk. I'm telling you. The kid's mother must have gone down if she wasn't evacked. There's a baby and it's alive. Get the baby, Dekk. Then we'll start sewing it up.'

He could see Dekk's head shake vigorously, his long red hair flinging out a thin haze of dust. 'I ain't goin' near it, Jon. It's unstable. I told you, there's a secondary hairline this side of the building and the whole thing could crack. I'm gonna have to knit that before I go anywhere near the goddamn edge. Look, I've checked the heats, there ain't nothin' but a handful of warm darters in there. Rats, for sure, and even they ain't happy. Nothin' else. No baby, Jon. The building's cold as a year in CrySis. So let's get with it, huh? If you'll just slide on down there and lay some tags at about fifteen em your side I'll stabilise the hairline this side. Then you can spread us a web and we can leave the hardcore and fomo and the rest to the C&C guys. Sound good?'

'You're sitting next to a hot rift, Dekk. You know you can't trust heat sensors there. If you don't get the kid, I'll do it. So decide.'

'There's nothin', man. Jon? Hey, you listenin' there?'

Jon caught the flashes of Dekk's mags catching the light. He raised his arms in an exaggerated shrug and rasped his fingernails over the bulb of his throat mike. He whispered, 'You're breaking up, Dekk. Must be the heat. I'm going across. Like you said, it could crack away any time.'

'Are you fuckin' crazy? I said there's a hairline! Jon? Oh, Jesus, you're a fuckin' nightmare.'

Jon laid an anchor charge from his toolbelt five metres in from the brink and watched the dust dance as the telescopic lance penetrated four metres into the ground and the slim carbon steel mast shot up to knee height. He waited for the secondary shock of the sublaterals to secure it, then slung a knot of plasteel cable round the masthead. Out of the corner of his eye he saw a shimmer of yellow as Dekk's crab commenced its slow jig along the far ground, nudging debris out of its path and knitting the hairline together in a series of dull explosive punches. It was all too slow.

He leaned back hard on the cable as he always did, though you could have slung an office block from that stanchion. Then he slid the long fat harpoon gun from its quiver over his shoulder and clicked the cable's free end on to a limpet charge and loaded the charge. He swung the gun up to his shoulder. He sighted briefly at the house and decided against it. Most likely the head would overpenetrate and bring the whole thing down. Holding his breath, he lowered the gun and squeezed the trigger.

The harpoon's kick nearly knocked him down, and its echo bounced down the rift. The chargehead dropped slightly faster than he'd anticipated, dragged by the trailing cable, whipping and hissing through the air. Ten metres below the building the charge slapped against rock. It imploded instantly and the tiny ratchet motor engaged, gathering up the loop of cable. The mast jetted out and the taut cable hummed as the sublaterals fired.

The yellow crab stopped for a moment, then carried on. Dekk's voice was a furious hiss in his ear. 'I don't give a shit about you, Jon, but if that charge had triggered the fracture I'd have lost my rig. You slipped the rift another half an em there. Just sit back and leave this to me, for Christ's sake. I'll be twenty minutes, okay? Then you can do what the fuck you want.'

Jon ignored Dekk. He surveyed the long fine line. Now he had a bridge.

He locked a slider over the rope, checked his charge belt and slotted the harpoon back where it lived.

'I know you can hear me, Jon, you bastard. Just turn around and this conversation isn't even history. I told you, there's no goddam kid.'

Jon double-checked the overhead slider and looked at the building. He tried to empty his mind of everything except that movement in the cot. The tiny hand waving. He felt the familiar taste of bile rising in his throat and swallowed it. Then he stepped over the edge.

The angle was too acute and he accelerated towards the far wall of the rift. He knew instantly he'd underestimated the width of it. The slider's friction grip wasn't intended for this degree of load. He was coming in too low and the rift was deep and hotter than he'd expected. Halfway over he swung his legs back and began to develop a movement ready to slam his feet into the wall, then realised he'd be too fast for that. He'd smash his ankles through his pelvis. He'd seen a spider do that before. The taut rope was keening above him as the slider played over it faster and faster. Jon threw himself sideways, hoping to slow himself at least a fraction but knowing it wouldn't be enough.

The brief low rumble gave him no warning. The line jerked violently and went abruptly dead as the rift shifted. Jon dropped into freefall. All the breath went from him. He started to remember something, a dream of pain, and the rift's jaws closed fractionally over him, taking a bite out of the light. There was a sudden lance of intense pain in his shoulder as he dropped, then the ratchet locked in and the line held again. The pain and the dream faded together. He flexed his shoulder, feeling only the old scar.

The line was slack now, and Jon's weight took the ratchet motor well beyond its automatic tension cutout. It wasn't going to regather itself.

He let himself swing gently. The breath that came back to him stung his throat. His body was pushing out sweat and the heat was evaporating it immediately. He was below the mast now, five metres out. The hairline must have slipped. The rock face in front of him was brown and rough, glistening faintly. Maybe he should have waited, like Dekk said. But his dreams were bad enough now without the death of some kid in a cot.

'Are you okay, Jon?'

'Yeah.'

'Well, fuck you.'

Jon reached for the overhead cable, observing how his hands shook. He began to pull himself towards the masthead, hand over hand up the rope's incline. The heat sucked the strength from his arms. He thought of the kid, scared up there and screaming, and moved on, not looking down. The bile rose again, and this time he couldn't swallow it.

With the last of the strength in his arms he swung himself forward on to the solid mast and hauled himself up to straddle it. He sat there shaking for long seconds, leaning against the hard rock until he could breathe and the ache in his arms and hands had receded, and then he started to climb. The exhaustion fell away as he rose towards the light, methodically locating handholds and footholds in the slippery rock. The visgel had by now extruded into a featureless overhang, but climbing it was easy. He punched his fists and kicked his feet into it to provide little adhesive grips that gently nudged him out again as he passed on, making his way easily up the slick orange expanse.

The electricity cables higher up he avoided. The power should have been shut off, but it wasn't always. He skirted the runnels of water and sewage, and then he had made it to the ruptured foundations of the house.

He came up on to the kitchen floor. Black and white ceramic floortiles had been shivered free and lay like a disrupted gamegrid. They shattered loudly under his boots. A blender hung from the wall by its cable. He glanced through the door and discounted the useless staircase. The kitchen ceiling was intact, so he shot up a piton and yanked the lath and plaster down around himself, then climbed up the wall and into the room beside the kid's room. He pushed the door open.

'Two things,' said Dekk. The feedback screamed through Jon's earpieces and Jon ripped them out. Dekk was standing there beside the cot. Through the window Jon saw the crab's pincer, not so bright any longer, raised and ready for Dekk to step back on to.

Dekk reached out an arm and flicked the mobile hanging low over the cot, setting tiny silver spaceships spinning, sprinkling fine plaster dust over the rumpled blankets.

'One. No fucking kid.'

Jon put out a hand to the mobile. One of the ships nestled in his hand, and he set it free again, twitching on its string and rocking all the others.

'Two. You ain't ever working with me again. This ain't the first time you've pulled something like this, and I've had it. You're fucking cracked, Jon.'

Jon turned away from Dekk and the cot and its slowly rotating cascade of spaceships to stare out over the rift. He blinked and ran the back of his hand over his eyes, wiping water and dust away. The movement over on the far rim took him by surprise. Usually by this time he was way down below, jinking from wall to wall, stitching and weaving, lost in the spider's process. Then C&C would be arriving as he was lifted clear, and as far as he was concerned the whole operation was sterile. Apart from glitches like today's.

Evacuated people were starting to gather on the far side, drawing up steadily and standing motionless along the rim, beginning to take in their local calamity. It would be fixed, of course. There would soon be another spider along to take over from Jon, then C&C would level the rift, and then they'd start rebuilding. But those people had lost everything.

Jon felt empty. He heard Dekk's voice as if from miles away, and the change in tone made him look around. He suddenly remembered he'd finally sent the message.

Dekk had a hand to his ear, listening. 'Yeah,' he said quietly. 'I got it.' He shrugged at Jon and shook his head. He said, 'So you quit already. Thanks for telling me ahead. Well, you're a fucking walker now, and this is off limits.'

'I was going to . . .'

He let the sentence trail away. Dekk was already halfway through the window, clambering on to the arm of his crab, and the lie would have been wasted.

TWO

A local tremor had rollercoastered part of Jon's direct route to Maze, and the demolition of a destabilised building forced him out into a wider loop. Wheeled vehicles were abandoned everywhere, shipwrecked on the quaked streets. Jon picked his way through them. They were useless now. They'd rust there until the emergency service autoids cleared them.

Maze was just within the quaked area, a sprawling two-storey building that had survived past tremors better than the collapsed architecture around it. Its outer wall was a long low façade of shadowblack glass, stark against the surrounding decay. The clear weather was still holding and Jon could read the vast words running along the dark glass from a hundred metres away. WANDERERS OF THE MAZE.

A copter in the red and yellow of Seismic swung above him, its speakers crackling. 'There has been a tremor two in this area. No further disturbance is anticipated today.' The announcement was casual and windblown. Tin cans and shreds of paper danced around Jon in the downdraught. The copter dropped and hung over him until he came to the building, then tipped sharply and clattered away. Jon thought briefly of Dekk and felt nothing.

A faint aura of ozone hugged the building. His filter buzzed clear, so he let the face mask fall to take stock of Maze. The tall letters glittered like dying coals against the obsidian background, dwarfing him. Jon walked slowly along the wall within the streetside corridor of scoured air. He reached the last word and stopped there.

Hunched beneath the M so that the apex of its arch met the letter's midpoint was an etched representation of the mediaeval dark wooden door that was the company icon. The door was thickly studded with hammered iron rivets. The plate of an ornate silver lock was set into the right of it, and at the left a pair of hinge plates snaked out to spread silver curlicues over the door's face, dividing and interweaving.

There was no handle to the door. There was nothing but the etched icon.

Jon put his palm to it. It was glass-smooth. Even the etching was an illusion. He guessed it was a holo.

He stood back and looked up. He couldn't see a scanner.

As he dropped his head the door blurred and faded. A slender arm in a blood-red velvet glove stretched towards him and hung there, cut off at the elbow by the darkness. On its outstretched palm was a pair of bLinkers.

The bLinkers were smaller than any Jon had seen before, even more compact than the military units he remembered from Dirangesept. They barely made an imprint on the glove. The eyeshades were hardly more substantial than corneal lenses, and in the concavities their jacketed neural exensors looked like minute Chinese thread noodles.

He lifted the shade loop with a finger. The exensors instantly twitched and began to probe the air. Jon suppressed his nausea with difficulty.

Leeches, he remembered. They don't enter *you. You* enter the machine. It had been bullshit then, and it was still bullshit.

Taking a sharp breath, he tipped his head back and slipped the shade loop over the bridge of his nose. He opened his eyes wide and pressed the shades gently down. The exensors were instantly crawling into the corners of his eyes, their spidery tendrils shedding cold sleeves of sterile jelly that slid down his cheeks like fat tears as he tilted his head forward. He felt the exensors fractionally displacing his eyeballs on their way to patch into the optic nerves. The brief retinal colour burst told him they'd made it.

He expected to wait but there was no delay, for which he was grateful. Immersion was rapid, the shuddering moment of scalp-to-sole paraesthesia that he loathed and a passing dizziness, the burning curling of his tongue and the echo of the soundless sound they used to call Mach Null.

And then something he didn't remember. An itching in his nostrils and a barrage of stinging scents; formaldehyde and mildew were there, and lemons and a sickening whiff of hydrogen sulphide.

Then nothing, and he almost reeled in the brief sensory vacuum. A pause, and inside his head was a deep, theatrical voice. 'Enter the Maze, chosen one.'

The door had reappeared with the lifting of the darkness of the shades,

15

and this time it was real, heavy and juddering open against hinges caked with rust.

Jon took a pace forward and stopped.

Maze was on show for him.

He was not in a building at all. He was standing in shade at the periphery of a bright forest glade. He glanced back. Amongst the trees a single piercing ray of light glinted on an old rusted black lamp-post. Jon shook his head.

He stepped out into the clearing. A breeze stirred the long emerald fronds of huge ferns above his head, and deep golden sunlight speckled the moss underfoot. He could feel the sun's warmth.

Visually, the bLinkers were astonishing. The colours were too bright, but that could be deliberate. The sound was fine; as he twisted his head, the birdsong overhead remained constant. Jon pinpointed the garish bird easily, yellow-winged and purple-breasted, with a crimson scimitar of a beak. It was perched on a flimsy branch that technically shouldn't have supported it, but that was probably a software override.

Jon knelt and picked up a round grey pebble, tossing it in his hand. There was a good tactile response, a fair sense of mass and density. It was too symmetrical, but it could almost have been real. He eyed the bird carefully, then flicked back his arm and lobbed the stone. The bird flapped lethargically away, its shriek of alarm matching the visual register precisely. The branch shivered to stillness.

It was the olfactory stim that impressed him most. The scent of grass was too prominent for the glade, and the hint of wood smoke on the breeze too spicy, but recognition was definite.

He took a pace forward and another smell, sickly and insistent, made him gag. He looked down and lifted his foot from a glistening coil of dung.

'Ho there, stranger!'

The reedy voice made him start, and he glanced around. He couldn't locate it.

'What would you be doing in the forest of the Lord of the Maze? Do you seek adventure, women, or . . .' The voice paused and sniggered. '. . . or trollshit beyond the dreams of avarice?'

Now Jon saw him. An elf maybe by his size, standing at the edge of shadow across the clearing. The glint of bright sunlight on a lichened rock at his side made him hard to spot.

The elf took a step forward and stood arms akimbo. There was contempt in his voice and the face matched with pinched lips, narrow eyes and pointed, lobeless ears. The bLinkered features were too perfect, though.

'I'm not a customer,' said Jon. 'Disconnect me. I have an appointment with Mr Kerz.'

He raised his hands to remove the bLinkers, but they weren't there. Just a numbness in his fingers as he felt for the shade loop. Part of the program. Around him he heard snickers of laughter, and a circle of dwarves, elves and men came out of the trees to surround him.

'I'm impressed. Now junk it, will you?'

The elf sneered. 'It should learn some manners. Does it expect the Maze Lord to grant it an audience with shit on its boot? Pibald, teach it some manners.'

A man detached himself from the circle, drawing a silver sword from a jewelled scabbard at his belt. The sword caught the light sharply. Without thought Jon reached down and found a sword hilt meeting his palm.

'Enough,' he said, lifting his hand clear. 'I'm not in the mood. Another time.'

The elf led a mocking chorus. 'He's not in the mood, not in the mood.'

Jon glanced at Pibald. 'Okay,' he said.

He drew his sword and weighed the balance of it in his hand. It was too end-weighted, not comfortable at all. He swung it experimentally, and for the first time the program showed its limits. The weapon handled as though the blade housed a loose bearing. It shifted unpredictably in his grasp.

Pibald was clearly used to compensating for the program. He advanced on Jon and touched swords. The sound was good, but there was a slight blur where the blades met, the software failing to rationalise the two viewpoints. The jar of Jon's sword in his hand was excessive for the light contact, and he nearly lost his grasp. Pibald came forward and feinted a lunge at Jon's chest, then made a fine cut to his face. Jon flicked his head back too late to prevent the blade nicking his cheek. It felt real and there was a convincing warm trickle of blood at the corner of his mouth. He was dimly conscious of the sound of cheering.

Pibald was standing back. Jon scythed his blade in a wide sweep, forcing

17

his opponent to parry two-handed. The shock sprang the hilt from Jon's grip, but before Pibald could take advantage Jon kicked his foot up into Pibald's groin. The real contact felt quite different from the bLinkered. Jon suddenly saw all the scene's faults, the grossness of the detail, the fuzziness of touch. Pibald collapsed, curled-up and groaning.

Leaving his sword on the grass, Jon walked up to the elf.

'Junk it now.'

The elf shook his head furiously. 'That was a contravention. No physical contact. We haven't finished yet.'

'I said junk it, you little shit.' Jon bent and scooped a thick wad of dung from his shoe. He reached forward and smeared it over the elf's face before he could recoil. The elf flinched and began to retch, and the scene flicked off.

Where the elf had stood beside a broad tree stump, a short stocky man with brushcut brown hair was vomiting on to an ash-grey desk console. His head was jolting and his cheeks bulged.

'Real, wasn't it?' said Jon. He read the name tag on the man's shirt. 'Now, Yani, would you like to tell Mr Kerz that Jon Sciler is here?'

Yani stared icily at Jon, slowly wiping the back of his hand across his mouth. The joints of his fingers were swollen, their tips white and bloodless. Red veins marbled his nose and cheeks. He looked to be at least in his fifties, old for a games player. Maybe that was where his bitterness came from. Maybe once he'd been something. Jon gave him a moment, then jerked Yani's head down towards the vomit puddling the console. Muscles bunched in his thick neck. He was fit and a lot stronger than Jon expected. Holding him still, Jon whispered into his ear, 'Just tell him, Yani, or I'll feed you your breakfast again.'

Yani jabbed a finger at the console. Bile began to seep into it, faintly revealing the key matrix.

'It's dead,' Yani muttered.

Jon heard another voice. 'Why don't you come straight up, Mr Sciler? Just follow my directions. Look to your left, there's an elevator . . .'

Leaving Yani, Jon realised that no one else had heard the voice. It was coming from the bLinkers. He raised his hands to remove them.

'I shouldn't do that just yet, Mr Sciler. It's a delicate unit, and it would be a pity to bother the neurosurgeons to go scrabbling about in there. Their touch isn't always as delicate as you'd imagine.'

*

Kerz leant forward on his desk, his chin resting on the tips of his long fingers, his head pivoting from side to side. Grey hair was receding from his temples and his ears were isolated, but a thin spur of tight silver curls tracked down his forehead towards the indented bridge of his nose, the sign of long bLinker use. He could have been almost any age. Jon guessed fifty.

'Jon Sciler,' he said. Kerz's tone was oddly precise. Listening to him was like hearing an antique voice chip. 'Sciler,' he repeated. 'You were a quake operative until recently, what they call a spider, yes?'

'I'd done it long enough. I wasn't fired. I quit.'

Kerz glanced at the sheet of paper in front of him. 'I see that. After nine months.'

'Most spiders last two months.'

'You misunderstand me, Mr Sciler. I was wondering why you lasted so long.' He waited a moment, then said, 'Your name is familiar. You were a Far Warrior?'

Jon nodded. It was obvious enough. Even now his movements retained the slightly exaggerated effect of bio-regenerated musculature.

'The poet,' Kerz was saying. 'Are you the poet?'

Jon stared blankly at him.

Kerz sat back and quoted, gazing at the pinlights of the high ceiling,

'We are the Far Warriors, we are the few
Who raised no hand in combat, shed no blood
And saw no field of battle, yet returned
Dehumanised and beaten, all but dead.
But dead inside, unburied and unmourned.'

He levelled his eyes again and Jon watched the black pips of his pupils slowly dilate. Kerz waited a few seconds more, then said, 'You wrote that?'

'A long time ago. I'm over it. Most of us are over it. I don't feel like that any more. You needn't worry.'

Kerz grinned wolfishly. His teeth were white and false, the acrylic gums a livid pink. 'I'm not worried, Mr Sciler. Quite the reverse. Would it surprise you to hear that a considerable number of Far Warriors seek what we offer – indeed, what we demand of you?'

'What do you demand?'

Kerz threw out his arms so that the sleeves of his jacket rode up his wrists, exposing long inches of pale hairless skin. 'We demand, Mr Sciler, that you devote yourselves to Maze, to the exclusion of all else. You who have been Far seem to find such a deal attractive.'

He was staring intently at Jon, but there was none of the usual prurient curiosity in those glittering green eyes. Jon struggled to comprehend it. It was the stare of a man observing a caged tiger – only it was not a visitor's but a keeper's gaze.

Jon held the stare, but Kerz didn't blink.

'Some are trying to find themselves,' he was saying. His tone was faintly derisory. Kerz was unconscious of it, though. His words had the smooth delivery of a practised speech.

'Many became Far Warriors for that reason. As I'm sure you know, Jon. In my experience, if they survived Dirangesept with their sanity, they often want to lose themselves again as quickly as possible. Maze provides that opportunity. I won't ask you how you have spent your time until you came to us, but I'm sure you understand me.'

He leaned back easily in his chair. 'What I like to say is, you may be able to help us, but we *know* we can help *you*.'

Jon stared at the screen. At the top, in orange letters that flickered like blown embers, was the notation, 'P.I. Preliminary Screening.'

A clipped sexless voice came from the vague direction of the screen. 'Answer each question aloud, as rapidly as you can. There are no correct or incorrect responses.'

The first question appeared on the screen, asking his name. When he answered, his voice sounded strange, as if the words were being sucked from his mouth. The next few questions required further personal details, which he gave. The fifth question made him blink at the screen.

My thoughts of death revolve mainly around:
         a) when it might happen
         b) the pain of it, if any
         c) what there might be after it

'C,' said Jon, after a moment. He felt slightly shaken.

The following few questions were innocuous again. Then came a question concerning whether he had ever played Maze, to which he answered yes, and then a string of connected questions.

When I enter Maze, I am:
      a) entirely myself
      b) a mixture of myself and my given character
      c) entirely my given character

In the role of my given character, I find myself:
      a) unrecognisable
      b) no different than I am normally
      c) more exciting than I am normally

When my given character dies:
      a) I am angry with myself
      b) I am disappointed at the end of the game
      c) I feel as if it is myself dying

Many of the questions seemed virtually the same, differing only in the phrasing.

There was a clock ticking somewhere at the edge of his consciousness, and it was beginning to tick faster and more loudly. He felt uneasy. The questions seemed to be coming more rapidly, and he had no time to think.

Interacting with different types of character, my behaviour is:
      a) always the same – my own
      b) generally in keeping with my given character
      c) always the same, but not that of my normal self

He answered 'C' to that, but somehow felt uncomfortable. He wanted to go back but the next question was already there and the clock was ticking urgently. His pulse was racing and he could feel the thump of his heart.

When I think of dying, I am:
      a) worried
      b) unconcerned
      c) excited

'No,' he whispered. He felt sweat run stinging into his eyes, and the question was gone. The room was echoing with his answer, but he couldn't remember what his answer had been. The clock's rattle was like gunfire, pounding in his brain, and the screen was flashing in black and yellow.

LAST QUESTION LAST QUESTION LAST QUESTION

The question burned on the screen. There was no choice of answer.

If I have a specific fear or phobia, it is . . .

THREE

After a week, the weather broke. He had known it would, really. Sometimes he still tried to convince himself otherwise, but there was no doubt, it was worse than before Dirangesept. Then, most days you could have walked the streets without a mask. Most days you could have looked up and seen the copters and microflites. Now there were six air-risk days in ten, and microflites were often just swift shadows in fog.

The streets were busy today despite an air-risk two alert. Seasonal volcanic dust with a few minor radioactive components. Visibility was a few metres and everyone wore filters to scurry between doorways whose irradiant safety-lights made them oblongs of crystal, the smog clawing and swirling around them like the mists in fortune-tellers' balls. Jon hated the streets when it was like this, but even with the job at Maze, if he got it, he wouldn't be able to afford a microflite.

He heard the siren of a tram behind him and waited until the high cables became visible, fluorescing in a vivid green that turned to scarlet as the tram approached. He started to trot, keeping abreast of the bow-wave of red light until a corroded post, a tram stop, congealed out of the fog. The neon light that should have marked it was shattered, exposed wires sparking and fizzing.

He was still panting when the tram rocked to a halt, its headlight punching a hole in the smog that only reached an arm's length from the dented and rusted prow.

There was no room aboard the tram and he let it pull away, the sweat on his forehead cooled by the mild stirring of scummy air as it passed.

He walked. This had been the market district. Now most of the shop windows were shuttered with steel and their doors padlocked or welded, and there were daily fights in the queues at butchers' shops and grocers' for ragged hanks of gristle and weed.

The shop he was searching for was next to a gun store whose scanners locked on to him as he glanced at the giant holo of the Koessler 9 mm SnapShot floating just beyond the doorway. The gun shrank to one—one and floated down to nuzzle anaesthetically against his hand. Jon moved past the store and the scanners lost interest. The gun snapped back up again.

This was it. INNER GAMES stood out above the lintel, the letters blood-red and quivering. Jon stood outside for a while before going in.

The door opened and closed with a synthesised tinkle of bells that didn't mask the suck and hiss of vent seals. The air inside was clean except for a subscent of machine oil. A pair of kids were playing with the teasers dangling from the walls. Jon read the holo title of the nearest, hanging letters that burned without heat. HELLSTAR K50. Jon had played one of the early Hellstars years ago, before Dirangesept. It had been a tedious slog through battalions of poorly realised insectoids. The kids were jerking their heads and hands rhythmically, wired to something called Disembowellers of Galvax.

Kei was there, at the rear of the shop. He nodded to Jon, then cleared his throat.

'Hey, you boys! You no buy, you go. Justa waste my watts, all'a time!'

One of the kids let his headset drop heavily. It ripped the teaser from the wall and cracked on the floor. He yelled back, 'You tried Warriors of Dirangesept yet, Kei?'

Kei's chair hummed forward over the floorgrid but the kid swayed back easily to avoid Kei. He turned and swaggered past Jon.

Jon jabbed out his foot, tripping the kid, and made as if trying clumsily to catch him falling.

'Watch it, sonny. Those brainsets make you dizzy.' He yanked the kid up by his upper arms, squeezing skinny neck and armpit flesh between his fingers and thumbs, briefly dead-arming him.

The kid shook his head and stumbled to the door. He stood there, not understanding why his hands wouldn't rise to buzz the palm plate. He had to wait for his friend to let him out. The other kid turned round in the swirl of fog. 'Haemorrhoid fucking android!'

The vent seal hissed them out.

'Call that a Japanese accent, Kei?' said Jon.

Kei shrugged. 'They can't tell the difference. You needn't have done that. They're my customers. I can handle them.'

Jon waved his arm around. 'This stuff sell?'

Kei grinned hugely. 'Like meat on the street. I even have to alarm the teasers or they'd walk. You should see the place after school, they're standing three deep at the sets. Hell knows where they get their plastic, though. These games ain't for dust.'

He swivelled and went back to the counter, sliding his hand out of sight behind it. The shopfront opaqued.

'This isn't social, Jon. You need a game like I need a bicycle.'

'Tell me what's around. I'm at Maze, but I'm blinded by the light.'

Kei's razored eyebrows lifted. 'No shit! After 'Sept, I'd have thought . . .'

'Hard times, Kei. Look at you. What you said before we came back.'

Kei raised a hand. 'We all said a lot of things. Okay. When did you last look at one of these toys?'

'Yesterday. At Maze. Before that was before the project. I'm out of date.'

Kei drifted towards Jon. 'You'll owe me one, Jon,' he said slowly. 'But you can clear it. I was going to come and see you anyway. I need a favour too.'

'Yeah?'

'There's a psychsupport student who needs help with her thesis. On Far Warriors. I was asked by the DVs if I knew anyone. I thought of you.'

Jon turned away. 'Well, you don't. I'm not getting involved with the Vets now. They've never done us any good.'

'They've never done you any good, Jon. You never let them.'

Jon flicked a teaser and watch it swing on the cable. 'Why don't you help her yourself, Kei?'

Kei tapped his chair. 'Unsound of body. One variable too many.'

'Sorry, Kei. I'll nurse my own wounds. I'm not being poked and published. It won't do any of us any good now. I'll just owe you.'

A needle of static spat from the chair's base as Kei shook his head. 'Agree to a meeting, Jon. Just that. It won't hurt. The decision's still yours. If you're not cooperative you're no use to her anyway. But no meeting, no help from me, Jon.'

Jon let out a breath. 'That important to you, huh?' The teaser had stilled. He flicked it again. 'Galaxy of Blood. Show me that.'

Nearvana had been Jon's choice. He arrived at the bar an hour late. He figured that if she'd heard of the place, she wouldn't show, and if she hadn't heard of it, an hour alone there would frighten her off. Sorry, Kei, she never made it.

Dark-haired, Kei had told him. High cheekbones. You might even find her attractive. Of course, you're old enough to be Chrye's father, he'd added. Chronologically.

The bar was in Holborn, at the top of the dead escalators in the closed tube station. The great steel shutters were never closed, though, and there was no aircon in Nearvana. On a clear afternoon it looked from a distance like the smouldering aftermath of a fire. On a bad one it looked like the mouth of hell. Nearvana was the place to go if you wanted to toughen up a lung disease or to get drunk and then mugged. Occasionally people at the bar were dragged down the dark silent escalators to the platforms. Nearvana was a place to go if you were a crowd, not a lone woman out of your depth.

Jon checked his nose filters and stood at the periphery of the bar, letting his eyes water and clear. Smoke marbled the air but Jon saw her immediately. She was sitting alone at a round matt black steel table against the grimy tiled wall, as he'd messaged her to for her own safety, and to scare her. It gave him a shock that she was there. And then, with his irritation at knowing he'd have to deal with Chrye now, he felt an instant of relief that nothing had happened to her.

He walked towards her, taking her in. She fitted Kei's description like a panther fitted the word cat. She was glancing around the bar casually, showing her ease. Her eyes were blue almonds and her black hair gleamed in the smoky gloom, seamlessly meeting the high neck of her jacket of dark cotton.

When he rasped the chair out to sit she took a moment to register his presence.

'Jon Sciler?' she said, then at his nod, 'I've always wondered what Nearvana was like.' Her voice was an effortless whisper, but it reached him through the cackle and grind of the bar as if only Jon was tuned to its frequency. Close up, those eyes shone like low blue halogens, and he read in them her pleasure at the opportunity to be here. At the edges of her smile he also read that she knew why he'd chosen the place.

At the bar, buying them both Pole water in fat aquamarine glasses, he observed her reflection in a mirror. Her head was tilted to one side, her elbow on the table, cheek cupped in a palm, and her lips were moving. He glanced across to where she was looking. Down the bar, a man was pouring a thick tongue of amber syrup from a dark bottle into a calibrated glass. Jon turned before the man could look up and catch his eye. He paid for the water and said quietly to the barman, 'That legal now?'

The barman blinked at Jon. 'Legal? Pardon me? Sure it's legal, legal as what he'd do to me if I told him it ain't. You want the 'fists in here, you're gonna have to pay 'em a lot more than I pay 'em to keep out. Now, can I get you anything to go with your water?'

'I'll get to the point, Mr Sciler,' she said, sipping from her glass. When she put it down the water maintained a slight tremor. Jon wasn't sure if it was the noise in the bar or her voice. 'I appreciate that you didn't want to see me. Kei told me. Did you know he's my great-uncle?'

Jon looked at the bangle on her wrist. Copper wires snaked round the silver core.

'He didn't tell me that.'

'I have a grant to research the effect of prolonged bLinker usage on the personality. It could be of use in the therapy of all kinds of psychological disorders. You could be of great help. You could—'

'—redeem yourself,' Jon interrupted. 'Couldn't you come up with something more original than that? I, a Far Warrior with all the guilt of the Dirangesept Project, could, by assisting you, heal myself.'

She flicked the glass with a finger. It hummed for a long moment. The ripple within built briefly, then returned to its previous simmer. 'Kei told me you were a cold bastard. Actually, you're probably wrong. I doubt anything could help you. Most Far Warriors are beyond help. Their problem – and yours, Mr Sciler – isn't unresolved guilt at all, in my opinion. Any more than it's a consequence of prolonged bLinker usage.'

She sat back and stared at him. Then she picked up the glass and sipped her water, as if this was a break between rounds and she was winning on points.

He said, 'Is that thing on?'

'What?'

He nodded at her wrist. 'I saw you use it. Are you recording this?'

She slowly smiled. 'I told you I'd never been here before. I wanted to take a few notes. What was that guy at the bar doing? I couldn't quite see.'

'He was taking flush.'

'Uh-huh?' She looked over. The man had a pack of cards and was shuffling them obsessively. His hands flickered like birdwings and his head was jerking to some inaudible beat.

'He's new to it,' said Jon. 'You get a couple of months before the arthritis hits you.'

Chrye held up her wrist. She fingered the bangle. A tiny LED flicked on. 'Now it's on.' She flicked it again. 'And now it's off. I wasn't recording us. You.'

She sipped her water again. Jon figured that was just about his round, but he felt adrift somehow.

'So what is my problem, then?' he said. 'In your opinion.'

'If you want to know, Mr Sciler, I think your problem is resentment of the blame thrust upon you by the world to which you returned from Dirangesept. If you're interested, I further think this resentment is justified. The politicians needed to blame someone, and once you were down the media were happy to keep on kicking. Still are. If there's no good news, bad news is fine. But that doesn't help you. Like I said, I can't help you.'

The card shuffler was cracking his knuckles now. He fanned the pack out on the bar and skimmed them together, endlessly repeating the operation. His foot was drumming against the stalk of the bar stool.

Chrye said, 'Actually, I believe you're also bound to have been affected by long-term use of bLinkers, but that will be a relatively minor thing.'

She looked at him and seemed to come to a decision. 'You're here under protest and I told Kei that was no good. It won't work. Thanks for the drink and have a good life, Mr Sciler.'

She slid her chair back and stood. She was taller than he'd expected. But he didn't know what he'd expected any more, except perhaps an argument. She looked at him directly and in the dark of Nearvana there was blue sky in her eyes. He couldn't work her out. Her dismissal of him was without rancour, just an acceptance of the situation.

'Sit down,' he said.

'Is there any point? Whatever you owe Kei, it's paid. Tell him I said you weren't suitable, if you like.'

'But I am, aren't I? You're still here.'

Jon wrapped his hand around his glass and looked down at it. The water was still. He realised that the bar was quiet and glanced around. The only sound was the whirr of shuffled cards. Everyone but the flush-head was trying not to stare at them. The barman was wiping down the bar with a dirty black and white chequered cloth in long, scything sweeps. In the calm, the flush-head's foot abruptly began drumming uncontrollably against his stool again. Jon could feel the vibration through the floor.

It struck him. 'How come they left you alone?' he said. Someone like you in Nearvana, he thought. It hit him fully what he'd done, asking her here, and that he'd just admitted to it.

She raised the hand without the wrist recorder. This bangle was gloss black and thick, set with stubby rubber spines. As she leaned towards him with it the whole bar seemed to draw in its breath. The flush-head's foot stopped beating.

Chrye touched the bangle gently to the rim of the glass of dead-still water in front of Jon. There was a faint click and the glass shattered. The fat cylinder of water held for an instant then collapsed on to the table and rolled into his lap. Jon heard laughter erupt and the bar eased back to life.

Chrye had slipped into the seat again. 'You only need to buzz the first one,' she said. 'The rest get the message. Now, can we stop fencing and discuss this like adults? What really bothers you?'

He took a breath and let it go. 'I'm damned if I'll do anything more in the name of Dirangesept. I've seen what people like you write. We screwed up because we're screwed up.'

Her expression hadn't changed. 'So screw us,' she said. 'I understand that. I haven't impressed you so far, Mr Sciler, so how about if I tell you a little about the Dirangesept Project as I see it? Then make your decision.'

Jon reached across the table and took a long swig of water from her glass. It tasted vaguely of metal. Even Pole water, he thought. Nothing was pure any more. Even the past was contaminated. He drank again and realised how dry his mouth had been. He put the glass down and nodded to her.

'Fine.' She stood again. 'How about we leave here first? Nearvana has fulfilled its purpose, don't you think?'

Following her out, Jon wondered whether she meant her purpose or his.

'Let's walk to the river,' she had suggested.

As they walked she talked to him, neutral words that he tried to respond to and failed. Images of Dirangesept slid across his mind, scouring the words away and silencing him.

'It's clear by the water, and the air's good again,' she said. 'They say we've got it like this for a few more days.'

He tried to look past what she said to him, to find clues to her soul, but he learned nothing except the depth of his suspicion.

Since returning from Dirangesept five years ago, after eighteen years in a ship spent frozen in CrySis, he'd hardly talked to anyone. Most Far Warriors, unable to find work or hold down jobs, had become reclusive on Earth. The Veterans provided some support, but they had never offered to help Jon. Not that he had sought their help. He felt they considered him part of their problem. And Starburn, of course. But he didn't resent it. Everyone needed a scapegoat, that was human nature. The Earth had the Far warriors, and the Vets, they had Jon now.

And Jon had Hickey Sill wanting to see him dead, and he didn't even have Dekk to talk to any more.

It suddenly hit him how isolated he was. He sneaked a glance at the woman beside him. She was talking and he realised he had no idea what she was saying. He wanted to speak to her, and at the same time he wanted to escape, to be alone in his room.

They walked on together beside the river. Eventually Chrye fell silent, and Jon wondered how to call a halt to this. The Thames rolled listlessly by, damped by a thick sheen of oil. It might have been a road except that it was so flawless.

'Dirangesept,' said Chrye at last. She kicked a pebble. Jon watched it skitter ahead, bouncing on the crumpled sidewalk before looping off over the water. For a moment it lay on the taut surface, then slowly, without a ripple, it was absorbed.

She started to talk as if to herself, reflectively, and Jon found himself relaxing. He might not have been there. He felt curiously calm. She had said the word and nothing had happened. Maybe it would be all right.

'You thought it would be like playing games when you awoke after the long sleep,' she began. 'You safe in the ships in high orbit, your autoids

30

down there on the planet. Clearing the swamps and jungle, rebuilding the city. A few indigenous animals to suppress. No danger, no risk.'

And we'd be heroes when we returned, Jon thought. He waited but she didn't say it. He relaxed a bit more.

'We'd trained with the bLinkers on Earth,' he said with difficulty. 'They were far more powerful than the game units back then. We knew what had happened to the first expedition, but we left Earth confident.'

'And when you woke up?'

Night was falling. They must have walked for hours in silence even before she'd said the word. Jon knew where they were, but he felt oddly lost. He shook his head. His tongue was thick. 'They were so fast.'

It was coming back. He should have known. He tried to clear his throat, feeling the saliva begin to congeal. 'No reaction time. No reaction time at all.' His legs stiffened and his chest clogged. He felt everything seizing up.

Chrye stopped. Jon was distantly aware of her taking his arm, but there was no feeling. He heard the echo of her voice.

'You've never talked to anyone about it, have you? I didn't realise. Jon . . .'

He couldn't answer. Dirangesept was upon him again. Chrye was gone. The Earth was gone. He was dying again.

A universe away, she was yelling at him. Her voice reached him like the echo of a whisper.

'Breathe, Jon. Breathe deeply. Jon, can you hear me?'

He heard the panic in her voice, but there was nothing he could do about it.

'Jon, breathe! Breathe!'

At last he heard a great roar, and it was his own, a desperate anguished emptying of his lungs. Then he was doubled over, and Chrye was pounding on his back with her fists. She shook with the effort, her arms working like pistons. It felt to Jon like the tapping of a baby's fingers.

Her room was even smaller than his. Books and papers slid into spills and drifts from every surface.

'I'll make us a cup of coffee,' she said, taking her jacket off. 'It'll be a cup, we'll have to share it. I had another but it broke. I hope you don't use sacch. There isn't any.'

He was still cramped and shivering. She looked back at him from the small cooking unit and ran fingers through her hair. 'Pull the bed down and get in. My credit's red, so it's the only heat you'll get.'

He managed to slip his fist through the ring to unfold the bed from the wall and began to fumble with his shirt. Bringing the coffee to him, Chrye stared at the scar tracking over his shoulder.

She sat beside him on the side of the bed. He tried to drink and she wrapped her hands around his, steadying the cup. Jon could feel neither Chrye's hands nor the cup's warmth. He could taste nothing.

'I've never seen Dirangesept stigmata,' she said. 'I've just read . . .'

'I don't often seize up totally,' he said. 'Usually it's just numbness and stiffness. Somatic scars – what you call the true stigmata – are rare.' He let her take the cup from him, and she sipped from it.

'You get to know your autoid well,' he said. He didn't know why, but the words were coming. He let them flow out of him. 'If a joint was stiff, you felt stiff. If it was lifting a load, you felt the weight. We expected that, we were used to it before we left Earth. On Dirangesept we were bLinkered twelve hours a day. We only yanked out to sleep. No game was ever that deep. We identified totally with our autoids. When they laboured, we sweated. When they were damaged . . .' Jon fingered his scar.

Chrye set the cup down on the floor and began to work at his shoulder. The muscles were unyielding and the scar was a smooth deep channel. The base of the scar felt like tissue paper over steel. She said, 'And if the autoid was destroyed?'

Muscles jerked beneath her palms. 'The beasts—'

'The stigmata should have been anticipated,' she interrupted him quietly. She ran a finger along the valley of the bone-white scar, noticing below it, striping his back, a pattern of longer, thinner welts. He was still shivering.

'Look,' she said. 'I'm going to get into bed with you. We aren't going to do anything. I'll just be there.'

He lay down naked and let her mould herself into his back, slowly appreciating the warmth of her. Her body was a salve to him. His breathing started to ease down and he felt the trembling begin to subside.

'There was little medical support on the ships,' he said at last. 'It wasn't expected to be necessary. After all, there was no physical danger. *We* weren't fighting. But as we lost autoids and the project began to collapse, the stigmata started to snowball.' He reached back over his shoulder and took her hand. 'There was no psychsupport at all.'

Chrye tried to hold him, but his body was shaking too much.

'We couldn't fight them. We couldn't.'

'I know that. You weren't to blame, Jon.' She turned off the light and pulled the blanket over them both. 'Try to sleep.'

FOUR

Kerz's long lean face filled the screen, the pixels defining it more rapidly than Jon could blink the sleep from his eyes. He wondered for a moment what time it was, what day. It was his room, though. He vaguely recollected rolling stiffly out of the girl's bed just before dawn. That was the last thing he remembered, glancing back from her door to see her nestled there in peaceful sleep, wrapped in the sheets soaked with his night sweat.

Kerz obliterated the memory. 'You're awake, Mr Sciler. Good.'

It wasn't clear where Kerz was speaking from, but he wasn't in his office at Maze. Behind him was a rack of shelving stacked solidly with vid cases. Kerz frowned abruptly at Jon, noticing the shifting of Jon's attention, and he leaned forward and made a movement off-screen. Abruptly his face was in tight focus and everything else on the screen was lost. The undefined background swam as he shifted fractionally to and fro.

He didn't wait for a response from Jon. 'I'm sending a messenger with some mindware. We're entering Maze in two days' time, and I'd like you to come along. The rules are for magic . . .' Kerz's hand swept across the screen in a dismissive blur. '. . . I know there's never been magic in Maze. We're trying something out, and you may be just what I need. You speak Chinese, don't you?'

Jon rubbed his eyes. 'Mandarin. I did, anyway. It's been a long time.'

'Mandarin will do. We can adapt. The tonal language is the important thing.'

Kerz's head tilted down to something out of Jon's vision. When he spoke again his voice was slightly muffled. 'I need a voiceprint to program the unit for recognition. Say, "Blue silk does not burn," in Mandarin, will you?'

Jon found it easier than he'd thought to remember the rises and reversals of the language.

'Again. Good. And once more. Now, "The gods are as fleas – innumerable, invisible and ineradicable."'

He waited while Jon translated the phrase. 'That should be sufficient. One moment.' Kerz's head tipped again, and Jon heard what sounded like himself reciting from the screen in a voice light with bells.

'Thick snow shrouds the skeletal trees
That mourn the burial of their leaves.'

The couplet seemed familiar, and it took him a second to realise he'd written it himself, years ago. Except that he'd written it in English.

'Excellent,' said Kerz. 'Now, the script for the magic system is basically pictographic, but you'll find the syllabary accompanying it close enough to Mandarin. I think you'll find it interesting. I'll expect you at 0600. Do you have a pen? I'll give you the location.'

'Just tell me. It's recording.'

'You'll find it's not, Mr Sciler. These machines can be adapted to receive rather more than is transmitted to them. Get a pen.'

Jon scrawled the address on a scrap of paper, then looked up at the screen. 'What about the job, Kerz?'

The screen was void.

Besides the officiator, only two of them were at the top of Primrose Hill for the scattering, as far as Jon could make out. A small knot of people stood further back, masked against the night's bad air. Some of them might have been friends wanting to be anonymous, but Jon had scrutinised them in the gloom and recognised no one. They were probably there for the show, or to see a Far Warrior go up if they'd done the research. But that wasn't likely. The papers hadn't made the connection.

A small grey jar on a rickety folding table on the grass held the ashes. The rocket with its black bulbous nose lay beside it, with a slender plastic tail and a stubby twist of purple touch paper. The other fireworks were in a box on the ground.

'I think it's time,' the officiator said. Jon had no idea who the woman was at his side. She hadn't acknowledged Jon, just standing there in a long dark coat, hands jammed hard into her pockets. Like Jon, she wasn't wearing a respirator, but there was a spidery black veil over her face, the lace scattered and stitched with tiny glass globes. Pinpricks of light shone inside the globes to throw shadows over her face. It was impossible to tell what she looked like. She couldn't have been a relative and there was no way she was from the Vets. It hit Jon how far apart they had grown, that there had been a girlfriend Jon had never met.

'The scattering of Marcus Lees,' the officiator announced, facing the hill's long downward slope into darkness. There was no echo to his voice. The night took away the words as he said them. He paused a moment, then knelt and drew a tall, fat firework from the box and moved away to the sand pit with it. He used both hands, screwing it hard into the sand, then bent and touched a nub of brittle yellow flame to the touch paper. The firework sparked and the officiator stepped away quickly. Sapphire jets streamed up into the sky, then turned in upon themselves and expired. As the night turned smoky a brilliant scarlet flower burst into life and faded, drifting away over Camden with the breeze, and more flowers, azure and golden and jade, bloomed and flowed over the sky.

'So we hope to be,' said the officiator. He motioned Jon and his companion back, then set a smaller conical firework in the sand and lit the fuse. The device whistled shrilly and sprayed a rising fountain of green and dull red for a few moments and died suddenly, leaving a sharp burnt smell in the air.

'So we are,' said the officiator briskly.

Jon glanced again at the woman. He wondered who would be there if his own ashes were being scattered, and found Chrye in his mind. Somehow he thought she would come. It didn't make sense after the way he'd treated her in Nearvana, but something in her eyes as they had sat talking in her room suggested she might see him as more than a Far Warrior, meat for her thesis. He had spent the night awake with her warm body huddled into his back, not moving for fear of waking her. Then when she had at last moaned in her sleep and turned around, he had dressed himself and silently left her.

Maybe she would be here, he thought, and he wondered how he felt about that. It struck him that he was thinking himself dead again. He shook his head clear and watched the officiator hold up the rocket by its tail and with his other hand pour the ashes in a steady pale stream into the firework's belly, then close it up and take it with the empty jar to the pit.

Jon's fellow mourner still hadn't moved. The officiator set the rocket aslant in the jar and sparked its fuse. For a moment the touch paper sputtered, and the dot of light disappeared. The officiator was swaying on his feet, undecided, when the fuse abruptly sizzled and flared. The rocket hissed and in one movement straightened and screamed up into the night. Behind it the ash jar cracked and fell apart. The only sign of the rocket in the sky was a brief disturbance of the drifting smoke left by the preceding firework. Gunpowder stung Jon's nose.

Jon craned his neck back. High above, far away, a tiny blur of red light penetrated the smoke. It had vanished before the accompanying muffled explosion reached the ground. There was nothing more.

'So we will be,' said the officiator.

In the echoing silence Jon looked to his side, but no one was there. The woman had gone. The crowd below was slowly moving up the hill towards him, and Jon fought off a second's panic. The leader was carrying a rocket and a jar. They had just been waiting for the next scattering.

Chrye had flipped up the bed and was sipping at a rewarmed half-cup of coffee. The door buzz startled her. She squinted at Jon's face on the security monitor and let him in.

He was wearing an old baggy shirt, and loose black jeans frayed at the heel. The filter clipped to his belt was an ancient opaque hognosed face-piece. Chrye couldn't remember seeing anyone ever wear such a thing. 'Let's go for a walk,' he said. 'It's my turn now.' He was standing there as if it was an arrangement already made.

She looked at him, not fully awake and cursing it. I missed something, she thought.

'Come in,' she said. 'Let me get dressed.'

She watched him pick up her papers and flick through them as he waited for her. She noticed his eyes register the thin book of poetry beneath a research paper, her worn copy of *Memories of Neverland* by Jon Sciler. He replaced the paper smoothly, covering the book again, not mentioning it.

Chrye had wanted to meet Jon Sciler since she had read his first book, *Far Warriors*. She had memorised that bittersweet poem, wondering how he must feel now about having coined the term. When Kei had first told her Jon Sciler was a friend of his and might help her with her thesis, she hadn't believed him.

Most Far Warriors were emotional cripples, had been even before Dirangesept. They were games players, avoiders of the real world. The

37

only reality they were comfortable with was a simulated one. She had spoken to some of Kei's DVs, and it had been useless. She had hoped Jon might be different, and he was. But while he seemed more likely to be able to communicate, he also seemed more damaged. There was a connection there, of course, and it excited her that she might be able to investigate it. How must it have felt to jot down 'Far Warriors' just before going into CrySis, and to wake up back on Earth a biological day later to find it a universal term of vilification? That extreme of resentment had faded, of course, in the years that had passed, but the effect on Jon Sciler must remain. Even the Vets had rejected him for it.

'Are we going anywhere in particular?' she asked him, pulling on a jacket.

'Not far,' said Jon.

After they'd walked for an hour Jon slid his filter over his face. Chrye still found the air breathable, but asthma was a common part of Dirangesept stigmata. She could see the wall of trees looming ahead.

She slowed down instinctively. 'Is this what you wanted to show me? I know about Hyde Park, Jon.'

Hyde Park was where the riots had begun when the withdrawal from Dirangesept had been announced. It had also been one of the first areas in London affected by a rift, and now it was a wild wood enclosing an unsealed chasm. There had been a poem in the *Neverland* book called 'A New Map of London', in which Jon had referred to it as Dr Jekyll's tomb. She had appreciated that – Hyde burying Jekyll for good, chaos overwhelming order.

People lived in the park. There were enclaves of tents and small shacks amongst the trees, and Chrye had heard that dwellings had been tunnelled out of the sides of the chasm itself.

Jon wouldn't answer her. She fell silent as they left Park Lane to follow a dwindling track into the shadowy wood. There were eyes behind branches, heads sliding in and out of sight. Chrye knew about this, but she had never been here.

'Don't worry,' said Jon. 'They won't touch us.'

She realised she was squeezing his hand. Her eyes locked momentarily on to a pair of eyes across the path. She looked away before realising that the staring white eyes were blind. When she looked back, there was no one.

She flexed her hand.

As they walked on, she began to be aware of more people around them, gathering out of the trees. These were not people of the park. They were walking in the same direction as Jon and Chrye.

'Jon?'

Now his hand was squeezing hers. She was tripping at his pace and her lungs were burning. She put on her filter, the carbon gritty in her throat.

'You're very good at understanding,' said Jon suddenly. 'It isn't as easy as that.'

She was still missing it.

'You think you know me. You've read my poems and you think you know me.'

She tried to shake her head, but he didn't see her. He was staring ahead, his masked face tilted up. Chrye felt someone jostle her. With a shock she realised that she and Jon were in the middle of a crowd, all moving forward, filtering swiftly through the trees. The man who had bumped into Chrye hadn't even noticed her.

There was silence as they all walked, except for the rustling of leaves and the tramping of feet on the hard earth, and the walk turned more urgent and determined, turned into a march.

Chrye found herself breathing quickly and shallowly with apprehension, and only when the foliage ahead seemed to be giving way to a clearing did she begin to relax.

Still urged forward by the crowd, Chrye glanced hesitantly at Jon. His attention was directed at something up ahead.

As they broke abruptly out of the trees, she followed Jon's gaze, and gasped at what she saw. An iron spire, blue-grey in the dead sky, reared high above the tallest trees at the summit of a great patchwork building of brick, wood and sheets of warped, rusting steel. Directly behind the building, stretching to either side, was the dark, wide chasm of the park.

The isolated building stood at the chasm's very brink. Chrye hooded her eyes and peered at the spire with difficulty. It resembled the nose cone of a rocket, and something was perched on its tip. From this distance it seemed to be a black bird, wings outstretched, but the bird was motionless, and as they came closer and had to tilt their heads further back to see it, it looked more angular. It looked like some kind of antenna.

She wanted to stop and see it properly but the crowd was a river around them. The image ahead nagged at her. Something about the shape of it was very familiar.

'Oh, no,' she whispered. She tried to stop, to pull Jon to a halt, but the crowd carried them on. In the open air, the noise of people talking had risen from a murmur to a din without her realising it.

She shouted, 'Are you crazy, Jon?'

He turned his face to her. His eyes were set behind the mask. She understood why he wore it. It was something to hide behind.

He said nothing.

She looked up at the crucifix atop the spire, at the skeleton with its burning eyes. 'Christ,' she murmured. The sockets of its eyes locked her into their empty stare, drawing her on.

She looked down with a sharp ache in her neck. They were almost at the doors of the church.

'Stop, Jon,' she yelled against the roar of the mob, but even if he'd wanted to, they couldn't have fought the current sweeping them irresistibly forward. Chrye could see the battered square steel doors rolled open. She nearly lost Jon as the river of people washed them into the squat building.

Instantly the atmosphere was different. A low, almost calm murmur boomed around the chamber. It was nearly full, but the pressure from behind was forcing those at the front to make more room.

Candles ringed the walls, and the sluggish movement of people buffeted the thousands of tiny flames, swirling the shadows and making the arched walls billow dizzyingly. The ceiling, crisscrossed with thick iron girders, seemed ready to plunge down and crush them.

There were no seats. The crowd pressed them forward until Chrye thought they would be suffocated, and then she heard the thunder of the doors rolling together behind them. She tried to look at Jon, but he wouldn't catch her eye. The smell of sweat in the church made her gag.

With the sealing of the doors, the babble of whisper and chatter died abruptly, and the candles subsided into stillness. The church set hard around them.

Far ahead was a raised pulpit of gleaming, burnished steel, and Chrye stared at it, mesmerised, understanding the silence. She felt her heart thudding, knowing where she was.

A huge, barrel-chested man was standing like a shadowy boulder on the pulpit. His long hair was lanky and black, and his dark beard seemed to begin just beneath his wide bright eyes. A black cape fell in thick folds from the cliffs of his shoulders.

The preacher of the Final Church, Chrye remembered. Of all places, why had Jon brought her here?

She glanced around. At least no one was looking at them. Everyone was staring at the pulpit.

The preacher slowly spread his arms wide, then drew them back into his chest. He opened his mouth and began to speak with a voice like thunder.

'Look at you all standing before me like poor parentless children.'

Artificially enhanced, Chrye thought. But she wasn't certain. It came from him so naturally. Chrye couldn't remember the preacher's name.

He paused, and his gaze tracked slowly across the congregation. 'Like poor curs. Like sniffing dogs without a trail.'

He waited. No one moved. His words hung in the thick air. He raised his arms, the cloak stirring behind him like restless wings. Chrye smelt sickly-sweet incense coming from somewhere.

He let go a vast sigh. 'Why are you here? What do you expect from me?'

The preacher stared at his congregation in silence. There was no movement. The candle flames were still.

'Do you expect me to say, "Look behind you, there is your God standing there?" Do you want me to tell you He awaits you with His arms open to enfold you into the great warmth of His endless love? Is that what you want?'

He leaned forward. 'Because if it is, then I will disappoint you.' His voice was low now, and harsh. 'There is no such warmth.' He raised a hand, palm out, and splayed his fingers wide, and continued.

'The warmth that is to come is the warmth of the volcano as it spews its puke upon you. The warmth that is to come is the warmth of the fever as it boils your blood. The warmth that is to come is the warmth of the sun as it sears your flesh.'

He drew a small breath. He whispered, 'Hell's warmth.'

Now the preacher pushed himself back and was silent for a moment. Chrye realised that the pressure from behind her had ceased. The congregation was recoiling from the pulpit.

The preacher leaned sharply forward again. His name came suddenly to her. Father Fury. But she had never thought it would be like this to see him. She had imagined him a sad, almost comic figure with a flock of the damaged and credulous. Here instead was a man of terrible power.

41

'Jon,' she whispered. In the dead silence her voice sounded to her as loud as the preacher's. She noticed the tremor in it.

Father Fury had begun again. His words shivered the candle flames ringing the pulpit.

'I shall not speak to you of God. God needs no prophets. God needs no apologists. When that time comes, God shall speak to you Himself. And that time will be soon.'

He nodded grimly. His voice was like fire. 'What, then, shall I speak to you of? I shall speak to you of Satan.'

Beside Chrye, Jon had stiffened completely. Chrye felt panic begin to shake her and tried to suppress it.

'Who amongst you knows where Satan is to be found today, as this world spins puking and belching to its end?' Father Fury roared. Then he leaned forward once more and continued in a sly whisper, 'Did Satan cause this?'

He shook his head, and Chrye heard a faint murmuring of agreement around her.

'No, Satan did not!'

The murmuring continued.

Father Fury punched out a splay-fingered hand and the church was silent, waiting for him to answer them. He whispered, 'Man caused this. It was man.'

He pushed himself back again, as if wearily this time. In front of Chrye, people were nodding.

Father Fury shrugged, rippling the folds of his cape like black water. 'Oh, Satan might have helped a little at first, nudged us now and then and prodded us on, but man is the instrument of his own doom.'

There were more people nodding their heads now, as Father Fury continued. 'But Satan is with us now, make no mistake. Satan is with us, and He is more powerful than ever.'

He let that settle like poison into his congregation.

'So where is Satan, if not in the men who by their greed and stupidity destroyed us all?' The priest waited a moment, as if expecting a reply. 'Is Satan in those who search for salvation in the emptiness of tarot cards and crystal balls? No, he is not.'

A murmur of agreement went up around the church.

'Is Satan, then, in those who attempt to escape their destiny with drugs? No, he is not.'

The murmur rose, and there were a few cries. Chrye kicked Jon's ankle, but he didn't move.

'The world must end, as Sodom ended and Gomorrah. And who destroyed those cities of evil? It was not Satan, but God. It was God! And the evil that is on this planet must die on this planet. What began on Earth must end on Earth.'

His fist struck the lectern with a force that shook the pulpit and drove a shiver through the congregation. Chrye felt scared, and felt fear all around her. There was a vinegary stink of piss. Her hand was numb, but she couldn't tell if it was Jon squeezing hers or her squeezing his. She told herself again that the preacher's voice was enhanced, but she didn't believe it.

'Only Satan would seek to flee the justice of the Lord,' he thundered. 'Only the Devil himself would seek to transplant the evil of man.'

He stopped again, and recommenced in a sly hiss that swayed the terrified congregation back towards the pulpit.

'So do you know, my brothers and my sisters, where Satan is?'

In the silence he answered himself, nodding his great head. 'Satan was on the ships that went to Dirangesept. That is where Satan was. Satan was in the souls of the Far Warriors. And, unless they repent, that is where he remains.'

Father Fury stared out over his congregation. 'They must repent,' he whispered. He leaned back and folded his arms, and stood motionless, waiting.

Chrye felt Jon's fingers flex and looked at him. 'Let's go,' she said quietly.

Jon shook his head without taking his eyes from the preacher. 'We have to see it through.'

Chrye became aware of a movement behind them. Someone was forcing their way forward. The shifting of the mass of people was accompanied by a rising murmur that grew into a rhythmic chant.

'*Repent, repent, repent.*'

She twisted round with difficulty. A man was pushing himself through the congregation. As he came forward a hand struck out at him, then another, and he was shoved and slapped. Chrye assumed he was being attacked for trying to work closer to the pulpit, but then he was lifted off his feet and carried high towards the preacher, the crowd parting as far as it could to let his bearers through. He was taken up the steps and dropped at the feet of Father Fury.

43

The congregation shifted as the man stood up beside the preacher. Chrye hadn't realised just how big the preacher was. He was at least a head taller than the man.

Father Fury put his hand on the man's shoulder. 'Do you repent?' he intoned.

The Far Warrior hung his head. 'I repent, Father.'

Chrye glanced quickly at Jon. Jon had frozen.

Father Fury stooped and drew out a thick black bull-whip from beneath the lectern, raising it high in the air. The whole church sighed at the sight of it. In a sudden movement the preacher cracked it back and flicked it down before the pulpit where it raised a devil of dust. Chrye had heard about the preacher's whip. It had seemed a pathetic device to her.

'Go down,' said Father Fury.

The Far Warrior stumbled down the steps and stood beneath the preacher. He faced the congregation, his arms at his sides, his head lowered.

Father Fury leaned over the lectern. He drew back his whip in a sharp arc. Chrye put her hand to her mouth.

The whip seemed to hang there for a moment, a languid black line etched in the heavy air. Then it cracked down like a bolt of dark lightning.

The strike seemed to pierce the man's flesh. His scream ran through the congregation. Chrye moaned at the shock of it. Around the church the candle flames began to dance. It was as if a spell had been broken.

Father Fury pulled back his arm and began methodically to flay the man. After a few strokes his shirt was shredded and fell away and his blood ran down, matting his trousers. The whip was a blur, seeming to fall again as it was raised. Drops of blood flicked from it like holy water from a censer. Chrye saw congregants who were splashed with the man's blood touch their fingers to it and then to their mouths, muttering prayers. She felt sick.

The man slipped at last in his pooling greasy blood and fell to his knees, but Father Fury flayed him until he slid face down on the slick stone floor and was still.

The preacher ran the flail through his fists. Blood dripped from them as if he had wrung it out. He looked up, and there was a terrible light in his eyes.

'This is your benediction,' he said. The softness in his voice was worse than anything that had gone before. 'Is there another who is ready to repent?'

To her horror, Chrye felt Jon begin to sway forward. She held on to him frantically and whispered, 'Jon, no!'

He blinked at her. He seemed dazed. He turned back towards the pulpit.

'Please, Jon. This isn't the answer.' She felt people staring at them. The chant was rising again.

'*Repent! Repent! Repent!*'

A hand reached out and clutched at Jon. Chrye knocked it away, and her wrist was caught from behind and held. She felt a scream rise in her throat, then a man shouldered his way violently between Jon and Chrye.

'I repent,' he shrieked.

Chrye's arm was abruptly released. The yelling man was taken instantly and raised up. He was carried towards the preacher like a twig in floodwater.

Chrye suddenly felt bile forcing her mouth open. She was vomiting and sobbing, the spasms jerking her body uncontrollably. Her hand was still in Jon's, and for the first time since they had entered the church he noticed her. She could see the tension in him subside. He said, 'We'll go now.'

She only said two things to Jon on the way back. As they picked their way through the trees of the park she said, 'Not all your scars are stigmata, are they, Jon?'

And then, giving him her doorcode, too shaky to punch it herself, she said, 'Father Fury. He was a Far Warrior, wasn't he?'

Jon let them in.

'Now you know something about Far Warriors,' he said.

FIVE

Chrye peered over Jon's shoulder at the tight columns of ideograms.

'Where are the translations?' she said into his silence. She felt a gulf between them. The process had seemed to begin well, but since he had taken her to see Father Fury he had withdrawn from her.

She knew it was her fault, expecting too much and pushing it too fast. She'd been over-confident in the beginning. By choosing Nearvana as the place to meet her, Jon had signalled how he wanted to play it, and she'd known how to deal with him there. But she hadn't anticipated that he'd be unable to assert himself in response, and she cursed herself because that should have been obvious to her. Jon Sciler had no control over his life. The vision and taut beauty of his poetry had blinded her to that. Now she saw that his poetry wasn't a sign that he could communicate, it was his replacement for communication. It was his control mechanism. He couldn't tell Chrye about himself, so instead he had taken her to Father Fury and simply shown her just how much she didn't know.

But at least he had taken her there, she thought, and held on to that.

'There aren't any translations,' he said. 'I have to work them out, if I can.' He answered her automatically, his voice as hard as the muscles of his shoulders. She wanted to reach out and rub the pain away, but the time for that was past.

'I'm in the way. I'll go,' she said at last.

When they had returned from the Final Church, she had sat with him in silence for an hour, and then he had stood up and left. He had shown her how much he needed her help, and she had been too numbed to speak to him. After Father Fury's sermon in the Final Church at the edge of the abyss, it had hit her that all she knew about the Far Warriors, about Dirangesept stigmata, was worthless. She had wanted to tell him that, but

46

the words wouldn't be said. She had wanted to comfort him, but couldn't move. Jon Sciler had revealed himself to her, and she had failed him.

So now she had come to him. He had opened his door to her and let her in without a word, then sat at his table and hunched down into the book as if she wasn't there.

Chrye was at the door, defeated once more, when he called out to her. 'No. Come here. Look at this.'

He spun the book around for her to see, and pointed at a sign, a pair of crossed arrows. He cleared his throat, and she wondered if he had spoken to anyone at all since they had left the Final Church. He said, his finger still on the page, 'Blockage, or confusion, or maybe a warning.'

That should be for us, she thought. She glanced at his eyes, but if he'd meant it he wasn't showing her. It seemed that every understanding of him that she reached only revealed a deeper complexity. She looked at the sign and tried to forget his past.

'But why arrows?' she asked. 'Why not sticks, or swords?'

'Look at these,' he said in response. He flipped pages. Chrye figured twenty pages in the manual, a hundred pictograms per page.

'See?' said Jon. 'The arrow is a common pictogram component. It crops up all the time.'

'So you figure it's an indicator of direction?'

She looked at him.

Jon looked straight back at her. 'Yes. I had figured that.'

He noticed the way she spoke, carefully unassertive. As if merely confirming his thought, not telling him. He could see her beginning to pick her way delicately through the maze of his defences, lighting the route not only for herself but perhaps for him too. No one had ever got this far, but then he'd shown no one else its entrance.

'There are a few clues,' he told her. 'It helps that I know the language is devoted to magic. The pictograms aren't spells, only the building blocks of spells. Look, here's one I've devised, I think.' He leaned back in the chair, his sleeve falling against her bare arm.

Chrye left her arm there, enjoying the contact and trying not to wonder if he'd meant it, and examined the four pictograms. A standing man, a flower, a wall, a broken sword. She couldn't see how they might link together.

'Tell me,' she said.

He tapped the paper. 'I'm guessing the flower can mean grow or create.

Nothing else seems appropriate. But I won't know until I try it. Tonight, maybe. If I've misunderstood the system, or misused any of the pictograms, nothing will happen, or the wrong thing.'

He spoke the sequence aloud, contorting his tongue around the syllables with difficulty. It sounded to Chrye as if the words had been broken and put back together wrongly.

'What should it do?'

He pursed his lips. 'It might create some sort of wall or shield. Beyond that . . .' He pulled a face at her. 'Whether a physical or psychic shield, only Kerz will know. I don't know how it might be used. The spell could be incomplete. Perhaps it's over-elaborate. I might be able to assume the first pictogram, the spell-caster. I don't know yet. I don't really know anything.'

Chrye ran her fingers down the page. Some of the symbols, like those for man and woman, seemed unambiguous. Others were almost entirely obscure. Horizontal wavy lines could mean water or uncertainty, mountains or getting lost, she guessed. In conjunction with other pictograms, they could probably mean all those things, and more. Even the most plain symbols must be adaptable. The little bird could simply be itself, or it could represent flight, or seeing from above, or it could be an element of death, the flight to the next world. She reached to flick the page, but Jon's hand brushed her away.

Jon stared at the list, seeing connections blossoming, the pictograms shifting and combining. There must be short cuts, refinements, spells of such elegance here. Here was creation and destruction, life and death. The power of gods and devils.

Chrye watched him consume the page. He has a photographic memory, she thought. And Kerz had known that, giving him the manual so soon before the entry. She wondered about Kerz for a moment. She wondered if Kerz had considered the effect of giving such a linguistic tool to a Far Warrior who was a poet. She touched Jon's shoulder, remembering the scars beneath his shirt, and wanted to touch them again, to soothe him. She wanted to tell him how much his poems had meant to her, but couldn't.

'Jon,' she said, watching him, 'it's a game. Remember it's only a game.'

He looked quickly at her, then away, barely swallowing the words. It's not. Not this time.

*

Jon couldn't sleep. In the darkness he lay on his bed shuffling pictograms and murmuring their sounds until it was time to leave for the game. Outside, it was cold, his breath bitter in the murky air. He whiled away the journey by rehearsing the few spells he had constructed, repeating them aloud until he had the streams of convoluted syllables rippling smoothly from his tongue. Once near the Angel an old street surveillance lens briefly activated above him and followed him for a few seconds out of the memory of some program-generated random curiosity. A few street lights were on, and the Islington roads before dawn were lifeless. He walked past the drab, withered trees of empty squares, hearing the hiss of a microflite above him once, feeling the arid warmth of its exhaust and glimpsing a faint shadow cast down through the gloom.

The spells comforted him like mantras, swarming in his head like the sounds of water over rock, and for long seconds he was almost able to forget how meaningless it all was when the Earth he walked was cracked and poisoned. The voice of Father Fury came suddenly to him. 'The Earth is your grave, and you cannot escape the grave.'

Wood Green bus garage seemed intact as he approached it, a vast brick shed, its few high windows splintered and dark. He walked around it; Kerz had warned him it would appear deserted, but it looked as if no one had been there for years. Someone had sprayed DEATH IS THE BEGINNING all over a wall in luminous yellow dripping letters. The gaping streetfront face of it was shuttered with tall gates of rusted steel.

He found the door Kerz had told him to use, with a rough cross chalked above the padlock. He knocked, and the padlock fell away. The door swung smoothly open.

Kerz stood smiling at him. 'Abracadabra,' he said.

Following him inside, Jon glanced back as the door closed. Outside, it was still gloomy. Within, it was windowless and as bright as day. But he could hardly see the far wall, or a wall to either side. The garage was an immense shell, its floor littered with girders and qualcrete blocks. It was as if something was being built or destroyed there, and Jon couldn't make up his mind which.

'This is our research site,' said Kerz. He strode away from Jon and bounded up a steel staircase hugging the wall. The noise boomed briefly and was swallowed by the immense space.

Jon followed him. At the top of the stairs was a gantry overlooking the floor. Kerz waited there for Jon to join him, then gestured outwards.

As far as Jon could see, the floor was an ordered complex of ramps, stairs, pits and walls.

'You're looking at over five thousand square metres, Mr Sciler. Precisely and meticulously landscaped. It looks random but every millimetre of it is logged and contained within the gamezone program.'

Jon grabbed the rail in front of him. The warm metal hummed. Somewhere in the building there was a generator. This place must use its own power, and it must need a lot of power. Jon gripped the railing hard, trying to take it all in. He was surveying a framework, a labyrinth, a stage set for Maze. It was the biggest gamescape he had ever seen. A small movement far across the chamber caught his eye, the flash of blond hair. There were a couple of men in grey overalls clambering around the gamezone. Jon supposed they were maintenance technicians.

Kerz moved along the rail. 'At the moment the scope of Maze is limited by the limitations of the bLinkers,' he said. 'BLinkers can give you sight, touch, sound. And our pharmatechs are giving us smell at last, and taste too. But bLinkers can't physically move you through space, or stop you dead if you hit a wall that isn't really there.' He closed his palm in the air and opened it again like a magician giving Jon a glimpse of the lines and creases of his destiny. 'You can get the impression of a small pebble in the hand, as you remember from the little scenario the other day, but that's about the limit in physical terms.' Kerz looked around, then gestured back at the stairs. 'You can't climb stairs unless there are stairs to climb, or fall into a hole if the real ground is solid.'

Jon nodded, hardly listening as Kerz walked him along the gantry. Their feet thundered on the metal.

'So Maze has been restricted to small, flat floor zones. Until now, that is. Programming this has taken years.' He made a quick outward movement with his hand, taking in the vast labyrinth, and added, 'It looks like the deep blue sea, but it's a paddle pool. The falls are minimised, and all the surfaces go to SwelGel on hard contact. You won't injure yourself out there.' He paused a moment, then pointed across the floor. After a second Jon made out a small group of people standing in a corridor far away. They were looking all around themselves, but not up. Jon guessed they were bLinkered.

'They're waiting for you, Mr Sciler. It's playtime.' Kerz waved Jon away from the balcony to a small cylindrical cubicle behind him. He slid the door open and motioned Jon inside. 'This isn't entirely new,' he told Jon. 'You've seen them before?'

'It's a solo. Visuals only. Pre-bLinker technology. I haven't seen one since I was a kid. We had better than this on Dirangesept.'

'We still use them to test programs. You're the only one using it because you're the only one casting spells. It's easier to monitor you here. You'll find this solo a considerable improvement on those you remember, anyway.'

Kerz slipped outside and the doorseal vanished. Jon felt the floor lurch slightly beneath him and took a step to balance himself. The floor jerked again, and Jon bent his knees and stood still, allowing the rollermat to centre him. The matt white walls were barely an arm's length away. He felt slightly claustrophobic.

'Look up,' came Kerz's voice.

There was a brief stab of light as the eyetrackers located his pupils.

He looked down, and was in a stone corridor. He walked forward and the rollermat glided smoothly underfoot. The walls of the corridor slid past.

He faced the side wall and took a step. This time the rollermat locked, and he advanced to touch the image of the wall. It looked perfect, but he felt the stubbled smoothness of polybubble.

Kerz's voice filtered through to him again. 'Try a spell, Mr Sciler.'

Jon stared down the corridor and cast man–flower–wall–brokensword. The words sounded like a flat stone bouncing from steel on to wood. About twenty yards away, at the level at which his eyes were fixed, a black pinprick flicked into view and began to exude a dark tarry substance that dripped to the ground, flowing more and more rapidly. As it hit the stone flags, it set hard. The barrier rose to the height of its source, then stopped.

'Good! Can you banish it?'

Jon substituted witheredflower for flower, and uttered the spell, his voice bouncing the flat stone back again. The barrier began to consume itself from the ground up but then abruptly stopped, leaving a thick black bar across the corridor. He wondered what he'd done.

Outside the solo Kerz laughed. 'Not bad, Mr Sciler. You'll make a wizard. Now, let me introduce you to your companions for the excursion.'

The rollermat stirred and Jon let it guide him along the illusory corridor. He found himself ducking beneath the black bar, and as it passed over his head the solo darkened. The program had assimilated the alteration.

Directed by the solo, Jon walked on, until rounding a corner he reached a widening of the corridor.

He realised the solo was rationalised with the gamezone below. Of the group of five standing ahead of him, Jon immediately recognised Yani and Pibald. It was clear that they weren't expecting him. Yani's diamond eyes narrowed. Pibald grunted something to himself.

The others Jon hadn't seen before. Two were women, and the third was a man standing awkwardly in a distinctive posture, feet apart and arms held slightly away from his sides. He had to be a Far Warrior.

Jon saw no sign of the same recognition in return, but few Far Warriors were still as striking as this man. Perhaps Jon was less conspicuous now. Or perhaps Maze employed so many that Jon was no novelty.

One of the women came forward and held out her hand to Jon. He reached instinctively to take it. At the edge of the polybubble a mild electrostatic charge struck his fingers. The combination of the primitive holo-effect with the static worked effectively enough, and the woman's hand seemed to slide synthetically into his palm.

'I'm Lapis, and this is Lazuli,' she said. They were, Jon saw, not similar but identical, wearing the same leather jerkins and trousers. Lazuli shook Jon's hand too, and he noticed that their eyes were of that perfect dizzying blue. Yani glanced hard at them both as they stepped back, and one of them pulled her lips together and made a small sound at him, shaking her head.

The Far Warrior glanced at Jon and murmured, 'I'm Footfall.' He was looking about nervously, and yet it seemed to Jon that he was somehow not completely involved in the situation. The others had the bright alertness that Jon expected of players, but Footfall lacked that. It wasn't boredom, though. He appeared truly apprehensive.

Yani sniffed. 'Let's waste no time in pleasantries,' he said. 'We'll see how he handles a real challenge.'

Lapis ignored Yani. 'What should we call you?' Or was she Lazuli?

'Sciler.'

'No,' snapped Yani, irritated. 'Hardworld names are forbidden here. You must have another.'

'What do they call you here, then?' said Jon.

52

Yani fingered the pommel of his sword. 'The name Demonslayer was bestowed upon me,' he said.

Jon looked him up and down. 'I bet you're a disappointment to your parents.'

Yani turned away.

'So, your name,' said Pibald. Jon noticed that Footfall was growing agitated, shuffling his feet and dragging the hilt of his sword up and down in its leather scabbard.

'Call me Starburn.'

The Far Warrior's eyes jumped to meet Jon's, suddenly and piercingly.

Yani wheeled round again. 'Why that name? Why did you choose that?'

Before Jon could speak, Footfall's head jerked and his arm moved in a blur. A crack of static burst against Jon's shoulder with the holo of Footfall's arm striking him and the rollermat swept his feet from beneath him. Jon was slammed sideways against the wall of the corridor.

There was a sword in Pibald's hand now, slashing over Jon's head. Ducking instinctively, Jon glimpsed a long scaled brown arm scything in an arc that would have decapitated him if Footfall hadn't knocked him aside. Pibald's blade hacked into the limb and a jet of brown fluid spurted into Pibald's eyes from the wound.

Pibald screamed and reeled backwards, dropping his sword and covering his eyes.

Jon crawled back, trying to keep up with the group as they retreated, the confines of the solo forgotten. He searched his brain for one of the spells, but the pictograms eluded him. He cursed his lack of a weapon.

Their attacker was a thin and gangling biped, tall enough to have to stoop in the corridor. It had lurched back at Pibald's blow, but now it sloped towards them again in near silence. Its attention was on the rest of the group, clearly seeing Jon as no immediate threat. On his knees, Jon flattened himself against the wall and the beast kicked past him.

Jon had a better sight of it now. The creature's head was little more than a swollen termination of its thick neck, housing a bulbous wrinkled sensory lobe – eye and ear combined, perhaps – at either side. It had narrow shoulders and hips, but its arms and legs were thickly muscled and its body was densely crusted by mottled brown warts. Jon guessed they were some form of active defence mechanism. Pibald had struck one of these. It looked like no part of its body would be safe to attack.

The wart hit by Pibald lay in folds that flapped at the beast's elbow. The creature seemed able to replenish its venom swiftly. The creases were already fading as the bladder reflated.

Through the beast's legs Jon saw the twins draw back their swords, and he shouted, 'No!'

They hesitated and in desperation he strung pictograms together and yelled them out, staring at the shambling creature's legs. 'Flower–rope.'

Nothing.

He added the symbol of a man walking. He switched the rope for what had looked in the manual like a vine, and inserted a convulsed pictogram that might stand for a knot, then screamed the spell at the creature.

This time the beast's stride broke. It flailed its arms and let out a little grunt of surprise, and stumbled. It took another uncertain pace, then its legs buckled in the thin black tangle of cord that Jon suddenly saw snarling them. It began to topple forward.

'Get back!' Jon yelled at the women.

With a piercing screech, the creature crashed to the stone floor, the impact sparking a chain of muffled explosions from the warts of its chest. Venom sizzled and oozed around it.

Twisting towards Jon, the beast tried to rise. Its chest was ragged and stripped of flesh where its own poison was eating into it. Thick straps of muscle peeled away and dissolved to reveal the bones of a white ribcage melting. The beast slumped. Its lungs began to disintegrate, still swelling and contracting.

Lapis and Lazuli pulled Jon to his feet. The creature was sinking into itself, as if slowly imploding. They watched it silently, the only sound the faint hiss of acid. Footfall ripped a tag of material from the hem of his shirt and dipped it cautiously at the edge of the pool. The scrap blackened and curled, and Footfall dropped it sharply. Only Pibald stood back, his white-knuckled hands grinding into his eyes.

Yani stepped forward and plunged his sword into the juddering heart as the brown wash of acid reached it. 'Die by the sword Skullsmasher, blade of Demonslayer,' he cried. A speck of red spat into his face and he leapt back.

'That's just blood,' said Footfall derisively.

Yani stared at Jon. 'Coward! If it hadn't tripped we'd all be dead except you.'

Jon ignored him and went to Pibald. Lapis and Lazuli were trying to examine his eyes, but they couldn't force his hands away from them. He was whimpering in pain.

Jon cast flower–eye–sun. The corridor grew a little brighter. Pibald still whimpered.

There had been a little vial symbol in the charts. Jon put it into the sequence in place of the sun, and added the symbol for a man beside it.

Now Pibald cautiously allowed the women to take his hands away. He was obviously still in pain, so although the spell had worked it hadn't been precise.

'Well done, Sciler,' said one of the twins.

Pibald wiped his eyes and said, 'Yes. Thanks, Sciler.'

Jon glanced at Yani. The little man sneered at him, but let the use of his real name pass. Starburn had struck a mark. They wouldn't use it.

Footfall said, 'And thanks for the sorcery that saved us all.' Jon had the feeling that Footfall was going to say something more, but he didn't. There was another look in the eyes of the haunted Far Warrior. It looked like pity.

'Onward,' said Yani. 'Skullsmasher thirsts for blood.' He waved the sword above his head and stamped his feet. Jon caught the twins exchanging a grin, curtailing it before Yani saw them. One of them noticed Jon registering it, and she rolled her blue eyes at him as Yani twirled his blade.

The dead beast was barely a puddle of brown ooze on the ground. Pibald's eyes were still streaming, though he was out of pain. Footfall was bending to help him to his feet when one of the women touched him lightly on the shoulder and whispered, 'Look.'

Jon turned with Footfall to see the corridor behind them filling with the shambling creatures. They were about five metres away. Jon met Footfall's eye and said, 'I don't think they're that fast. We'll back off and try to get some dead space, give ourselves a few minutes to think.'

Footfall nodded, hoisting Pibald upright. 'Lapis, Lazuli, take the lead, check it's clear ahead of us.'

The creatures were coming forward more rapidly, jostling and crowding each other in the narrow corridor. As the rest of the group began to get moving, Jon glanced at Yani. He had half expected Yani to slope off with them, but Yani was standing his ground, sword in hand. 'Who elected you leader, Sciler?' he said coldly.

'If you've got a better idea, yell it out,' Jon said. 'Now would be a good time.'

Yani didn't reply.

'I don't know why you're complaining,' Jon couldn't resist adding. 'This looks like Skullsmasher's lucky day.'

SIX

The area immediately surrounding Maze was slowly being cleared of the quaked rubble. There seemed to be no urgency. A safety barrier had been erected with a guard booth where Jon was given a pass stamped with a photograph he didn't remember having been taken.

The building was the same, but the Gothic door was being scuffed metal this time, and through the wall's dark glass he could make out the silhouette of a surveillance lens. Maze had nothing to prove to Jon today. Maze opened the door for him, and Maze closed it soundlessly behind him.

The atrium was deserted. Jon paused, half expecting Kerz's voice to direct him. Yani's desk console was unattended.

He walked around the console and let his fingers float over the keys. The palm-sized screen was dull. 'Now, where are we?' he murmured.

A face bloomed on the screen, wearing a familiar sneer. 'We're in fairyland, Mr Sciler. And we're going to go up, up, up in the magic elevator to the first floor, and then we'll skip down the corridor until we come to a big grey door. And on that big grey door we'll see an itty-bitty sign that says "Reality Validation". And we'll go tappety-tap on the door and we'll tippy-toe inside. There. Are we clear?'

'Fuck off, Yani.'

Jon killed the screen.

A wedge of clinical light leaked across the corridor as Jon opened the door. The woman behind the desk didn't look up at him. She murmured, 'Please sit.'

He didn't, and she raised her eyes. The whites of them were faintly cloudy, blurring into her brown irises.

'I can come back,' Jon said.

She waved her pen at him. 'You are . . . ?'

'Jon Sciler. I thought you were expecting me.'

She blinked an instant longer than was natural, and Jon guessed at an implanted retinal display. Her eyes took a moment to refocus on him.

'Yes.'

The desk between them was a long wide arc inset with banked monitors. Jon could see the faces of a couple of the screens at the far end of the curve. Ranks of five-digit numbers were steadily scrolling down their displays.

Her chair was on tracks and she hissed down the desk towards Jon, reaching perfunctorily over the monitors to touch fingers with him. 'Dr Locke,' she said shortly. 'Thea Locke.' Her hair was cropped short except for a straight fringe of brown above her eyes. She smiled as if it was an exercise she'd been shown a long time ago and forgotten, and gestured at the chair opposite her. 'Would you sit, Mr . . . ?'

'Sciler. Jon Sciler.' He tried to pull the chair forward but it was fixed to the gleaming white floor. The pores of the air-exchanger were like a scattering of coal dust there. Jon sat back, the seat rocking as he settled in it.

The woman tracked away back up the desk, murmuring, 'Bear with me.'

Jon swivelled his chair around. The wall facing Dr Locke's desk was a lightwall, set to a lifeless grey. He swung back. She was writing on a yellow pad, staring at one of the screens. The wall behind her was black glass. He wondered if he was being watched.

He rocked hard on the chair. It squeaked and Dr Locke glanced up for a moment, a frown tugging at her fringe. Jon grinned at her and rocked again, picking up a rhythm.

She dropped her pen on the mat and looked at him.

'What did you think of last night?' she said.

'Interesting. I'm not the first to experiment with magic, am I? The routines are advanced. How far have you got?'

Dr Locke shook her head and picked up her pen.

He tried again. 'Have we all been Far Warriors?'

She said, 'How are you getting on with the rules for magic? I watched the scan of last night's excursion. It seemed to go well.' She glanced at a screen. 'Tripping the boilbeast, a healing spell – that was good, resolving blindness too – the shield barrier, of course, and a bridge spell. And then destroying the bridge.'

She met his eyes. 'That was a sweet reversal. There was a lot of noise, though, so we didn't get a clear record of how you did that. You can jot it down for me, save me some time on the printout.'

'Couldn't you lip-read?'

'Tonal language. Remember?'

He felt dismissed by the flatness in her voice, as if he'd lost a chance to be taken seriously.

'What kind of scan do you get of the excursion?' he asked, expecting nothing. But she reached below her desk and brought out a disc.

'I'll show you. It's a composite, an overview. Turn around.'

The lightwall went to black and flashed a rainbow colour test, then Jon saw himself from above with the group, just before the first boilbeast. The image blurred and slid, and fixed again at the chasm.

'Talk me through, Mr Sciler.'

There had been over a dozen boilbeasts pursuing them. Pibald, his vision still impaired, had nearly bolted off the edge before Footfall could stop him. Jon saw himself gazing over the drop. It had looked bottomless. He'd felt nauseous poised over it. Mists gathered down there. He remembered thinking there were blues and greens down there, but the mists were only formless grey shapes. Pibald and Footfall were at his side, the others out of shot behind them.

He turned to look at Dr Locke. 'How deep is it really?'

She nodded him to turn back, and the screen shifted. Two men stood on a steel walkway at the edge of a pit a couple of metres deep. From the overhead viewpoint he couldn't see their faces, but they must have been Pibald and Footfall.

The screen shifted again and Jon saw himself back alongside them, the gamescape restored. The drop still made him uneasy.

The spell had been easy to formulate but hard to control. He watched the screen as the memory flooded back.

'I made a false start here.'

A black slab materialised high over the centre of the chasm and began to flow across to the far side. It set abruptly as it struck the rocky edge, and the unsupported centre creaked and sagged. The black substance fractured and the half-bridge splintered away, plummeting endlessly down to be lost in the mists.

'It still doesn't look like two metres,' said Jon.

'Forget that,' said Dr Locke impatiently. 'What did you do?'

'I built it out from each edge in turn, the second time. I directed it with my eyes. It took me a while to work that out. I like that. It's a good touch.'

On the screen the bridge flowed hesitantly up and over the chasm in two separate parts that fused in the middle. 'It doesn't look very solid. It wasn't easy to concentrate with all the noise.'

Jon looked at the others on the screen. The frame seemed to expand to contain the entire party, moving out when they separated, closing in when they came together. He watched them holding off the boilbeasts while he was fumbling with pictograms. They had figured out a strategy of going for the warts that lined the beasts' flanks and pointed sideways, or else stabbing at their feet, which were wart-free. Pibald and Yani were laying about themselves furiously, while Footfall was keeping them at bay more efficiently.

Footfall was a fine swordsman, Jon realised, watching him. He hadn't quite appreciated how fine at the time. The beasts were still bunched together, and Footfall was darting in beneath their flailing arms and deftly using the flat of his blade to trigger their envenomed warts at each other. The panic and confusion it created was worth as much as the physical damage.

Lapis and Lazuli fought side by side. There was something odd about the way they fought. They stood too close together, yet their swords flew without ever interfering. It was breathtaking to watch. Jon had never seen such swordplay. Their weapons worked in combination as faultlessly as a pair of chopsticks.

'They're constructs, aren't they?' he said suddenly.

He glanced back at her. She grunted, staring intently at the screen. 'Interesting, isn't it? Seeing what you missed. Anything there you don't remember? Anything you do remember that isn't there?'

Jon shook his head. He watched Yani. Demonslayer.

Jon turned around to face her. 'The boilbeasts,' he said. 'It doesn't make sense that they have no resistance to their own acid. It wouldn't happen.'

'Mm-hm. You might also have noticed that they screamed rather loudly for creatures with no mouths. What you played here isn't a fully integrated macro-scenario. It's a testing shed. Would you concentrate on the screen, please?'

He swivelled back to the lightwall. 'How's the bridge done, physically?'

It had been – felt like – more than software. He watched them cross it, watched himself destroy the bridge as Footfall, the last of them, stepped off it. The bridge suddenly just wasn't there, and three boilbeasts fell whirling and screeching into the abyss, the echo hanging behind them for long seconds.

Dr Locke reversed the film and closed in on the bridge as it was forming, cropping the players out of the frame and freezing it. She shifted the display from bLinkered to actual and threw the scene forward. Jon watched hydraulic ramps and struts telescope from slots in the steel walkway and elevate smoothly into the skeleton of Jon's bridge.

'Okay?' She flicked back into the bLinkered view of the black bridge, then cut the picture. 'Enough.'

'Is everything I create made of that black stuff?'

'Perhaps. That's one reason you're here. Black's a default colour. Your spells can be more specific. You created a bridge, not a stone bridge, or a wooden one.'

'But what I can do is still limited by what your hardware can deal with. Suppose I try something beyond it?'

'Again, that's why you're here. Now, let's start.'

She was punching keys and checking her screens and monitors. He could see them reflected in her eyes and in the glass behind her. He thought he recognised the stretch and tic of an EEG.

Apparently satisfied, she extracted a pair of bLinkers from a vacpac and reached forward to hand them over to Jon. She peered at him, judging his reaction as he hesitated before tipping his head back to set it in place.

'These are readers, not feeders,' she said. 'I'll be recording your responses every session.'

He straightened, squeezing his eyes closed. The story still didn't quite fit. 'If the computer can read my spells and enact them, then it must be programmed with all the possibilities. So why do you need me?'

She raised her eyebrows and sat back.

'It's not a computer. It's an AI. Artificial Intelligence, Mr Sciler.'

In the black glass over her shoulder he saw a tracer spit across a screen. She leaned forward to touch the screen and it greyed.

'We can't yet accurately predict what the AI will permit,' she said. 'It seems to depend on the scenario, the player and a few other variables.'

'What other variables?'

'AIs . . .' She shrugged. 'Micro-fluctuations in ambient temperature, power surges, bloody-mindedness or boredom. You're hooked up to five in parallel. We want to compare what they'll allow you to conjure up, how they'll interpret your spells. The tests here in the laboratory will be controls. There are two other environments. One is the gamezone, like last night, only fully bLinkered. No solos.'

Last night, Jon realised, hadn't been his acceptance after all, but a final test for him. He had been given the solo so that if Kerz had decided not to accept him, Jon would have left Maze without realising how far they'd advanced.

'And the other environment?'

'Let's not run before you can walk, Mr Sciler. Or fly before you can run.'

She seemed to have relaxed. Her attention was on the screens. Jon prodded her gently.

'Fly? That's not possible. The gamescape hardware won't permit that.'

'That's right,' she acknowledged. 'But the bLinker gets around it. Not perfectly yet.'

Jon nodded.

'Our pharmatechs are working on the middle ear. Balance, position, equilibrium – they're all controlled by three spirit levels in the middle ear. They tell you you're motionless, that you're falling, they signal pitch, roll and yaw. They can be fooled too, as any spacer knows. As you know, Mr Sciler. We can limit the extremes of pain as well, where we need to. So you shouldn't need to go through what you may have suffered on Dirangesept again. Ah, we're ready.'

The screen displays reflected in the glass had stabilised into travelling sawteeth and trembling bright horizons.

'Now, if you'll turn around once more, we'll commence. Forget I'm here. Just do what you think the question demands.'

Jon swung round. On the lightwall were white words against jade.

CREATE: WATER

The lightwall went blank then gave him a picture of rolling mountains.

'What does it want? A glass of water, a thunderstorm, a river? What?'

'It's up to you. The AIs will interpret it too, remember.'

Jon tried a long spell to bring rain from the sky, but although the words felt right, the range of his vision was too narrow. He could concentrate on a patch of cloud and it would darken, but as he shifted his gaze the dark

62

patch, instead of spreading, cleared. He looked down at a depression in the foreground of the image and attempted a lake. A small patch of water welled up, little more than a pond. Jon rubbed his eyes. When he looked again the lightwall was blank. Then there were more words.

CREATE: FOG

A picture of a deserted street faded up and focussed. Tall timbered houses leaned over a road of rough cobbles. Jon put a spell together and introduced a thread of mist twisting out of a doorway. It followed his eyes like a vapour trail. He led it around the street, trying to thicken it, but the thread was too fine and he ended up with a scrawl of faint grey twine that just seeped away. He tried to adjust the spell and succeeded only in stabilising the scribble of mist.

He looked around at Dr Locke. She gestured for him to continue.

COPY: KEY

This time he was given a wooden table with a metal key sitting on it. After a moment the scanner began to pan around the table, rising and falling, giving him a full view of the key. Jon managed to produce the template of a key after a quarter of an hour. He followed the teeth of the original with his eyes, then he tried to trace the outline on to his model. It was hopeless.

After half an hour his head was pounding.

Dr Locke cancelled the wall and told him to stop. He stood up and stretched, feeling the cracking of his bones. She was writing as he left her. 'Magic isn't easy,' she said without looking up. 'We'll continue tomorrow, Mr Sciler.'

SEVEN

'Ghosts,' said Jon.

Chrye couldn't see anything, but a moment after he'd said it she heard the approaching thin giggling through the mist of fine grey ash. It had been falling for two days, deposited from a month-old eruption in the Sumatran string. Kentish Town was ankle-deep in ash. The council was spraying it with gel to bind the particles and then ploughing the stuff into the nearest rift, but it was a losing battle.

Jon pulled her into the extinguished doorway of a newsagent. Behind the glass a handwritten note was unevenly taped at eye level, the corners of the paper yellow and curling like ancient parchment. The ink had faded and the words, 'Back in five minutes', were hard to make out.

The feel of Chrye's bare wrist in his palm did something to Jon. He realised it was the first time he had touched her without the reaching-out being for his own comfort. Until now, it had been Chrye touching him.

He could hear them getting closer. They sounded crazy. He pulled Chrye as far into the shadows as he could, then hooded his eyes against the reflection and peered through the glass. Inside the shop a pile of tabloids was propped against the door. The headline of the topmost paper read, 'NY TO FOLLOW SANFRAN INTO SEA IN THREE YEARS.' And beneath it, 'ATLANTIC TO MEET PACIFIC IN TEN.' Jon squinted at the dateline. Over a year ago. Maybe the time scale had been pessimistic, but the tectonic disruption that had destroyed most of America would eventually consume the rest of the world. Asia and Australia were further down the track than Europe, according to satellite pictures, and Africa was close behind them. The only argument seemed to be whether the end would be caused by ripple or domino effect.

There would be no reprieve. The Earth was dead from the moment

ReGenesis triggered the chain of nuclear devices it had set along the floor of the Marianas trench in the Pacific Ocean. The Christian fundamentalists had anticipated the tidal waves giving them their new American dawn, but not the effects on the planet's crust and the release of trenched radioactive waste.

A sharper flurry of billowing ash blew past the doorway. Here they were. For a moment more Jon held Chrye's hand loosely in the recess of the doorway as five of them went by, grinning, their skin as clear as smoked glass and as tight as plastic. They were wearing skintight black T-shirts and bleached jeans cut off at the knees, and fluorescent yellow boots. They weren't wearing filters. Their necks were traceries of hyperoxygenated capillaries, and thin tubes snaked from their wrist cuffs to the feed-bulbs in their hands. They clenched their fists as they moved, pulsing the drug through the clear tubes into their veins. Their eyes were pools of neon.

Chrye watched them dance by. 'How was it, coming back to this?'

Jon moved out on to the street again, remembering. 'It was as if we'd landed on the wrong planet. Another hostile one. But this time we were flesh-naked.' He swept his arm in an arc, the ash washing around him. 'This was worse, of course, the air, the pollution, the tremors and rifts, but our reception . . . none of us was prepared for it.'

She touched his arm. 'It was understandable. Thirty-seven years you were gone. Eighteen years of hope, a year of confusion and disbelief as the information started to filter back, and then eighteen more years of media-led anger feeding on despair,' she said. 'My generation was brought up to revile the returning Far Warriors.'

Jon glanced at her, wanting to understand her. 'Why don't you?'

The ash was gathering more thickly, folding around them as they walked. The street became as intimate as a bed. Jon felt himself drifting, weightless. He thought of the warmth of her hand and looked for a moment into her eyes. Their blue reminded him of Lapis and Lazuli, but the colour of Chrye's had a depth that theirs lacked.

'Chrye,' he said, almost to himself. 'I've never heard the name before.'

'I was born as you entered orbit over Dirangesept,' she said. 'When there was so much hope. That year most of the babies were named after flowers. My mother remembered chrysanthemums. She told me they were so beautiful. I think she imagined great fields of chrysanthemums on Dirangesept. Yellow chrysanthemums.'

She fell silent. Jon had a sense he should say something to her. He couldn't.

The ash was growing still denser. It was clinging to them, but now Jon felt it was sealing them within themselves. He felt isolated from Chrye.

'Where are we going?' Chrye said. 'We've done a circle. We're nearly back at your place.'

'That's where we're going,' he said. He glanced at his watch. 'There's someone you're going to meet sooner or later if you're going to be visiting me again, and I'll feel better about it if I'm with you the first time. You've missed him so far, but that won't go on. I'm pretty sure he's off duty this afternoon, so he'll be back there by now. I want it to look coincidental.'

Chrye sensed tension in his voice and tried to make a joke of it. She said, 'Who is this mystery guy? Is he good-looking?'

'His name's Hickey Sill.'

Hickey Sill was a runt with a swagger. He lived in the room below Jon's.

Hickey was standing in his doorway watching them come up the stairs, as Jon had guessed he would be.

Jon paused and rested a hand on the metal rail. It was cold and greasy with sweat. He wiped his palm on his trousers. 'Hickey,' he said.

Hickey's eyes darted beyond Jon to Chrye. His lips split open.

'Girlfriend, eh? Bring her in. Plenty enough for three.'

Jon started up again. 'She's not my girlfriend.'

Hickey's mouth split wider. 'All the better. She wouldn't say no to a drink with a pacifist, would she? What's her name?' He stepped out of the doorway. Jon stopped three steps below him, his eyes level with Hickey's. He could smell the stuff on Hickey's breath. He took a step up.

'Aw, be nice,' said Hickey. ' 'Cos if you don't be nice, I can be a lot more not nice back.' He put a hand out to Jon's shoulder to steady himself. 'My, what big muscles you have, Mr Wolf,' he said.

Chrye touched Jon's arm. 'We'd be happy to have a drink with you. And my name's Chrye,' she said. 'You're a pacifist, then?'

Hickey pushed himself off Jon. ' 'S better,' he said. He headed back into his room.

Jon gave Chrye a warning look. 'Don't worry,' she mouthed.

'Yeah, I'm a 'fist,' said Hickey Sill. 'My trig.' He pointed up at a wall covered with pictures torn from fleshzines, of girls sprawled wet and naked over indefinable, glittering chrome machinery. The biggest photo tacked to the peeling wall, overshadowing the others, was of a pacifist autoid squatting down on its three articulated legs. Across the top of the picture was scrawled in childish lettering, 'The **Fist** In Pacifist'. Scattered amongst the girls were more images of the same autoid running, its legs telescoping, and of the arms extended.

Hickey brandished a brushed-silver atmosflask. 'Impounded this morning,' he said. He giggled. 'Still hot.' He shook the smooth cocoon then unscrewed the top and poured three glasses of deep red liquor. He gave Jon the smallest, and the next to Chrye. Hickey raised his to the room's high naked bulb and squinted at it. Something moved there.

'Fire down below,' said Hickey and drained the glass. He sat down abruptly, and his head dropped.

'Count from twenty,' Jon told Chrye. He took her glass and poured their two measures back into the flask. He couldn't quite make out the larvae. They were a thickness of colour, swirls of crimson in scarlet.

'. . . two, one,' said Chrye. Jon screwed up the flask and tossed back her empty glass as Hickey belched and looked sharply up, directly at Chrye. She lifted the glass to him and smiled.

'He told you about Dirangesept?' Hickey asked. 'Never told me shit. Not surprised, of course. Couldn't kill a bunch of dumb animals. How they had the fucking nerve to come back . . .' He gestured at the picture on the wall. 'I've got blackeyes there, and hardhands, and scattergas . . .' He shook his head in disbelief. 'An' that's nothing. I've read what they had up there, military autoids fucking loaded with death.'

Jon stood up. Hickey didn't even register it. Chrye watched Hickey's eyes. The quivering pupils were directed at her, but there was nothing there.

'I could hardhandle this whole fucking city with half my weaponload,' murmured Hickey dreamily.

Chrye looked at Jon. His back was to her. He must have listened to this a thousand times, not daring to argue with the crazy pacifist. Hickey Sill was an extremist, but what he said was what everyone thought of the Far Warriors.

'What's this, Hickey?' Jon was in the corner of the room.

Hickey rose uncertainly to his feet. 'Ah. Sssh.'

Chrye beat him over to Jon. On a small plastic table a metre-long widescreen was set up with a headset and keypad.

'Is it a game?' she said.

'No.. Impounded,' said Hickey. He leered at her and pushed her aside. 'On loan.' He picked up the keypad and flicked it. The screen became live. It showed a dim street in three-sixty with a few degrees of crossover at each end. A brick wall filled half the screen, curled tatters of fading, air-eaten posters partly concealing fragments of graffiti.

'A remote scanner?' said Chrye.

'No,' said Jon. 'I think I've seen one before.'

Hickey Sill giggled and his fingers did a jig over the keys. The picture brightened and the wall slid back.

'Blackeyes on, up and rolling,' announced Hickey.

'He's got a transceiver,' said Jon quietly. 'Illegal. Very expensive. They're used to hack into pacifist autoids like Hickey's trig and override them. Cuckoos, they call them. They're not usually very effective, since the frequency codes change hundreds of times a second. They just jam them, most of the time. But if you know the code routines, like Hickey knows his, you can program the cuckoo . . .'

'Sssh,' said Hickey, squinting at the display. 'Better park it. Walls have eyes.' The wall returned to its former position.

'. . . then you can moonlight from home, run all sorts of little errands. Hickey here could get busted for the atmosflask, but for possession of a cuckoo he could . . .'

'Could nothing, Mr Far fucking Warrior,' interrupted Hickey. ''Cos the guy who gave me it ain't missing it no more, so if anything happens I'll know where to go.' He pointed at the screen and palmed keys. A three-fingered metal claw came up close, flexing, then folded into a seamless ball. Hickey shifted his thumb and the hardhand slammed away into and through the wall. Hickey pulled the hardhand back up to the screen, brickdust eddying around it.

'Now,' Hickey said, 'how about another little drink?'

Jon had told her Hickey wouldn't be there this time, but Chrye had still run up the stairs past the pacifist's room, holding her breath. She'd recovered quickly, but now, looking at the book lying on the table between them, her breath caught again.

It had to be a journal. It had a maroon leather cover, and was so thumbed that it wouldn't lie flat any more. On the top right corner an ornate S had been carved into the leather.

He kept a journal, she thought with excitement. Jon Sciler had kept a journal. She had hoped he might have done – a poet would. She thought of her studies, and of what might be in Jon Sciler's journal of Dirangesept, and found herself remembering lines instead.

> Here we are our own gods.
> We reinvent and reincarnate ourselves.
> Here we are our own devils,
> Consigning ourselves to our own limbos,
> Delivering ourselves to our personal hells.

She stared at the book. It looked as though there had been words on the cover, but whatever there might have been was obliterated by dense scribble that had scored and even ripped the leather.

Jon stirred the book around the table with a finger. 'Let me tell you something,' he said. 'Let me tell you about someone.'

Chrye lifted her eyes to him. 'All right,' she said. She watched the breath he took, long and slow.

'He was really my only family after my parents died, and I was his, I suppose. We grew up in an orphanage. His real name was Marcus Lees. He never used it. He called himself Starburn. Starburn was a flickpage hero back then. An orphan. I remember his catchline – "Last of His Race from the Depths of Space". Starburn had lost his memory, except for the occasional flash of recall. Grew up thinking he was mad but human, realised much later that he was from another world.' Jon grinned faintly. 'The usual story. You ever seen those things?'

'Who hasn't? I never heard of Starburn, though.'

'You weren't born.' He sighed. 'Starburn had a pet too . . .' He saw Chrye's confusion. 'The flickpage hero. He had a crazy wolf that had been found by his adoptive parents in a wood. The wolf had been brought up with the family dog, thought it was a dog.'

Chrye said, 'Nice touch that, him and his wolf, both thinking they were less than they were.'

Jon stopped and looked at her. 'Yes. Yes.' He took a sip of his drink. 'We used to go to the game halls together. He was always beating me, whatever we played. The highest scores were all topscreened and they were all columns of Starburn. He got a real slam out of that.'

'What were Starburn's powers?' She saw him hesitate, and laughed. 'The flickpage hero. Did he have any?'

She could see him relaxing now. He had stopped pushing the book around and was stroking the cover with a finger as he talked, running his finger over the monogram. Chrye suddenly thought, Sciler? Starburn?

'Travel at light speed, I think. And other stuff, a bit weird.'

'What about limitations? That's standard in the flickpages, isn't it? Isn't there always an Achilles' heel? Was there anything like that?'

'Oh, yeah. If I can remember. His powers only worked at night. The Earthbound – he called humans Earthbound – were scared of him. They thought he was a vampire, and the wolf a werewolf, of course. Oh, and something else. There was a constellation in the sky that had to be visible for his powers to work. It couldn't be a cloudy night.'

'He had problems, then,' said Chrye dryly.

Jon nodded. 'And hair just like Marcus's. A little red streak. I suppose that's why he identified with him so much.'

'Natural enough. Go on.'

'We stayed close after leaving the orphanage. Bummed around the arcades. Made money that way. We knew all the games. I was good, but he was unbeatable. I did the setups, Starburn did the rest.'

He took his finger from the book.

'Then Dirangesept came along. Starburn enlisted us both like they were paradise tickets.'

'Did you mind?'

'I'd have gone to hell with him.' He laid his hand over the book. 'I didn't expect to.'

Chrye waited, watching his eyes, their flecks of green in brown.

'They took us, we were among the first. We were perfect. Young. No family, game crazy, high quotients on the lot – reflex, spatial anticipation, learning ability. Starburn was a special prize. Having him was perfect for the project. All the players he'd beaten in the halls couldn't wait to join up. He was their armour and their sword. Just as he was mine.'

'Did you feel bad about that, Jon? Responsible for them?'

He glanced at her. 'I did. Not now.' He fell silent.

Chrye said tentatively, feeling she'd suddenly lost him, 'Did you blame him for all the deaths? You know that's wrong.' There was so much more inside Jon, Chrye sensed. She wanted to reach out and touch him.

'Of course you know why he enlisted, Jon.'

He rubbed his eye. 'Oh, yes. Dirangesept. Space. It might have been *the* constellation. He was insane for a while up there, I'm certain. He thought he was Starburn come home to save his planet. But, hell, he was still good.

He lost fewer autoids than anyone else. He couldn't save us, though. He couldn't even save himself. He was only human.'

Jon took a breath and continued. 'The stigmata were the start of it, then back here the suicides and self-mutilations began.' His voice began to catch. 'As you know.'

Chrye nodded.

'Back here on Earth we lost touch for a long time. Someone said he'd joined Maze. It surprised me at first. Then I started getting these letters from him. We never met again, though. He wouldn't see me. He said in his letters there wasn't the time.' Jon ran his tongue around his lips. 'The letters. He became obsessed with the stuff he was testing for them.'

He looked at Chrye and then away. 'His letters became more and more agitated. I stopped reading them. I wrote back, but although he kept writing, he never seemed to acknowledge me. It was just all this vague stuff about the game. And that I should join Maze.'

She nodded again. 'I did wonder . . .'

'No. No. I didn't. That was the last thing I was ever going to do. If he wanted to, fine. He wasn't my closest friend any more, the friend I'd gone to Dirangesept with. He was a crazy stranger. In the end I was throwing the letters away without opening them.'

'I don't understand. You've joined Maze.'

'Listen to me, Chrye. The letters stopped coming. I thought . . . I don't know what I thought. It didn't seem to matter.' Jon picked up his mug and took a swallow of the lukewarm coffee. His throat was dry. 'Then I read he'd died, killed himself.'

He stopped. The words seemed to bounce round the room. His eyes were stinging and he rubbed them, not understanding at first that he was crying. He didn't know when he'd last shed tears. He hadn't spoken to anyone else about Starburn's death. Not even to Kei. He wasn't sure whether Kei knew Starburn was dead. Probably he didn't. The name Marcus Lees in the news wouldn't have rung bells for anyone but Jon.

Except that there had been someone else at the scattering, he remembered. Someone else knew Starburn was Marcus Lees, and knew him well enough to attend his scattering.

'I'm sorry,' said Chrye. 'You must have felt you'd let him down. But you didn't. He was clearly deeply disturbed.'

'Listen to me, Chrye. It's impossible. He didn't kill himself. He was murdered.'

'Jon, you know how many Far Warriors—'

'You aren't listening. It would have been physically impossible for him to do it. They said he was found drowned in a reservoir. He couldn't have done that, Chrye. He had a phobia about water.' Jon was on his feet, breathing heavily. He wiped his hands over his face.

Chrye waited for him to sit down again. 'So that's why you joined Maze.'

Jon stroked the cover of the book with a trembling finger, then pushed it over the table towards her. 'A few days after his death I received this. He must have sent it just before . . .' He shook his head helplessly. 'I open it and close it, but I haven't been able to sit down and read it. I want you to. This is your field. I want you to tell me about him.'

Now it makes sense, Chrye thought. She felt relieved to know why he was cooperating with her. He needed something from her. He needed her help.

She just didn't understand why it also felt like a rejection.

EIGHT

Jon waited for Kerz to speak. He had the feeling that something was about to move forward at Maze. Something was about to change.

Kerz was in no hurry. 'How are you getting along at Reality Validation?' he said at last, slowly.

'I can't tell. Dr Locke won't say.'

'Then I'll tell you. You're progressing very well. Remarkably well. And you've been very patient. Do you have any questions?'

'Yes. These tests have been going on for a month now. I know the spells but I haven't seen what they'll do in a zone. It's like learning a language from a book and never going where they speak it. It seems pointless.'

Kerz nodded. He pushed the tips of his index fingers together hard and watched as they blanched. 'How are you sleeping? Do you dream at all?'

'What do you think? Of course I do.'

'Anything out of the ordinary?' He lifted his arched hands and sighted at Jon along his fingertips.

'What's an ordinary dream, Kerz? I still dream of Dirangesept.' Jon shrugged. 'That's all.'

Kerz let air between his fingers. Their colour seeped back. 'You're ready for the next stage, Mr Sciler. It's time to speak the language. I know it's been frustrating for you, but we've had no choice. You had to pass all the tests before we could show you their point. Security . . .'

He rose to his feet and moved around his desk, walking Jon towards the door. 'We have something new for you,' he said. 'You're up and running. And you're fast, too. It's time to see how fast you are.' Kerz stopped at the door and turned around.

'One last thing. You will have noticed the confidentiality clause in the contract you signed with us. That's standard. I'd like to remind you of it.

You must discuss nothing of what you experience and learn here with anyone else outside of these walls. Anyone at all. That includes fellow players. Do you understand that? And do you accept it? If not, your contract terminates right here and now. And the same if you ever contravene it. Ever, Mr Sciler.'

'That's fine,' Jon said smoothly.

'Good. Let's go, then.' Kerz ushered Jon into the corridor, and Jon started towards the elevator.

Kerz had halted by the door. 'Where are you going?' he called.

Jon looked round. 'The gamescape in the old bus garage. I assumed . . . Where is the zone, then?'

Kerz grinned. Jon noticed how regular his teeth were. 'You'll be accessing it here at Maze.'

'Here? But . . .'

'Old technology, Jon. Out of date now, or just about to be. This is a fully internalised zone. There is no physical arena. No muscleware at all. We made a major technical breakthrough a short while ago, which is the reason for all the secrecy. Our bLinker technology provides total motor bypass. It'll be just like you're asleep, only the dream's the game.'

Jon stared at the chrome curves and shivered. It wasn't the cold. The room was as warm as blood. He hadn't seen a CrySis pod since the Dirangesept ships.

'Claustrophobic?' asked Dr Locke shortly. She glanced up at the bank of screens on the wall. She had looked straight through his nakedness, which made him even more conscious of it. He wondered what she did see. Soft hardware, he guessed. His mind jumped, and he wondered what Chrye had seen when she had looked at him naked. For both women he was a cache of raw data, but there was a difference in Chrye's gaze. Dr Locke just wanted technical access. He wasn't quite sure what Chrye wanted. He was seeing her again in Nearvana, sitting there, touching her bangle to the glass. Then he thought of Starburn dead and had the sense of everything breaking apart, everything except Chrye.

'If you're claustrophobic, I can ease it.'

Jon shook his head. 'No drugs.'

'I didn't mean drugs. Once you're bLinkered, I can directly—'

'I'm not claustrophobic.'

Her attention shifted back to the screens. She said over her shoulder,

'You're not going into cryonic stasis here, if that worries you. We're just using the CrySis pod's monitoring equipment. It's convenient.'

It didn't help. Jon eased himself into the pod and let the clear bodygel flow around him. It welled uncomfortably into his ears and rose until he could feel the cool meniscus circle his forehead, cheeks and chin. It was as if he were wearing a mask of air. Dr Locke glanced at him. He felt even more exposed.

'Now, Jon,' she said. Her voice sounded distant through the viscous gel. 'Once you're in the zone we can't reach you. You won't be alone, of course, but we can't communicate with you. The zone's freestanding.'

He twisted his head towards her. The gel damped his movement. He could feel the gentle dragging of his hair against his scalp. 'How do I get out?' he asked her. His own voice sounded alien. The gel nudged the corners of his lips. 'Time limit?'

'Uh-uh. You can stay there as long or as briefly as you like, but you come out when you want.' She paused. 'You'll have an exitline. It has to be a word or phrase you won't forget, and that you're not going to need in the zone other than to exit.'

Jon thought. 'Chrysanthemum,' he said.

She didn't react. She bent towards him and he opened his mouth for the airline. It tasted of plastic and menthol. He bit hard on it as she slipped the bLinkers over the bridge of his nose. Then her hand moved out of sight and the pod's ridged carbon lid began to slide down. The gel meniscus eased up to swallow him, and he thought he heard her say, 'Remember, magic will be different.'

Jon lay in the blackness of the pod, waiting for Mach Null. The wait was interminable. He lost all awareness of the gel and the mouthpiece. He moved his limbs, or thought he did, but there was no sensation. He felt disembodied. He wondered what had gone through Starburn's mind at this point. This must be the game Starburn had been working on.

His thoughts began to wander. There had been something in the way Hickey had leered at Chrye, watching Jon's reaction to it. Hickey was unpredictable. Maybe it had been a mistake to introduce him to Chrye. Maybe he should just have kept her away from him altogether.

It wasn't happening. He should have been in the zone by now. Something had gone wrong. Without any sense of the gel supporting him, he began to feel nauseous. He didn't know why. He didn't think he was claustrophobic. Panic surged for a moment and his heart lurched, then the feeling of fear went away and he seemed to sleep.

Bile rose in his throat, waking him. He tried to swallow but it welled up stinging until he gagged and jerked up reflexively, his eyes wet, tear ducts stimulated by the bitter taste. He opened his eyes, realising that he hadn't struck his head on the canopy of the pod, and rubbed the water away.

He was lying in a bed. He tried to sit up, but his body was unaccountably stiff and sore. He hauled himself on to his elbows, feeling worse than he'd ever felt with the stigmata.

Something had gone wrong. He licked his lips, aware of a consuming thirst. His heart was thumping.

The light was dim and he couldn't see well. He waited for his eyes to accommodate to the gloom. He felt cold. The room was cold, his bed sheets were ice-cold. He shivered briefly, fighting off panic, and lay back down. Exhaustion overcame him and he slept again.

When he woke again and looked around, the darkness began to resolve and in time shapes formed around him. He squinted until he could focus.

More beds stretched away in every direction. This was not a gamezone. It was real. He was in a ward, a vast hospital ward.

It wasn't quite right, though. It shouldn't be so cold in a hospital.

Maybe he had a fever. That would explain the muscle ache. He rolled his shoulders. They felt like they'd felt orbiting Dirangesept, immediately after emerging from the years of CrySis.

There had to have been a hardware malfunction. The pod must have failed.

Still, it shouldn't be so dark. He looked at the beds. There were shrouded shapes on them, but no movement at all. Jon felt his skin crawl. All the patients lay serenely on their backs, creaseless sheets drawn up to their chins.

Jon felt an urge to throw his sheet off and run, but something froze him. He suddenly wanted this to be the gamezone, but there was nothing false about it. He put the corner of the freezing sheet into his mouth. The rough cloth grated against his teeth and drew saliva, as it had when he'd been a child in the orphanage, alone in bed and scared of the dark, but there was no comfort in it now. He spat out the lint it left on his tongue. It was all real. The silence was the heavy silence of a huge room. The smell was the smell of rot and death. Every sensation was real, but the strongest of them was his own fear.

He knew where he was. This was a morgue. Everyone here was dead.

He wiped his mouth with the back of his hand. There was several days' stubble on his chin. He peered at his hands. His nails needed cutting. He ran his fingers through his hair. Long hair.

He flicked his eyes around the room, desperate to find a fault. There was none. No detail gap. No blur while the program caught up. He held a finger up to his nose as close as he could focus, then looked sharply at a far bed. There was the normal physiological delay in refocussing. No gamezone's infinite focus. It was perfect. It was real.

He tried to control his breathing. He was hyperventilating and shivering at the same time. He tried to think back. He remembered going into the pod, and then there was a blank. Then he'd woken here.

Something must have happened while he was in the pod. Or maybe he'd been in the zone, and somehow entered a catatonic state. He'd heard stories, everyone had. Fucked software, fucked pods, fucked bLinkers. Fucked players.

Maze must think he was dead.

He began to calm down. He wasn't dead, though. He wasn't dead. He was alive.

He looked for a name tag on his wrist, but there wasn't one. Hardly surprising. Kerz had had his corpse anonymously disposed of. Maze wouldn't want their failures found. Like Starburn's death? Jon wondered how many others there had been. Perhaps that was why Maze liked to use Far Warriors. Displaced people. No dependants. No questions.

Would Chrye ask questions? He cast the thought aside. It wasn't necessary. He was alive.

He checked his pulse. Slow, if anything. Must be the cold. It was getting hard to think, to think straight. He had to get out.

He sat up painfully. He was so stiff. He felt like he'd been here for years.

A movement caught his eye. It was almost shocking in the stillness. Someone was silently moving among the beds, a woman dressed in a dark smock and a long flowing skirt. A mortuary attendant. She must have seen him. She was threading her way towards him.

He watched her approach his bed, staring at her, and all thought was driven from his head. She stopped beside him and nodded, smiling. Jon just stared at her eyes.

'Hello,' she said, obviously unsurprised at the rising of a dead man. She reached for his wrist and took his pulse. Her hand was warm and dry. 'You're with us,' she said. 'And for the first time. Welcome to Cathar.'

She twisted her head away, and Jon noticed another figure, far away among the beds. The woman at his side beckoned and called out in a low voice, 'We have a waker here. I'll deal with him.'

Jon thought he caught another movement at the corner of his eye, but he couldn't fix it. Something low down, just above bed height, a quick flash of dark red in the drab room. What had she meant, 'for the first time'?

The woman beside Jon turned her eyes back to him.

His head whirled. Her hair was brown and extraordinarily thick, pulled back at the nape of her neck and roughly plaited. She had high sharp cheekbones, but not unnaturally so. It was her eyes. The irises of her eyes were huge and so yellow that even in the gloom they almost glowed. They were impossible eyes.

He stared. She was impossible, but she was real. All of this was real. He was certain of it.

He pulled his hand away from her. He felt dizzy. He looked into those incredible eyes and whispered, 'Chrysanthemum.' As he said it, he was not certain any more that it would work. He wasn't even sure that he wanted it to.

NINE

Jon shook his head. 'Not *déjà vu.*' He frowned. 'It was like a familiarity. Like I'd been there before, in dreams maybe. Yes, maybe that's it. She said I was a waker for the first time, but maybe that was only in this body. That body. Maybe . . .'

Chrye saw Jon beginning to drift. She touched his hand and he jerked.

'Tell me, Jon.'

He looked at her as if he'd never seen her. As if she were the dream.

'You said you exited the zone when you saw her for the first time. Go on.'

'Mm. I'm sorry.' He shook his head as though flies were buzzing around him. 'I don't seem to have it right now. Sometimes when I think of it, the memory's so real. No wonder they're paranoid about secrecy. It was incredible.'

'You told me you came out for two hours . . .' she repeated patiently.

He stared at his hands on the table. 'Cathar, she called it. I think Starburn called it that, in the journal. I remember seeing the name. I don't know if it's the name of the village, or the country, or what. Cathar.' He flexed his fingers, turned his hands over and back again. 'Two hours,' he murmured. 'Jesus, it seemed . . . I just sat there in the CrySis chamber. I couldn't believe it. Dr Locke took me through it, then I went back there again.'

'Jon.'

He sighed heavily. 'She said her name was Jhalouk. She said she'd been the one tending to me, washing me, cutting my hair and shaving me while I'd slept. Apparently it's a common thing, we wake for the first time and it's such a shock that we exit almost immediately. They clean us up, and

79

wait, and we return later. Well, some never return. She says there's a long period of adjustment, of acceptance.'

He had a few days' stubble now, Chrye had noticed. In this world. That troubled her. And he'd said, 'Back *there*.' 'Jon,' she said harshly, 'Cathar is a game program. It's the best you've seen, but it's mindware. It doesn't exist.'

'I know that. I do. It's just that everything was so *real*. With bLinkers, or in the solo, it was only ever simmed, a sort of hobbled reality. It was play. But this . . . She was as real as you are, Chrye.'

'In the game. But you're out now, Jon. Think of it as a dream. It's as real as life when you're in it, but as soon as you wake up you know it for fake. And now you're out of the zone . . .'

'But you can't go back into a dream, Chrye.'

Chrye gave up. 'Go on, then. Tell me the rest.'

His cheeks were stinging mildly, and when he put a finger to his chin it was smooth. He explored his cheeks with his palms.

'I put some balm on after I shaved you,' Jhalouk said awkwardly. 'Perhaps too much. I'm sorry.'

'It's okay.' He felt uncomfortable with her. In the dim light of the sleeping chamber she was looking at him with concern. He looked away, his eyes ranging over the still room. Empathy. How the hell did they program a construct with empathy?

'Are you ready?' she asked him.

He forced a grin.

'You must close your eyes as we leave the sleeping chamber,' she said. 'The sunlight will damage them.'

She led him through the rows of beds. He glanced at the lifeless faces framed by plump soft pillows as they passed. There were men, there were women and there were children. Of course there were kids, he thought. Kids would play the zone too, once it was released.

Jhalouk was talking to him. Sometimes wakers arrived at night, she said, and that was better, but now it was mid-afternoon, with the sun strong and Jon's eyes dark-tuned. Jon murmured something back to her, seeing the plot logic. Squint at first, accustom yourself only gradually, and you'll be more inclined to accept the zone's daylight visuals.

So at the tall door of the chamber he'd obediently closed his eyes and she'd taken his hand. Her warm hand was small and her palm and the pads of her slender fingers were calloused. He explored her hand with his, astounded by its detail, and heard her laughter. He ran his finger along her deep lifeline.

Then suddenly he felt warmth on his face and there was diffuse light glowing through his eyelids. There was more. There were voices speaking and shouting, and above – definitely *above* him – was the shrill keening of birds. He leaned slightly forward and someone brushed roughly past him. Jhalouk said a few sharp words to the other person that Jon didn't catch. He caught a whiff of pipe smoke that made him cough, and as it cleared he realised that the air he was breathing was untreated. It was good air.

'Walk forward now. Keep your eyes closed,' the girl said.

He heard the clatter away to his left of something approaching rapidly, and recoiled instinctively just as she tugged him back. The clatter was in front of him and past with a cuffing of wind on his face.

'Horse and cart,' Jon murmured appreciatively. He felt his heart thumping.

'I'm sorry,' she said. 'I didn't see it. It's all right now. Come on.'

There was a transition underfoot from flat stone to cobbles. He could feel their unevenness through the soles of the sandals she'd given him, and he could feel the sun on his feet between the thin straps. He lifted his face to the sky.

'Aah.' His eyes were closed, but he smiled. When had he last smiled? He thought the corners of his mouth would crack.

'Be careful, there's a step here.' Her small hand squeezed his.

'Salt,' he said abruptly. 'I can smell salt.' He remembered the rough olfactory pharmatech when he'd arrived at Maze the first time. He realised how synthetic that had been in comparison.

'Of course,' she answered. 'Sit down here, that's it, slowly. We're by the sea.'

The seat was smooth stone, almost too warm against the backs of his thighs. He'd put on thin trousers in the cold dark chamber along with a thin cotton shirt and the sandals. It felt like cotton, at least.

'You can lean back. There.'

His back pressed against two broad bars of slightly yielding wood. He could feel them moving with her weight beside him. A shadow flicked between his eyes and the light, and her palm was touching his eyelids.

'Open your eyes gently.'

Despite her guarding hand, the sliver of sunlight was blinding. He closed his eyes again, suddenly scared. He felt himself standing on the brink of something, the soles of his feet on solid ground but his toes dangling, and he would open his eyes to see . . . what?

She laughed, and he tried to see the logic path. Easy so far. They've found a way to bypass Mach Null, hardly a significant advance. She was a construct seen by half-light, and it's all been non-visual stims since then. It's just getting to me. Starburn is dead, but he's still getting to me.

He opened his eyes. Her hand was still there, her fingers a lattice between himself and brilliant light. She began to withdraw them, and he grabbed her wrist.

'Wait.'

Something changed. He had taken control, even if only to hide behind her hand. Until that moment he had acquiesced, let her – let the program – guide him. By grabbing her he had changed the parameters. He was playing.

'Ouch. You're squeezing my hand.'

He let her go. She left her hand over his eyes, and the brilliance of the light gradually became bearable.

There had been emotion in her voice. The instinctive reaction against unexpected discomfort, sharp reproach. That subtlety of emotion from a construct, even a construct built by an AI.

'I'm sorry,' he said. 'I wasn't quite ready.'

She's not a construct, he thought. She was a player too. Of course. Just because she leaked it that the players in this zone were what she called wakers, that didn't mean everything else was a construct. She'd be an in-house player from Maze. She was a guide. It made sense.

He thought he had it then, just for a moment. Until he opened his eyes.

The water was so blue that he gasped. Across the bay were mountains, their cool rising slopes a play of emerald and jade green. The sudden sense of distance, the perspective, made him sit back hard into the seat. He let his gaze drop slowly, over the water and across the quay's edge until he was staring at his feet in their soft leather sandals. There was no fade. There was no blur or pause. It really was a beautiful piece of pharmatech, he told himself. He told himself again, then gave it up.

He looked more closely at the harbour. A narrow stone jetty pushed out from the quay, and within a low breakwater a few small boats rocked at anchor. The boats were clinker-built, shallow-keeled and high at bow and stern, with low cabins amidships. The ropes securing the vessels could be followed down through the water, he saw, all the way to the seabed, perhaps waist-deep here. There were flames of coral down there, and the flicker of shoals of darting fish.

Learn the zone, Jon thought. He looked again at the boats and noted the stylised eyes painted at bow and stern. They could be significant, and they could be no more than the scrawls of superstition.

He thought of sea myths, legends of the seas, and his heartbeat quickened at the thought of so much possibility. Along the quayside were men opening their nets to dry and for repair, laying out the fine mesh between cables of dark stone weights and thin lines of mottled cork floats. Jon looked along the jetty's waterline for a tide mark, wondering if this was low tide or high.

Beyond the breakwater a sailing vessel pulled into view, its full pale sheet drawing Jon's eye. He also saw a small island far beyond it that he hadn't noticed at first. It seemed slightly indistinct, as if somehow, despite being surrounded by clear bright sea, it lay in shadow. He thought almost in relief that the program had a glitch, but then realised that the island was a bare rock outcrop. It sat strangely in the general scene. Looking more closely, he noticed an ugly building of stone grafted on to the small wave-whipped island.

The sailing vessel had almost reached the jetty. As it came alongside a couple of men leapt ashore and began hauling on thick mooring ropes, dropping them in loose figures of eight around double-stubbed iron stanchions. The small boat slipped back briefly, sliding off its own wash, and the ropes gathered the slack, then took the strain, snaking and tightening around the stanchions.

Forgetting Jhalouk, Jon got to his feet and walked over towards the boat, stopping beside the stanchions. He could hear the hemp creak and see the fibres twist. He rested a hand on the crown of a stanchion. It was warm, and there was a faint shiver as the rope strained and shifted. The vessel was secure at bow and stern, but it was still bucking heavily from side to side.

He looked down on to the deck and saw why. The three men who were the boat's crew were struggling with something he couldn't identify, thrashing about on the slippery boards. One of them abruptly swore and reeled away from the confusion. The boat rose on a small wave and sank back and away from the jetty before the mooring ropes yanked it sharply back. It tipped abruptly and the sailor lurched further, off balance and yelling, then tumbled over the boat's low rail and into the water.

He surfaced quickly and was heaving himself up a rope on to the jetty before Jon could move to help him. Bright sprays of water flew from his clothes and dropped like jewels in the sun, staining the stone jetty black before fading almost instantly. His slapped wet footprints lasted moments longer. He leapt back on to the boat and landed on his feet, not quite losing his balance as the boat juddered with his impact. The other men adjusted easily to the abruptly shifting deck.

The complexity of it was astounding. Jon tried to replay it in his mind, the clean arc of the man's leap, his wet shirt flapping, the boat's reaction, the compensating moves of the others. The pure equations of it all, and the whole thing just a throwaway line.

Now Jon saw what the men struggled with on the deck. They had a great sea turtle that was at least as long as the men were tall, and as broad as a barrel. It had been turned on its back and partly secured in some form of harness that trapped its flippers against the underside of its shell and muzzled its jaws, but one of the front flippers was still free, and it was this that had knocked the sailor away in a last gesture. The turtle was worn down and exhausted, and the three men were finally able to secure the flipper and stand back to watch it rocking silently on its shell, its bullet head twisting slowly from side to side. Jon watched the jaws working against the muzzle. The men were panting, leaning against the sides of the boat, staring at the captive animal. The boat rocked gently. Jon listened to the turtle's shell grating against the boards.

Jhalouk was by his side. 'It's a valuable catch,' she said. 'Turtles can be trained to tow boats and to set and gather fishing nets.'

Suddenly Jon felt overwhelmed and drained. 'Jhalouk, I'm going to exit.' He rubbed his eyes. 'I mean sleep. I'm too tired.'

She looked alarmed. 'No! Wait.' She led him back to the seat and sat with him. 'Don't go to sleep here,' she told him. 'I'll take you to my house. You'll be staying with me for a while. But you must lie down before you sleep, or you can damage yourself.'

He didn't understand her. He drew a deep breath and shook his head. 'How can I hurt myself by sleeping?'

She smiled. 'You wakers don't sleep like us. When you say your charm word, you just slump like puppets with cut strings. If you had been standing on the jetty, you might have struck your head or even fallen into the water and drowned. You must be careful. You're newly woken. There's a lot for you to learn.'

She pulled him gently to his feet and pointed up the hill. 'It's steep, but it isn't far.'

His legs felt like lead. 'Tell me more about wakers,' he said as they walked. The path was steep and tiring, winding through alleys with houses to either side.

'There are sometimes children born to women in Cathar, children who live but have no life. They are tended in their sleep, cared for, and they grow old and die. We tend them in halls like . . .' She waved a hand down towards the sea front far below them. 'Very rarely they awaken, as you have. Sometimes they bring strange memories, sometimes none. Sometimes they awaken just once, briefly, and never return.' She turned her head and smiled at him. 'I wasn't sure if you would. You looked so shocked to see me.'

They had left the houses behind and were rising through fields of some pale green crop that Jon didn't recognise. The path was levelling off and the hillside becoming rockier. Ahead of them was a white-walled house with a wide balcony. Jhalouk turned off the path towards it. She was saying, 'Wakers leave us from time to time. They can usually control their absences, and they must be careful – their unoccupied bodies can be damaged easily.'

She climbed through a small gateway on to the balcony and held out a hand to Jon, pulling him up on to the tiles. Her voice became almost reverential, and she took a sidelong glance at him. 'But they can do magic.'

'Stop there, Mr Sciler.'

Jon yawned and stood up.

'No, we're not finished. I didn't say that. Drink your coffee. I want to backtrack again.' Dr Locke glanced at a monitor. 'We don't get such a good readout of this zone. We get some pictures but it's not comprehensive, and it's not always accurate either. So I'll need you to take me through it in a lot more detail in order to correlate your experiences with my scans.'

'Why don't you get the detail? You got a good picture from the last game.'

'You've got more questions than me, Mr Sciler. Are you sure you're the

85

right side of the mirror here? Just do your job and I'll do mine. I'm good. I don't know if you are yet.'

Jon crossed his arms and sat back. 'I'm not a rat in a maze, Doctor. Don't treat me like one. I'm not playing ding-the-bell here for you. If you want feedback, you give me some in return.'

She pushed her chair away from him, fizzing hard along the track, then clicked back slowly. 'Very well. There are several reasons. This zone was fully internalised, so we can't use plots of your motor activity to provide fixes. Also this was more "real" to you, so your own emotional and intellectual responses were a great deal more complex. You were snowstorming my readers. The time will come when we can either filter it selectively or read it all, but not with today's systems.' She glanced away at a monitor. 'Yes, I get some pictures, but you're not seeing them – they'll do more harm than good. Make you lazy and dull your memory.'

She flexed her fingers and clicked her nails on the desk. 'Okay. Your first thoughts. Recap. Good entry. You liked it.'

'After the shock. We've been through that.'

'And now we'll go through it again. Any more comments? The hall of sleepers. Anything you forgot first time? You were a little shell-shocked. You saw a second attendant in the background. Did you notice anything else?'

He shook his head.

'You're sure?'

'Yeah, I think so.'

She stared hard at him, then jotted something on a screen printout before looking up again. Jon wondered what she'd written. Two short hard lines had completed it – she'd either cancelled it or underlined it, and Dr Locke wasn't the type to make errors. The printout curled itself up.

'Okay. Go outside. The street.'

Jon hesitated. 'The program,' he said. 'It was incredible.'

Dr Locke held up her fist. She flicked up a finger. 'The girl.' Another finger. 'Street noise. Carts clattering . . . Take me through noises.'

'Horses . . .'

'How many?'

'Two – twice. I heard horses twice, separately. No, three, once by the jetty. I heard one behind me there just before the boat docked.'

She stared at him, then wrote. 'Go on. Birds.'

'I don't know how many. Constantly, once we were outside. Sea birds, I guess. You want me to describe their wing markings?'

'Yes, but not now. Secondary detail's your homework. Continue. Other animals, people.'

'There was the turtle. On the boat, three men. That whole thing was . . .'

Dr Locke was nodding as she wrote. 'Yes?'

He stopped. 'Doctor?'

She raised her head. 'Yes?' In her eyes he saw an odd expectation, and for a moment what resembled greed.

'I thought it was real.' He breathed out hard. 'I actually thought for a time it was real.'

There was just impatience in her face now. 'Three males on the boat with the turtle. It isn't real. You only said two horses last time we went through it. It's vital you remember it all for me. Every detail. I can't correlate otherwise. This isn't a game.' She caught herself. 'Here in this room, it isn't a game.' She paused. 'Okay. We'll stop there for today.'

She gathered in her papers and swivelled her chair. She keyed a thumb pad set into the black glass wall and it split open. It wasn't a one-way screen. Racks of labelled discs sat shelved there, ceiling high. She turned back to the desk and flicked a disc from beneath it, then twisted round and rose to file it in the wall. She stretched up towards a high shelf, her fingers riffling along the rows, searching.

Jon stood up carefully and glanced at the desk. He couldn't see her notes except for the top sheet, but the long printout was bunched loosely beside it. It looked like a brain scan, thin black lines jerking rhythmically up and down, stuttering forward. He saw the scrawled note she'd made and an arrow indicating something on the scan. Her writing was difficult to read upside down, and a slight gloss on the scrolled paper caught the overhead light. He couldn't quite make out the words.

Dr Locke had found a slot for the disc. She was reaching to slide it home.

He leaned forward and gently flattened the printout with a fingertip. Her thick underlining had scored the paper and it snagged his nail as he withdrew. The printout bounced and recoiled, jarring her pen. He stretched out but couldn't make it. The pen rolled to the edge of the desk and dropped on to the floor at her feet.

Dr Locke turned sharply.

'Sorry,' Jon said. 'Does this go up there too?' He was holding out a disc that had been on the desk.

She flushed with anger, snatching the disc from him and examining her desk. She pressed her palm down on her notes and then turned them over, and bunched the rolled printout in her hand and stuffed it under the desk.

'You never touch anything in here, Mr Sciler,' she said furiously. 'Do you understand that?'

The wall was still open. She reached a hand behind her and fumbled to close it. The heavy sheet of glass moved slowly. The shelves were tagged with names. Jon caught a few of them. Most meant nothing to him, odd names. Then up high, his own, Jon Sciler. There was a shelf reserved for him.

'You can go, Mr Sciler. I'll see you tomorrow.'

The wall closed off, finally covering the central name on the longest shelf. The shelf was tagged Marcus Lees, and it was totally bare.

TEN

'There on her desk,' Jon said slowly. 'She was filing the discs away and I saw her notes on the desk. She'd written something on a printout, a few words.'

Chrye shrugged. She didn't want to encourage this. She kept her voice damped down. 'What had she written?'

He closed his eyes, remembering it. Chrye looked at his face, knowing it so well now.

'She'd written, "Cathedral. Very early." I thought I might have misread it, but I'm sure that's right.'

'Cathedral?' She wrote the word down and stared at it, seeing the soaring arches of a great church and smelling sweet and pungent incense. It didn't seem like Cathar. 'You didn't mention a cathedral to me. Was there one?' Chrye frowned. 'The building on the island?' She played with her pen, rolling it over her palm. 'Does it matter, Jon? It's the game. What's the importance of it?'

'It didn't look like a cathedral. But it was far away. I couldn't really make it out.'

Chrye thought of the welts on Jon's back. 'Have you seen Father Fury again? Have you been back to the church?'

'Not since . . . No.'

She sighed and threw down the pen. It beat a little dying rattle on the table. She drew a breath and then said, 'Jon, do you really know why you're doing this? You said you were through with it after Dirangesept.'

Jon felt the change of atmosphere in the room. He rubbed his hand across the back of his neck and watched Chrye as she brought her bag on to the table and opened it. She took the book out and let it lie between them. Starburn's journal. His fingertips itched as if charged.

89

She said, 'You know what he says in here, don't you? And it was in his letters too, wasn't it? About this zone being real? You didn't tell me because you knew what I'd say. I'd have told you to get the hell away from Maze.'

'I was right, wasn't I?' he said. 'You don't believe it was suicide either, do you?'

'Are you crazy, Jon? Why would they kill him?' She raised her hands. 'Never mind. We're not even going to discuss that.' She held the book up, holding it between them like a shield, and he saw her anger in the way the journal quivered in her grip.

'Look what they did to your friend,' she said furiously. 'They let him believe they had accidentally stumbled on a real zone, where magic worked, and that he was involved in the mapping and colonisation of it.'

Her voice was rising and she worked to hold it down. 'Hell, Jon! He was perfect for it. Maze picked him for his mental state just like the Dirangesept project picked him for his game skills. He wasn't testing the game for them – they were testing the game on him, seeing if it would send him over the edge. And it did. Maze needed Starburn's guilt. He was desperate for the zone to be real. Don't you see that, Jon? It wasn't a game for him. We could all be wakers, Jon. Don't you see that? It was his second chance to save the world.'

Jon looked away. Without thought Chrye reached forward and swung at him with the book. He made no attempt to block her. The crack as she hit him hung in the air. Her strength shocked her.

He straightened and levelled his eyes at her, and for a moment they stared at each other. Chrye watched his cheek redden. He seemed to lose focus. She flinched when he stretched out his hand towards her, holding still with difficulty, bracing herself against the blow. Instead he just touched his finger to her cheek and said, 'You're crying.'

'Of course I'm bloody crying,' she said through the salt of her tears, thinking, Why *am* I? She held up the book again. Her hand was shaking once more, and she put the book down. She tried to pretend it was anger still. 'I've read it. And you know what?'

She waited for Jon to react, but he just sat there. So she said it. 'I think he realised at the end that the zone wasn't real. That it was all a mistake.'

'A mistake?' His voice rose. 'You call all of this a mistake?'

She wiped her palms across her wet cheeks. 'Not like that. He didn't just *want* the zone to be real. He *needed* it to be real. And when he found it wasn't . . .'

'He killed himself. Yeah, great deduction.' He slapped his hand on the table. 'End of story. Cue credits. Except that he didn't kill himself. He couldn't have killed himself like that. Remember?'

'So you keep telling me, Jon.' She found her temper rising again. She put her fists under the table and clenched them, trying to cut her nails into her palms, but they were bitten too short. She opened her mouth, knowing it was wrong to say to him what she was about to say but unable not to.

'You know, Jon, when I first met you I thought you were different from the other Far Warriors. You had a bit more distance from Dirangesept. You'd sorted out your guilt a bit more.' She wanted him to say something – anything – but he just sat there and let her go on.

'I was wrong. You've just displaced it further. You loaded it all on to Starburn. He was your scapegoat.' She frowned. 'What did you tell me? "He was their armour and their sword. Just as he was mine." It was Starburn who failed up there on Dirangesept, wasn't it, Jon? It wasn't you at all. Recognise it, Jon?'

She could see it in his eyes, the hurt far greater than her slap, but it was too late. 'You said he had a phobia, Jon. Well, I had access to the project's preflight med/psych checks as a research source for my thesis. After you told me that I looked up Marcus Lees on the roster.'

Jon nodded once. Chrye wanted to stop, but it kept coming, like a nightmare. She could see what she was doing to him, and she couldn't stop.

'Marcus Lees had no extreme phobias. Mild claustrophobia. He didn't like the CrySis pods, which is a healthy response. But anything serious? Uh-uh.'

Jon nodded again. No surprise to him, she saw, and that made it a bit easier.

'So. I think Starburn killed himself because he realised the means of his redemption were an illusion. All right, maybe he had a thing about water, but not quite a phobia. Maybe drowning himself was the most extreme form of self-punishment he could imagine. And he wouldn't be the only one, would he? Look at the ministry of Father Fury.'

She wanted to be done with it now. 'Marcus Lees killed himself. And when he killed himself, all your own guilt catapulted back again. So you

91

had to deal with that. And you dealt with it by telling yourself he was murdered and you had to avenge him. And now you're getting sucked into the same cycle, Jon.'

He opened his mouth, then closed it. Chrye felt heady with the power of what she'd told him. She wanted to apologise, to say something that might reduce the hurt she could see in his eyes.

'No,' he said flatly.

She picked up the pen again and started to play with it, running her nails hard along the pen's ribbed grip. 'Jon, you can't . . .'

'No. You're wrong.'

'Jon, it's no good denying . . .'

He raised his hand, and she stopped.

He began slowly, not looking at her, looking at the book on the table. 'You know what Dirangesept did to us. You know something about the damage, the stigmata. You know about guilt, responsibility, paranoia, about the brain.' He jerked his head up and jabbed a finger hard at his temple. His eyes were wide, unblinking, piercing hers until she looked away. She knew she'd taken him too far.

She found herself staring at the journal, thinking she had to cool him down somehow, but her mind was blank. His palm smacked down on the book, the blow jarring her as much as if he'd slapped her face.

'You listen to me now. You listen to me.' His voice trembled. His fists were white on the table, his knuckles like veined marble. She hadn't seen such passion in him before.

'You think you've worked it out? You know what Dirangesept did, but you don't know how, do you? You don't know what happened up there. Okay, I'll tell you about Dirangesept. That's what you want, so I'll tell you. Then you can tell me I'm crazy. Then you can tell me anything you want.'

Alone, Chrye made herself coffee with a tablespoon of two-day-old grounds and half a teaspoon of fresh and settled back on the bed with it. She flicked the screen on and speed-played the first ten minutes, watching the acceleration magnify the uncertainty in his face. She slowed it when Jon began to speak and then she leaned forward to view the tape for the fourth time.

'The Far Brigades took nine years to prepare,' he was saying. 'We set off nine years after the first expedition, the colonists, were destroyed.'

On the screen he stopped and frowned as a thought struck him. 'We must have passed the few who returned in space, in silence, without acknowledgement. Some of them still alive now.'

Chrye supposed so. There had only been twenty or thirty survivors anyway, according to the records. They'd gone to ground back on Earth, out of shame and despair probably. Their homecoming had preceded the Far Brigades reaching Dirangesept, and no one on Earth had been interested in reminders of failure.

The year of the Far Brigades' arrival had been the year that Chrye had been born. She hadn't told Jon about her birthday. The coincidence was uncomfortable, somehow, smacking of destiny and strange omens. She believed in neither, but reading Starburn's journal had left her feeling uncomfortable. His paranoid world view had been oddly plausible, and she didn't exactly know why. She had tried to analyse it logically, and it had come down to the fact that the whole idea of an alternative reality was just ridiculous. It was ridiculous.

But a small seditious voice within her kept whispering how did she know it wasn't possible?

She froze the picture and looked at him. He'd been twenty-one, twenty-two on Dirangesept, and now, after eighteen more years in CrySis, and five years on, he was biologically twenty-seven. It was hard to believe he was four years older than her. Sometimes he seemed a child. Sometimes – now, frozen in confusion – he seemed twice her age.

She made herself restart the tape, aware that she was displacing, knowing what was to come.

The tape stretched his voice slightly, giving it a burr of tension. 'There were a thousand of us in the Far Brigades, highly trained, in ships with ten thousand autoids. Far more than we'd possibly need. Ten machines each. They thought any we'd lose would be due to technical malfunction. Ten each was playing safe. Ten each was overkill.'

Chrye watched the only smile of the three-hour tape try itself out briefly on his face, and resisted the urge to leave it there and walk away. It was a sad smile. She wanted to touch his face on the screen now, just as when he'd made the smile she'd wanted to reach forward and touch his cheek. She'd wanted to say something stupid like it's all right, knowing it wasn't all right at all, and it was getting less all right all the time now.

'It took eight years to adapt the new generation of autoids and bLinkers for Dirangesept, and another year to train us to use them. Our autoids had everything. They were supposed to be unstoppable, invincible. They had scanners that could see everything, weapons that could stop anything. And they had us to operate them. So we slept well in CrySis. There was nothing to fear.'

Jon worked his knuckles into his eyes. Chrye wondered if he'd had a full night's sleep since then.

He continued. 'When we entered a geostationary orbit over Dirangesept, the CrySis pods opened. We ate a meal while the carriers dropped with our autoids. Our first food in eighteen years. I couldn't swallow it. We were directly over the remains of Alpha Colony. It was the fourteenth of May, 2055.'

It was the fourth time she'd heard it from his lips, and she still shivered. The day so full of hope for the Earth. The day she'd been born.

'As we ate, we stared at the colony on our screens, the pictures relayed from the descending carriers. It was greener down there than anything I'd ever seen. There was hardly a thing to see in all the green, just a glint of titanium here and there. It had been a city ready for ten thousand people. Now it was a jungle burying scraps of tinsel. We couldn't believe it. We'd heard how almost everyone down there died when the beasts attacked the colony, but we expected the city to be there.

'Ten minutes before touchdown we dispersed to our solitary cells and bLinked. Mach Null, just like the simulations back here on Earth. No different. Starburn and I were in the first carrier. I could see him – his autoid – everyone in the carrier was staring at him. It was crazy. For the first time I saw how crazy it was. We were all up there on the ship, every one of us, alone but safe, and at the same time we were packed together in this tiny carrier hurtling down towards Dirangesept.

'It was cramped in the carrier. I could smell the oil like rancid breath. I could feel the flanks of the autoids to either side of me like flesh against my flesh. We dropped. And there was this silence. I tell you, all the simulations were exactly like this, but this was totally different. Everyone felt it. And then, in the silence, Starburn just raised his fist. His hardhand. He raised it high, and he opened and closed it, ball to claw to ball again. It was so solid. It was the promise of safety. And as one, we all copied him, in silence, all of us in our own little cells in the security of the ship, all of us petrified, but a little less so now.

'The pilot blasted a clearing in the forest and landed the carrier in it. For a moment as the engine died there was peace, then the hatch opened and hell came in screaming.'

He took a long, shuddering breath. 'I wasn't near the hatch, so I survived. Five or six of us were nilled immediately, a couple more panicked and nilled each other along with a few of the beasts, and then the smoke and fire gave the rest of us a few seconds. I heard Starburn yelling orders so loud they distorted, and we were lasing a hole through the carrier's outer. We lost five more getting out.

'That was how it started, and it never let up. My group was meant to guard the perimeter while the colony was rebuilt, but it was hopeless. What you heard back on Earth was nothing to the truth of it. There was never any hope. We weren't wanted on Dirangesept. By the end of the first day we'd lost a few hundred autoids. We said it was bad luck, the difference between simulation and reality, but we already knew.

'They were beautiful when occasionally we saw them. I can't describe them. They were like fabulous cats, I thought, though others said not. Bears, eagles, you name it. Starburn said they looked how they wanted us to see them, but sometimes I think they looked how we wanted them to look.'

Chrye's own voice intruded on to the soundtrack. 'How did Starburn see the beasts?'

Jon said, 'Wolves. He saw wolves.'

'Go on.'

'Whatever we saw, we all agreed they were beautiful. And they didn't so much move as flow. Except when they were moving in attack. Then you hardly saw them.'

He seemed to fold into himself for a moment. System shutdown, thought Chrye. 'But your scanners recorded them?' she asked.

'At the last minute. Barely before visual contact, usually. That's why we couldn't just blast them from up high and safe. The ship's scanners never registered a thing down there. It was like they didn't exist till we hit the ground.' He stopped again for a moment, then continued, 'Starburn was the best of us. He cut most of his scanners, just switched them right off. He only left the basic sensory ranges open, human-wavelength eyes and ears. He said he could concentrate better that way, he developed a feeling for the beasts' presence, an instinct. He'd be up ahead of you and just fling out an arm to the side and throw a det. So fast. It was uncanny. It was like magic, like he was throwing a spell in a game.'

Jon shook his head slowly. 'Jesus, did they scream when you killed

95

them. It went right through you.' He shook his head again. She could see him almost disbelieving the memory.

'I tried it too, nulling my scanners. It worked for me, though not as well. I was never as fast as Starburn. But we were losing autoids all the time. At the end of each day we'd rendezvous and set up a safe zone, cleared, mined and wired, and we'd cut back to the ships, and try to sleep, then bLink again. Sometimes we'd return to dead machines – the beasts had somehow penetrated the safe zone and destroyed us.

'But that wasn't the worst of it. After a while the beasts changed their tactics. Instead of ripping us apart with their claws, or beaks or teeth or whatever they had, or destroying the autoids while we were asleep, they'd trap and disable us. That was when we really began to feel pain, when the stigmata began to escalate. You see, we were running low on autoids, and Command thought we were pulling out unnecessarily, wasting the hardware. Orders changed. We were told to remain bLinkered until our autoid was rendered totally inoperative. Until death. Death after death. And they were slow deaths down on Dirangesept. You didn't forget them.

'My last death was just before the project was aborted. Starburn died with me. We were on patrol together in deep jungle. He was ahead of me. There'd been no progress rebuilding the colony, and morale was nil. We knew it was almost over.

'Starburn wheeled around and lased a tree and I heard a hit, a terrible cry of agony. It was a trap – the beast sacrificed itself for the distraction. Starburn took another pace and I saw him disappear. They'd floated a raft of twigs on a water pit.

'I remember thinking they knew it would be him, his scanners would be off. I ran to the pit and knelt down beside it. It was deep and murky but I could see him there under the water, tangled in some sort of weed net. He was struggling, tearing at it with his hardhands, but they weren't meant for that. And the silt he stirred up was scattering his lasers.

'I was stupid. I forgot it was just an autoid. It was Starburn, and I was going to save him. I tried to talk to him but his comms were out. There were no direct cell-to-cell comms on the ship either by then – they'd cut the facility when they stopped us from bLinking out of disabled autoids. Every function we had was bLinkered. So he couldn't hear a word I said. I lay down on the bank and stretched my arms out towards him, reaching down into the water. But I couldn't quite touch him. It was too deep.

'I heard a cracking and splintering above me, but ignored it. By the time

I saw the long shadow rushing towards me over the water, it was too late. They'd felled a tree across my back, pinning me where I lay. I tried to push myself up, to throw it off, but there was an agonising pain across my shoulders. I couldn't draw back my arms. When I'd reached out for Starburn, I'd exposed my autoid's shoulder joints. They'd been ready. They'd pushed thorns, long hard thorns, deep into the joint assemblies and jammed them. How had they done that? How had they known to?

'The pain in my shoulders and across my back was unbearable. I was paralysed. Below me, in the water, Starburn wasn't struggling any more. The silt was settling and I could see him clearly. He was face up, and he was staring at me. The water was seeping into him, only it wasn't just water. Water wouldn't seize up an autoid. My arms were in the water, and they were going numb too. It must have been some sort of corrosive agent.

'All I could do was watch. Inches away from me, Starburn was dying. I watched the light go out. I watched him as he died.

'But the worst thing, the worst thing of all, worse than the terrible pain, was the knowledge that he couldn't see why I wasn't helping him.

'And then, from the greenery across the water, the beast came out. It just seemed to materialise there, without disturbing the foliage. It sat on its haunches and stared at me. It was like some animal buddha. It had huge eyes, piercing green eyes with black pupils that I could see had a notch out of them, that's how close it was.

'I was staring at it, and there was a question in my mind. Why are you trying to kill us?'

Jon blinked and added slowly, 'But it wasn't *my* question. It wasn't *my* thought.'

Chrye froze the screen and sat for a long time before letting it continue.

'It sat there watching the life go out of me. All it could see was this disabled machine, half in the water, but it was looking into my soul. It was deeper into me than I was into my autoid. And I was deep. I was in agony.' Jon squeezed his eyes closed. 'Stigmata,' he said. He shivered, then drew a long breath.

'Eventually, I passed out. I died too.

'After that, Starburn and I hardly spoke. I felt guilty, somehow, though it wasn't my fault. I don't know what he felt, whether he blamed me or not.'

Chrye had wanted to speak to him then, to suggest that Starburn might have felt ashamed at failing – at not only failing but at being seen to fail by his faithful disciple, Jon. That could have destroyed the superhero fantasy Marcus Lees had had of himself, and if that had been his only self-image . . . She had let it pass, meaning to return to it later, but she never had.

'We were separately reassigned to different duties, and shortly afterwards the pullout was ordered. No one wanted to stay there, but there wasn't any comfort in the announcement. We went into CrySis for the return to Earth. The mood was bad. I don't know what it was like back here, but in those ships, believe me, it was worse. We crawled into those pods like we were piling the dirt over us. Some of us didn't want to wake up again, I know that.

'You know all about the reception we got, of course. The bad news had preceded us by years, Chinese-whispered back along that great chain of comm satellites. The first fury of it had died down and a dull contempt and resentment had become ingrained. To us it was just hours before, but we emerged from the ships to a whole world bitter at our failure. We'd never even been soldiers. We'd never expected pain. It had been a game we'd been told we were going to win. And now we were told we were responsible for the world. For the end of it. We all slunk away. Starburn and I lost touch.'

He rubbed at his eyes and yawned. Chrye could see the exhaustion etched on his face.

'And then the letters started coming. And then I read he'd died like that, and I got the journal. That's the whole story, Chrye. And that's why Starburn couldn't have drowned himself. After that death on Dirangesept, it was like he had rabies, he was so terrified of water. He couldn't drink, he had to chew ice. If it was raining outside he stayed in his room. He couldn't even take a piss with his eyes open. Starburn drown himself? Oh, no. He was murdered.'

Chrye woke to the sound of white noise from the machine. An image of Jon was locked there blurred and flickering between frames, his mouth fractionally opening and closing as if he was struggling for air. She brushed the hair from her face and stopped the tape. His face faded and the screen went grey, taking with it all the light in the room. He should be here, she thought, checking the time. It was past two a.m. The windows were dark and the room was cold.

The thought kept looping in her head. He should have arrived by now. She uncurled herself stiffly from the sofa and dialled his number, feeling unaccountably anxious. The call-tone see-sawed for two minutes before she gave up. Maybe he'd got back late and was asleep, not wanted to disturb her. But she didn't think so.

She wrapped the sheet around her and tried to sleep. When eventually she did, it was to wake sweating as the first light filtered through the window. The remnants of a dream faded away, images of death and the sound of a distant scream.

She tried Jon's number again, and let it ring unanswered for ten minutes before cancelling the call. Don't get involved, she thought. But maybe it was too late.

ELEVEN

It tasted like coffee, like a coffee brewed with rich nuts. It was sweet too, and raisiny. It tasted better than any coffee he had ever drunk.

Jon looked down, staring over the ocean, nursing the warm cup between his hands. Last night he hadn't fully appreciated the long steep climb to the house, but this morning the view took his breath away.

The house was high above the sea, at the summit of the village. Looking down over the red-tiled roofs meandering down the hillside to the harbour, he could see a dirt road stretching in either direction around the broad curve of the bay like a pair of open arms. The road was empty of traffic. There was little activity down by the quay, just a couple of small figures moving slowly, and most of the boats were at sea. The few that remained rocked at anchor.

He raised the cup to his lips again and drank the perfect, strong brown coffee slowly right down to its dregs, enjoying the gritty feel of the grounds on his teeth, and then he wiped a finger around the cup's base and brought it up to his nose. The aroma was deep and almost treacly.

Jon sighed with contentment. It was all there, in that cup of coffee. But standing above everything was the taste. Maze had sequenced taste.

He refilled his cup and looked around, conscious despite everything of a vague disquiet that he couldn't shake off.

The source of it wasn't anything in Cathar. The morning in the zone was perfect. He'd woken in the bed he dimly remembered Jhalouk helping him to climb into before his last exit. His eyes had opened to a brilliant bar of sunlight on the rough brick wall by his side. Just like before, no Mach Null. It had seemed natural, like waking anywhere.

Chrye wouldn't mind when he failed to turn up, he told himself. By the time Dr Locke had been through her schedule of spell-tests with him it had been nearly midnight, and when she'd told him he should sleep there at Maze, Jon had been too tired to argue. She'd suggested that he might rest better in the CrySis capsule and, despite his dislike of the pod, he'd folded himself into it to sleep there. His last thought had been that he'd have more to tell Chrye when he did see her. He felt bad about it, though.

And then he'd woken here, thirsty with the aroma of coffee coming through the window. There was a jug and basin in the corner of the room, so he'd sluiced water over himself, sucking air at the coldness of it, and then without thought had slipped on the clean soft white shirt and maroon trousers that must have been left there for him and opened the door, following the smell of coffee. He could have exited, but he hadn't.

There had been no sign of Jhalouk, just a pot of coffee on the wooden table that stood on the stone-tiled verandah, and six chairs, six cups and a heaped bowl of cakes he had yet to try.

The sun had been slowly lifting in the sky to the left of the village, and the sea within the breakwater was disturbed by a sharp breeze that lifted wispy white licks from its surface. Beyond the breakwater the water was torn up more severely, and Jon watched the fishing vessels rearing and pitching out there.

He sat down at the table and poured himself another cup of the coffee, wondering who the other chairs were for.

'Well, look who's died and come to heaven.'

Jon recognised the voice as soon as he heard it and swivelled round, the legs of the wooden chair grinding on the stone.

'Yani,' he said flatly. He nodded to the others. They were all there. He should have guessed.

'You didn't like Demonslayer, did you?' said Yani. 'But I'm called Janus here. It's easier for the saps to remember. You should be able to manage it too.' He sat down and took a cake. Pibald did the same, and the girls too, their movements as synchronised as before.

Footfall took the chair with its back to the wall of the house. His face was crumpled and anxious, just as it had been when Jon first saw him.

'How long have you been here?' said Jon, to no one in particular. He noticed what he had said, as if the place were real. It was so easy. It was like drinking the coffee.

He realised abruptly that he had known that Dr Locke intended enabling him straight from sleep. That explained the feeling of disquiet.

He felt no better for identifying it. It struck him that he had no idea what time it was. It was morning here in the zone, but he could have been in CrySis for hours, minutes, days even.

Pibald answered him. Beside him Janus – it was easy to think of him as Janus, and Jon wondered why he'd chosen the name – had his mouth stuffed with cake, crumbs trickling from his chin.

'A while. Long enough to acclimatise.' Pibald sipped appreciatively at the coffee one of the girls had poured for him. 'Long enough to develop a taste for this.'

Jon took a cake from the bowl and bit into it. It was sweet and soft and tasted of cinnamon, and with the unexpected spice and texture he had a sudden flashback to his childhood. There was a strawberry soyshake in front of him in a tall fluted glitterglass and the same taste of cinnamon was in his mouth. He was with his mother and they were sitting at a table at a small street kiosk. He couldn't reach the ground with his toes. His mother had turned around half away from him to talk to someone he couldn't see, just a stranger who had asked for the sacch, but she had responded to him while Jon was still saying something to her. The moment was frozen. Jon could see the tendon stretched in her slim neck and the blade of shadow in the angle of her jaw. It was the moment that Jon had realised with sharp anxiety that he wasn't the only focus of his mother's life. It had suddenly hit him that everyone and everything around him existed independently of him, that it would all carry on happening even if he weren't there to see it.

The shock of it had almost made him choke. He had hoped never to feel like that again.

'What's wrong, Sciler? Something gone down the wrong way?' Janus laughed.

Jon stood up from the table and dashed across to lean over the balcony. He felt his cheeks bulge and sweat break out over his forehead. There was only the coffee in his stomach and it spewed out, arcing darkly down and spattering over the rocky hillside. His eyes were wet and stinging. Below the balcony a lizard paddled out from beneath a stone, its spine a vivid crimson patterned with purple flashes, and began delicately to lap at the liquid. After a moment Jon turned his back to the wall and rested there, breathing deeply and shivering.

'You all right?' Pibald asked.

Jon couldn't speak. He tried to swallow the acid in his mouth.

'Don't worry about Sciler,' said Janus derisively. 'I think he just discovered he's stepped right into another pile of shit. Only this time it won't just wipe off.'

The man's eyes shone with venom. Jon twisted round and spat the taste away. The lizard had vanished. There was a disappearing flash of red in the undergrowth further down the hillside, too fast for him to lock on to. As he turned back, his eye caught Footfall's.

He knows it's real too, thought Jon suddenly, then corrected himself uncomfortably. He thinks it's real. Jon tried to hold his glance, but Footfall looked quickly away. Behind him the doorway held a woman's silhouette, and Jon shaded his eyes as Jhalouk came softly on to the verandah. Pibald's head jerked up too. Jon smiled and Jhalouk nodded back, her yellow eyes registering him. She went to Pibald and let him kiss her on the cheek. As she pulled gently away from him she raised her arm and brushed his face tenderly with the back of her hand. Jon looked down, feeling unaccountably foolish, then glanced at the others. There was nothing to be read in their faces. He wondered if they had noticed his reaction, what they might have seen in him.

This has all been happening for a long time, he thought. It's not back-plot, it's history. Thoughts slewed around his skull, colliding and conflicting. If it's a program, if the zone's just a synaptic illusion, she could be a player, like I thought, and there could be a relationship between them. This could just be another place to meet.

And if she's software? He rubbed his eyes, trying to unscramble it. We look the same here as outzone. Janus is the same little shit I saw at Maze, with the same mean mouth and tiny eyes, not even adjusted to seem elfish this time, and Pibald and Footfall are as they were in the other games. So maybe they can't change us physically in this zone.

He rolled his shoulders, testing them for their customary stiffness. The muscles moved freely. He wondered about the stigmata and reached a hand under the neck of his shirt. The familiar track of the deep scar was still there.

So they couldn't change physical features. Or chose not to.

But Jhalouk had those impossible eyes. Must she be software, then?

She was sitting down beside Pibald, and Jon wondered whether they had slept together. The question repeated itself. Is she real? Because if she's real, then the zone's real.

There was pressure on the back of his hand. He started.

'How are you feeling?'

It was Lapis, or it was Lazuli? Whichever she was, she wasn't real, even if the zone was real. Dr Locke had told him that, he seemed to remember.

'Not too good,' he said.

'Try not to think about it,' she said. 'Just be here. It hits everyone at first.' She squeezed his hand and released it. Jon thought there was a glance between her and Footfall.

'Some worse than others,' murmured Janus derisively. 'Some never get over it.' He raised his voice. 'Pass the cakes over here, Lapis, before Sciler throws up over them.'

Jon could see a difference in the way they had their hair now. Something at least was different. They both had long, thick, dark locks, but Lapis tied hers loosely back while her twin left it free.

'Look,' said Footfall sharply. He was leaning forward and pointing out over the bay. Jon followed his finger to see a boat bumping out over the swell from the far side of the cluster of rocks that was the strange island. The boat was unlike the fishing vessels of Cathar. It was sleeker and sitting low in the water. It was painted dull black too, while the hulls of the fishing boats were blue and white and varnished so that they shone in the sun.

Pibald and Jhalouk crossed the balcony. Jhalouk's hands pressed into the brick of the balustrade until her knuckles blanched.

The black boat was making directly towards the nearest fishing craft, crashing through the heavy sea, unaffected by the buffeting of waves. It had a dark square mainsail raised and a smaller foresail, and the wind that swelled them was so constant that the ballooning curves of the sails were set rigid.

'That's Nyla's boat,' said Jhalouk quietly. 'He has a wife and three children.'

Jon knew she meant the fishing boat.

Pibald put his arm around her shoulder. 'There's nothing we can do,' he said.

Jon stood up, aware of a sharp tension in the air. The twins were rising from the table. Footfall was already at Pibald's side, leaning forward and shielding his eyes with a hand. Janus reached across the table to grab a cake in each fist before trotting over.

Pibald murmured, 'He's seen it.' The fishing boat had moved with a sudden jerk. Jon guessed it had cut its nets adrift.

Jhalouk didn't move. The fishing boat was raising a sail and leaning hard into the wind now, pushing away and tacking furiously. White water flared from its stern as it began to make way towards the harbour. The black craft adjusted its direction, moving implacably to intercept the other boat. Somehow the wind at its heels was stronger and more favourable.

Jon watched the race. His heart was beating faster and he didn't know quite why. It seemed clear that the fishing vessel would make the safety of the harbour. It had a good lead. It was tacking while the black boat was oddly able to move in a straight line, but it was scything through the water now at a tremendous speed.

'He'll make it,' Jon said into the silence.

Janus let out a huge laugh and Pibald glared at him.

For the second time, Footfall said flatly, 'Look.'

As he said it, the wind seemed to drop around the small boat. Its sail slumped in folds on to the deck.

The sudden becalming made no sense. The other fishing vessels around the bay were all moving too, and their sails were filled as they made urgently for the harbour.

'Oh God, no,' said Jhalouk. She slumped against Pibald. He put an arm around her.

Jon didn't understand. Something terrible was about to happen, or maybe it had already happened.

There was a peculiar smell in the air, pushed in by the sea breeze. It wasn't the coffee. It was like there had been a fire far away, and then rain. As if something slightly foetid remained, hot and moist.

'Magic,' muttered Footfall.

Yes, thought Jon. Of course.

Footfall glanced at him. 'There's nothing we can do. He's cut their wind.'

Jon leaned forward, trying to make out the detail. The black boat came alongside the other, and its sail also went slack. Jon made out five or six figures on its deck. There were only two on the fishing vessel.

He's cut the wind, Jon thought. Who is he? Who is using magic?

Everything seemed to be happening at half-speed. The distance between the boats and Jon telescoped. The circle of quiet water enclosing the scene might have been a stage. He saw what was happening with absolute clarity.

Jhalouk wrenched herself free of Pibald and stared wildly around. 'There must be something. Footfall! Can't you do something?'

Footfall shook his head. 'He's too strong. It's too far. I can't.'

'You can try! You must. You know what will happen to them.'

Footfall opened his mouth and closed it. He shook his head again.

A swirl of ropes flew through the air from the island boat. The ropes whipped taut and the vessels were drawn together, rising in a brief kiss with the noiseless collision. One of the men from the black boat leapt across. He appeared to hang for an instant in the air, and as he landed a faint wooden clack sounded, like the tolling of a cracked bell.

The sound didn't fit the picture, Jon realised, and he felt a mingling of disappointment and relief. Before he could decide which had been stronger his brain told him it was the sound of the boats coming together, stalled by the distance. The clack of the two vessels echoed mournfully along the hillside.

It was like a signal. Everything had taken place in silence until this moment, but now time accelerated again.

'Six against two,' Pibald murmured. Jhalouk had buried her head in his shoulder, unable to watch.

'No hope,' said Janus. 'No help either. So no point agonising.' He poured himself more coffee.

Jon had a sense of real lives at stake out there. Jhalouk's anxiety was radiating to the group. She was connected to the little boats bobbing about together and Pibald was comforting her. And the thread that linked Jhalouk to the boats and Pibald to Jhalouk touched Jon and bound him in.

Tears were running down Jhalouk's cheeks. Pibald tried to wipe them with his sleeve. 'Jhalouk, there's nothing anyone can do. Footfall would help them if he could. You know that.'

Only Footfall could do magic here, Jon realised. But Jhalouk had told him only wakers could do magic, and they were all supposed to be wakers here, except for Jhalouk. Even if Lapis and Lazuli weren't wakers, Pibald was, and also Janus. So. So perhaps not all wakers could do magic.

Perhaps Jon couldn't.

The boats were rocking out there in their circle of calm. The men struggled with each other in little clumps, falling and regaining their feet like cartoon animations. It was impossible to make out their faces, and at this distance only Jhalouk's reaction gave the fight any gravity.

Jon felt connected to it, though. He could distinguish the pirates from the fishermen. The fishermen were desperate, their arms flailing wildly, while their attackers were beating them down with their fists in a manner that was oddly mechanical.

'It's like clubbing fish,' Lapis murmured beside him. There was a long sadness in her voice. She was right, Jon saw. The hopeless desperation of the fishermen, all their panic and energy, was useless against the pirates. Their resistance was unfelt, and soon they fell to the deck and lay still.

Their attackers appeared neither exhausted nor jubilant. There was no pause in their efforts. With the same undiminished strength they dragged the unconscious fishermen to their own boat and set the deserted vessel adrift. A pinprick of flame spat into life in the hand of one of the pirates and he drew back an arm and tossed the lit torch on to the fishing boat's deck. It lay there guttering indecisively for a second and then flared. The flames took hold swiftly and a ribbon of pale smoke unfurled over the boat. The charmed circle of water began to froth as the wind broke through. The fire bloomed like a contagion.

Jhalouk was weeping against Pibald's chest. He was stroking her hair slowly and rhythmically, and whispering in her ear.

The pirate vessel was almost hidden by the pall of smoke. Its sails were raised and its course was towards the island.

Jon was sick with helplessness. He felt drained and defeated in a way that was terribly familiar. The sense of distance and connectedness and the utter loss of hope felt like something at the core of his being, and it was exposed like a sliced nerve over a flame.

He looked at the others. Lapis and Lazuli had their arms around each other and seemed more one person than they had when they had been indistinguishable. That closeness shared made him feel as though he had lost something that he had never had. Even to watch them made his pain worse. He yearned to have that comfort.

Footfall was sitting at the table, his head cradled and his face hidden in his hands. Janus was nodding to himself. There was a smile on his face and his eyes were wide and shining. He caught Jon's glance and said, 'That's done, Sciler. Enjoy it? Now you've had your introduction and induction.'

Anger welled up suddenly in Jon's gut. He was trembling with fury. 'It isn't done yet, you little shit.' He turned round to the sea, aware as he did that everyone was staring at him. He didn't care. He was huddled within himself, and pages of pictograms rolled before him. His head was buzzing.

Out at sea, the wind was blowing the smoke away from the burning boat so that the pirate vessel was in clear view. It was about to round the spur of the island.

But there they were, waiting for him. He pulled them out, five glittering symbols that he could see so sharply that he might cut his tongue with the saying of them.

Jon held the boat in his gaze. He could see the spell lying there in his mind, but as he began to curl his lips around the first pictogram the others started to fade and even the first blurred. His tongue seemed to thicken and his lips turned to rubber. He forced the syllables out, though, into a wind that hadn't been there when he'd started. The wind was blowing directly at him and he tried to duck his head away. The choking wind followed him.

He recalled the boat, and lifted his head back up to fix it in his eyes. He could just remember the next pictogram, and brought it out into the wind that was growing fiercer. It was all around him, jostling him. He reached out and leaned forward to brace himself against the wall. His eyes were streaming so that he couldn't see the boat any longer, and he had to bring up a hand to wipe the water away, nearly falling back as the strengthening wind punched at him. Now as the third pictogram came, the wind was in his throat and bloating his lungs, and he could hardly force out the breath to utter it.

The fourth component he could barely remember, the wind and the noise of it threatening to empty his mind and his will, but at last he said it.

Through the mist of stinging tears he saw that the boat was at the island and about to disappear. Jon wasn't sure about the final pictogram any longer. It was smoky and indistinct. When it came out he hardly heard it above the deafening gale that he thought would any moment raise him up and hurl him down the hillside.

Then, with the last syllable held in his throat, for an instant there was nothing. It was as if he were standing in a vacuum. Everything went away, the wind and noise all withdrawing from him like a tremendous tide going out all in a rush, leaving him beached and drained.

The black boat was still in sight, a hairsbreadth of sea between its prow and the rocky outcrop that was about to envelop it. The spell was all but complete, and Jon was a catapult at full stretch.

A sharp crack sounded behind him, and Janus swore loudly. He must have dropped his cup.

Jon shook away the distraction. There was a fraction of the final syllable left to be uttered in the silence. It came easily, sounding like a soft whisper in a deep cave.

As he watched it, realising he had allowed his gaze to be distracted from the boat, a large boulder detached itself suddenly from the island's profile and tumbled awkwardly into the sea. An instant later the stern of the boat slipped safely out of view.

Jon's legs seemed to lose their strength. He fell, grabbing awkwardly at the wall. There was nothing in his hands to grip with, and he felt himself sliding down. It was as if he were in a faint without quite losing consciousness. There was nothing he could do about it.

Then just before he hit the ground there were arms beneath his shoulders and he was lifted up and carried to the table. Jon knew without seeing him that the arms were Footfall's.

'Drink this,' said Lapis. 'You'll need to rehydrate. Magic drains you.'

'Yeah, even if you screw it up,' said Janus.

'Shut up,' Pibald said with sudden vehemence. 'At least he tried. You don't give a damn about any of this, Janus. I don't know why you're even here. All you do is stuff your face and piss on everything. Why don't you just exit for ever?'

Janus kicked the fragments of his coffee mug across the verandah and made a gesture at Pibald. 'And why don't you save your energy for something useful, like trying to get your little local friend pregnant?'

Jon tried to twist his head to see Pibald, but found the effort beyond him. He heard Jhalouk murmur something to Pibald, then Footfall said, 'This is pointless. I suggest we all cool off a bit. Sciler will need a few hours' rest.'

TWELVE

It had been raining steadily for hours. The sound of the rain enveloped him, blown over the bare ground by gusting wind. Jon had seen films of squalls rippling through fields of tall corn back when the corn still grew thick and strong, and this was how the rain fell in small unfinished patterns. The odd memory gave him a strange impossible nostalgia. He could see it now if he closed his eyes. The sound of the rain beating on the street became the hissing of corn. It was as if he had seen it in reality, but where he had seen it was in the zone, the wind brushing over meadows far away behind the hillside he had just departed.

He was shivering and exhausted. He had exited the zone before anyone, then left Maze after the shortest debriefing Dr Locke would let him escape with. The security fence around Maze had been strengthened, and there was still no indication that rebuilding would start in the cleared area. Jon had walked away from the gate until he was sure no one could see him, then settled down as comfortably as possible in the doorway of an empty building at the edge of the area to wait. Janus had left a while after him, shrouded in a hooded brown stormproof but instantly identifiable, and Jon had dropped his chin into his chest as the short man passed.

Footfall came out an hour later. Jon recognised him by his height and by his walk, the stiff stride of a Far Warrior. He was wearing a long grey coat down to his ankles that billowed as he strode into the rain, then quickly grew dark and heavy with water until it was flapping against his legs. He wore a broad-brimmed hat, the bouncing rain smudging its edges. He had a full face respirator too, and blunt black boots studded with thorny rain. He was easy to follow.

Jon let Footfall take him twenty minutes from Maze before catching up. He passed Footfall and stopped in front of him.

Footfall's head was down. He moved automatically to sidestep Jon. Jon put his arm out, keeping his palm open. Somewhere off in the distance behind Footfall, like a smooth boulder in the road, was the dark silhouette of a pacifist trig. Its limbs were withdrawn. It was motionless. John didn't remember passing it.

Footfall came to a halt. He raised his head and peered at Jon.

The street was deserted apart from the two of them standing in the lancing rain. The rain sounded like it had been going on for ever and the world was going to drown, just like sometimes in a quake it seemed to Jon that the world would crack itself apart. It never felt to him any more that the Earth was going to make it.

A veil of water cascaded from the brim of Footfall's hat. He tilted his head back, displacing the flow. His eyes were wide, swollen under the convex glass of the mask. Jon couldn't read him at all. There were no clues. He tried to search Footfall for a way in but the man just stood there as if someone had given up carving him because the rock was too hard. Chrye would know, he thought.

'Sciler. What.'

It wasn't even a question. Jon was lost here. He didn't even know what to call him. Footfall wasn't his name. Jon had intended making out it was coincidence, but Footfall had been expecting him.

It came with a rush. Of course he had. Jon had triggered it before, in the first zone. Only Janus had picked it up then, but Footfall must have registered it. He had been waiting for Jon ever since then. That was his in with Footfall, and that was his first question answered.

'You were in the zone with Starburn. We have to talk.'

Footfall's eyes flickered. The lenses exaggerated the reaction. It was as if he'd flipped channels somewhere inside. 'No. Starburn's dead. He killed himself.' He hunched down and made to shoulder past Jon.

Jon grabbed him by the sleeve. Footfall's coat was sodden. Jon wasn't dressed for rain and didn't have gloves. The faintly acid water squeezed from the cloth made his fingers sting. He held on and felt the thick seam of Footfall's coat start to give. It wasn't even an old coat. Nothing lasted now. Everything was biodegradable.

Jon relaxed his grip slightly. 'Starburn was murdered,' he said. 'Someone killed him. It wasn't suicide.'

Footfall stared straight at Jon with his magnified eyes. He looked slowly around the deserted rainswept street before leaning towards Jon and whispering, 'It's not like you think. Leave it, Sciler.'

He wrenched his arm from Jon's fist and began to run.

Jon shouted, 'Wait,' then flicked his head around, his nerves jangling. Nothing was moving but something on the street wasn't as it had been. The rain was still drumming down, quickly swallowing the sound of Footfall's retreat. There was nothing else.

Except that the trig was standing closer. Jon took a slow step backwards, and the trig started unevenly to rise on its three legs. It was only as tall as him, but it seemed vast and looming.

Jon took another step and turned and ran blindly into the rain. Footfall had vanished.

Fifteen metres, he thought. It hadn't been closer than that. He could out-accelerate it for the first three, then he'd have maybe ten paces before it was on him. So forget outrunning it. Where is it now?

His ears were selling him only the white noise of the rain, the stinging rain like a paste against his face, and he had no time to slip the mask down so he was sucking in the water along with the harsh air and feeling it tickle and burn like jolts of basement whisky. His throat was on fire.

Where was it now? Jon felt as if he'd been running since yesterday, but the little counter in his head quietly sang six steps, seven steps, eight . . .

He made a sharp left turn into an alley, nearly losing his footing and feeling his ankle wrench. The alley was as narrow as a doorway but deep enough to be a passage to somewhere, and in the impenetrable lattice of rain that bounced from the walls and paving it lost all perspective. It was like staring down into a whirlpool. Jon plunged into it.

Ten steps, and in front of him there was a brick wall. Dead end.

He swung round to face the mesh of dancing rain, and saw it holding the faint dark outline of the trig. A bead of light flared in its belly and swept out into a bright cone that arrowed towards the side wall. Through the rain Jon made out the pattern of bricks caught in the etched circle of light.

The spotlight began to track up and down in a search pattern, splaying across the puddled ground and crawling back along the wall. Jon flinched uselessly as it slid towards him. There was nothing to hide behind, just a mess of sodden paper and ripped plastic packaging. He hunched down and tried to melt into a corner.

The light found him. Its blinding radiance slapped him against the wall and pinned him there.

This is it, he thought numbly. He shielded his eyes and waited for the sharplight to condense, for the heatbolt that would finish him. His chest trembled as the bright cone stroked down from his neck to his groin and travelled slowly back up again. It came to a halt in the centre of his chest and contracted to a hard and shining coin. Seconds passed. Minutes passed. The only sound was the rain and it was deafening.

'Do it, for God's sake do it,' Jon screamed into the rain. His control had gone, and his voice broke. 'Do it,' he sobbed. The water was a part of him now. It drummed on his head and drained from his feet. It flowed through him as if he wasn't there. He couldn't tell if he was crying or if he'd pissed himself.

Instead of condensing to a point, the circle began to grow wider and carried on growing, diffused by the rain and spreading intoxicating colours that spun and licked outwards.

Jon clenched his fists, watching the bright disc expand. He felt the heat of the scattering sharplight, and from the disc's centre the colour started to drain.

For a moment it made no sense, and Jon thought he was hallucinating. Then he realised – the microwave component of the honed sharplight was boiling and evaporating the rain. The brightness at the rim intensified into a halo that fell around Jon, and for a fraction of a second as the light blinked off Jon was left staring through a perfectly clear tunnel. At the end of the tunnel was the alley's entrance, and filling it, burnt on to his retina, was the motionless black trig.

The rain came down again like a curtain.

THIRTEEN

Chrye wasn't certain Jon would be there, but she had prayed Hickey Sill wouldn't. She struck out instantly on Hickey. His door was open when she got to the corner of the stairs on the floor below. She dropped her head and tried to sneak past but he was standing there waiting when her boot hit the first step.

'I appreciate that,' he said in a voice she guessed was meant to be friendly. The sinus occlusion from whatever blend of drugs he was on clogged it up. He sounded as if he was talking through water. She just nodded and made to go on past him. Hickey blocked her, one hand on the wall and the other stretched across to the stair-rail.

'I said I appreciate that.'

Chrye took a pace back. She could smell the stuff. He was sweating it. His face glistened.

'You look tired, Hickey. Why don't you get some sleep?'

''S what I mean.' He nodded slowly. He was slurring now, but he hadn't before. He'd been practising the opener while she came up the stairs, sharpening the consonants, she guessed, but that was as far as it went. Jon had told her Hickey had the building bugged and lensed. Paranoid, psychotic, Hickey Sill was the ideal pacifist for the world's end. He grinned happily at her.

Great, she thought, returning his grin as neutrally as possible. Jon Sciler spends all his time in a make-believe world trying to solve a crime that may be in his own head, and this crazy 'fist Hickey Sill spends his time waiting for me.

Hickey widened his grin. His teeth were somewhere between yellow and green. Chrye looked past him up the next flight, wishing Jon there. He wasn't. He wouldn't have heard anything, the way she'd come up trying to avoid Hickey, and Hickey's voice wasn't loud.

She recognised true danger in him. Ticks in all the P-boxes. She had thought he was just a fantasiser before, but now she knew he was for real.

'Yeah, I 'preciate it,' he repeated. He shifted his grip on the rail.

'What do you appreciate, Hickey?' He couldn't be ignored, that would be a mistake. The little bit of his brain that was engaged enough to articulate that phrase was sufficiently alert to trigger more, and he wasn't predictable.

'I 'preciate you try'n notter 'sturb my sleep. 'S a hard job, pas'cation.' His head nodded heavily. 'So I 'preciate it.' His eyes were watering now and beginning to close. Whatever it was, it was shutting him down at last. His sweat-lubricated hand slid down the rail and he nearly lost his balance.

'Let's get you inside,' Chrye suggested. She helped him to stand, turning her face from his breath. It was like something a long time dead. She staggered inside his room with him. She looked at the bed in the corner and decided against it. It was covered in crushed food cartons frothy with mould.

Hickey attempted to rally himself as she let him drop on to the couch, and tried to bring her down with him. There was a dull cable of drool running down his chin. She pushed him back on to the worn leather and he fell instantly asleep.

Chrye glanced around the room. Nothing seemed to have moved since Hickey had dragged her in with Jon to drink with him. She looked around, taking it all in.

A greying of dust had settled over everything except the screen in the corner. There was a scuffed trail of wear on the carpet between the screen and the couch, and another between the screen and the small cooking unit. Then there were the pathetic pictures of women and of his trig tacked up and curling away from the wall, and that was it. There was nothing more. Jon's identical room above Hickey's was bare too, barren of ornament and memory, but in Jon's case it was a conscious making of space. Jon lived inside himself. Hickey's room was as empty as Hickey Sill.

He's never had a woman, she thought abruptly. And he could have had women if he'd wanted, a pacifist, even one as revolting as Hickey. There were no mementos of love here, no souvenirs of rape, even. Hickey wasn't interested.

She crossed her arms over her chest and hugged herself as the next conclusion hit her with a jolt. Hickey Sill doesn't want me. He just wants what he thinks will hurt Jon if he takes it. So I'm disposable.

She stared down at Hickey and shivered. She straightened her back carefully and was at the door when something made her turn round.

Hickey was sitting up wide-eyed. 'Be you and me soon, Chrye,' he said clearly. ' 'Cos I know where. I've been looking and now I've seen him.' He frowned sombrely. 'Yeah. What he deserves, mister Far fucking Warrior.' He closed his eyes and fell back and started to snore.

'He wants to kill you, Jon,' she said. She was still trembling. It hadn't started until Jon had looked at her as she stood in his doorway right above Hickey's, and said, 'Are you all right, Chrye? You don't look good.' Then he'd had to lead her in and sit her down. Her head was shaking so much she couldn't even focus on the chair.

'He . . .' She was going to tell him Hickey Sill wanted to take her from Jon first, maybe kill her too, before or after he killed Jon, but she held that back. She didn't want to complicate it, she told herself. 'He said he's seen you, or something.'

Jon sighed. 'I thought so,' he murmured. 'He gave me a warning. Look, don't worry. He knows he can catch me as I come out of Maze now. But if he's going to kill me, he's only going to do it off duty, with that cuckoo and his trig. He wants me dead, but he doesn't want to lose his job over it. That's why I'm safe here. He's not going to risk any connection. But he can't spend all his time waiting outside Maze for me either. He's got to work and sleep too. I've got time.'

'Maybe we can take the cuckoo . . .'

'No. He'll be waiting for that. Don't ever think Hickey's stupid, Chrye. If I break in and take it, he'll have it all on tape, he'll come looking and he'll be able to kill me on duty. I'm blocked solid. What he told you, Chrye, he didn't just let it slip. He knows what he's doing. Telling you was part of it.'

He picked up her bag from the floor. 'So. You brought it?'

She looked blankly at it and said, 'What?' Her head was still full of Hickey Sill.

'The journal,' Jon said impatiently.

Chrye couldn't believe he could just switch like that. Displacement, she thought. She had a flash of Hickey Sill's wild, mad eyes locked on hers.

116

Maybe that was what she needed too, some kind of displacement activity. It seemed everyone else had something. Reality was too much.

'Ground rules,' she said. 'If we're going to do this, if I'm going to help you find out what happened to Starburn, we do it properly. We establish some rules.'

He hadn't taken his eyes from the book since she'd set it on the table. In the time since she'd last seen him, Chrye realised, the journal had taken on a new meaning for him. Something had happened in the zone. She left her hand resting on the curling leather of the cover, struck by a sudden feeling that he might make a grab for it.

'One,' she said. 'And look at me, Jon. I'm not screwing around here.'

He half raised his head.

'When we arrange to meet, we meet. You turn up. No excuses. Because if you're right and Starburn was murdered, then you're probably also in danger. So I need to know when to be worried. Okay?'

'Okay.' He was looking at her now, sitting tautly.

'Two. You're not having this book, Jon.'

He exploded up from the chair. 'That's just crazy. The book's our one advantage over them.'

'Calm down. Listen to me.' She held him with her eyes until he subsided again. 'There's a lot of stuff in the book, but your reaction to the zone has to remain virgin. They'll soon know if you've got hidden information, and if someone at Maze was involved in Starburn's murder they'll already have you under glass. They'll know he was a friend of yours. And another reason. I think there's something odd going on in this game, and I don't want any foreknowledge you have muddying it.'

Jon said sharply. 'What do you mean, something odd?'

'That first debriefing you had. I can't put my finger on it, but Dr Locke asked you some peculiar questions. I don't know what she was after yet, but she wasn't just after your opinion of a game, Jon. If something you get from the journal screws it all up for them, Maze will ditch you and we're lost. We're a long way behind them, Jon.

'And one final thing. If I'm going to get anywhere, I have to know what Dr Locke knows, and the only access I have, other than from you, is in these pages.' She tapped the book's cover. 'So, Jon, are we straight now?'

She waited for him.

'We're straight,' Jon said.

Chrye leaned back. She could feel the tension leaving her shoulders. She opened the book and smoothed her palm over the first page.

'Fine,' she said. 'First, there's nothing that gives us any idea what Cathedral could be. No mention of it. Now, I'm not going to give you any detail, as we agreed, but you don't need to go in there quite as blind as Starburn. So, if you like, I'll tell you a bit about Starburn's final months.'

Jon smiled to himself. Stick and carrot. But he didn't mind. He didn't mind at all. Looking at her, head down over the open journal, he remembered the warmth of her body nestling into his rigid back that first night and wondered again how she could have had such immediate trust in him to do that.

'It's the same writer all the way through, I'm sure,' Chrye was saying. 'Sentence structure, grammar, vocabulary – it's all consistent.'

She glanced up and made a face at Jon. It was a face that said they were working together now, that they were a team. Jon tried to respond, but it was hard to dissect the warm reciprocal feeling from the dread that shadowed it, and his smile was quick and brittle. He and Starburn had been a team, and it had failed. Jon couldn't just slide back into it with Chrye. Maybe that was how her trust was so easily given. Maybe it had never been tested and found wanting.

'But there's a progressive personality change,' Chrye went on, turning a few pages. 'It starts without a mention of anything but the game he's working on, and there's no confusion about its nature. It's all hardware and software, players and constructs. Then, as he gets more involved, his objectivity begins to fray.' She shrugged. 'That's okay, I'd expect it. He kept his own time log, here at the back.' She flicked through to the end papers then swivelled it round so Jon could see the meticulous charts.

'Daylight hours, sunrise, moonrise, it's all here. A zone day lasts twenty-three hours and fifty-two minutes.' She frowned suddenly. 'That is very odd.'

'Why?'

'If you're creating such a thing, why not make it dead on twenty-four hours? It'd be far simpler. This way, it's crazy.'

Jon said carefully into her silence. 'Something else. Perhaps it's connected. The zone, well, it's faultless. I don't understand it. Kerz and Dr Locke explained it to me, all to do with internalising motor function, but it's *too* good. I've seen most of the development of virtuals, and it's been a series of little leaps. What this zone represents isn't just an improvement.'

He stopped there, letting the words hang in the air, and Chrye wondered if he was waiting for her to say it. That maybe it was real. That maybe in this real place there was a twenty-three hours and fifty-two minutes day–night cycle.

She steered uncomfortably past the trap. 'I did some calculations of my own, extrapolating from his log. It could explain what follows. Maze kept him there well over forty per cent of wide-eye realtime. That's illegal as well as predictably psychologically damaging. And he was highly vulnerable to begin with. He was selected for it.'

'As I was,' said Jon. 'Don't look at me like that. The difference is that we've got the book. Even if you won't give it to me.'

Chrye stared at him. She liked that. She fingered the book as if for the first time. It meant something new to her. All of a sudden it was something between Jon and herself, not between Jon and Starburn. She liked it that this cord linking Jon and Starburn was beginning to fray. There was a long way to go, but this was the start she needed.

'And I've got you,' he added.

'What?' She felt herself flushing.

'I've got you,' he repeated. For a moment he wasn't quite sure why he'd said it. 'I mean, to interpret the book. To make sure nothing happens to me. Starburn had no one. You're my psychsupport, Chrye.'

The colour was going from her face. 'Oh. Sure. So, let's go on.' She bent over the book, covering her confusion. 'He enters the zone, just like you did, Jon. A few days spent acclimatising, learning the ground rules, and the game begins.' She flicked through the book. 'Then he begins to get agitated, talking of something from the zone escaping and spying on him, stalking him. Of course he never quite sees it, can't describe it. Classic paranoia. Textbook.'

She hesitated for a moment. Maybe she shouldn't have told him that, but she'd done it now. She decided to go on. 'The psychosis is interesting, though. He starts to document events outside the zone as well as within it. And when he does, there's still no confusion between what happens in-zone and out. That does surprise me. No characters carry over in either direction except this unseen observer, or stalker, or whatever we call it. He knows exactly where he is. It's clearly a paranoid psychosis, but the parameters are unusually well defined.'

119

She leaned back and closed the journal, then sighed and lifted it to the light as if the black silhouette was going to reveal more that way. 'Or else I'm completely wrong. The journal could be total fiction. Or else someone could have been stalking him for real. It's impossible to diagnose a psychosis from such a limited source.'

'And he's dead now.'

'Yes. So we can never come to a conclusion.'

'Unless we accept the apparent suicide,' Jon said dryly.

She licked her lips. 'You know, if you hadn't told me about his phobia, and I'd been the coroner, I would have accepted suicide. Though I'd have damned Maze publicly for setting him up like that. I wonder why no one did?'

'We don't know what information the coroner had access to. And no one had the book, remember. Starburn sent it to me just before he died.'

Chrye nodded. 'So. What have we got? Someone may possibly have been following him, and he was murdered in a rather unnecessarily involved way that appeared to be suicide but was clearly not to anyone who knew him. Why?'

'Maybe they were torturing him. Trying to make him tell them something.'

'Something in the book, you mean? There isn't anything here. It's just a diary and a game journal. It isn't even a good record of the zone.'

Jon opened his mouth, then paused. Eventually he said, 'You thought there was something odd about the debriefings. Well, there's something else I haven't told you about Maze.'

'Oh? What?'

'Have you heard of something called PI?'

She shook her head. 'It isn't familiar. What is it?'

'I took a psychometric test at Maze at the first interview. It was titled "PI Preliminary Screening". There were a lot of questions, rather weird ones.'

'Can you remember any of them?'

'A few.' They were etched in his skull. He watched them re-form on her pad in her neat handwriting.

Chrye's frown deepened when he had finished. Shadows crawled over her forehead. She doodled flowing abstract patterns around the tidy paragraphs for a few minutes. 'PI,' she murmured. 'You're sure that's all?'

'I told you. "PI Preliminary Screening".'

She wrote it down and circled the words heavily. 'Well, it's nothing I've ever heard of. And the test's not like any psychometric I've ever come across. Those questions. Death wish and identity slip. It's a curious combination to be searching for.'

'Perhaps they're trying to eliminate them.'

'No. The whole sequence was focussed on it. It was identified by the first few questions. The only point in pursuing the string was to quantify it. This wasn't a dumb questionnaire, Jon. It was on a screen. It was a smart test. The computer chose each question on the basis of your answer to the previous ones.'

'There's more,' he said hesitantly. 'It may mean nothing.'

Chrye had a bad feeling about what he was going to say. 'Yes?'

'At the end I was asked if I had any phobias.'

She felt her breath catch. 'Oh, no,' she whispered. 'What did you answer?'

'I don't think I said anything. I can't remember. I haven't got any phobias I know of.'

'Did Kerz say anything about the test?'

'Uh-uh.'

She put the pen down. 'Well, maybe they're trying to eliminate phobic situations from the game now.' She wondered if she sounded at all convincing. 'Maybe they think they screwed up there with Starburn somehow.'

'So will I have passed the test?'

She made a fist and hit him on the shoulder, wanting and not wanting to hurt him. 'Sometimes . . . sometimes I still don't know you, Jon. I hope to God not, but you're in the game. So I guess you did.'

He stood stiffly to his feet and stretched his arms out. 'Well, that's a good thing.'

'Jon,' Chrye said despairingly. 'Is there anything else you haven't told me?'

He cocked his head to the side and said, 'That's funny. That's exactly what Dr Locke keeps asking me.'

REAL SKILLS, it said over the main door in a script made of stylised guns and swords. Jon headed through the foyer towards Information. The booth was dark and looked empty, but something was happening, someone was there in the shadows.

The guy behind the counter was V-helmeted, head jerking, staring left and right and then ducking away out of sight before leaping up with both hands levelled, tracking left to right and pumping absent guns around the hall. Jon waited a moment before pushing the 'Attention' button on the counter. The guy swore and mimed holstering the guns. He flipped up the visor. 'Yeah, what's it you want, player? We got it, just say what it is, huh? I get better things, y'know it? Menu's up there plain enough.'

Jon slid his eyes down the board behind the man.

'I don't see eyetrackers. I don't seen screenmarkers.'

'Ain't gottem, that's why. Game skills for players, that's what we got here. Guns we got, blades. You wanna use a kris, a kukri, scimitar, sabre, we gottem. Shoot a long bow, Uzi, sharplight, Koessler, we gottem. What you want, you're looking the wrong place.' He made to drop the visor back down.

Jon said slowly, 'Listen to me. I need something custom-built. I need someone who can do that for me.'

'Ain't no call for custom stuff. Any game you name, we got the skills here, learnem here. No game we ain't got the skills for. You hearin' me? Hand skills, weapon skills.'

'I understand. I'm asking the wrong question. I'd like to speak to whoever builds your hardware. Just point me there and you can go right back to the OK Corral.'

'Why'ncha say so? Jesus! Communicate, man. What it's all about? Enda the corridor, door marked "Maintenance". See? Wasn't so hard. Only needed to ask.' He grinned. 'Wagon train, anyway. Surrounded! Clint Wayne's Quick Draw – new game from Id/Entity. Pickin' off the Sioux. It's fuckin' *blood*.' He clicked down the visor and looked over Jon's shoulder and swore again. His arms were as if they were cradling a shotgun. He tracked and fired, the big gun not giving him the kick it should have if the hardware had been any good.

'Missed,' Jon said. He moved off down the corridor.

The seminar room was big and empty enough for words to bounce round the walls. Chrye arrived ten minutes late, rattling her way through the stacks of steel and plastic chairs towards the oval table. Her tutor looked up and raised her painted eyebrows, ignoring Chrye's apology and its faint echo.

Chrye sat down and opened her case on the table. Bad start, she thought.

'Well, Chrye, shall we begin?'

'I'm not sure Jon Sciler is a suitable subject for my thesis, Ms Schaefer,' Chrye said.

There was a silence which her tutor plugged with a sigh. Chrye felt the echo of the sigh like a rebuke.

'Really?' Ms Schaefer said. 'And why is that?'

'He's accepted a job at Maze, the games company. He's testing bLinkered games.'

'Why should that disbar him? I don't see it as a problem.'

'He's suffering more than ever from bLinker effects now. I don't think he's a suitable subject – he needs treatment, Ms Schaefer. I don't think my position is ethically tenable.'

Her tutor tapped her pen on the table impatiently. 'Chrye, you have a first-class degree in functional psychology. You're close to him. You're in the best position to help him. If he's willingly exposing himself to this situation, we both know he won't withdraw from it to seek help. And no one can force him to. For you to attempt such a thing would be unethical.' She walked to the window and stood there with her back to Chrye for a moment, her angular figure framed by the tumbling grey ash that had been falling all morning. She turned around again.

'I'd be prepared to adjust your remit to incorporate his situation, if that would set you at ease. We can be sure of his safety, and your thesis can be more wide-ranging than originally intended. That would suit everyone concerned.'

'I'm still not sure.' Chrye looked at Ms Schaefer. It had taken Chrye six months to find a suitable subject and now this was happening. 'I'm having a problem over something else too. Jon has become convinced that a friend of his from the Dirangesept project was murdered at Maze. At a conscious level this is his reason for joining them, to discover the murderer.'

Ms Schaefer didn't react. Chrye continued. 'He's very convincing. The friend is certainly dead, and Jon gives plausible reasons for it being murder.'

'And naturally it's all post-rationalisation. Chrye, you're getting sucked into his world-view. I don't need to remind you that transference works two ways. You must be careful not to get too close to . . .' She fixed Chrye with a glance. 'To Jon.'

Chrye felt her face redden. 'Okay. I'd like to discuss the company, Maze,' she continued. 'As I said, Sciler's friend worked for it before he died, and he sent Sciler a journal written during his time there. I'm extremely concerned about some of the techniques they used at Maze. This man Lees became clearly paranoid in a very unusual way, and I have worries over the ethical base of the company.'

'I take it you've seen this journal. Do you have it?'

'Yes.'

'Can I see it?'

Chrye handed it over to her tutor. Watching her start to flick through it, Chrye said, 'You'll see Lees was kept bLinkered for long periods – the day–night cycle in the zone is just short of twenty-four hours. When he began, he was bLinkered during the day, came out to sleep. But as he became immersed, the shorter days in the zone forced his biological clock to creep. In the end he'd gone into reversal. His days were being spent in the real world, his nights awake, bLinkered, in the zone.'

Ms Schaefer nodded, then looked up at Chrye. 'You're theorising sleep deprivation, aren't you? It's a good point. But, according to this, he was always in a CrySis pod when bLinkered. Is this relevant, Chrye? What do you know about CrySis time?'

'Uh, yes.' She felt stupid. 'REM sleep. Even if he was bLinkered, CrySis time is equivalent to REM sleep. So there was no sleep deprivation.'

'Good. But I agree, the day–night discrepancy seems odd at first glance. You haven't done much game psychology, Chrye, have you? No. In the past, games were predicated on the illusion of victory. Now, with the world . . .' she waved an arm vaguely towards the ash-blurred window '. . . they're based more on the illusion of survival. Of hope.'

Chrye shrugged. She knew all of this.

'All the companies, Maze included, employ psychologists. They fund research externally, carry it out internally. An effective virtual game, Chrye, is close to reality, but not too close. They're drawing a fine line. It's in the game companies' interests to hook players, and they'll be using everything they can to do this. The techniques they use will be close to the edge, but the world's close to the edge. The government's on the anvil and the hammer's falling. Their attitude is that it's better that people play games than they take drugs and go berserk in the streets at this time.' She pulled herself up. 'All I'm saying here is that the old rules don't always apply. There are games, but there's no playing field any longer.'

She stopped abruptly. 'Sorry. My hobbyhorse, I'm afraid. With the present government's attitude, games companies get away with murder. Metaphorically speaking. But if your research shows up anything dangerous at Maze, Chrye, we'll do what we can.'

She took a deep breath and released it slowly. 'Where were we?'

Chrye said, 'Sleep deprivation.' She had never seen her tutor like this. Ms Schaefer was usually totally detached. For some reason she was involved here.

'Okay, that's ruled out by the pods, but my feeling is that this day–night discrepancy will act as a form of drug dynamic. When you mentioned sleep deprivation you were on the right track, Chrye. Players will, within a week or so of solid play, become disoriented. Day and night outside the zone will lose their meaning. Players adjust to the game clock and find it hard to readjust. Every game sold will be identically time-set to create a solidarity among players. My guess would be that Maze will market the game as playable at night.'

Chrye nodded. 'Jon goes to Maze at about ten in the evening to play. He comes out after debriefing, sometimes as late as noon.' She thought, And if you're drawn into believing this game zone could be real, then the immutability of the zone time reinforces it.

Ms Schaefer was saying, 'If, as the book says, all motor function is internalised, the players won't need pods. That'll just be a research requirement. Once they're bLinkered they can lie in bed, even sit in a chair.'

She shook her head. 'It's a massive leap. I don't know, Chrye, but if Maze have got this far, maybe the game even provides REM sleep equivalent outside CrySis pods. Maybe players get a full night's play and then a full day's function too. Maybe they'll push the game as an alternative to sleep. God knows how many people suffer from nightmares these days, that's reason enough to play. But either way, as the zone clock slowly takes over, they'll be completely hooked.'

She sat back. 'It's very, very clever.'

'It's brainwashing,' Chrye said.

'Maybe it is. If it is, you're in the position to prove it. But be careful. No one's going to be interested in scares over a game that, bottom line, maintains public tranquillity. And until the game's on the streets, Maze is going to be as protective of its wares as any drug dealer.'

'Great. And that leaves me . . .'

'With my full support. But keep it all between us, Chrye. It's just a thesis, nothing's changed. You haven't discussed any of this with anyone else, have you?'

Just Kei, she thought. 'No. No one else.'

'Good.' She laughed. The sound was brittle and she cut it short. It came off the walls like a screech of feedback. 'Maybe paranoia's contagious after all. This is just a game we're talking about.'

'Okay,' said Chrye. 'One final thing. I've been trying to find out about a smart psychometric test Sciler was given at Maze. It was just titled "PI". I can't find anything.'

'PI?' Ms Schaefer pursed her lips. 'It means nothing to me. I don't suppose . . .'

Chrye pulled out the list of questions from her folder.

Her tutor sat reading quietly and then muttered to herself, 'PI, PI, PI.' She looked up at Chrye. 'Personality Indicator, Paranoia Index? I don't know. If it's a smart test, we could probably work backwards and get his responses, go from there.'

'I've done that. Highly imaginative, creative, emotionally blocked, introverted . . . but that isn't what's being measured here.'

'No, it isn't. You know, Chrye, the first part of the sequence and some of the later parts remind me of the psychometrics in the initial Dirangesept selection procedure. The first project, I mean. Selection wasn't so refined then. A test similar to this was used to deselect potential martyrs and heroes. This, of course, isn't a deselection process at all. It isn't quite looking for potential suicides either. It seems incomplete, too. Was there . . . ?'

'Phobias. The last question was, "Do you have any fears or phobias?" Jon's dead friend, who presumably underwent the same test, had a form of hydrophobia. And he was subsequently supposed to have drowned himself.'

'Well, that's interesting, isn't it? I have no response to that, except that if he did, it would be the ultimate proof of success of aversion therapy.' She smiled thinly, then said, 'I didn't mean to be flippant.' She held up Chrye's handwritten notes on the test. 'Preliminary test, it says. So we know there's more to come.'

She let the notes go and stood up. 'That's it for today, I think. It's going extremely well so far. Oh, do you have a copy of this?' She held up Starburn's journal. 'No matter. I'm going to read it properly and I'd like to show it to a few people. I'll have it duped and return it to you when we meet next week. You have more than enough to be getting on with, Chrye. And I'll see what I can find out about PI for you.'

FOURTEEN

Chrye stood outside the smoked-glass doors of the Pacification Bureau beneath the glow of the blue lamp with her hands stretched high. Her skirt was riding up around her hips, and she knew this routine wasn't necessary. She just needed to pass once through the scanner's field. But she kept turning around until the voice from the speaker grille told her to stop. 'Just one more time, hands a little higher please. And a little more. Okay, you're clear.'

The doors opened and closed around her as if they resented the air she brought in. She went straight to the raised desk in its glass cage and tried to keep her voice level when she got there.

'I called ahead. Chrye Roffe. I wanted some information on a case.'

The officer peered at the screen on his desk. 'Hold on one minute for me. Just replaying your security check. Can't be too safe.' He squinted at the screen, easy over the time he took. 'Okay. You ain't carrying nothing I don't have on file now.' The pacifist leered at her, leaning forward over the console to look her slowly up and down. 'Them blue frilly panties suit you real well.'

Chrye touched her lip. 'You might want to wipe your mouth,' she said. 'I'm not sure if it's just drool or you're leaking brain there.'

He stared at her for a few long seconds, then drawled. 'There's a note here. You're accredited. Look a bit old for a student – what'cha studying, eh? How to get screwed by men in uniforms?' He stuck his tongue out and panted at her, then looked pained when she just gazed back at him. 'Joke, okay? What'cha studying?'

'Psych. I'm specialising in personality defects. I thought I'd start here.'

He frowned. 'Smart little fucker, aint'cha?'

'Look, why don't you read the note? Or maybe you'd like me to read it for you.'

He looked uncertainly at her, then examined the screen again. 'Lees, Marcus. Yeah, I got it here. Suicide.' He dabbed a finger at the monitor. 'It's searching. See, suicide ain't the end of it.' He grinned at her. 'Got a whole department devoted to suicide evaluation now. So many bastards killing theirselves, we can't keep up with them all. Wasn't a relative of yours, was he?'

'He had no relatives,' Chrye said.

'I know that. Testing, see? Sign of a good 'fist.' He looked at the screen again, muttering. 'Searching, searching, here we go.' He put his finger to the screen and squinted closely at it. 'Ha! Case got referred to CMS, and they referred it right back to Crime. Got stamped suicide confirmed. No action. Case closed. Looks like you wasted your time here, student.'

'Where do I find CMS?'

The officer laughed. 'CMS? Sure, go right ahead. Captain Madsen. See that corridor, go right along it till you find a blue door says CMS. Gonna have to push hard, though, no one's been in there a year or two. Tell him front desk sent you.'

He was speaking into the intercom as she walked away down the corridor.

The blue paint was flaking off the door and lying on the floor's scuffed grey tiles. Chrye pushed the door open.

The office was tiny and empty. It was obviously a secretary's office. There was a keyboard and monitor on the desk, and grey files piled on steel cabinets. The monitor was humming. It looked like someone had left the office moments ago. Behind the desk was another door, paned with frosted glass.

As she made for the inner door the hazy silhouette of a head and shoulders swelled behind the glass, and the door opened.

'Ms Roffe? My secretary just popped out. Come in. I'm Captain Madsen.'

Chrye glanced at the chair tucked under the secretary's desk. There was a thick greying of dust on the seat.

Madsen gestured for Chrye to sit, waiting for her before taking his own seat. His desk was covered with files which he pushed aside with a sweep of his forearm. He looked about fifty. There was a few days of stubble on his cheeks and chin and stretching down his neck as far as his Adam's apple. She noticed that his pale brown hair seemed thinner on the right than on the left.

'What can I do for you?'

'I don't know if your front desk told you, I'm Chrye Roffe. I'm a psych student. I'm studying the effect of virtual environments on the personality. I'm particularly interested in suicide.' She tried to flatten out the crumpled 'Please help Ms Roffe' letter that her tutor had given her at the start of her doctorate, passing it over to Madsen. 'I was wondering if you could talk to me about a case, a suicide which seems to have been referred to your department. This is my begging letter.' It often worked no better than one. After the front desk, and looking at Captain Madsen, she didn't have much hope for it this time.

Madsen glanced at it and let it fall to the table. 'What was the suicide's name?'

'Marcus Lees.'

Madsen looked at the letter again, this time reading it through.

Chrye said, 'I believe the front desk called my tutor to confirm it earlier in the day. I don't think it was the officer on duty now.'

Madsen leaned forward and spoke into the intercom. He flicked it off and asked Chrye for her photo ID, then said to her, 'I'm not directly connected with the Department of Pacification. I'm an investigator for Home Affairs. I'm based here for convenience – 'Fist's convenience, not mine.' He folded her letter and handed it back. 'I don't need to draw out the notes on the Lees case. Trouble is these days we're so overloaded with suicides, Ms Roffe, and everyone who does it makes it special. They want to get their name in the news when they die, bizarre murder case, that sort of crap. We don't have the resources for it. Real crime's off the scale.' He passed her back the letter, then leaned back in his chair. 'Cult stuff helps. You know where you are with a cult. Cults make our lives easy. You ever heard of the Eighth Day? Before your time, I guess.'

Chrye had an odd sense that Captain Madsen had just slipped away from her and into himself. She wasn't even sure he knew he'd asked her a question. She nodded and said, trying to bring him back, 'I've heard of it. It was a cult based on a non-interactive game. A small games company produced a simulated environment, a sort of paradise around which you could drift in a disembodied state, just observing.'

Madsen sat back in his chair, staring up into the bare bulb hanging from the ceiling. His right hand went up to his ear and he began to spin a

130

hair around his index finger, twirling it around and around. He's gone, Chrye thought.

'That's the one,' Madsen murmured. 'The game was called The Eighth Day. It didn't do too well on the streets at the time, everyone was into slash'n'shooters. Eighth Day was sharp visually, very inventive, but it went see-through on the shelves. Then someone decided it was real. Someone thought wouldn't-it-be-nice-if . . . and the next thing they had themselves a cult. They recruited for a few months, then they hired the Albert Hall. The leader, or one of the lieutenants maybe, had beefed up the program so that each of them could see whoever else was in the zone as sort of 2-D cutouts, identical shadows—'

'Souls, they called them,' Chrye interrupted. 'They'd all played the zone before, but it gave them a sense of belonging, seeing all their fellow souls in that safe and beautiful environment. This was the first VR-led consensual mass suicide. It was part of my degree course.'

'And now it's just an acronym on my door. Yes. It was just after the first Dirangesept project had failed. I wasn't in the department then, I was a 'fist on foot patrol, working what they still used to call the graveyard shift. Jesus.'

He's locked on to this, Chrye thought. She remembered the case study, remembered wondering how people could be so willing to let their lives go. Curious now, she waited for Madsen to go on.

He crooked his head. 'I was walking through Hyde Park when the call came. I used to like it there, it was peaceful the way the trees were beginning to grow. You could still see the stars through the branches. The night never bothered me.' He was tugging at his hair now. 'I wandered over to the Albert Hall at four in the morning after someone living nearby called up to say it was odd but no one had come out and that the hall was completely quiet. When I got there it was dark, like it was simply closed up for the night. All the doors were locked, there was no sign of movement. I shone my torch inside, saw nothing. I thought either it was a hoax call or the caller had slept through them leaving. It was possible. The Eighth Dayers weren't a rowdy lot. But the caretaker didn't respond when I knocked at his door. So I forced the lock and went in. I pushed all the switches I could find in his office, but nothing worked. I went through into the inner corridor, went right around it twice, and still nothing. By then I was feeling more than a bit jittery. I didn't want to go any further.

'Anyway, eventually I took a breath and pushed open the doors to the auditorium. All the lights were out, remember, and of course there were no windows in there, so my eyes wouldn't adapt to the dark beyond giving me the vaguest of shapes. I had my Nitelite on my belt, but I didn't like using that. But I didn't want to be a target either, so I wasn't about to shine my torch in there. So I put the Nitelite on and I looked around.'

Madsen was tugging hard on the hair entangled in his fingers. He wasn't even aware he was doing it, Chrye realised.

'Everything looked grainy with the Nitelite. Grainy and gloomy. I did a quick sweep of the place. It was empty, that was my first reaction. I wanted to turn right around and leave but, of course, I didn't. I looked again, slowly, and I saw that the symmetry of the place, and the silence and the stillness, had told me the wrong thing. It wasn't empty at all. Quite the opposite. Every seat in the Albert Hall was occupied. Every single seat had someone sitting there.

'I still didn't think they were dead or even comatose, although their heads were lolled forward. I thought they were still just bLinkered, into the game. I took a step towards the nearest person. My footstep sounded like thunder. I could hear the echo of my breathing.'

His right hand jerked and he pulled out a few more strands of hair, then paused to examine them before letting them fall to the floor. He went on. 'It was a woman. Her arms were in her lap, her hands like stacked saucers. She was wearing a long shirt and a jumper, and a headset like the rest of them. I didn't want to touch her head, it felt like disturbing her, so I tried to take the pulse at her wrist. I lifted her hand and held it, and there was no resistance. It was as if she was showing how she trusted me. I nearly cried, holding her hand there.'

He squeezed his eyes tight closed for a moment, a line of creases appearing on his forehead like a set of shutters being rolled down. Chrye waited for him to go on. There was nothing for her to say. She knew the facts, but she'd never heard the story. Now it was real.

'Anyway, there wasn't a pulse, but I was shaking hard and it could have been that. I couldn't really concentrate, I kept looking around as if they were all about to wake up like zombies and start coming at me. So I held her head up and tried to take the carotid pulse, which wasn't there either. She was dead. I took off her headset – old type, non-invasive – and looked into her eyes. It was weird, staring into her eyes with the Nitelite. Her pupils were wide as moons and I could see right through them to the back of her retinas. It was like a blueprint of some place. I just stared. It was like I needed to understand it. Like I could somehow understand it.'

There was a long silence in the room. Eventually Captain Madsen's eyes came down until they met Chrye's. She shifted herself in the chair, moving her head enough to be sure he was focussed on her again and his story was done. She swallowed and said, 'And that was what made you join CMS.'

'That's it.' He began to wind some more hair into his fist, then seemed to realise what he was doing. He lifted his hand to pat his ruffled hair down and said, 'It's a long time ago now, but I wake up every morning and it seems like it happened last night.'

'You wouldn't forget that sort of thing,' Chrye said inadequately. She wondered whether she should suggest returning another time, but he seemed abruptly alert so she decided to try it. 'The Lees case,' she reminded him.

He exhaled once, hard, like a diver surfacing from deep down, then rubbed his hands together, seeming surprised to find hairs twined in his fingers. 'Yes. Marcus Lees. The situation is, unless there's a definite indication of violence, it tends to get ignored. He was found drowned in a reservoir, no marks or bruises, end of case.'

Chrye said, 'But you said you remember it. Why's that? And why was it referred to you, to CMS?'

'To answer your last question first, referring it to CMS is a way of concluding an awkward case. No obvious violence, so they don't call it murder. It saves the department some money and keeps the unsolveds down. But now and then a case hits a few too many connections with other cases and they can't just bury it. That's the trouble with the analysing computer. It isn't coincidence-proof, and it keeps records. When it starts flashing its little red lights you can't just tell it to go play in a rift. So in this case the readout suggested a possible link with other cases, and one of the options for pursuit was CMS.'

'What was the link with other cases?'

He paused and looked at her, smoothing his hair down again. Eventually he said, 'It was tenuous. Lees was found floating in a reservoir, a freshwater reservoir, but he was found with apparent deposits of seawater in his lungs and stomach. You asked why I remembered the case, and that's why.'

'Seawater?'

Madsen held up his hands. 'There wasn't much left, he'd been floating awhile. It could be done. He could have taken an anti-emetic and then drunk a gutful of salt water before jumping in and swimming out to the middle of the reservoir. It could have been an assisted suicide – which I know is technically still murder, but we don't actively pursue them – or, yes, it could have been murder. It's hard to tell. Like I said, he'd been there a good week before we fished him out. So we can't be sure. Lees could simply have been having a go at a name-in-the-news suicide. That's what the coroner decided.'

That wasn't impossible, Chrye thought. Except for his phobia. She said, 'You still haven't got to why it was referred to you.'

'The thing is, the reason it flashed red lights on Anal – on the analysing computer, sorry but we call it that – is that in the last year we've had a few suicides with odd features like in the Lees case. Detail discrepancies. Well, Anal likes that sort of thing. One of them was a guy set fire to himself in his bed. We found the can of petrol in what was left of the room. It could have been a set-up, like Lees could have been, like anything could be. I mean, if you start staring at anything close enough, it'll drive you crazy.'

'But there was a discrepancy in that case too?'

'That's right. The pathologist thought his body had burnt at a far higher temperature than anything else at the scene. Like it had been in a furnace.'

'I don't suppose you remember whether the guy was phobic about fire, anything like that?'

'No idea. Why?' Madsen frowned.

'Well, if it was murder following torture, say, made up afterwards to look like suicide, then a phobia gives it an extra twist.'

'Ms Roffe, you've got a sick brain. Was Lees phobic about water, then?'

Chrye hesitated. She made her lips into a smile. 'I don't know. I'm just interested in why VR-users commit suicide. Far Warriors especially. Marcus Lees was a Far Warrior. I don't suppose the burnt guy was a Far Warrior?'

Madsen's eyes narrowed. 'Look, Ms Roffe, this is a confidential interview. You clearly aren't a fool, and if I don't tell you, you'll just go away and work it out for yourself, and if you do that maybe you'll work out more than there is to work out. There are these cases Anal picked up and collated, and CMS was one possibility. What the pacifists can do is send Anal's list to us, marked "Possible suicide, possible CMS". Now, whatever this Lees case is, it isn't CMS.'

Madsen sighed. 'I'm generalising here, but there are three main classifications with multiple murder.' He began to tick his fingers. 'Spree killings, when a lone guy goes berserk, a one-off brain-boiler. Then mass killings, which are usually premeditated and may be at more than one site and by more than one perpetrator, and which this department investigates where appropriate. And then there are serial killings.' He put his hands down on the table.

'So they send the Lees file to me, marked "Query suicide, query CMS", and I send the file back "Not CMS". That's all I can do. And they mark it "Conclusion, suicide". Anal switches off its red lights because the file's been referred on, investigated and resolved. It should never have come to me in the first place, but that wasn't my decision, and Anal can't override a human decision to go for a cheap twenty per cent option over the expensive seventy-percenter. So, yes, Ms Roffe, there could be a serial killer out there.'

The door of the office bumped open and the nose of an unmanned refreshments trolley poked through.

'You want some coffee?' Madsen said.

'Yes please. No sacch.'

Madsen walked round the desk and picked up two coffee discs from the trolley. He gave one to Chrye and took the other back to his seat. Chrye thought, He told me about the burnt man so that he could feel he had to tell me about the serial killer. He has no one else he can tell.

The trolley withdrew and the door fell back, not quite closed. Madsen kicked it shut.

Chrye held up the white disc. 'Thanks,' she said. She yanked the rim out from the base, telescoping the cup into shape and activating the sealed coffee tab. She could feel the heat gathering through the insulated plastic. Madsen passed her a jug of cold water from his desk and she filled the cup, dispersing the seal and cooling the superheated coffee down to almost drinkable.

'Technology,' Madsen said. 'Still tastes like shit.'

Chrye grinned at him. Madsen was okay.

'You don't think too much of the pacifists, do you?' she said.

'I don't think too much of this coffee, but I drink it. It's all there is here. It keeps me awake. It's just that I'm old enough to remember what real coffee tastes like.'

'Do you know a pacifist called Hickey Sill?'

Madsen pursed his lips and said casually, 'He a friend of yours?'

'No. I think someone should keep an eye on him. He hasn't got the personality to be bLinkered. But I don't want to say anything officially. He knows me, and I don't want anything traced back to me.'

Madsen grimaced, sipping his coffee. He said, 'Everyone knows about Hickey Sill, Ms Roffe. He has a high clear-up rate, one of the highest. He's very successful. And you're right, he shouldn't be allowed on the streets. But, for what it's worth, they know about Hickey. His toes are over the edge.' He drained his cup and balled it in his fist before lobbing it into the corner to slide down a hillside of crumpled white cups. He said, 'You know it's a bad thing, but can you give it up?' He shook his head. 'Uh-uh.'

He stood up and held out his hand. 'I think we're done, Ms Roffe. It was good to meet you. It really was. As for Marcus Lees, I think you'll agree that he's not a suitable subject for you to pursue, there being a question over the suicide. Might not even be too safe, considering the alternative, people involved still being around, maybe.' He paused. 'I sound melodramatic, don't I? But I'm serious. There's a line from an old, old film. I'll always remember it. It goes, "The world is a den of thieves, and night is falling." Goodbye, Ms Roffe.'

He opened the door for her and closed it behind her. Through the grimy pane of glass she could see him standing there, his hand raised to his head, making small tugging motions at his hair. She wondered how long it would be before his hand would be arching right over his head to get to the last roots, or whether he'd start using his left hand instead.

She made her way back to the front desk. The officer there called out as she passed, 'Madsen tell you his little story, huh? His Eighth Day story? He tells everyone that. You know he wasn't even there, don't you? It's all in his head.' He tapped his skull.

Chrye smiled goodbye as if she hadn't heard him. He made her wait before buzzing the door open for her, and as it closed behind her she heard him shout through the diminishing slit, 'Hey, joke!'

She let it go, walking home slowly, words shifting around in her head like pieces of a puzzle. Whatever Madsen was holding back was the key to it all. She had everything else, she was sure. She knew she could work it out.

Inside her room she sat down at her table with a mug of coffee and spread a blank sheet of paper in front of her, staring at the white rectangle and spinning a pen in her hand as she replayed the conversation with Madsen in her head.

Anal had put the CMS option as a twenty per cent possibility. Madsen had played that down. It didn't quite make sense, so she worried at it a bit. She wrote '20%' at the top of the paper and began to doodle around it as she thought. Twenty per cent was cheaper than the serial killer bet, but it was still pretty high. It wasn't just a forget option like Madsen had made out.

So there had to be another connection between the victims, one that would be significant to CMS. That meant membership of some organisation.

She drew a circle on the sheet of paper, beneath '20%', and wrote 'Far Warriors' inside it. They were all Far Warriors, Madsen had just about admitted that, but for twenty per cent there was something more. It wasn't the phobia thing. Madsen hadn't even known about that.

It was Maze. It must be Maze. Madsen knew it. That was the twenty per cent factor. All the victims, all the phony suicides, had worked at Maze – she'd bet on it.

She sketched out another circle, cutting it partially through the first, and wrote 'Maze' inside that. She began to shade the intersection, thinking.

Madsen would have concluded that the killer was a psychopath with a grudge against Far Warriors, who probably worked at Maze, like his victims. It was a twenty per cent option, so Madsen must have tried to investigate it after all. And he'd got nowhere. If he'd made inquiries and drawn a blank, he'd have told her.

So Maze had blocked him. And that meant that the killer was inside Maze. Maze was involved in the murders, actively or passively. Maze knew.

The pen's nib was squeaking. Chrye realised she'd gone right through the paper and was scratching the point into the wood. She stared at the mess she'd made of the paper, at the ripped intersection of the two circles, and thought, Cathar.

She took another piece of paper and wrote,

1. All victims phobic?
2. All victims involved with Cathar?
3. Murderer involved with Cathar?
4. Cathedral – virus?
5. Connection???

She chewed on the pen, going back over her thoughts. Maze had blocked Madsen. That must have taken quite a bit of influence, even if Madsen wasn't Pacification-backed. Ms Schaefer had told her that the government turned a blind eye to a lot of games company stuff, but this was surely more than just a commercial company operating on the edge.

It came back to the game. Everything came back to the game. It had to. And to Cathedral, whatever that was.

She put the pen down. Jesus. Maybe Starburn was right. Maybe Maze had stumbled on a gateway to some other world. That would be something worth protecting. Maybe even worth protecting a serial killer over.

She laughed. It sounded brittle and crazy in the silence of her room. She said out loud, 'Joke,' but that didn't sound any better.

FIFTEEN

'Hey, Dr Chrye! How's my favourite relative on this beautiful night?'

It was the same every time she saw him. She let the door seal itself behind her and smiled at him. 'Wrong and wrong. I'm not a doctor, Kei, and it's a foul night out there,' she said. She left the rest of it hanging. His parents had died in a microflite crash during an ash storm, his older sister – Chrye's grandmother – had died of an environment-related immuno-deficiency disease, and his younger sister had committed suicide after her third stillborn child. They had all been alive before Kei had left to be the salvation of the planet. Now Chrye was his only relative and the Earth was doomed.

'Won't be long, though,' he said. 'You'll get there. How are you getting on with Jon?'

She squeezed his shoulder and bent to kiss his cheek. He held her tight for a second against his barrel chest, driving the air from her lungs.

'You know I can't talk about that,' she chided him, straightening. 'But I like him.' She hoisted herself on to the edge of the counter and sat there kicking her heels against the polished steel plinth, staring around the shop. The inner chainlink walls had dropped for the night, protecting the games and giving the place the feel of a prison cell.

Kei examined her. 'Don't get to like him too much, Chrye,' he said.

'What do you mean by that?' She felt her face colouring.

Kei shrugged. 'He's . . . just that he's a Far Warrior. We're all chewed up. You know that. I put you in touch with him to help your thesis. That's all.'

'Everyone's chewed up, Kei. Not everyone's like Jon.' She tried to smile. She hadn't expected this from Kei. 'Not everyone's like you. Anyway, I'm trained in damage. It's what I know.'

She pushed herself off the counter, closing the subject, and said, 'Kei, I have a question for you. I wondered if you could tell me anything about someone called Marcus Lees?'

Kei frowned. 'Who?'

'He was a Far Warrior. Marcus Lees. You might have known him as Starburn.'

Kei made a face. 'Oh. Everyone knew Starburn. Jon especially. He and Jon were like finger and thumb. Jon must have told you about him.'

'What can you tell me, Kei?'

Kei moved past her towards the back room. 'I'll fix us some food if you want to go over this. It's a whole story.'

She followed him through the doorway. 'New chair,' she commented. It glided smoothly on an airbed.

'Yeah, I'm not used to it yet. I'm getting some nausea. Motion sickness, of all things. But it gets me out a bit more. I don't have to worry so much about getting stranded by quake damage.'

'Business is good, then? It looks expensive, your chair.' There was a brandmark on the back of the chair. A winged wheel.

'People always buy games. It's okay. But no way could I afford this. I got a deal through the Vets. Jon knocks them, but they're okay.'

The back room of the shop was where Kei lived. It had once been a single grand high-ceilinged ballroom, but when Kei had bought the house and opened the shop, he'd had it adapted to his needs. There were two floors now within the same vertical space, connected by a long shallow metal ramp hugging three of the walls. It was a perfect living-space for Kei in his chair. Chrye could just about stand upright on either floor without knocking her head. A vast Victorian crystal chandelier still hung by a long gilded chain from the centre of the true ceiling, its globe suspended within a cutout in Kei's upper floor. It illuminated the lower floor from above and the upper from below, and was always faintly on the move within its frame. Kei called it his seismograph. He said the rattling of the crystals and the oscillation of the light gave him advance warning of quakes.

Chrye always felt intimidated by the immense chandelier. 'One day that light of yours is going to come down and squash you flat, Kei,' she said.

He laughed at her. 'The Victorians knew what they were doing. The house will come down before this baby does. And when that's about to happen she'll give me enough warning to get clear.' He glided forward until he was directly beneath the chandelier. It swung gently over him, encouraged by the wash from his chair. He seemed connected to it, as if there were some crackling bond of energy between them. The hundreds of bulbs cast a swirling, fractured light over him, and when he finally moved away the disturbed air pushed the chandelier into greater motion. Broken light swilled over the walls. The stacks of boxed games stored at the rear of the room seemed to stir and twitch in the shadows.

Kei grounded his chair by the cooking unit. 'Well, you wanted to hear about Starburn. He was the best there was on Dirangesept. If anyone could have cleared the planet, he could. But in the end it got to him like it got to us all. The fight went out of him. I don't know if it was just Dirangesept, though. There was a lot of talk up there. Then he and Jon fell out.' Kei threw a speculative glance at Chrye. 'Jon tell you why? No one else ever knew. There was a lot of blame thrown about, natural enough. Damaged people, there was a lot of damage. But, then, you know that,' he said deliberately. 'Of course you do.' He rubbed the thin stick of his thigh. 'A lot of damage.'

Chrye ran water into a pot and set it to heat. She looked around for something to put in it.

'Noodles in the cupboard there,' Kei said, pointing.

She dropped a few knots of dry noodles into the water and watched them uncoil and start to swell. She didn't need to be looking at Kei to know his pain.

Kei eventually started again. 'A lot of us joined the project because of Starburn. Because of him and because of Jon. Did Jon tell you that? When it went sour, there was a lot of talk about him and Jon being responsible. It wasn't fair, but no one was thinking straight. How maybe the pair of them wouldn't wake up after CrySis, back on Earth. Just talk, but it wasn't easy for them.'

The light was settling now, becoming as stable as it ever was. The chandelier was swaying just enough to make Chrye feel edgy. The room seemed out of focus and vaguely unreal. She didn't know how Kei could live in such a place.

Three minutes. She drained the noodles over the sink and divided them into a pair of blue-glazed bowls, then set the bowls on the table and sat opposite Kei. Twin pillars of steam rose between them.

'Starburn's dead,' she said.

Kei picked up his chopsticks and lifted a few strings of noodles, then let them fall back into the bowl. He dripped soy sauce on them and watched the blackness leak down.

'He was murdered,' Chrye continued. 'Whoever did it tried to make it look like suicide to anyone else. Anyone but Jon. And he was working for Maze, Kei.'

Kei tipped his head back and swallowed a hank of noodles. 'Ah. I wondered why Jon signed up. He's got himself another little mission, then. The great avenger.'

'That's not funny, Kei.'

'Hear me laughing? If Jon wants another try at being a hero, what can I do about it? Anyone could have killed Starburn. Why blame Maze?'

'Maze employs a lot of vets.'

'You're saying a vet killed him?'

'It looks that way to me, Kei. And it looks like the killer was sending Jon a signal at the same time. They knew he'd follow Starburn, and I think they want to murder Jon too.'

Kei raised the bowl to his lips and let the dregs of the sauce slide down his throat. He wiped his chin with the back of a hand, then grunted and dropped his palm flat on the table. The dark stain of soy on the back of his hand looked for a moment like old blood to Chrye.

'That's crazy,' Kei said. 'Why not just tamper with the CrySis pods on the way back from Dirangesept? It would have been easy enough. Why wait so long?'

She felt Kei didn't want to know. He was blanking her. She said, 'I'm not sure it's like that. A lot of the psychological damage from Dirangesept will have got worse, not better, back on Earth, with the hatred here. And I think the games at Maze may have compounded that damage. I think someone killed Starburn to expiate their own guilt, and the next step's to kill Jon. That's not going to help either, of course. Starburn probably wasn't even the first. Whoever's doing this isn't going to stop until everyone's dead who had anything to do with the Dirangesept project.'

'Except the killer,' said Kei. 'If you're right, which you aren't.'

Chrye shook her head. 'He'll kill himself at the end of it. When it hits him that none of this has helped.' Chrye pushed her noodles away, unfinished. 'He or she. You don't seem too concerned by this, Kei. You're a target. And Jon's your friend. I thought he was, anyway. He seems to think so.'

Kei flicked the rim of his empty bowl with a long fingernail. The porcelain sounded dull and cracked. 'It's a theory, Chrye. I'm not convinced. Anyway, what can I do?'

It hadn't been a question, just a shrug-off, but Chrye used it. 'You can get me a list of vets who joined Maze.'

'Uh-uh. Not even for you, Chrye. That's privileged information. Comes under the Vets' privacy regulations. Look, why don't you tell the 'fists about this?'

'They already know. They won't do a thing. They'd be happy to let you all wipe yourselves out. Far Warriors are blamed for most of the city's crime as it is.'

'So tell Maze what you think's going on. Let them sort it out.'

'And alert the killer. Sure thing.' She shrugged. 'Okay, forget that. Maybe you can do something else for me.'

'What, then?'

'Some time ago, wasn't there a game that got infected with a virus? The hacker was never caught, but the virus was dealt with. One player ended up in a coma, I think, and died later.'

Kei said, 'And?'

'You deal with games, Kei. I know a bit about general hacker psych, but I don't know anything specific about game hacking. I'm interested.'

'What's this to do with Jon?'

'Nothing at all. It's a tangent, Kei. I'm working on my thesis, remember? Virtual environments, personality? One of the issues is what makes a hacker fix on virtual games, what effect does an infected game have on a player – does it ruin the game, or what?'

Kei sighed. 'Your Far Warrior killer's become a hacker, is that it? Well, that's crazy. Absolutely.'

'Kei, can you help me or not? I remember that the virus was dealt with, and there haven't been any more since. Games have been clean. Now, that probably means the hacker was found and employed by a games company as a programmer. You speak to the games companies, and you've told me people are always coming to you with their own games. I thought you might know. I'd just like to talk to him, that's all.'

'The guy in the coma had a pre-existing brain tumour, if you remember. His death was a coincidence.'

She held a hand up. 'I wasn't making a connection.'

Kei said, 'WarStar. That was the game. I'll see what I can do, Chrye. I'm not promising you anything.'

'What's that?' Chrye asked as soon as Jon let her in.

The blank roll-down screen filled the far wall of Jon's room. He'd finished rigging the ceiling mount up beside the light fitting and removed the bulb from its socket, so the room was shadowy with the brittle halogen light from a single long-arm lamp on the floor.

Jon reached up and clicked something black and compact on to the ceiling mount, then twisted the connector at the end of its dangling flex into the bulb socket. He stepped down from the chair and said, 'Okay. Can you switch that on for me?'

Chrye flicked the light switch. Two tiny bright lenses on the face of the ceiling-mounted device caught the halogen light, flashing and shifting.

'Standard eyetracker,' Jon said. He pointed to the screen. 'And that's just a flatscreen TV. There's a proper lightwall in Dr Locke's office, but I can't afford a lightwall. What I've rigged should be good enough.'

He pointed to the metal frame of the TV. It stood slightly away from the screen, and Chrye realised it was a separate device. A small dark disc sat in the top right corner of the frame, intruding into the screen's territory.

Jon said, 'And that's the last piece. A screenscriber.'

'Great,' said Chrye. 'Very impressive. What's it all for?'

'I'll show you. Look away from the eyetracker for a second while I lock on. Okay, you can look up now.'

Jon was staring intently at the screen. Chrye waited and Jon said after a moment, 'I've drawn a circle. Let's have a look at it.'

The disc flew from the corner of the frame and rapidly marked out a rough circle in the centre of the screen. The ends of the circle didn't quite meet. The scriber erased the circle and withdrew.

Chrye said, 'I still don't get it.'

'Magic. In Cathar magic depends on eye coordination as well as knowledge of the spells. This is to practise. I can do it blind, like I just showed you, or it can show me what I'm doing . . .' He looked back at the wall and Chrye watched the scriber come down and steadily mark out an almost perfect circle on the screen.

'Or I can do it with interference.'

He switched on the TV. The room was flooded with submarine light and a picture faded up of a rift somewhere in a heavily populated centre. The sound came up. '. . . pictures from Birmingham this morning.' The rift faded and the newsreader's head flashed up. 'Other news. The government continues to deny rumours of preparations for a new Dirangesept project, accusing games companies of fuelling the rumours to boost sales of linked games. Rice imports show signs of stabilising, and soybean production is up for the third consecutive month. The cryonics company Cold Comfort are taking on new staff after an increase in orders for CrySis equipment. And now the weather . . .'

Jon switched the TV off and the scriber came down. The circle was hopelessly out.

She looked at his face, remembering what she'd thought of him that first time in Nearvana. Not good-looking despite that brushed-back brown hair with its faint streaks of smoke, and the lines of his face too hard, his eyes liked polished stones. Now she saw him differently. She saw him as a haunted man bound by loyalty and friendship. And maybe it was the light, but his eyes were softer now, his face more open. Maybe some of his stigmata were easing. She said, 'Jon, do you remember exactly when you got the journal from Starburn?'

'Why?'

'You said it was just after he died. I've been doing some research, and there're a couple of things that worry me. Starburn wasn't the first to be killed. I think there's a serial killer at Maze, targeting Far Warriors, and I think that Maze know it. They might be turning a blind eye to it, or they might even be involved in the killings, for some reason. I got this from the officer who investigated it, and he told me Starburn had already been dead a while by the time the body was found. At least a week. So when did you get the book?'

'I got it the day after it was reported,' Jon said numbly. 'The day after he was supposed to have died.' He looked at her. 'Christ. Whoever killed him sent me the book.'

Chrye nodded. 'I wonder what made Starburn join Maze. I wonder if he was doing for someone what you're doing for him. It looks to me like someone at Maze is working their way through the Dirangesept project, reeling you in and killing you one by one. Be careful, Jon. I don't want you to be next.'

Jon couldn't sleep. He checked the window readout and nilled the filters

145

and let the heat swim in, feeding his restlessness with it. The moonlit street beneath shimmered in the haze. A pack of dogs prowled along the buckled pavement, sniffing and probing the crevices, searching for rats. He watched them round the corner then slipped on trousers and a jacket and gently eased open the door of his room. He glanced down the stairwell. There was no light beneath Hickey's door. That was one good thing about the hours Jon was keeping – they weren't coinciding with Hickey's right now.

He looked at his watch again. There was another hour before he had to leave for Maze, but Dr Locke had told him he could enter the zone any time he liked now, as long as he stayed afterwards for debriefing.

He headed down the stairs and into the street. The moon was round and dusty. With the respirator on he could hear his breathing like a ragged pulse, reminding him that for the moment he was still alive. He wondered where Footfall lived, and the others. It struck him that he'd never been kept waiting by Dr Locke for his debriefing. Maybe there were other debriefers there, one for each of them.

Inside the security fence the cleared area around Maze was swept flat and bright with broad-beamed searchlights. Nothing was going to be rebuilt there. It was all security. It probably always had been, the quake in the area no more than a story.

The atrium was empty, so he went straight up to the CrySis chamber. There was no one there either. He walked around the room, running his hands over the chrome and carbon curves of the pods. There were twenty pods altogether. Several of the others were set and waiting like his own. The rest were closed down. It was impossible to tell whether they were occupied or not. He came out again and walked down the corridor towards Reality Validation, conscious of the way his boots squeaked on the tiled floor. He stopped at the door, knocked loudly and called out, 'Dr Locke.'

There was no answer. His words hung in the air as if they had nowhere else to go. He looked both ways along the corridor. There was still no one in sight, and no sound except the guttural hum of the air-conditioning. Jon pushed the door, expecting it to resist, but it swung smoothly away from him. He felt his breathing quicken.

He slid inside and closed the door, then went around the desk to the black glass filing cabinet. With the light off he could just make out the shadowy racks of cassettes behind the glass. It took him a second to locate the crack of the door, and he ran his finger down it until he found the thumb pad and catch.

It wouldn't give. He tried cautiously again, and a low light came on in the room behind him, throwing his shadow sharply on to the face of the cabinet. He stood still, letting his hand fall to his side. Without turning round, he tried to see around his silhouette in the glass. All he could make out was the reflection of the low curve of the desk and its rank of monitors. The light source was directly behind him.

A soft voice spoke from behind. A woman's voice, sounding crisp in the darkness. Dr Locke's voice.

'The cabinet is locked. Please submit your access card.'

He waited a moment for her to say something more, but she didn't. He turned slowly around, preparing an apology, but there was no one else in the room. The central screen on the desk was live and facing him, empty of words or pictures, just glowing like a window of brilliant jade. The voice had come from the screen.

'The cabinet is locked. Please submit your access card.'

Jon let his breath go. The door had been unlocked because everything in the room was protected. After a few moments the screen greyed out.

He was about to open the door to leave when he heard footsteps outside. He backtracked quickly and crouched down behind the desk. The footsteps passed by.

Jon waited a minute and slipped back into the corridor. He returned to the CrySis room. He thought one more pod was down than had been just before, but he couldn't be sure of it.

He coded open his clothes locker and undressed. The metal floor was warm and sticky against the soles of his feet. He rolled into the pod and bit on the airline, then waited impatiently for the gel to rise around him.

It wasn't dawn yet in Cathar. There was no sign of life in Jhalouk's house. Jon dressed quietly and climbed down the hillside into the village. He took the road west, walking slowly, relishing being alone, and by the time he reached the small inlet he'd spotted the previous day, the sun was smearing the water with silver.

From the house it hadn't been clear quite how well concealed the inlet was by trees. Jon almost walked past it. He wandered down the warm sand to the water's edge and stood looking out. It was as peaceful as he'd hoped it might be. He kicked off his shoes and listened to the pale blue water sawing at the sand and watched it throw shavings of froth over his bare toes. Then he made his way on round and into the inlet.

He'd expected a small sandy bay, and it mostly was, but the far arm was a rocky bluff dressed with trees and thick with shadow. Where the sand petered out a small path led awkwardly up and into the rocks, and from the beach a short jetty of bleached wood pushed out into the water.

He let the salt breeze play on his face for a while, then walked up the beach towards the rocks and let the path take him into the shadow of the trees. The path curled and twisted for a few metres, and then there was light ahead and the path opened into a clearing. Jon was reminded for a moment of his first visit to Maze, and he glanced around to see if Janus was there. There was no one, only a wooden shack hunched in the shadows. He went up to the door and knocked. There was no answer, and he pushed at it gently. It didn't open.

There was no sign of a keyhole. He reached through the window and managed to undo the latch, then shoved the door open and went inside.

There was a wide bed there with thin yellow sheets strewn over it, and a wooden table in the centre of the room. A clay oven sat in the corner beneath a chimney. The oven was cool to the touch. What caught Jon's eye was the wooden cot in the corner. It was a tiny, beautifully made cot for a newborn baby. The cot sat on rockers and Jon pushed it with a finger to set it moving. It was old, but it had obviously barely been used. The rockers were slightly rough, still unsmoothed by use.

He looked around again and saw two cupboards. One contained men's clothes, and there were dresses in the other. Behind him the cot stilled to quiet.

He looked at the bed, trying to work it out. There was just one pillow and it was isolated on the left side of the bed, crunched into a ball. One person had slept there, but had slept roughly. There was a pair of man's longjohns lying on the sheets, and a mess of crumbs and spilled water on the table.

He went back to the cupboard with women's clothes, and this time noticed a musty smell to them. He looked from the bed to the cot and across to the table, then reached out a hand to the dresses in the cupboard and touched the shoulder of a blue dress hanging there. The surface of the cloth powdered at his touch and his finger came away with the colour. He rubbed it away on his trousers, not knowing what to think, then jabbed at the palm of his hand in sudden panic, feeling the solidity of everything suddenly in question, then managed to calm himself. The clothes were old, years old. At the bottom of the second cupboard he noticed a dusty box of unworn baby clothes. He didn't dare touch them.

A noise from outside jarred him, and he closed the cupboard quickly. He realised he had no idea how long he'd been standing there. He opened the front door carefully, but no one was in sight. There was an axe leaning up against the door frame and he picked it up, swinging it over his shoulder. After a last glance inside the shack, he closed the door behind him, reaching through the window again to flick the door latch back. As he did so, he heard a long, keening cry from the trees that made the hairs on the back of his neck stand up. It began like something human, and then it rose and kept on rising until it trailed away seconds later, the howl of a creature in terrible torment. The silence that followed it was total. There was no echo. The air felt like ice. Jon stared around the clearing, his hand clenched round the axe handle, waiting for something more but not knowing what could follow that cry.

After a while the silence became less brittle. Jon skirted around the edge of the clearing and walked into the trees, keeping clear of the path. Holding the axe by its head, he used the sharp blade to mark delicate notches in the trees at ankle height each time he shifted direction, marking his path, making his way towards the sound of water again. Eventually he came out beside a small rocky stream as it emptied into the sea. He clambered up over the rocks until the sea was out of sight, then stopped and sat by a pool of almost still water where the stream collected itself before rushing onward and the darting shapes of tiny fish glittered in a fat spear of light coming down through the trees.

For the first time in Cathar he had a feeling of peace. He sat quietly and let his mind empty, listening to the rhythm of the water tumbling down through the rocks.

He stayed there until the light coming down through the branches softened and the heat began to slacken, then got to his feet. He felt stiff in his bones. He took the axe into the trees and began to cut himself some saplings and lengths of a tough vine that seemed plentiful, and dragged it all to the stream. Then he followed his trail back to the clearing and returned the axe to the shack. Whoever lived there hadn't got back yet.

It took him the rest of the day to build himself a shelter from the raw materials. When he was done he had a deep crawl space at the stream's edge, strutted and cross-braced with wood and camouflaged with rocks and stones. He walked around it, adjusting foliage until he was happy it couldn't be seen. Then he returned by way of the clearing to the shore.

The sun was lower in the sky, and the shore was as deserted as it had been earlier in the day. Jon stepped on to the jetty and walked to the end. It creaked on its palings and moved with him, as if he was neither on land any longer nor quite at sea. On an impulse he closed his eyes. All that he could hear was water. Beneath him was the sharp bump and gurgle of waves against the boards and posts of the jetty, and behind was the rhythmic massage of water against the beach. Back and to his left was the brittle splintering of the sea against the rocks, and all around he could hear the soft slap of waves overthrowing themselves. Here, Jon thought, you could be blind and know what distance was, and space, and perspective.

He opened his eyes again and looked down, noticing a damp pile of fish scales by his feet, pearly and translucent. Someone had been fishing from here.

A swift shadow flashed over the jetty and Jon looked up, surprised. High above him a great dark eagle, barely flexing its broad wings, flew above the contour of the trees and vanished behind them. Jon stared after the bird, following its entering trajectory. It failed to appear where it should have, and he wondered whether he had lost it in the sky, or whether it had ever existed, or whether it had existed only briefly and just for him.

Then it was visible again, its course changed, drifting out over the bay as smoothly as a cursor across a screen.

Chrye checked the security monitor. Every time the doorbell rang she expected it to be Hickey Sill. It wasn't him this time. Whoever was there was about four feet six and pin-thin. Chrye could see 'MUNCHOMA' picked out in gold thread on the scarlet baseball cap, and when the head tipped back she saw it was a young girl standing there, wearing a bright blue smock and carrying a covered white plastic platter. Chrye could smell curry through the door.

'Wrong address,' she called out. 'I didn't order anything.'

The delivery girl stepped back. She read out Chrye's address in a high, trembling voice, then said more sharply, 'Order called in by Kei Roffe. And it's losing heat, ma'am.'

Chrye hesitated, then opened the door. The delivery girl looked about fourteen, with long brown hair caught in a rough ponytail. She came past Chrye, and as she did the picture on the security screen beside the door went to snow. The girl flicked the door closed with her heel. She looked around and made for the table Chrye was using as a desk. Chrye just had time to gather her papers out of the way before the tray hit the table.

The girl rubbed her hands together and flexed her fingers, saying in her fragile voice, 'Jesus, that's a fuckin' weight. You're Chrye, yuh?'

Chrye just nodded at her.

'Kei said you wanted to talk to me. You got any buzzies on right now? Better switch them off 'cause I'm gonna run a sweep here and it'll bleach anything you got listening.' She was shifting the foil food cartons from the tray and stacking them neatly on the table. When she was done she licked her fingers, clicked the tray's base out and began to mess with a miniature keypad housed in a cutout within the tray's insulated wall. Chrye's security monitor went from snow to dead.

The girl said, 'Okay, we got limbo. Now you can get us some knives and forks. Hope you're hungry. May even have some real meat here, don't hold your breath.'

Chrye stood still. 'You're the hacker?' She laughed. This little girl wasn't a psychopathic Far Warrior. 'What's your name?' Chrye asked her.

'MaryAnn. You hungry or not?' The girl began ripping the tops from the cartons, reading them out as she went. 'Meat in batter, noodle curry, cheese-fried rice, egg tacos.' MaryAnn looked at them and then at Chrye. 'Ah, well,' she said. She trailed a fork across the oily surface of the curry and added, 'Looks better on the holos. Rice is probably the only thing you can believe.'

Chrye laid a pair of plates on her small table and watched MaryAnn serve out the food. Chrye wasn't keen on fast food any more, the strong spices and garish colourings usually masking food substitutes.

MaryAnn took a mouthful of rice and swallowed it. 'Could be worse. Just. Okay, what can I do for you?'

Chrye said, 'I don't know. I have a friend working on a game that's in development, and I think there may be a virus infecting it.'

MaryAnn shook her head decisively. 'No maybes. It's a virus, you'd know. What does it do? What makes you think it's a virus?'

'I think I know its name. Maybe it means something to you. Cathedral?'

'Uh-uh. Weird name for a virus. Viruses get real sloozy names. Zygote,

Footnote, DataSlurp. Cathedral's a bit oiky. Still . . .' She considered, chewing awkwardly on something in the noodle curry and then spitting it on to her plate. 'Could be an oiky hacker.'

Looking at the slim coil of translucent green rubber at the side of MaryAnn's plate, Chrye felt her appetite leave her.

Undeterred, MaryAnn dug a fork back into the bright yellow curry, saying, 'What does it do, this Cathedral? Lens me in here. Focus me down.'

This is going nowhere, Chrye thought. She couldn't even understand what the girl was saying. 'I suppose it may not be a virus,' she said. 'I just thought, the name, I thought viruses have names like that.' She saw MaryAnn pulling a face at her and struggled to remember what she needed to tell her. She thought of Starburn's journal and said, 'The game seems to contain a construct that follows the player all the time.' It was all sounding ridiculous to her, like paranoia. Like Jon had sounded to her.

'Not a virus, whatever it is.' MaryAnn was still wolfing down the food. She wiped her mouth with the back of her hand, then rubbed her hand on her jeans, leaving a long saffron streak on her thigh. 'Definitely not a virus,' she repeated. 'Double-def. Tell you why. Hackers want to make a wow. They like to shatter. You've made a virtual world, hacker'll put a black jag through it, hacker'll fuck up a primary colour, screw the shadows, de-render curves. Or they'll scratch a deep cut into the audio, paste in some white noise. Nothing subtle. Hackers aren't like that. They'll just foul up anything sensory.' MaryAnn ran her tongue over her teeth and grinned at Chrye. 'Weird guys, hackers, cross between cat-burglars and neurosurgeons, but what they like to use, once they're in, it's a sledgehammer. This is Maze we're talking about, right?'

Chrye nodded her head, then froze. 'Do you work for . . . ?'

'Uh-uh,' said MaryAnn. 'Just a guess. Maze is shut up tight right now, and I know what's happening everywhere else.'

She frowned suddenly, then belched, putting her hand to her mouth too late. When she took it away there was a smile on her lips. 'Jesus, pardon me. I think that meat was reorganised soya. Tasted even funnier than usual. Definitely wasn't dog. But listen, just 'cause there isn't a virus doesn't mean everything's nice and sloozy. Sounds to me like the game's still a bit fuzzy, that's all. Maybe that's why it's not on the streets yet.' She belched again. 'Anyway, you want some more help, get a readout of the game, then tell Kei and I'll scrute it for you. Now, I gotta get back to the shack.' She played inside the food platter again and clicked the base back down. 'Okay, you're all reset now. Wait till I'm gone and you can power up again.' She stood up, then added, 'Oh, and that's eighteen-seventy for the food.'

Chrye watched MaryAnn skip down the stairs to the street, the tray slung over her shoulders. She wasn't sure what was happening now. She had thought she was getting somewhere with the virus theory, but now it was all uncertain again.

Except that Starburn had been murdered, and Jon's life as well as his sanity were at risk while he worked at Maze.

She began to clear the remains of the food from the table. The soya meat was disintegrating, becoming textureless. The tacos and rice had turned to mush. Except for the fragment of rubber, the whole meal had probably been semi-stabilised soya. Chrye closed her eyes to spill everything into the waste tub.

A wave of exhaustion slid over her. It came down to two choices, she thought, sitting down heavily again. Either she managed to stop Jon working there, or she did everything she could to help him find out who had murdered Starburn, and why.

There was a third possibility. She could back right away from Jon Sciler and pretend she'd never met him. But she knew that wasn't a choice any more.

SIXTEEN

Jon entered Cathar early again, waking in the crawl space and almost sitting up before he remembered where he was, clattering his head on the lattice of branches. Light was slanting through and into his eyes, and there were the brittle sounds of birdsong and water. He edged out into the open air and stretched himself, feeling stiff and ravenously hungry.

He realised he hadn't eaten at all the previous day in the zone. The program didn't know or care that he had eaten soya rissoles in his room an hour ago. Or maybe this was part of the separation. He was getting used to the routine of day following day, switching between London and Cathar and never sleeping in either zone.

He smoothed down his hair, correcting himself mentally. Either place. But that also wasn't right.

When he knelt down in the small pool to sluice the freezing water over himself, small fish darted around him, tickling his skin. He stood on a rock already warm from a bar of sunlight and shook himself. The water flew glittering from his body.

He felt bursting with life. He thought, What if it is all a program, a gamezone? It was always with him now. It felt like Cathar belonged to him. Even when he exited, he was never really tired any more. Cathar seemed to charge him up.

He drank water from the stream, letting it run like ice down his throat, and then headed back towards the clearing. The shack was deserted, but when he looked through the window he saw the table cleared.

The tide had come and gone during the night and he walked slowly along the beach by the high mark, kicking through ragged knots of dark brown seaweed. He felt like a child searching for treasures among the flotsam, but there were only shards of wood and a few bright shells caught up in the puffy webbing of seaweed.

He looked out to sea and his eye was drawn to a small rowing boat rounding the rocks at the far arm of the inlet, nosing up a wash of white water before it. The prow dipped deep in the water and every wave that struck it threw water into the boat. The sole figure in the boat was occupied in bailing water over the side. There was no sign of how the boat was powered, but it ran a deliberate and steady course along the coastline. It was headed for the jetty.

As the boat drew closer, Jon hooded his eyes against the glare of the sun and squinted at the figure in the vessel. The semi-profile seemed familiar. It was a man, but there was something defective about his outline, though it was hard to be sure with the sun bright behind him and his constant activity. The man was shirtless and the muscles of his chest shone with spray. Jon couldn't fix on quite why his outline appeared wrong. Something told him it wasn't a program flaw.

He could see the man's face creased and dark now. He was clearly fit, but no longer young. The bleached white hair at his temples flared out like a pair of vestigial wings, fluttering at his ears as he dipped into the boat to bail out water, dipping and bailing rhythmically without a glance to his course or to Jon standing on the shore staring at him, mesmerised.

It can't be, Jon was thinking. It can't be him.

The boat shifted direction slightly as it came nearer and Jon saw the man more fully. His left arm was cut off at the elbow and he held the bailing bucket in his right hand, lifting it out brimming with water with as much ease as swinging it back empty. The stump of his left arm was a matting of livid scar tissue and it swung wildly about as if it had its own life. Jon remembered it vividly. Balance. He uses it to balance himself. He always used to do that.

The sudden thump of wood under his feet told Jon he had stepped on to the jetty without even knowing it, and it was too late to conceal himself. The man had looked up and seen him. The boat was bumping at the planks at the far end, shivering the woodwork all the way down to where Jon stood.

Jon hesitated, then walked to the jetty's end and held out his hand for the rope to be thrown to him. The man stared at him briefly and then ignored him, looping the cable smoothly around the tall pole at the corner of the jetty and hauling the boat in by it one-handed, easily coiling the slack from hand to elbow and then in a swift movement making a figure of eight of the heavy rope and locking it over the boat's rowlocks.

'Do you know who I am?' Jon said without thinking.

The jetty was moving more with the boat moored to it, and Jon felt as though he was floating on the wallowing boards. In his mind he saw Mr Lile against the grimy dormitory walls, running his right hand through those feathery wisps of hair, staring hard from Jon to Starburn and back and saying, 'Which of you two was it this time, eh? Or shall I just choose one of you? Jon? Marcus? Come on now. One of you salted the aid worker's engine.' There had been an odd break to Mr Lile's voice that he couldn't ever quite control. 'This is no joking matter, you two. You don't make my job any easier by doing things like this. You know we're dependent on Community Aid.' He had sighed, the sigh soft in his throat. 'I promised the aid worker you'd be punished, and I'm not breaking my word. Jon, I think it's your turn. Step forward.'

Jon saw himself taking a pace forward to receive the punishment. He felt the jetty move under his feet as he held his hand out to Mr Lile. The palm of his hand was a child's palm, small and pale and shaking. Mr Lile said, 'Five strikes, Jon, for the waste of a bag of salt.' He grinned at Jon. 'Five strikes from my left hand.' He took off his jacket and shook his head at Jon, then his left arm rose and fell five times like a pump handle, swishing through the air as if there was a hand at the end of it to strike Jon's palm. 'Now, for God's sake don't do it again, and have the grace to apologise to Mr Mellor next time he comes. And if you do anything like that again you'll get my right hand.'

'I know well enough who you are.'

The man even spoke with Mr Lile's voice. But that wasn't possible. He couldn't be a player if this was a gamezone, and he couldn't be here if this was somehow real. Mr Lile had died while Jon had been in CrySis on the way to Dirangesept.

The boat was stacked with wicker cages which the man began throwing over the side and into the sea. As they flew through the air Jon caught hints of bright purple through the mesh, and the flash of claws. He stood back as the man jumped on to the jetty.

Jon said, 'Then who am I?'

He had asked the question intending to challenge the man, or perhaps testing the program or the zone, but as the man stood there and looked hard at Jon, Jon realised that the question came from somewhere deeper inside himself. And as the man stood without answering, hand on hip, water dripping from his trousers on to the planking, Jon became less sure of himself, and the answer he awaited seemed crucial.

The man turned away to secure the boat, and Jon saw a thick shadow drift through the water beneath the jetty.

The program's searching, Jon thought, waiting for the man to respond. He felt a surge of disappointment at suddenly seeing through it. It was a game after all. Maze had done some research, they'd dropped a construct of Mr Lile in Cathar for some reason and they hadn't expected me to ask this question.

The man turned back and began to walk down the jetty towards the beach. Jon fell in beside him, aware that the shadow in the water was keeping pace with them both.

'What do you want me to say?' the man said roughly. 'I haven't seen you before, and I know everyone in Cathar, so you're a new waker. You have their look . . .' He waved his stump at Jon. 'That look of superiority and wonder. That will pass.'

They were nearly at the shore, and the man jumped down into the shallow surf. Jon bent to sit on the jetty's edge. About a metre out the shadow knuckled out of the water and kept coming, a turtle like the one Jon had seen in the harbour, but this was far bigger. Its head was the size of a man's.

The man looked across at Jon. 'You want more? By the look of you, you're the son of Harel and Showen. You have Harel's eyes. Though you're no more a son to them than a rat to a bird.'

There was a bitterness in his voice that Jon couldn't work out. 'I don't understand,' he said.

The turtle had come almost out of the water and was nuzzling its head into the palm of the man's hand. The man took a knife from a sheath at his belt and began scraping at the turtle's shell with the fat iron blade, chipping away barnacles and crustings of salt.

He looked across at Jon. 'You wakers. You think you're gifts to us. You imagine we bless your arrival and give thanks to God when a baby slides dull-eyed and listless into the world. Do you think we celebrate when a child is taken from us into that hall of living death, and when the husk of our child is taken by one of you, from wherever it is you come?' He wiped his knife-blade clean on his trousers. 'You come and you go, and what about us, left here in Cathar to live and die?'

Jon said nothing, not understanding the sudden outburst. The man gave the turtle a thump on its shell with the knife's hasp and the creature turned awkwardly around in the surf, entering the sea and becoming a shadow that slid away and vanished. The man sat and stared after it, oblivious to Jon.

Jon thought of his mother, the little he remembered of her before her death, and he thought of Mr Lile's orphanage where he had met Starburn.

'What's your name?' he asked the man.

'Lile.'

Jon didn't know how to read that, whether this Lile was somehow an aspect of the real, dead Mr Lile, but if Cathar was a zone and Maze had found Mr Lile by research and recreated him here, then maybe they had gone even further back in Jon's life. An excitement welled up inside him. Maybe they had discovered more of his past than Jon knew. 'Harel and Showen,' he said. 'My parents . . .'

'Harel and Showen are dead.'

The word stabbed into Jon. He felt that something had been held out to him and then snatched away in an instant, exposing a great hole at the heart of him. His head dropped into his hands, and when he raised them Lile was looking at him. Jon wiped his eyes and he was seeing Mr Lile in the small office that looked over the tarmac playground sprouting with moss and weeds, and Mr Lile was telling Jon his parents were dead and he would be living at the orphanage now. He hadn't believed it then. He'd left the room skipping, and then he'd met Marcus Lees and they had invented Starburn and elaborate stories of their real families to whom they would be returned when the dark forces had been defeated and it was once again safe.

Dead. His parents were dead.

He heard Lile talking, and thought he was still a child in that tiny office. 'Harel and Showen died a year ago.'

'How?'

Mr Lile had told him it was a car crash and quietly said, 'Don't you remember, Jon?'

But he remembered nothing and had never asked Mr Lile for more, not wanting detail to muddy the bright fantasies. Now he had asked the question.

'Calban took Harel in a raid. Showen drowned during a storm a week later. You were their only child. She was a strong swimmer, but she had no land to swim to any more.'

Lile stood up and stretched his arms, just like the Lile Jon remembered used to do. As he flexed his fingers and made them into a fist, the rounded tip of the stump twitched as if yearning for what had been stolen from it.

He looked at Jon again, then jumped back on to the jetty and climbed into the boat rocking calmly there, reaching into the water by the prow to haul on a rope dangling from it. As the webbing of straps emerged to be folded into the boat by Lile, Jon recognised it as a harness and realised that the turtle had been towing the boat.

Lile started swilling his hand over the side of the boat again in a regular pattern, pausing occasionally to slap the water's surface, and Jon saw the turtle's shadow rise to nudge against Lile's hand, then slip deep beneath the boat and rise again. This time when its head broke clear Lile took one of the cages from its mouth. He patted the turtle's head and the turtle slid down and away. Lile clambered back on to the jetty and walked past Jon, making his way up the shore. The cage swung from his hand, shedding water like a trail of black pips on the pale sand. He said to Jon, almost reluctantly, 'Are you hungry? This is more than I can eat alone.'

'Fine,' Jon said. He watched Lile start up the path towards the shack, then followed him.

A pile of neatly chopped wood was stacked up against the side of the shack. Jon hadn't noticed it last time. It crossed his mind that maybe it hadn't been there before, but maybe he just hadn't noticed it, or maybe Lile had only chopped it yesterday. He wondered what was in the wicker pot.

Lile reached around the window frame to undo the latch, not apparently concerned about Jon seeing him do it. In the open doorway he turned and said to Jon, 'Set a fire.' Then he closed the door behind him.

Jon collected kindling for the fire's base from chippings at the base of the stack and made an airy pyramid above it with twigs and thicker branches, then realised he had nothing to light it with. Lile hadn't emerged from the shack, and Jon wasn't inclined to disturb him. He formed a spell and began it, staring at the wood.

It seemed easier this time. Maybe it was the scale of it, or the proximity, or maybe it was just not his first time in the zone. The ideograms still tried to wriggle away from him, and the wind hurled itself at him, but the spell let itself be said, and with the spell's end a spurt of flame licked up from the kindling. Then, like last time, he felt the backlash of lethargy wash over him and slumped back on the ground.

He opened his eyes to see Lile standing over him. There was a cleaver in his hand and a terrible empty look on his face. He raised the cleaver high, the blade blinding in the sun.

'Wakers,' Lile said flatly. 'Look at yourself. You're dead. I know what your magic does to you. You haven't the energy to move, have you? You don't know who I am and so you do your wonderful magic trick to impress me, and you allow me to kill you.'

Lile's head went back, and he brought the cleaver down.

Jon tried to move his head out of its way, but his strength had gone with the magic and Lile followed him easily with the heavy blade. At the last moment Jon screamed and closed his eyes. He heard a grating thud that shook his skull and felt metal cold against his cheek.

He opened his eyes sharply.

The blade was buried in the ground beside him and Lile had turned his back on Jon. He was facing the trees, his arms slack at his sides.

Jon rolled slowly away from the cleaver and got to his knees, rocking there until he could feel his strength beginning to return. His heart was thudding slow and hard and his breath was coming in long gulps. 'What the hell did you do that for?' he shouted eventually. He noticed that the fire had gone out. The spell hadn't worked. He hadn't held his concentration on the flames quite long enough.

Lile took a long time turning around. He looked down at Jon with contempt and said, 'Look at yourself.' He dug in his pockets and held up a pair of shells, conical opalescent shells studded with rough black excrescences. Then he unstrung a small leather pouch from his belt and poured a stream of what looked like grey ash into the larger shell. He paused to tell Jon, 'We don't *need* you in Cathar.' He started grinding the smaller shell into the ash like a pestle into a mortar until smoke rose and sparks jumped in the air, and then he reached over the fire and spilled a blue gobbet of flame on to the wood.

Jon watched the fire take. Lile said, 'Sizzle shells and dried barb-bird guano. It's easy if you know. But you know nothing here, you wakers. There isn't a thing you can do for us that we can't do for ourselves.'

The fire was spitting now. Jon had nothing to say to Lile. Lile suddenly jerked his head and said, 'Your friends are here for you. Go with them.'

Jon turned his head to see Lapis and Lazuli coming into the clearing. Lile ignored them, ripping the cleaver from the ground and stalking towards his shack with it. Jon found himself able to get to his feet. He took a step after Lile, but Lapis put a hand on his arm and said, 'There's no point, Sciler. No one can talk to Lile.'

Lazuli took him by the other arm and said, 'We're having a meeting in the village this afternoon. We need to decide what to do about the raids.'

As they left the clearing, Lapis looked quickly back, then she leaned close to Jon's ear and whispered, 'You should stay away from Lile.' He could smell a sweet, musky perfume on her neck. He seemed to remember it from somewhere, but he couldn't place it.

'Why?' he asked her. 'What do you know about him?'

She looked at Jon curiously. 'You know about wakers?'

Jon stopped. 'Lile's not a waker, is he?'

Lazuli laughed and tugged him on. 'Lile? Don't ever accuse him of that, Sciler.'

'Jhalouk told me something,' he said. 'The bodies are ready for us. They're like our other bodies back in London. It's like we pre-exist here.'

Lapis said, 'That's right. But they don't just spring into being. They have to be born just like we do. And they are born when we are born. At the same time.' She glanced at Lazuli as if for confirmation.

Parallel worlds, Jon thought. She's telling me Cathar is a parallel world.

'Every now and then a mother in Cathar gives birth to a stillborn baby. Only it isn't quite stillborn. It's in a form of coma, we think. It has certain basic reactions. It grows if it's fed. And if we get to Cathar we inhabit the body waiting for us here.'

Lazuli took over, almost interrupting her twin. She touched Jon sharply on his elbow to get his attention. He had a sudden, brief sense that there was a slight tension between them.

'It's considered an honour in Cathar to give birth to a waker, but not everyone likes it. Many of the bodies are never taken. They age, wither and die without ever becoming conscious. There are hundreds of villages along the coast and inland, and every village has its hall of wakers.'

Lapis added, 'Imagine being a parent to such a child.'

'Harel and Showen,' Jon murmured.

Lapis glanced at him. 'What?'

'Lile said they were my parents. They died before I came.'

161

'We don't know who ours are,' said Lazuli. 'It wouldn't mean anything to us.'

'Or to them,' said Lapis. 'Mostly they have other children and forget about the wakers they bore. Mostly.'

They were on the coast road heading for the village. A horse and cart rattled past them in the other direction, the cart loaded with mottled yellow fruit the size of melons. Dust swirled behind it. Jon coughed, and he noticed that Lapis and Lazuli simultaneously brought up the wide sleeves of their shirts to cover their mouths against the dust. He realised that this was the first time he'd had any respiratory trouble in Cathar.

'Sometimes wakers don't stay long in Cathar,' Lapis told him when the dust had cleared. 'They come for a few hours a day for a while, then never return again. We think they're coming here in their sleep and they imagine Cathar's just a dream.'

Jon looked at Lapis and then at Lazuli. They were each lightly holding him by an arm, and it was disconcerting how when one briefly tightened her grip or loosened it, the other did the reverse. And they were making eye contact with him more than they had before. It was as if they were somehow competing for his attention. He tried to concentrate on what they were saying. Were they suggesting Cathar could be reached by chance, during a night's sleep?

'Some people never come to terms with it, though,' Lazuli said.

With what? Jon wondered. With the fact that it's real, or the fact that it isn't?

Lapis said, 'Lile's one. That's why you should keep away from him. He's dangerous.'

Jon thought he'd misheard her. 'Lile?' he said. 'But you said he's not a waker.'

Both women shook their heads. Lapis said, 'Of course he isn't. That's not what we meant. Lile's wife died in childbirth, years ago.'

Now it made sense. Jon said slowly, 'And the baby was a waker.'

'That's right. Lile never comes into the village any more,' said Lapis. 'But some time ago the waker who claimed his child's body came upon him by chance.'

A long, mournful cry sounded behind them. It echoed in the hills, and there was a whinny of alarm from the horse away down the road. Jon turned to see it rear up sharply, pawing at the ground and tossing its head, teeth bared, whinnying with fright. The driver of the cart leaned forward to calm it, stroking its flank. A sharp gust of wind carried his voice clearly back along the road. 'Steady now, it's gone away. It wasn't after us.' The cart was slewed across the track. Behind it a pile of smashed fruit was already attracting flies.

'How did you find me?' Jon asked Lapis, puncturing the abrupt quiet.

'Everyone's been looking for you. You didn't return last night, and we were worried. With what's been happening . . . Where were you? Why didn't you come back?'

Jon said, 'I won't be staying in the village. I've found somewhere to sleep. Don't worry about me.'

He expected one of them to ask why he wasn't prepared to sleep in the village, but neither said anything. They walked on.

'But you came straight out here to find me,' Jon said. 'How did you know to come here? I could have been anywhere.'

'The villagers saw you heading in this direction yesterday morning.' Lapis hesitated. Jon stopped and looked straight at her, but she wouldn't meet his eye.

Lazuli said quickly, 'We just thought you might have come this way.'

Jon ignored her. 'Go on,' he told Lapis. 'You were going to say something.'

'You mentioned – before – that you knew Starburn.'

Jon guessed she wasn't sure whether it was breaking the rules to tell him that, to talk about things outside the zone. Unless she was a construct simply stalling while the program decided whether to slip the information out to him. But there was something more to her hesitancy that he couldn't read. The palm of her hand was warm on his arm, and her stride had adjusted to his. Lazuli was slightly out of step with them both.

Lapis said, 'Starburn was in the body of Lile's son. We thought you must have known that. That's how we guessed you'd be there.'

Jon glanced out at the sea. Starburn was Lile's son. He tried to make some sense of it, then let it go. Maybe there was no sense to be made, no reason to be found. It was just Cathar. The sea flashed with the sun like a great swathe of indecipherable machine code, and the island sat blackly in the heart of the sea.

'Tell me what happened to Starburn,' Jon said.

He was looking at Lapis, but for some reason she shook her head. Lazuli answered him.

'Calban took him to his island.'

Calban, Jon thought. He remembered the name vaguely from Starburn's journal. 'Tell me about Calban,' he said.

Lapis said, 'Wait till we get to the village. When we're all together. Then we can talk.'

They were nearly there. There was more activity than he had seen before in Cathar. The quayside swarmed with people and carts, and the hillside was swollen with movement.

'This is how it started last time,' Janus said, putting his coffee on the table and leaning back on his chair. There was an edge to his voice. Jon couldn't work him out at all.

'What happened last time?' Jon asked.

Footfall was staring off over the water towards the island. It was about noon and, despite the shimmer of the surrounding sea, the island was as dark as ever. It seemed to absorb light, just as it appeared to consume the attention of everyone in Cathar, no matter what they were doing. In the streets everyone constantly glanced at it as if it were a wound that refused to heal.

Pibald said, 'It happens every few months, quite regularly. Calban raids the village and takes men away with him. He also takes wakers, but no one knows why. He uses the village men as slaves, but the wakers are never seen again. They just disappear on to the rock. We assume he kills them. We're the only real threat to him.'

'Hah,' said Janus. 'What threat have we ever been to Calban?'

'Last time. What happened last time, Janus?' Jon repeated. Janus just grinned back at him.

Pibald answered Jon. 'A series of raids on fishing boats over a period of a week or so, the men kidnapped like you saw yesterday. Calban uses them as zombie-slaves. Everyone calls them shades. He seems to be able to exert some sort of mind control over them. We don't know how he does it.'

'He can do magic,' Footfall said. 'We know that. According to Jhalouk, no one has ever been as powerful as Calban.'

Jon asked him, 'Is Calban a waker?'

'Jhalouk says not. He's the only Catharian ever to have the power. It seems to have tipped him over the edge. He killed his parents and his elder sister at the age of twelve, stabbed them to death, then rowed himself over to the island before the bodies were discovered. The villagers sent a boat over with some men to fetch him back, and the boat never returned. They sent another, and the first boat sailed out to meet it. You saw a repeat yesterday of what happened then. After that Calban was left to himself on the island, and nothing was seen of him for ten years or more. The villagers thought he'd died there. As you can see, the island's quite barren. There's only the house the shades must have built him. No one knows how he survives.'

'Sorcery,' Lazuli said. 'That's how he survives. You can sometimes smell his magic on the wind. Though the villagers say he eats the flesh of the men he kidnaps. It isn't impossible.'

No one spoke for a moment, then Pibald said, 'His first attack on Cathar was a few years ago. That was a failure. He attacked in daylight with a few boats and was beaten off. Then he began raiding with more success, at intermittent intervals, taking a few men and the occasional waker.'

He stopped and rubbed the back of his hand wearily across his forehead. Pibald believed it, Jon realised. And he was in love with Jhalouk. Really in love, as if they had a future together in Cathar that he could safeguard.

'All of that was before I first awoke here,' Pibald continued. 'Then a few months ago he attacked in the early morning, under cover of fog. There's often a thick sea-mist at dawn, and Calban pushed one in before his fleet. The mist cleared as the boats landed to either side of the harbour.'

Jon noticed that Lapis and Lazuli had clasped hands on the table. Their fingers were knotted together and their knuckles were white with pressure. It was as if they were trying to fuse with each other. He looked into their faces. There was no sign that they were even aware that their fists were joined. Lazuli was gazing away over the sea, her eyes unfocussed, but Lapis was staring straight back at him. He looked away quickly, unnerved by the intensity of her gaze, and found himself observing Janus. Jon raised his eyebrows at him, expecting Janus at least to smirk in response, wanting anything to break the sudden atmosphere of foreboding, but instead Janus took over the story.

'The village defences were suckered perfectly. They split to cover either side of the harbour. It was beautiful to watch – it was like they were the Red Sea and Calban was Moses. You should have seen it, Sciler. Pibald and Footfall got sucked out left and the women went right, and when the whole setup was locked on and lit up, Calban just sailed in centre stage and stepped off his boat on to the quay right here, and the quay was as clear as Sunday in Bibletown.'

'Except that it wasn't quite empty, was it, Janus?'

It took Jon a moment to realise it was Lapis who had spoken. There was fire spitting in her voice.

Janus threw his arms up. 'Jesus, are we going to go through this all over again? He didn't have to be a fucking hero. This wasn't the OK Corral.'

Pibald said quickly, 'You don't have to be so cocky about it, Janus. That's all.'

'Starburn was there, wasn't he?' Jon said.

Janus caught himself. 'I'm not justifying myself to you. Any of you.'

Footfall suddenly said, 'It wasn't your fault. Nobody ever said it was. Lapis?'

Lapis swept her free hand slowly across the table and inspected her palm for a long moment. Then she formed a tight smile with her lips and aimed the smile at Janus. Jon was glad it wasn't meant for him.

'That's right, Janus,' Lapis said. 'I never said it.' She held the smile on Janus until he looked away. It was the first time Jon had seen him look uncomfortable.

'I don't care who tells me, but I want to know what happened,' Jon said, trying to control his voice. There was the same excitement welling up that he had felt when Lile had been telling him about Harel and Showen, as if he was about to hear a real truth here in Cathar. He tried to dull it but couldn't.

No one said anything. There was a look of immense sadness on Pibald's face. Footfall was frowning as if thinking of something else.

Pibald remembers it, Jon thought, and Footfall does his best not to.

Janus was beginning to grin again. He was unquenchable. Was he the one? Jon wondered. Was he the killer?

The silence burned around the table. The sounds of Cathar at work cocooned them. The clattering and crying-out, the animal noises and the whisper of the sea were like the syllables of a spell binding Jon to the conclusion that all of this was real.

Jon couldn't bear it. 'Tell me. Someone has to tell me.'

It was crazy. In his mind was a vivid picture of Starburn's corpse floating in a reservoir somewhere in London, and he was looking around the table here in Cathar half expecting someone to tell him exactly how Starburn had got there.

'Okay. Why not?'

Jon didn't want it to be Janus, but there was nothing he could do about it. He sat back and listened.

'Starburn knew Calban was going to show up there. And I knew he knew. Difference is, I also knew there was nothing he could do about it. Not a thing. But Starburn wouldn't accept that. He had to be a hero.'

'And that's another difference between you and Starburn.'

'Be quiet, Lapis,' Jon said. He hadn't seen that it was her, but he knew it. He felt he was beginning to know her apart from her twin.

Janus raised a finger at her. 'Yeah, and here's one more. I'm alive. You done?'

'Just tell it,' Footfall said neutrally. 'We haven't time to waste.'

'Tell *her* that,' Janus said. 'Well, they were just standing on the quayside staring at each other like they were a pair of statues.'

'Could you see Calban?' said Jon. 'Did you see his face?'

Janus shook his head. 'I was way back. I could see what was happening from where I was. There was no point in coming out. Especially after I'd seen what I saw. The fog came on to the quay after Calban like coat-tails. Like it was attached to him. And it was around his head like a helmet somehow, only with the visor up so his eyes showed through. Yeah, I saw his eyes, Sciler. Yellow eyes, Catharian eyes, only they shone like piss in moonlight.'

Jon watched the memory flicker over Janus's face and tried to read it, but couldn't. He wondered again why Janus was here in Cathar.

'They threw some magic about,' Janus said. His voice slowed down as he recalled it, and he screwed up his nose. 'I could smell it like camphor and maggoty flesh. The air was thick with it. It didn't last long. Then Starburn just walked towards Calban and the fog came out to meet him. I couldn't see anything more. The fog stirred around for a while and when it lifted, abracadabra. No Calban, no Starburn.'

'He fooled us,' Footfall said. 'I doubt Janus could have done anything except get himself taken as well.'

'That would have been something,' Lapis muttered.

Footfall ignored her. He said to Jon. 'Starburn was the best of us at magic. Janus can't do much, and the twins . . .' He shrugged. 'Pibald has some small ability, and so do I. But judging by your first attempt yesterday, you have a lot of potential, Sciler. Maybe you could be as good as Starburn was.'

Pibald stood up. 'So there it is, Sciler. Starburn is gone and you are here. And Calban will return soon. I suggest we prepare ourselves and Cathar better than we did last time.'

Janus shot to attention and snorted, 'Aye-aye, cap'n. All hands to the burning deck.'

Lapis took Jon's arm and walked him away from the table. Jon was aware of her warmth again.

'He's dead. I know he is,' she said quietly. 'This must be stopped. There must be no more murder, Sciler.'

Tears tracked her cheeks. Jon lifted his arm and used his sleeve to wipe the water away, feeling a sudden tenderness towards her.

'No more death,' she said.

'I know,' he told her.

Lazuli came up and joined them. She took Lapis's hand and stroked it. Looking from her twin to Jon, she said, 'It has to end, Sciler. Calban must be stopped.'

A shadow flickered over them. Jon glanced up to see another great bird soaring high overhead, or maybe it was the same one he had seen before. As he watched, it caught an updraught and began to spiral up into the clear blue sky, diminishing as it rose until it was a dot, a pixel, and then nothing at all.

The twins had gone when he dropped his head again. Until Lazuli had mentioned Calban, Jon had had the strange feeling that he and Lapis had not been talking about Cathar at all.

As the last of the gel seeped out of the pod and the lid rose, he saw Dr Locke's face staring down at him. The abstracted look he'd always seen in her eyes had gone and in its place was something else. Her cheeks were glowing. She was clutching a sheaf of coloured printouts in one hand, and the other hand was gripping the pod's rim so hard that her knuckles were white.

Jon started to raise himself out of the pod. He spat out the mouthpiece and caught a sudden strong scent of machine oil, so powerful that it made him catch his breath and sink back for a second.

Dr Locke frowned at him. 'Quickly, Mr Sciler. That was a productive excursion, and it will take us a while to examine it. Dress yourself and come straight to my room.' The languorous drawl had gone from her voice.

She turned on her heel and disappeared.

Dr Locke didn't mention his presence in her room the night before. Jon tried to read her eyes, but that new indecipherable look was still glittering there. Maybe she didn't know. Maybe she didn't care. She popped a bLinker pack open for him and gestured him to sit, and started flicking on her screens.

Slipping on the bLinkers didn't bother him any more. He hardly noticed the tendrils stroking their way around his orbits of his eyes.

'All right, Mr Sciler, tell me about it.' She was running her fingers through her hair, over and over. Jon thought she was worried about something, but that wasn't it. She was excited. Something had happened in the zone that she wasn't prepared for. That made two of us, Jon thought.

He sensed the lightwall coming on behind him. He could see reflections shifting over the black glass of the cupboard in front of him, and as he spoke to Dr Locke he could see her attention wandering, her eyes losing their focus on him and flicking over his shoulder to whatever was happening there. He wondered whether she was watching his experiences played out as he recounted them for her. How did she know it had been productive? What did she mean by it?

'Go on, Mr Sciler. I haven't all day to waste.'

'I was standing beside the jetty . . .'

It was more vivid than memory. He began to run through it for her, the memory seeming more solid than her room. She was writing all the time, referring constantly to a stack of printouts on her desk. They looked like relief maps of islands in blues and oranges and reds. There were three on each sheet, the top two distorted ovals, mirror images of each other, and the bottom one not quite a circle, indented at top and bottom. Every sheet was the same, but the colours and the areas picked out were different. He suddenly realised they were brainmaps, left, right and rear views.

When he mentioned Lile for the first time, she didn't react. He wanted to stop and ask her about him, but it felt like showing weakness to ask her. He began to feel angry with her for the effect Lile had had on him. He went on with the story as if Lile had been just another construct.

She didn't say a word until he got to Lapis and Lazuli arriving at the clearing. Then she held her hand up and interrupted.

'Go back to Lile for me. You recognised him, yes?'

Jon nodded. He realised he didn't want to tell her anything about Lile. Lile wasn't her business.

Her voice rose. 'You tell me everything, Mr Sciler. Everything. Not just what you see, what you hear. I want to know what you think. I must know everything.'

She leaned back in her chair and waited, clicking her pen on the pile of printouts.

Jon eventually broke the stand-off. 'Lile,' he said. 'I don't understand . . .'

'I've told you before, Mr Sciler, you don't need to understand. That isn't your job. It's mine, and you aren't making it easy.'

'Easy? Making it easy?' Jon shot round to face the screen. Lile filled the frame, the cleaver held high and ready to drop. Jon turned full circle in the chair, then stood up and pointed at the screen. 'I thought this was a game. This isn't a game at all. I don't know what the fuck it is, but it isn't a game. Yes, I recognised Lile. You know all about him, don't you? You put him there for me. What was that supposed to do to me?'

She was playing with the consoles on her monitors, not even listening to him. The reflections in the glass behind her were different now. Jon realised he was seeing a videoscan of his brain. The areas of colour were adjusting and rearranging. A burst of intense red with an orange halo sat shivering in each of the three images like a warped target.

Without looking at him, she said, 'Have you finished, Mr Sciler?'

'No, I haven't finished. If it's a game, then I'm the subject, aren't I? You're playing it on me.' He leaned forward and rested his hands on the desk and said, 'I want to talk to Kerz right now.'

'That isn't possible. We must carry on.'

'It isn't possible, Dr Locke? Are you sure of that? Because until I get to talk about this with Kerz, this session is suspended. So if you don't want to waste any more of your precious time, you'd better get him.'

'Take your hands off my desk, Mr Sciler.' She picked at keys on her main console and stared at the screen. 'Mr Kerz is unavailable. I told you that.'

Jon shrugged. He said mildly, 'What was it that guy called himself in Cathar? Lime? My short-term memory never was good.'

Dr Locke stood up, her face crimson. She grabbed a disc out of the input slide and opened the black glass door to throw it on to a shelf.

Pushing the door closed with one hand, she snatched her access card from the main console and hissed, 'Mr Sciler, you wait here.'

The monitors and the lightwall greyed out as she slammed the door behind her, and the reflection in one of the black glass doors skewed a fraction to the side. Jon stood up and stared at the widening crack between the doors. The lock hadn't engaged. She'd left the cabinet open.

He went round the desk and swung the door out.

There were six names on the shelves. Marcus Lees was no longer one of them. He read them from the top down. Jon Sciler. Yani Dromou. Kuta Chevalir. Teomera Sequiera. Anders Sosa. Daedalus.

Daedalus. Jon vaguely recognised the name. Something about the first Dirangesept project. It had been connected with that.

He pushed the glass doors closed and looked on the desk. The sheaf of printouts was sitting where she'd left them. The brainmaps were meaningless to him. There was a string of numbers in the top left corner of each sheet. He flicked through the pile and drew a single sheet out. The paper was thin and the colours had bled through it. Jon folded it and slipped it into his pocket, then went back to the chair and waited for Dr Locke to return.

Chrye sharpened her pace when she saw the pacifist trig ahead. She couldn't just walk past them any more. One day it was going to be Hickey Sill behind those shiny big blackeyes, and Chrye knew it would be Hickey in a mean mood. She tried to remember the pictures in Hickey's room. Was this Hickey's trig?

There was no way of telling whether the trig was active. She tried to relax. Until they moved they looked like dead metal either way.

Suppressing a need to turn around, to cross the street at least, she drew level with it. Its legs were three stubs holding the round black thorax inches from the ground, and the head was semi-retracted. Chrye could see herself stretched across the bulbous blackeyes. Dead metal. She was almost past and in its shadow when the head extended abruptly and the blackeyes swivelled, following her. Chrye felt her heart pound. She froze.

'Stop. You there. Stop now.'

She wondered whether it was worth running. Then she wondered if she was going to collapse. Her legs had turned to mush and her heart was a drum. She waited for Hickey's move. That was all she could do.

'I said stop. No further warning will be given.'

Chrye looked at her legs. They were quivering. What was this?

Across the street she caught a movement. Everyone else had stopped, but now someone was breaking into a run, a man carrying a silver aluminium case that suddenly began to swing wildly. Ahead of him people were hitting the ground. A scream nearby freed Chrye. She dropped flat.

Beside her the trig started to rise, its three legs silently extending. Chrye glimpsed the streaking flash of its sharplight and with a screech of ripped steel, sparks flew from the silver case. The runner tossed it away, spinning, a purple trail sailing from the laser's gash. The case fell beside a woman on the ground who touched the seeping purple with a finger and put it cautiously to her mouth.

The trig was already past Chrye, moving at first in a crippled lope but rapidly accelerating away.

It was obvious that the drugrunner had no chance. He wouldn't make it to the next corner. Chrye didn't care. She was safe. It wasn't Hickey. She watched the trig draw level with the man and run him hard into the wall. The man picked himself up as if nothing had happened, though his left arm was dangling awkwardly and clearly broken. In his right hand was a fat grey gun.

'Hey, you know me, man. You ain't supposed to do this.' He hesitated, then lifted the gun until it was centred on the trig's glossy belly.

'Put down the weapon,' said the trig. Its amplified voice echoed down the street. Its hardhands slid out and swung at its sides like antique clockweights.

The drugrunner said, 'Fuck you,' to the tick tock of the hardhands, marking time. He licked his lips with a tongue stained purple. He was smiling.

Chrye saw the gun kick and heard the charge zing away. Stupid, she thought.

She'd been waiting for it but the trig's hardhands came up and slammed together faster than her eyes could follow. They sandwiched the gun hand between them and this time the drugrunner screamed. He held out his arm and stared at the mangled weapon. A thread of blood trickled from the barrel. The man's hand seemed to have disappeared. Between his wrist and the gunbarrel was just a mess of reddening metal and bone.

That was unnecessary, thought Chrye. But she was relieved it was over. She waited for the trig to take the drugrunner away.

172

'Put down the weapon,' said the trig again, more loudly.

Chrye got to her knees, staring. The street had been starting to ease back to life, but with the trig's repeated order the movement stuttered to a halt again. The woman beside the shattered silver case had been lapping intently at her palm, smeared with the bright drug, and she froze there, her hand held to her mouth.

The man shook his hand violently. What remained of the gun wouldn't be released. He was fused to it. He began to whimper. The drugs and adrenalin had been shocked off and he was panicking. He kept shaking his hand as if he could shake away the pain with the gun.

In what seemed an idle movement, the trig cuffed the drugrunner's head with a hardhand. Chrye watched sickly. The crunch of bone was audible across the street. The drugrunner lurched back into the wall, the side of his face caved in and blackening quickly with blood.

'I ca't drop it, you fuck.' The man's voice was rising in terror. 'Ca't you fucking see that?'

The trig struck him again, on the jaw this time. The man still tried to speak, but he couldn't any more. Bubbles of blood filled his mouth, dropped to the ground and burst brightly. He was waving his gun hand desperately in the air.

'Put down the weapon. No more warning will be given,' said the trig.

Chrye looked away as the hardhands fell. She heard the trig returning to its post beside her. Chrye stood up shakily. She heard the giggle in the trig's voice as it whispered, 'Put down the weapon.'

Chrye backed off, looking at herself in the oval blackeyes of Hickey Sill's trig. Hickey stared back at her and said, 'I never knew bio-engineering was so easy. Some days, work's nothing but fun, huh? Say now, how about a date, pretty girl? You wouldn't like to end up like that, would you?'

'Come in and sit down, Jon,' Kerz said lightly. He added, 'This isn't normal at all.' He waited for Jon to sit, then said, 'Well, well. You have agitated poor Dr Locke. She isn't used to players of her games who won't play nicely with her afterwards. Whatever did you do to make her so emotional?'

'Lile,' Jon said. 'What's Lile doing in the zone, Kerz? What's the point of putting him there?'

'Ah. Is that what this is all about? Well, you've no need to worry, Jon. Are you concerned that we've done some research on your background?

It's like vetting, just like the secret services used to do when they were recruiting spies. We did all that when you first applied to us.' He smiled at Jon and spread his arms wide. 'Surely that doesn't surprise you? Maze is the largest games company in the world and we're jealous of our secrets, as jealous as any government. There's a lot to lose, as you must have realised by now. We know a great deal about your past, Jon. We know for example that you aren't a natural cooperator. We're not critical of it, we have no desire to change it. We simply know it. Dr Locke certainly knows it.'

He paused and fiddled with a pen. There was a pen on his desk but no paper, and there was an executive toy, a holo of a tiny dog running around the desktop. Occasionally the dog stopped to bark tinnily at the pen in Kerz's hand. Jon wondered what Kerz did in his office when he wasn't exercising the dog. There was another door behind him that Jon hadn't noticed before. 'Would you like something to drink?' Kerz said. 'I think Dr Locke can stand to wait a few minutes more.'

'I don't want anything. I just want to know what's going on here.'

'I understand that,' Kerz said, nodding. 'We didn't mean Lile to upset you, Jon. Quite the reverse. We expected him to be a pleasant surprise, something familiar, something to make you feel at home. If it shocked you to see him, then we apologise. We're only human after all.' Kerz held the pen out of reach over the dog's head and watched it jump up at the nib.

'We know how Cathar behaves under most stresses,' Kerz said. He began to draw the dog towards the edge of the desk, the dog barking and leaping ineffectually. 'We've been live-testing it for a very long time. It represents a great deal to us. It could be our ruin if it goes wrong.'

Was this it? Had Starburn been murdered because he'd discovered lethal faults in the program? But that didn't make any sense. Nothing was making sense. It still made no sense that Lile was in Cathar. Jon tried to follow what Kerz was telling him.

'You complained in your little outburst to Dr Locke that you felt she was testing you, rather than the game. Well, in a sense that's quite true. Cathar is very real, isn't it? Remarkably so. It can be quite confusing, this degree of verisimilitude, and up to a point that's all to the good. But you yourself know what game players are like, Jon. They want to convince themselves it's real, at the very least while they're immersed in the game. That, too, is all to the good. But, again, up to a point.'

Kerz's voice was soft and reasonable. Jon felt he was losing his anger and he wasn't ready to. 'Up to what point, Kerz?' he said. 'Why don't you get to the point, if there is one?'

Kerz was dangling the pen over the edge of the desk, the dog still jumping and yapping at it. Kerz twitched his fingers and let the pen drop to the floor. The dog launched itself after it, yelping wildly as it fell, and flicked out of existence.

Kerz reached down to pick up the pen, his thin pale neck stretching out of his collar. 'Now and then, players are going to imagine that they recognise the constructs in Cathar. That's inevitable. We need to know they can handle that. We need to be confident they won't . . .' He trotted his fingers towards the desk's edge and leapt them off. 'So, yes, Jon, we were testing both you and the game. Your reaction to Lile was significant, and we'll be reassessing Cathar as a consequence.'

He tossed the pen on to the desk. The dog reappeared beside it, snapping and growling again. 'So, all's well once more,' Kerz said.

Jon felt lost in the tangle of words. He had no response to Kerz. In his head he was seeing the tiny holo falling again, only this time it was Starburn, and when it reappeared on the desk it was himself yapping ridiculously at Kerz.

Kerz stood up and added, 'Dr Locke doesn't understand that her testers are rather less robust than her games. Frankly, I don't always understand her. She knows more about games than you or I ever will, Jon, and yet she hasn't the faintest comprehension of the concept of play.'

He shrugged. 'One last thing, while you're here. I've been meaning to mention this to you. You might consider keeping a journal of your thoughts on Cathar for us. I have a notebook here you could use.' He pulled a book from a drawer beneath the desk and handed it to Jon. 'Now, back you go to Dr Locke. I'll tell her not to be so rigid with you in future. She should be able to remember that for the rest of the day.'

SEVENTEEN

Jon sat in the Angel Café thinking of sleep, nursing a glass of water as the rain tracked down the window beside him, watching shadows of raindrops slide like a disease over his hands and the glass and across the metal table. Chrye was late and the air was bad out there and getting worse. Fog was coming in too. He rubbed the window with his sleeve, wondering if he could see a figure standing out there, over the road, motionless and without a respirator.

Since Dirangesept his sleep had been interrupted by nightmares that woke him screaming and remembering only whirling colours, blues and greens spinning through his head. Now with his nights spent in Cathar he didn't need sleep at all, but he missed it more than ever.

He stared through the streaming window and recalled other memories of Dirangesept for the first time, and found them oddly comforting. Chrye had been the difference. Since meeting her, he was increasingly able to think of Dirangesept without the panic overwhelming him.

The beasts hadn't been the only life on the planet. They were just the alpha life form. Even if they were alpha triple-starred. There were plenty of other animals there as well; its ecosystem was complex and complete. But it was the sounds of Dirangesept that filled his thoughts, the infinitely layered sounds of the alien jungle.

Under the brittle hum of the aircon system he closed his eyes, letting it all flow back to him.

Listening to Dirangesept was like staring out of light into the night sky and seeing only darkness, but gradually beginning to make out a few bright stars and then more and more until the sky seemed so full of stars that the darkness was just their thin pale matrix. On Dirangesept the background noise was a soft buzz so uniform that it was like silence until

176

you started to listen to it. Then you made out the distinct, hollow clicks of wing casings, the sharp rasps of body scales against bark and stone and the brittle throat rattles and croaks. And then beyond them the fainter rhythmic slappings, the soft whistles and whines, the burrs and the rustlings. And when you had processed all of those sounds there was still beneath them an endless procession of almost inaudible snuffles, sighs and moans, patterings, tickings and sounds fading away beyond comprehension and the human ear. The warnings, the enticings, the calls to mates, to young, to prey, to the living planet.

Jon had never tired of it. At nights on Dirangesept when he had secured his autoid as well as possible and was supposed to have exited, he had often remained bLinkered under the darkening sky and nined his ears to let it all flood in and fill him with life.

Now there was just the hum of the café's aircon in his ears. He opened his eyes and squinted through the glass, tracing shadows through shadows. Something, someone, was out there.

Chrye came coughing through the door. A twenty-minute walk and the filter in her mask needed replacing. The day hadn't been scheduled as air risk one. Jon was already there, staring through the window as if he hadn't seen her. She called his name and startled him. The door swung back behind her but the catch didn't quite engage, and he stood up and went quickly as if to shut it. Sitting down and wiping her eyes, she glanced round to see him standing in the open doorway, staring down the sodden, windblown high street. There was nothing to see beyond him except the faint outlines of struggling figures caught in rain and mottled fog. It looked like he was gazing into another world, a place of loneliness and despair. Perhaps she was just seeing things the way he did now.

A waiter shook a fist at him and shouted, 'Chrissake shut the damn door.'

'What is it?' she said as Jon came back. 'Did you see someone?' Did you see Hickey Sill? she meant. Her phone slate was stuffed with Hickey's calls. She was twitchy in the streets now, changing direction whenever she saw a trig.

'No. No one there.' He sat down. She could see he was lying to her.

'What are we going to do about him?' she said.

'Who?' Jon seemed distracted.

'Hickey. I'm talking about Hickey Sill. You know he's stalking me. I can't go to the 'fists about him. It seems he's their golden boy. I think he's close to doing something violent. He threatened me in the street.'

'Hickey,' he said, but he didn't seem to have heard her. She wasn't sure how much was real to him at the moment. She opened the back of her mask and pulled out the filter. It was damp and black and smelt of sulphur. She dropped it into the ash tray and put in a new one.

The waiter came over and jerked his head at Chrye. 'You never heard of the Resp Law? I could throw you out for that. Both of you.'

Chrye took a breath, anger suddenly erupting inside her. 'Your door doesn't close properly. You have no functioning vent seal. You could be closed down for that. Don't quote the Resp at me.' She swung her arm around, taking in the empty café. 'Who else is here on a day like this? Christ. Do you want business or should we go somewhere else?'

The waiter picked up the ash tray and looked at the filter. He seemed to slump. 'I guess it's a bad day. No sense making it worse, huh?'

Chrye nodded. 'Yes. Bad day.' She glanced at Jon. He picked up a glass of filtered water and sipped from it. She said to the waiter, 'I'll have the same.'

The waiter wandered off. Chrye thought about trying to tell Jon about Hickey and decided it wasn't worth it at the moment.

He started to turn the glass around on the table, staring into it. It didn't look any different that way to Chrye. He said, 'I saw the cassettes of the wakers in Cathar in Dr Locke's office. She's taken Starburn's name off the shelves. There were five other names as well as mine. They have to be Janus, Pibald and Footfall, and then a woman's name, Teomera something, and a man called Daedalus. Just Daedalus. He was the only one with no other name.'

He looked at Chrye and went on, 'I've heard of a Daedalus. He was in the original Dirangesept expedition. I've tried to do some research on him, without much success. He's supposed to have been a hero, saved the lives of a lot of the colonists on the planet, but I couldn't get any reliable detail. And since his return there's nothing. He seems to have vanished.'

The waiter came with Chrye's water and a fresh ash tray. She waited until he'd gone before saying, 'I haven't heard of Daedalus. Was that his real name?'

'I think it must be. Starburn was under his real name on the Dirangesept roster and at Maze. Daedalus appears as Daedalus in both places. I know someone I can check it with, though. I'll do that.'

'Okay. What about the woman?'

'Teomera? Either I haven't met her yet, or she's Jhalouk. Which would mean Maze can alter your appearance when you go there. And I don't think they can do that, or they would have done it with the rest of us.'

You don't think it because you still want Cathar to exist, Chrye thought. Jon wouldn't meet her eyes, though, which troubled her. She said, 'There are the twins, Lapis and Lazuli. Could Teomera be one of them?'

He hesitated there and Chrye didn't know how to read it. His eyes lost their focus for a moment. She took a gulp of water.

'I don't know,' he said slowly. 'Their movements are so synchronised.' He started to say more, but stopped again. 'The wakers would have to be twins, and there's just the name Teomera on the shelf. I don't know.'

He's covering something up, Chrye thought with a shock. He saw Hickey outside just now and told me he hadn't, and now he's keeping something else from me.

'Go back to Daedalus,' she told him, recovering herself. 'Who is he in Cathar?'

There was that evasive look again.

'Jon?'

'I'm not sure. I'm not sure any more.'

'What do you mean? Jon, talk to me. We have to know who's real and who they are, or we're getting nowhere.'

His face seemed to crumple. 'At first it was so simple. There were players in the game and there were constructs. And then the players were wakers and now Cathar might not be a game.' He held up a hand to stop her interrupting and she was almost relieved. She wasn't sure how convincing she would have been, disagreeing with him.

'But at least I thought I knew who existed only in Cathar. Whether or not Cathar was real. Now even that's gone.' He fell quiet.

'Something's happened, hasn't it? Tell me, Jon.'

'I saw someone in Cathar who can't be a player and who can't exist only there.'

His voice tailed away. Chrye had to tell him to go on.

'I told you I was sent to an orphanage when my parents died. It was where I met Starburn. I was in a bad way for a long time. The manager befriended me, put me back together. His name was Mr Lile.' Telling it to Chrye brought it all back again, but now, somehow, the memories were tainted by Cathar. He saw Mr Lile raising his amputated arm in mock punishment again for sabotaging the aid worker's vehicle, except this time his elbow hinged into an axe handle and the axe blade was falling.

'Jon.'

Her hand touched him on the cheek and he flinched. He said, 'I saw Mr Lile there. He even called himself Lile. He didn't know me, but it was him. I told Kerz about it and he spun me some story about testing my reactions, but he was lying.'

'How do you know he was lying?'

'I've been thinking about it. Either Mr Lile is Daedalus – except I know Mr Lile is dead – or there's some other way to get to Cathar, independently of Maze.'

And which also means, again, that Cathar is real, Chrye thought. It always comes back to the same thing.

'What do you mean, Jon? How do you know Kerz was lying?' Chrye repeated. She still couldn't just tell him, don't be stupid, Cathar doesn't exist.

'Lile had a medallion around his neck. It was an old sixpenny coin on a silver chain. It was the only thing I had that belonged to my parents. There was a rule in the orphanage – no jewellery. But Mr Lile let me keep it. He unthreaded the chain and put it in the safe in his office, and I held on to the coin with its tiny soldered loop. We were allowed to earn a little money by running errands, and I kept the coin with that money. When I left the orphanage he gave me back the chain.'

Chrye remembered her fingers chasing down the nape of his neck and along the blanched depths of his scar. She wondered how back then, weeks ago, she could have been confronted by his anguished soul and imagined it was all so simple and that she could help him escape his past. Now he had drawn her into his madness and it seemed all she could do was to hold on to him more tightly.

'You don't have it now – the chain,' she said, not knowing what else to say.

'No. Mr Lile died while I was in CrySis on the way to Dirangesept. Starburn and I woke up to the news. Heart attack. He was about sixty.'

'"Orion's arrow",' Chrye said suddenly, remembering. 'You wrote that for him, didn't you? That "Drawn arm of stars that loosed us on our course".' It was his arm, wasn't it?' She looked at the tears welling in his eyes, watched them run shining down his cheeks and into the corners of his mouth. She understood the poem now, even if it was all she did understand.

'I let it out in space over Dirangesept,' Jon said. 'Just before we went down for the first time. It was meant to be in his memory, good luck or something, but then it all started to go wrong. The coin must still be there, hurtling along with its chain like a bright, tiny comet and its tail. But no one knows about it. No one ever knew about it, Chrye. Maze *can't* have known about it. Even Starburn never knew about that. But Lile was wearing it in Cathar.'

Chrye shook her head. Dirangesept had been a sleep away, a long, frozen sleep, but it had been there when the Far Warriors had woken up. It had been there. Cathar was different. Cathar surely only existed during the sleep, disappearing as soon as the travellers awoke. So how could this be true about Lile?

'Maybe your Mr Lile isn't dead,' she suggested helplessly, knowing he'd have an answer to it. 'Maybe he told them.'

'No. He'd be over a hundred years old now and, anyway, I checked the records this morning. He's definitely dead.'

'Maybe they hypnotised you, extracted the information?'

'Such a tiny detail? How long would they have needed to get that deep? I'd have hours, days of lost time. I'd know.'

'So how do you explain the coin, Jon?'

'I don't know. I just don't know.' He shrugged, then abruptly dug his hand into his pocket and dragged out a crumpled scrap of paper, flattening it on the table. A pool of spilt water began to soak up into it and he swore, shaking the liquid off.

Chrye grabbed the paper from his hand and stared at it, at the three brain profiles with their linked patterns. 'Where did you get this, Jon?'

'I took it from Dr Locke's room.'

She said slowly, 'They've been brainmapping you. This is a picture of your brain in three dimensions.' She pointed at the central hub of dark red and said, 'This indicates an area of high oxygen uptake. When any part of the brain is working particularly hard, it uses more oxygen. That's what they've been doing with you. This is just a snapshot.'

'I'm sure they have video readouts of the whole time I spend in Cathar,' Jon said, then added, 'Though that still doesn't explain why I'm connected to the AIs during the debriefing sessions.' He looked at the paper. 'Okay, how do you read this?'

Chrye jabbed her finger at the brain map. 'Your amygdala,' she said. 'I'll bet this is when Lile was having a swing at you with the cleaver. The red core's much bigger on the left view, and see how it's located to the left of the posterior view? Well, that's your left temporal lobe. Your fear centre.'

Jon stared at the skewed target. 'It looks very well developed,' he said dryly. 'If I can get the whole readout, could you interpret it, then?'

'Not worth a damn. No one could without a precisely corresponding visual and verbal transcript of the experience. Without that it's as about as much good as sifting entrails.'

'So what do we do, then?'

'I'll show this to my tutor if that's okay with you. We're meeting again tomorrow.'

Her finger came away from the doorcode panel sticky and stained faintly with purple, but Chrye was too busy thinking about brainmaps and the name Daedalus to question it any further than putting it down to kids buzz-running. She closed the door behind her and slammed on the locks.

Even then, turning round to see her work all over the floor and the furniture tipped everywhere, she just started gathering up the papers and reordering them. It wasn't the first time she'd been burgled and her place trashed. But she'd have to replace the computer and she wasn't sure how she was going to pay for it this time.

She dropped the papers on the table and saw the computer still there. Her heart began to thump. She stopped dead still and saw the shape of a man sitting on the floor behind the bed. He'd pulled the bed down.

Hickey stood up slowly. There was a broad grin on his face. Chrye realised she'd been too busy looking behind her to look right ahead. Jon hadn't seen Hickey at all. Hickey had been waiting here for her.

'Now I reckon this counts 's evidence, Ms Roffe,' Hickey said happily. He was wearing skintight blue surgical gloves and waving a tiny bright purple plastic pouch in the air. In his other hand he was holding her copy of *Neverland*. He let the book fall to the ground and screwed his heel into the cover, ripping the binding apart. 'Oops, dropped it,' he said.

Chrye started backing towards the door, rubbing her stained finger on her trousers. 'Get out of here, Hickey,' she hissed. 'Get out now or I'm calling the 'fists.'

Hickey spread his arms wide. He wriggled his fingers. 'Hell, girl, here they are. In person. Faster'n a speeding bullet. Never off duty, Chrye. How's it go, now? Scene one: Officer Sill saw you behaving strangely on the street, said hi – we being friends – then noticed traces of moonbeam on your fingers. Scene two: you asked Officer Sill in and offered him a little action.' Hickey Sill stood up unsteadily. 'Cut to court . . .'

'Get out, Hickey, and take your shit with you.'

She looked at her finger. The stain was still there. She turned around and tried to work the door, but there was no time. Hickey's smooth blue hands were snaking under hers and rising, yanking her arms up into the air and behind her neck. She caught a brief whiff of his breath; he was already on something. He brought his hands back behind her head and locked his fingers there, jerking her face hard down on to her chest. Hickey was strong. She tried to kick back into his shins but he was wearing high boots.

She heard him say, 'That's no way to talk about this high purity 'beam. Some fuckwit dealer died for this, remember?' He paused. 'Hey, I'm a fair man. You're gonna be doing three years' dark time – might as well know what you're doing it for. Might as well 'preciate it.'

He kicked her feet away and started to drag her back towards the bed. She could hear the excited rasp of his breath in her left ear and struggled to breathe. At the bed he adjusted his grip on her arms and let her head come up. She instinctively started to take a huge breath, and halfway through it Hickey's hand slapped on to her mouth with a palmful of moonbeam that she took straight down, fast and deep into her lungs.

Hickey threw her on to the bed and grinned at her.

'Well, girl, I reckon you got a real giant leap there. Feel good, huh?'

It was beginning to take already. Her skin was tingling and she felt sweat starting to run off her. She tried to roll over and thought stupidly that Hickey was trying to help her, but he was only dragging her trousers off.

'Did I mention scene three?' he panted. 'Okay, scene three: Officer Sill tampers with the evidence. Yeah, I like that. An' your boyfriend's gonna fuckin' love it.'

The sweat was plastering her trousers to her skin and Hickey was having trouble working them over her hips. She tried to open her legs to hold her trousers up, and Hickey's mouth twisted in a grin, misunderstanding it. 'Hey, girl, you're ahead of me.'

Everything was starting to go foggy. Chrye couldn't speak. She saw

Hickey's eyes like red moons swimming over her and stuck her tongue out at him, managing to pout her lips.

'Wanna kiss, huh?' He leaned over her face, his breath rancid with whatever had given him this strength.

She held the pout until his lips were on hers, and made herself give him an open-mouth kiss, licking her tongue around the inside of his mouth and using the last of her strength to blow moonbeam into him. He pulled away from her and grinned crazily. 'Whoo-oo,' he sighed. She heard his long, echoing giggle bouncing around inside her skull, and then his full weight crashed down on her. She tried to shove him off but her hands were rubbery and he pushed them away easily, laughing.

She lost consciousness.

Hickey Sill's laughter was still rattling around inside her head along with an avalanche of razor-studded rocks when she woke up. Her trousers were down around her ankles and her shirt had been ripped off. She thought, I'm alive, and then didn't let herself think anything else for the moment. She waited until she could predict the ceiling's movements, then rolled carefully off the bed and on to the floor which was bucking insanely. Except inside her head, there was no pain. She guessed that was due to the moonbeam. Hickey was curled up in a nest of paper over by the table, snuffling quietly to himself and trembling intermittently. For some reason his piece of the room didn't seem to be moving.

Chrye waited for the floor underneath her to quieten down and managed to crawl to the bathroom. She struggled out of her clothes and left them on the floor, then sat on the toilet and checked herself thoroughly. She put her head in her hands and sat there for a long time. Hickey hadn't touched her. He must have passed out pretty quickly, she thought. Thank Christ. She heaved herself into the bath, turned the tap on cold all the way and held her head under the lash of brown water until the last of Hickey's giggles had been washed away and the rocks in her skull had started to blunt. Then she lay on her back and drank down water straight from the tap until she couldn't taste moonbeam any longer.

After that she wrapped a towel around herself and went back into the other room. Her head was clearing. She looked at Hickey who was shivering more violently, his arms and legs jerking and his eyes opening and closing crazily.

'Moral is, Hickey,' she muttered, 'don't mix your drinks.'

Hickey didn't answer. His eyes were screwed shut now and his jaw was wide open, lips stretched out tight and white. A high screech came from his throat and cut off abruptly. She used a chair leg to push him over and forced herself to go through his pockets, feeling nauseous at the idea of touching him. Along with his wallet there were a few blister packs of ovoid purple tablets that she didn't recognise, and slotted into a long stitched pocket beneath the armpit of his jacket was a thin metal club, about fifteen centimetres long and four in diameter. By its sheen she guessed it was titanium. It had a ribbed rubber grip, and when she flicked a tiny black contact on the grip another ten-centimetre spike of metal jolted out of the club's end. Chrye stared at the club and then at Hickey slobbering on the floor. She held the club over his head, suddenly shaking, and then brought it down gently, not quite touching him on the skull with it. She breathed out slowly before retracting the spike and sliding the club back into its concealed pocket.

She sat down and called Jon, but cut the connection after the first ring. She didn't want to know he wasn't in. She felt fragile enough.

Then she thought about the 'fists, but after what Madsen had told her about Hickey, she knew she couldn't call them.

So she dressed herself and sat and waited for Hickey to come out of it. After another half an hour of random spasms, Hickey's body quietened. Chrye started clearing up around him, smoothing out the ripped and crumpled pages of *Neverland*, murmuring to herself the opening lines of 'bLink Twice'.

> In the orbit of the eyeball
> In the mirror of the lens
> I no longer see my image
> I no longer know myself.
> I reflect upon reflection,
> I reflect, reflect, reflect.

The lines comforted her. Even just saying them, she felt Jon with her. She felt he was part of her now.

An hour later Hickey woke up.

Chrye made herself lock eyes with him and said as steadily as she could, 'That was great, Hickey. You want to do it again, get in touch. I have to go out soon, though, so you'd better go now.'

She hustled him out the door and watched him stumble down the stairs, then locked and bolted herself inside. She figured Hickey would wonder about it for a while, but he wouldn't be sure enough to come back to her for a few days. Maybe by then she would have stopped shaking.

EIGHTEEN

Jon hadn't been this way out of Cathar, east of the harbour. After a few minutes the twins led him down a muddy track off the road, back towards the shore. The track headed towards a dense maze of rickety wooden houses at the water's edge.

'This is the reef,' said Lapis, gesturing ahead at the shacks. 'This is where we live.'

It didn't look like a reef. Jon couldn't remember seeing it from Jhalouk's house up on the hillside. There had been a bluff beneath the house, though, so maybe it had been concealed. The whole mass seemed to be shifting as he watched it, its outline moving against the sky. Something about it wasn't right. After a moment it didn't bother him, though. He knew everything in Cathar could be explained. It was the explanations that worried him.

'This is Cathar as much as the rest of the village,' Lazuli said. 'It isn't pretty, but we feel safe here. This is where we come from, where we were born.'

Jon glanced at her, not sure how to take what she was saying, and looked at Lapis who just nodded and said, 'Last time Calban attacked Cathar, we were here.' She swept her arms across the promontory of shacks. They seemed to be tipping into the sea in an arrested avalanche.

The stone path turned to wooden boarding as Jon followed the twins, and under the boarding was rippled wet sand. Jon began to see that the outermost shacks were on stilts and the paths between them were raised walkways over the water. From the shore it wasn't possible to tell where the land ended and the sea began. He understood it now. This rickety network of housing was the reef.

'This way,' Lazuli said. Here on the reef she seemed to take control, and

Jon realised that until now Lapis had been the slightly dominant personality. As they walked on to the boards Lapis swayed, almost losing her
balance, and reached out for Jon's arm. She didn't release it again. It felt
comfortable to Jon that they were balancing each other. Lazuli walked
steadily ahead of them. It didn't appear to concern her any more that
Lapis was attached to him. The connection between the twins had shifted.
Lazuli kept breaking off her conversation to wave and shout greetings to
people. The reef was full of life.

Lazuli led them through the shacks until they reached a fenced outpost
at the end of a long and isolated walkway. They surveyed the sea and the
houses around them. The sprawl of shacks looked like it would be
wrecked by a high wave.

'How did you fortify this last time?' Jon said.

'You can't,' Lazuli told him. 'We didn't know what to do. We had an
arc of pontoons set around the perimeter of the reef, loaded with wood
and set to burn, but when Calban sent the fog in he cut the cables and sent
a wind to push the pontoons back towards the reef. By the time we
realised what had happened it was too late. The outer fringe of the reef
was ablaze. We had to hack the burning houses into the sea.'

'What about Calban's men?'

'They landed safely beyond the reef and came up behind us. We were
trapped here.'

'Away from the centre of Cathar,' Jon said. 'Away from Starburn.'

Lapis said, 'And that's more or less what happened to Pibald and
Footfall over to the west. I think Calban just wanted Starburn. The rest
was a diversion.' She squeezed Jon's hand. 'I don't want that to happen to
you, Sciler.'

For a moment there was silence. Jon felt a tension between the women.
Lazuli glanced at her twin and said shortly, 'I'm going to see Skain. I'll be
back later.'

The walkway boomed under her feet and she disappeared into the
network of passageways. Jon stared out over the sea with Lapis. In the
late afternoon the water's surface was almost undisturbed. There might
have been a film over it, beneath which it swelled gently and subsided.
Jon could feel the reef on its stilts moving with the sea. He felt that
everything was connected and that he was part of it all. Lapis was holding
his hand.

After a while she sighed, then without speaking she drew him back into the labyrinth of the reef and led him to a small shack. Jon had to stoop to enter it. He made out two narrow beds, a table and chairs and a squat iron stove in the corner, its smokestack cracked and blackened. The rest was in shadow.

'We live here,' Lapis said. She sat down on one of the beds and gestured for Jon to sit beside her.

The hut was shifting in a subtle rhythm, and Lapis seemed to be falling into him. She stroked her fingers across the back of his hand. There was a gentleness to her that there hadn't been with Chrye.

'Is this real?' Jon said, watching her fingers trace along the veins of his hand.

Lapis smiled. 'You don't know if I'm real, and you're asking me that.' She leaned forward and he smelt a perfume on her, the scent of roses, and she kissed his lips. 'Is this real?' she whispered. 'Or this?'

He pulled away a little. He thought of Chrye again, Chrye waiting for him, because that was what she was doing, he knew that. It was in her eyes and her voice. At the beginning he hadn't wanted it, and then later he hadn't wanted to admit it.

Lapis was caressing his cheeks and her hands were working softly around his eyes, ruffling his hair and reaching further to the nape of his neck. She leaned to pull him closer and he didn't resist as her hands slid under his shirt to pull it away.

Chrye was waiting for him, waiting patiently, and she trusted him. But this was Cathar and Lapis had slipped his shirt off, her hands on his shoulders stroking him. He remembered Chrye working at the pain there, easing it away. This was different. But he hadn't been ready for this with Chrye, and she had known it. Perhaps he was ready now, except that this wasn't Chrye.

He leaned on to Lapis's shoulder and let her kiss his neck. She took his hand and fed it into the coolness under her dress.

He hesitated, and Lapis looked at him. Her eyes were bright. They were waker's eyes, always so pale and blue, but now suddenly he thought there was a flash of yellow to them, there and gone. The sun was low and golden in the window, and maybe it was only that. His hand was high on her thigh and Lapis covered it with hers, holding it there and then rubbing it so that his palm was moving on her skin, moving higher into the cleft between her legs. The house was moving with their rhythm now, or maybe theirs was that of the house, of the sea swelling beneath them. Her face was flushed and sheened with sweat. 'Love me,' she whispered. 'If it isn't real, what does it matter, Jon? If I'm not real, what can you be doing that's wrong?'

He raised himself from her and she pulled his trousers away and then her hands were on him. She fell back on the bed and he was on top of her and then inside her, moving like the sea beneath them.

He cried out as he felt the surge of his coming and then like a long vibrant echo her own, and in the dying of it all he thought, She called me Jon.

The shack was creaking around them, moving gently. Looking up at the ceiling Jon could make out the constant easing of the planks and he could see the sky between like streams of bright fluid. Everything was shifting. Nothing was solid. Nothing stood still. He sat up.

He looked at her and said, 'You *are* real, Lapis, aren't you?'

She was crying, her body shivering with tears.

'You know about me,' Jon said. He remembered the rockets bursting over Primrose Hill and thought, Lapis was the woman at Starburn's scattering. Starburn told her about me.

He put his hands on her shoulders and said, 'Tell me what's happening, Lapis.'

She pulled him to her and held on to him tightly, still crying. 'I don't know. Am I real? I don't know if I'm real. I was real to Starburn, and he was real to me. I want you to be real for me, Jon.'

'What about Lazuli? What is she?'

'She's part of me. She's as real as I am.'

Jon pushed her away gently and went to the stove. There was a barrel of fresh water by the wall with an iron scoop hanging on a rope beside it. He filled a pot and put it to heat, then found a jar of coffee and poured a short stream of it into the steaming water.

He heard Lapis dressing herself behind him. She came up and touched him. 'I'll do that,' she said, composed again. She found a pair of mugs and took them to the table, sitting down with him. 'You asked me about Lazuli. I can't explain it properly, but I had a twin who died as we were born. I always felt her with me, all my life. Then when I joined Maze they made a construct for me, a sort of mimic.'

Jon nodded. 'In the first zone I played. Yes. But I thought you were both constructs.'

'Then I came here to Cathar, and we found each other again.' Her eyes were shining. 'It was wonderful. It was the same for her, it had been all along. She was as alone in Cathar as I'd been in England. Without each other we were lost.'

She poured the coffee for them and sipped at hers. 'But now we're whole again.'

'Lazuli's eyes,' Jon said. 'You both have wakers' eyes.'

'Not always. You may have noticed, sometimes in a strange light . . .'

Jon nodded.

'Lazuli wasn't quite a waker, just as I was incomplete in England. When we were born here in Cathar, they thought she was dead, but she survived, sort of.' Lapis gave an odd smile. 'Until I awoke here, Lazuli was . . . adrift, really.'

'What happens to her when you exit?'

'I only exit to debrief now when she sleeps.'

'And what happens to you in London without her?'

'I know she's here, I know I'll return. It's okay.'

Jon knew she was lying, but he left it. Whatever Starburn had been to her, she wanted Jon to be now. He wondered what that might be.

She put the coffee down and tilted her head, listening. 'Someone's coming. Something's happened,' she said.

The coffee was jumping in her mug. Jon realised the floor was shivering. This wasn't the sea.

Outside the thud of footsteps rattled and stopped as the door of the hut flew open.

Lazuli stared at them, at Lapis. 'Calban's men,' she said. 'Shades, about twelve of them. They must have landed along the coast. They're coming towards the reef.'

A small group of men from the village preceded the shades by about ten metres, backing away from them. The shades walked smoothly, swinging clubs in their hands, not in step but maintaining an easy pace. As the crowd came closer Jon saw that the clubs were dark with blood.

One of the Catharians detached himself and ran up to Lapis and Lazuli, shouting incoherently.

'We need missiles,' Lazuli said to her twin. 'We mustn't get close enough to let them use their clubs.'

'Get crossbows from the reef,' Lapis told the Catharian. 'Quickly.'

'There isn't time,' Jon said. 'Look how fast they're moving.'

One of the shades seemed to notice Jon. He stopped and pointed his club, and the group changed direction.

They're after me, he thought. Just me.

Lapis said, 'Get back, Jon. There's nothing you can do. You can't use magic, it's too much of a risk. If it doesn't work . . .'

She was right. He'd be helpless.

There was an eagle above him, circling, or maybe it was a vulture watching for the pickings of death, one of Calban's camp followers. He glanced up at it and was sure it was the same bird he'd seen before. It swooped low and rose again.

'Go back to the village, Sciler,' Lazuli said quickly. 'We'll deal with this.' She drew the sword from her scabbard, and Lapis did the same. The twins looked at each other and Jon couldn't tell for a moment which was which.

'No,' he said. 'They'll kill you.'

'Go. There isn't time.'

Calban's men broke suddenly into a trot, and the Catharians yelled and began to scatter. Jon pulled one of them to a halt as he ran past and wrenched the sword from his hand. Lazuli shouted to him, 'No! This isn't your skill. Just run.'

The leading shade jerked abruptly and slumped to its knees. It reached up to its shoulder and yanked out a fat crossbow bolt, then stood again and carried on, already overtaken by its companions.

'They can be killed,' Lapis said. 'Head or heart, or loss of blood. But not by you. Run, Jon.'

The pair of them stood side by side in front of him. The first of the shades was nearly on them.

Jon ran off the track and into the scrub, thinking to be able at least to outpace the shades and lead them away from the village. The foliage was only knee-high but the roots caught at his ankles. The shades were fast. They loped easily through it, hardly slowed at all.

Jon heard a grunt behind him and feet crashing through the brush, closing on him. One of the shades was close enough for Jon to hear its breathing. The ground was rockier and beginning to rise, and Jon veered sharply left. He vaulted over a boulder and turned in the same movement, swinging the sword in a wild arc. He saw the shade try too late to jerk back its head as the sword's blade swept into and through its neck and the headless body fell back. Not my skill, Jon thought. Fine, I'll settle for luck.

He looked back. There were three still right behind him. Lapis and Lazuli had cut the others off and were trying to hold them at a distance while a group of Catharians edged round to shoot them without risking the twins. Two more of Calban's shades had fallen, and another fell as Jon watched, a crossbow bolt jutting from its eye.

The others were fanning around the twins now, trying either to surround them or to present harder targets to the crossbows, or maybe just to bypass the twins, to reach Jon.

And while he stood and watched them, the three right behind him were closing in. Stupid, he thought. Keep going.

He glanced up at the slope and decided against it. It was too steep. He'd only have to lose his footing and slip back to be caught. He caught a glimpse of red up there, the red a streak tumbling down the slope over to the left where he was heading, and there was a shadow there too, sliding down over the hillside even faster than the slash of red.

Shadow of a bird, he thought, waiting for carrion.

He carried on, breathing hard now, parallel to the slope but heading away from Cathar and the twins. After a few metres he glanced back again to see the three shades strung out into a line by his change of direction.

They weren't slowing at all. Far behind him the other shades had closed in on the twins, not bothering to come after Jon. Not needing to, Jon thought. There were four of them left down there, four on two, though the villagers had given up their crossbows and were rushing towards the twins with swords.

Jon had his own immediate problem. He stopped dead. The ground at his feet dipped abruptly into a gully, a drop of two metres. No way round it, and the same rise on the other side. He didn't want them backing him into it and risk an uncontrolled fall, so no other option.

He crouched on to his haunches and dropped down, flexing his knees as he hit the ground, and began to work his way down the gully. The vegetation was thick and he made slow progress high-stepping through it. He used the sword to sweep the thick vegetation away from his face.

He could hear them above him. He heard the crash and thud of one of them jumping into the gully after him, maybe five metres back. And the others overtaking him up top where the ground was easier. Bad mistake, he thought. I'm trapped. Shit. He heard the crash again as another one leapt into the trench somewhere up ahead.

There was a shadow above him and it was red, not the bird but too fast to be one of the men. He ducked instinctively and the red blur was right in front of him and heading away down the ditch, low in the foliage and fast, some kind of animal. A moment later he heard the scream, a human scream that came channelled back along the gully, and he carried on towards it, nothing else to do. He reached the shade's body a few paces on. Its head was a mess that Jon stepped over.

Two left, then. One behind him, and the other one where? And the animal, but Jon wasn't going to worry about that.

Further on he had to squeeze past a thick buttress root jutting into the gully and almost blocking it. He stopped beyond the root and stepped back quickly, pulling himself into its shelter. There was no room to swing the sword or even to hold it ready without it poking into sight, so he held it by his side and waited.

The shade stopped at the other side of the root. Jon could hear it breathing, slowly and steadily. He dug his hand carefully into the wet earth behind him and pulled away a handful, lobbing it ahead where it made a small sound.

The shade's hand reached carefully around the root and Jon flinched out of its reach. The fingers were short and grimy, nails ripped. After a second the arm followed it, and at last the head. Its face stared blankly at Jon. There was no expression in it at all. It could have been dead. Jon shot himself forward and smashed into the arm with all his weight, holding it against the far wall of the gully before the shade could force the rest of his body through the gap.

The shade's strength was incredible. The buttress root must have been as thick as his thigh, but it shook and cracked under the impact of the club on the other side as the shade tried to burst through. Jon couldn't shift his body enough to bring up the sword. He could barely hold the shade's arm. He heard the club splinter on the root and the shade gave up on that, hurling Jon back into the wall of the gully and crashing clear of the root barehanded. Off balance, he lifted the sword hilt and managed to wedge it into the wall under his arm as the shade came at him, hands high and set to strangle him.

The shade hadn't seen the sword. Jon felt the weight of it and the tightening of its hands around his neck as the shade impaled itself on the blade. Then the pressure failed and the blade cracked, and the weight of the shade slumped against Jon, crushing his ribs. He could barely breathe.

The weight was on top of him. He couldn't push it away, and the sword's pommel was pinning him back against the gully wall.

He felt himself beginning to faint, his breath becoming shallow as his lungs couldn't expand to draw air, and all he could smell was acrid blood and the sweetness of vegetation. Darkness was coming in from the corners of his vision, and then there was a movement to his left. The noise was muffled by the shade's body pressed hard against him, and the shade's body suddenly lifted away from him.

Jon slumped down to the ground. He coughed violently and sucked air, and looked up to see the last shade in the gully with him, its club high and falling at him, the shade's head and the club silhouetted against the sky, and there was nothing at all that he could do about it.

Everything slowed down for him. Above his head a flash of silver was looping across the sky to intersect the shade's arm. The arm seemed simply to detach itself at the elbow as the sword crossed it, and as it and the club whirled away, spilling cords of blood, the sword continued its arc and sank into the shade's neck.

Blood was everywhere. The sky was a red Rorschach. In the middle of it the shade's head rolled to the side in what seemed like uncertainty to Jon, but then it just kept going. The body followed it. The sky returned suddenly to blue.

Lapis jumped down into the gully. He knew it was her.

'Are you hurt, Jon?' she said. Her voice was dull, though. She must have used such force to kill the shade, and there was nothing in her voice.

He shook his head. There still wasn't enough air to talk, and it was hard enough to breathe.

She put his arm around her neck and helped him to his feet, then began to work her way with him along the gully. Jon didn't feel connected to her at all.

The ground slowly came down to meet them, and by then Jon could breathe again, painfully. Lapis hadn't said anything else. Something was wrong.

Jon looked up as they walked back towards the reef. Lapis was gripping his wrist too hard, striding along. There was a group of Catharians standing on the shore. The bodies of the shades were piled up nearby, but the Catharians were ignoring them.

'Lazuli,' Jon said, knowing suddenly what had happened.

Lapis pulled him towards the Catharians, and they parted to let Jon see

Lazuli's body lying awkwardly on the sand at the tide's edge. Lapis knelt beside the body of her twin and took her hand, just holding it. The surf came in around Lapis's ankles and played with Lazuli's hair, arranging it and rearranging it in a perfect fan against the sand. As if undecided, Jon thought. As if it somehow mattered how her hair looked.

'Lapis,' he said, but he couldn't think of the next words. There didn't seem to be any. The sand was stained red beneath Lazuli's stomach, and the sea was coming in white and returning red, and each time the red stain beneath Lazuli was renewing itself. A fog of tiny flies was forming on the surf around Lazuli's wound, and Jon waved his hand in a useless attempt to disperse them. A few moved along the air stream of his arm to gather around his head. He tried to brush them away but they wouldn't go, spinning around his eyelashes, flicking at his nostrils and dipping into the corners of his lips.

'They killed her,' Lapis said. There was nothing at all in her voice, not even disbelief. It was as if she was just testing the words. She tried them again. 'They killed her.'

A few of the Catharians made to lift Lazuli from the water's edge, but Lapis reached out and knocked them away. The sun was disappearing beyond the reef and the reef's jittery shadow was crawling over the shore towards them.

'Let them do what they must,' Jon told Lapis softly. The flies were still around his face, flying into his mouth as he talked. They tasted like caraway pepper on his tongue. He looked around at the crowd and said, 'What happens? Will she be buried?'

A man behind Jon answered, 'There will be a pyre, Sciler. Fire will take her to the world of no weariness tonight. We shall prepare her.'

Someone else touched Lapis's shoulder and said, 'She is weary no more.' And another one did the same, said the same words to her, and then everyone was whispering to her. Lapis shrugged the first one away, but as the hands continued to touch her she began to cry.

It was dark when Jon reached the house on the hill with Lapis. Janus was sitting at the table and there was no sign of anyone else. There were candles on the table and a fat white fish in a bowl of oily broth. Its head and tail flopped over the sides of the bowl and the fish seemed to be swimming in the light from the flickering candles. Janus had a plate of bones like pale needles in front of him and he was taking flakes of fish from the bowl with his fingers, filling his mouth and then pulling out bones one by one as if he was moulding the fine translucent curls out of the white flesh with his thin, stiff lips.

'Where's everyone else?' Jon said. It was getting hard to talk. His chest was stiffening. He thought he must have cracked some ribs. He brushed again at the haze of flies that had followed him from the beach. His eyes were stinging with them now and he had to keep wiping them from his nostrils. Lapis hadn't spoken since they had finally left the shore, and dusk had been falling by then. He had glanced back once through the plague of flies to see Lazuli's body being wrapped in a blue cloth and carried along the sand towards Cathar's harbour.

Janus waved a hand at the flies and said, 'Well, what's happened to Miss Razor-tongue, then? Lost her voice along with her reflection? Doesn't want to play with the grown-ups any more?'

'Shut it, Janus,' Jon said. He sat Lapis down at the table, then sat next to her. She was like a doll, neither resisting him nor helping. Jon said, 'It looks like Calban isn't giving us time to get ready for him. What the hell have you been doing all day? And where are the others?' He stopped, wheezing painfully.

'Janus has been with me, Sciler. We've been reviewing the defences.'

Jon tried to twist round to see Footfall, but his ribs resisted the movement. His mask of flies adjusted itself. 'A boatload of shades landed beyond the reef,' he said through it. The flies moulded themselves to the shape of his breath.

'I heard. And I heard about Lazuli. She's weary no more, Lapis.'

Jon looked at Footfall in the candlelight, thinking, He uses their rituals. He's just like Lapis. This is where he exists.

Footfall came to the table and put a hand on Lapis's shoulder, saying, 'I heard she died bravely.'

'But she fucking died, didn't she?' Janus said. He took a long thin fish bone from his mouth and added, 'Whatever the fuck she was. Can't you do something about those flies, Sciler?' He moved away down the table, taking the bowl of fish with him.

Jon stared at Janus, wondering what he knew about the twins and how he knew it. Janus made a winding motion with his hand. 'Let's move on, then. Calban hasn't declared a truce.'

Jon realised Lapis was clutching his hand tightly. He tried to pull himself free, but her grip was strong. His ribs were hurting even more, and the skin of his face felt suddenly uncomfortable, as if it was setting hard. He wiped his free hand over his forehead, brushing away a soft crust of flies, and his palm came away red, flaked with the drying blood of the shade Lapis had killed. Flies crowded around his hand. Jon wiped his hand clean then rubbed hard at his face, bringing all the blood away and the rest of the flies with it.

'Lapis saved my life, Janus,' he said, watching the insects swarm over the shreds of dried blood on the ground.

'Yeah. And the question you have to be asking yourself now is why.'

Jon stood up. 'Nothing's for nothing with you, is it, Janus?'

'That's right. That's exactly right, Sciler. And I'm still here. I was here before you came, and I'll still be here when you're dead and gone.'

There was a movement beyond Janus's shoulder. Footfall caught it at the same time as Jon. He spun round and then apologised to Pibald. 'Sorry. I'm jumpy.'

'We all are,' Pibald said. 'Lapis, I'm sorry about Lazuli, but . . .'

'She's weary no more,' Janus said sarcastically. He waved his arm around, scattering the candle flames and throwing light and dark around. 'What the fuck is all this? Just because there's a body to burn this time, we're going native?'

Jon looked at Lapis, expecting her to say something, even to attack Janus, but she still just sat there. Then he thought, What did Janus mean by that? Haven't there been bodies before? Has Calban taken them all?'

Pibald said, 'Jhalouk told me the pyre's ready. If you want to come, Lapis.'

They walked to the top of the cliff, climbing further up the slope from Jhalouk's house and then continuing until another steep incline took them to a lookout at the head of a valley. The valley walls stretched away to left and right, interrupted by spurs of hillside. The lookout point was a clearing, and in the centre of the clearing was a pyre of wood. There was a latticework of branches in the heart of the pyre and through the wood Jon could make out the body of Lazuli wrapped in a white shroud.

'I want Sciler to fire the flames,' Lapis said, staring at the pyre.

'It's her right,' Jhalouk whispered to Jon. 'It's an honour for you. You must use magic, it's the custom.'

Footfall seemed about to say something, then stopped. Jon noticed him look at Lapis and then at himself. There was something between them, Jon thought. Or else there had been. Footfall had expected to be asked to ignite the pyre.

Lapis glanced at Jon, indicating for him to start. He stood and built the image in his mind of the fire burning, seeing it as if in memory, as if he was recalling what had happened already, so that it could be more real. He imagined the heat on his face, the brightness of the flames making him squint. He saw the words of the spell written in the flames, the flames spelling them out for him in their flickering, and for the first time he felt in charge of the sorcery. He felt he was its conduit instead of some kind of half-blind miner digging away at muddled ore. This time it wasn't like trying to light a tiny fire under the eye of Lile's scorn and failing. This time it was magic. It flowed from him, and even when towards the spell's conclusion the wind tore at him and ripped the syllables from his tongue, wiped the spell from his brain, he drew breath and memory together and continued to the spell's end.

The pyre blazed and spat. Jon fell back. He felt someone catch him and knew it was Lapis. She sat next to him and squeezed his hand, saying nothing. The fire bored up into the sky, smoke rising like dark hoar breath against the pale blue evening.

There was only the fire for a while, and the evening seemed to advance quickly. Beyond the funeral pyre the sky darkened until the smoke was bright against it. Lapis stood and moved away to stare down the valley. The sky above was still deep blue but at the valley's end a wedge of darkness was advancing. It was taking out the blades of hillside to the valley's flanks one by one, and thunder was bounding along the valley to drown the fire's crackle and bang.

The villagers were starting to draw back now, and the fire's clean sting of smoke was tainted by sulphur and something else, something oddly like licorice. Jon glanced at Footfall and saw him nodding at Janus. Jon was too slow to catch Janus's response. Janus and Footfall were surveying the hillside behind.

The pyre was burning fiercely and its smoke was stretched up into a cone with a swirling black tip. The sky directly above seemed brighter than ever, and behind the approaching thunder there was a wind pushing along the valley that lifted leaves from the ground around Jon and was starting to fling the trees into a frenzy.

Along the valley the darkness stepped closer, eating up the valley's spurs to left and right, swallowing what was left of the day. Clouds of small birds spun overhead and vanished towards Cathar and the sea. The villagers were beginning to head the same way, slapped on by the wind. Jhalouk dragged Jon to his feet. 'Come on,' she said. Pibald wrapped Jon's arm around his neck and started to walk him away from the pyre. Lapis stayed where she was, ignoring everything, her eyes on the pyre.

'Wait,' Jon said to Pibald and Jhalouk.

Footfall and Janus were talking together at the clearing's edge, peering at the surrounding hillside.

A strap of lightning speared down into the valley floor, leaving a weal on Jon's retina for seconds. The darkness was almost overhead now like a solid thing and there was more lightning. It was as if the sky was curdling, becoming jelly and then cracking with the brilliant gashes of lightning.

The fire had gone crazy in the wind, spinning out of control. Lapis was sitting shaking her head rhythmically, humming to herself, her mouth stretched in a lunatic smile. The thunder was growing louder now and it was in synchrony with the lightning. The storm was directly overhead, and it still hadn't started to rain. The air felt rigid, like huge boulders grinding thunderously together, with the lightning flashes as their sparks.

Jon shrugged Pibald away and turned around to scan the hillside, sniffing cordite and licorice until he saw what he knew would be there. And then he shouted to Footfall and Janus and pointed with the last of his strength. 'There he is.'

Their eyes met, Jon in the clearing and Calban up among the frenzied trees on the brow where the hillside started to dip down towards the village. As the fatigue finally overtook him, Jon saw Footfall and Janus set after Calban.

And then the rain fell.

Ms Schaefer shook the brainmap in her hand. 'This is standard stuff, Chrye. As you said, it's a snatched shot from a neurological mapping procedure. It's a composite technique, tweaked a bit, but you can see they're basically using positron emission tomography and functional magnetic resonance imaging. Old techniques, but they work.' She looked up at Chrye.

Chrye nodded. 'PET and fMRI. Yes.' She was finding it hard to focus. She kept seeing Hickey.

'But they're using infrared too. See the blurring here? They've super-imposed another reading on the display.'

Chrye hadn't noticed that.

'Which is interesting,' Ms Schaefer went on. 'Infrared is non-invasive, but less accurate. PET and fMRI are easy to set up and monitor in the CrySis pod, so maybe we're getting a further answer to the pod question . . .' She touched the paper to her lips and breathed lightly on it, setting it fluttering. 'But why use the infrared? It would seem redundant, wouldn't it?'

'It's a game they're testing,' Chrye said, feeling she was losing it. 'Why use any of them? What's the point?'

Ms Schaefer put the paper down. She said carefully, 'Good question. Very good question, Chrye. The obvious answer is that they're checking the subject's response to the software, to the game. I would think that the AIs are being used to that end, in some way. But I think there's more, and there's nothing sinister in it. It's research. There has been extensive research carried out on brain function in virtual environments, but what they're doing at Maze lies in uncharted waters.'

'How?'

'Think about it, Chrye. The cerebellum, for example, regulates subconscious activities like balance and movement. But Maze have managed to supersede those functions. The bLinkered player no longer has to move or be moved physically. Now, does that mean that their software *overrides* cerebellar activity, or is the cerebellum somehow bypassed? That would be question one.' She glanced at Chrye, checking she was still with her. 'Question two, visual stimuli – does their software feed or bypass the visual cortex? Likewise other stimuli. Question three, Jon's motor responses, his speech and actions – at what point does the software read them, and at what point does the software disable them?'

Chrye picked up the brainmap and stared at it. 'They aren't sure what's happening in there, are they?'

Ms Schaefer laughed awkwardly. She seemed to pull away from Chrye in a manner that Chrye couldn't quite define. 'Oh, I wouldn't go that far,' she said. 'They're checking their systems, that's all. There shouldn't be any risk involved.'

'No risk? How can you say that? People have been murdered.'

'You don't know that, Chrye. Even if there is a killer, nothing we have discussed indicates that anything going on at Maze is directly connected with it. Maze is building the ladder as it climbs, Chrye, and there's nothing wrong with that. These are unusual times.'

Chrye started to say, 'But last time you said . . .' then stopped. 'Maybe you're right,' she finished.

Her tutor smiled. 'I think so. Oh, and before I forget, here's the journal back again.'

Chrye slotted it into her bag. 'Who did you show it to?' she asked.

The pause was hardly there, but Chrye felt it like a chasm between herself and her tutor.

'I didn't bother, in fact. I just read it myself. The writer was clearly suffering from paranoid delusions. I think we both got a bit worked up by it last time.'

Chrye stood up. 'So what should I do about Jon Sciler?'

'I think you should simply carry on with your thesis. Keep me informed of your progress, Chrye, exactly as usual. And, of course, make me aware of anything else that arises, like . . .' she indicated the brainmap that Chrye had picked up '. . . and between us we can ensure Mr Sciler's wellbeing. Not, as I say, that there's any risk to him at all.'

NINETEEN

'What are we doing here, Jon?' Chrye asked, following him down the frozen steel escalator of Highgate tube station. At the bottom the barrel-walled platform was lit by skinny bars of neon every ten metres, the pasty light dulled by the cracked green tiling. The platform was silent and deserted.

'I want to show you something,' he told her. He opened the door of a comms booth seamed against the concave wall. The clear visthene sides were greening with age. 'Come inside.'

Even with the comms equipment long ago ripped away it was close with two of them inside, and Jon wouldn't tell her anything else except to wait and be patient. She leaned against the visthene panels and stared at the fading advertisements across the tracks, trying to ignore his tension. One for a cult book she had read years ago. *Kill Yourself First – An Existential Response to the Virtual World*. Flanking it, adverts for scented respiration filters, games, WaterPur tablets, everything you needed to cope on a guttering planet.

'Jon, I trust you, but what—?'

'Listen. They're coming.'

She could feel the visthene bowing with a rush of air from the tunnel's far end. At the same time she was aware of a squeaking, chittering noise and a ragged brown carpet started to unravel and roll towards them both from the tunnel mouth and up from the tracks beside them.

'Rats,' she said aloud, the word a menacing hiss in the tiny booth.

'They can't get in.' His voice sounded detached. She hadn't heard him quite like that for a long time. She didn't like it. She put her hand on the door handle but the rats were already at the booth and scratching at the visthene.

'Christ. Jon?'

The noise was louder and Chrye realised there was another sound as well, a rustling and flapping. The carpet of rats and mice and other long-tailed scuttling things Chrye had never seen before rolled thickly into the curved walls and washed up them to break back in high seething waves, surf-white with bared teeth and then speckled with blood as the rodents attacked each other in their panic. The walls of the booth rattled but held.

The air pressure in the station increased and the buffeted visthene wobbled, and the gaping tunnel mouth was suddenly full and alive with movement and the rustling noise. The maw of the tunnel seemed to ripple darkly and flow outwards, growing and splintering over the tracks and platform.

Chrye realised what was happening. The tunnel was choked with birds driving a piston of air and all the vermin before them.

The birds kept coming and the sound of their crying-out and the terrified screeching of the rats boomed inside the visthene walls. In the open space of the deserted station the flock of birds formed into a corkscrew, plunging down on the right and rising on the left with rats and mice and the other things in their claws and beaks. They whirled along the platform towards the booth in a dizzying spiral. Chrye felt dizzy and disorientated, as if she were falling towards the birds in a helpless spin. She lurched against Jon and slammed the palm of one hand against the pane of cold greasy visthene in panic, crazily afraid that she might simply crash through it and tumble away down the platform.

It seemed to take an instant and for ever for the vortex of birds to reach the booth. Chrye pushed herself back against the other wall. The visthene was bumping against her with the impact of the birds, and Chrye just stared as they took the rats into the air and were away. She felt Jon's arms around her and buried her head in his shoulder.

Eventually the noise began to recede and she opened her eyes to see the maelstrom of birds whirling away again down the platform and back towards the tunnel with their prey. They filtered into it and vanished. Chrye felt as if she had somehow risen again.

Jon was holding her tight. She pushed him away and looked at him, ready to be angry, and saw that his eyes were squeezed closed. He was shivering. His eyes had been closed all the time. He had seen none of it.

She shook him until his eyes opened. 'What – what was that about, Jon?'

'I haven't been back to Father Fury. This is where I come.'

'Why? What is there here for you?'

She waited but she could see that he couldn't answer her. She walked him out of the station and up the hill, searching for a quiet place. She found Highgate Wood.

Only one entrance to the wood was still open and a permanent ash warning was posted there. In the wood fallen ash was never sprayed by C&C to be bulldozed away as riftfill. Month after month it collected.

She closed the gate behind Jon. He was silent. The trees were tall and grey all around them, seeding the ground evenly with ash as the wind stroked through the branches. Ash swarmed about their feet. Chrye thought of the whirl of birds and tried to work out why Jon would go there. It made no sense. She understood Father Fury, but not this.

She gave up. 'Talk to me, Jon,' she said. 'Tell me about Cathar.'

'It's impossible.' His voice was thick with despair. 'Calban's ahead of us at every turn. I was too tired to go on and I had to exit, but I saw Calban. He wanted me to see him. And I sent Footfall after him with Janus.'

'What's wrong with that, Jon?' He was drifting away from her like the ash. She felt as far away from him now as when she'd first met him and he'd said the word Dirangesept and collapsed into himself.

'Jon. Answer me.'

He looked around as if he didn't know where he was. She felt scared for him.

'Jon, start again. Tell me what happened.'

He took a breath. 'Lapis is real,' he said. 'Lapis is Teomera Sequiera. Her twin was a Catharian—'

'A construct, Jon,' Chrye interrupted.

Jon shrugged listlessly. 'Whatever she was, Lazuli never really existed on Earth. In London, Teomera Sequiera was born the only survivor of twins, but in Cathar her twin survived too. Until yesterday. Lazuli was murdered by a group of Calban's shades. They nearly killed me as well.'

He stopped abruptly and Chrye wondered what he had been about to say. Eventually he went on. 'Just before I exited, Footfall and Janus set off after Calban and I think it was a trap. I don't trust Janus and I'm afraid for Footfall.' He kicked at the ash, raising it like smoke around his ankles. 'It was odd, but I half expected to recognise Calban. He stared at me, though. As if he knew me.'

Jon hesitated and Chrye said, 'Yes?'

'And Lapis has completely flipped. She may have been crazy all along.'

That wasn't it either, she thought. She looked across at him, but he had turned his head to peer behind them. Chrye could see about fifteen metres of monochrome trees. Her eyes ached for colour.

'There's no one else here, Jon. Who else would be here? We're crazy to be. What is it?'

'I thought . . . nothing.' He carried on walking as Chrye stopped at a tree with a small poster tacked to the trunk. An image of some animal showed faintly through the dusting of ash and Chrye ran her finger across it. She read the text, the words 'Lost Cat', in a childlike scribble. 'Please Help.' She wiped the whole page clear but there was nothing else except the picture, a colour still of a black cat streaked with silver. The cat seemed to stare at her until ash began to cloud it over again. She wiped her finger over the cat's eyes once more, wondering whether there was something familiar in them. Ahead of her Jon seemed to be merging with the ash, the Earth dissolving him away, and she had to trot to catch up with him and make him solid flesh again.

He said, 'I'm sure Lapis was sleeping with Starburn in Cathar, and I think she was at his scattering too. I think she's the killer.'

Chrye took that in. 'Teomera,' she murmured.

'She doesn't know if she's even real herself. I think she attaches herself to people to try and convince herself she is.'

Chrye thought about that, trudging through the ash. 'And when they reject her, she kills them. Or perhaps they fail to convince her she's real, or she thinks they realise she isn't real. Any of those is possible. Perhaps killing them is revenge, and perhaps it makes her real to herself for a while. That makes sense, Jon.'

They walked on through the grey trees. Clumped ash fell from the branches, plopping to the ground to leave soft-edged craters. Jon was still glancing back, staring at the ground, at their receding wake of twin furrows in the floor of ash. Chrye said, 'So how does she kill them? Starburn wasn't the first, we know that. According to Madsen there were no signs of drugs in their systems, and all the deaths were violent. How did Lapis subdue them? Didn't any of them resist? And what about the subsequent cover-ups? She can't have done that too. Not alone, anyway.'

'Janus knows something about her,' Jon said. 'I don't trust him at all, but he definitely knows something. They hate each other.'

'Perhaps he rejected her and he's still alive?'

Jon nodded slowly. 'She blames Janus for Starburn's death in the zone. And that's another thing. We don't know he actually died there. All we know is that Calban took him to the rock.'

'But he can't still be alive, can he, Jon? He's dead. *Really* dead.'

Jon said nothing for a minute and Chrye looked at him, knowing he was thinking of Lile. She said, 'Well, whether he died in Cathar or not, we don't know what happened to him there. The journal ends before that. Starburn stopped writing it just before Calban took him. And you're right, Starburn was definitely sleeping with Lapis in the zone. It's in his journal. Although there's no mention of him seeing her outside it.'

'There wouldn't be,' he said. 'Outzone contact is forbidden between players, and the journal was written for the benefit of Maze. It wasn't his own private journal at all.'

She glanced at him and he went on, 'Kerz asked me to start a journal. He even gave me a book to keep it in. It's exactly the same as Starburn's.' He shot a glance at Chrye and said, 'I have to avoid writing about you. It isn't easy.'

Chrye wondered how much to read into that. He never told her anything about his feelings. She thought there must be something in there, at least some thought for her, but she wasn't sure and she didn't want to say anything in case he withdrew from her altogether. Perhaps she was just projecting her own feelings on to him, creating a place inside his head that didn't exist. She said, 'So we can't believe everything in the journal. He was hiding stuff from Maze all through it.'

'He was hiding a relationship with Lapis from them. If she is the murderer, if she's killed others before Starburn, Maze won't necessarily have had any idea it could have been her.'

'But they would have cared about the murders, wouldn't they? They wouldn't just have ignored them, surely?'

'No . . .' He paused. 'Unless . . . unless it didn't matter to them any more. Unless the victims had already died in Cathar.'

Chrye considered that. She said, 'Perhaps we've been looking at this all wrong from the beginning.'

'How do you mean?'

She slowed down. The children's playground was on their left, the slides and swings unevenly rimed with ash. They looked complex and incomprehensible. Chrye said, 'We've been looking for a killer and we've been trying to work out what's going on at Maze, and trying to find a link between them. Well, what if there's no link? What if there are two things going on at the same time, but unconnected? What if Maze has some piece of research going on, something connected with Cathar, that they're desperate to keep the lid on, and quite separately there's a serial killer operating within the company? Now, as long as the killer keeps to their own patch and doesn't interfere with what Maze is doing, perhaps Maze is quite happy to let the killer carry on, rather than bring in the 'fists and risk compromising their research?'

The playground was behind them. Jon stopped and stirred a foot through the ash until he'd made a small clear puddle of earth. The dull brown soil looked like rich chocolate to Chrye, but ash almost instantly began to speckle it. Jon said, 'Perhaps Maze is even carrying out the cover-ups after the murders, just to keep the whole thing quiet.'

'Maybe,' Chrye said. 'And something else, Jon. If Lapis is the killer, she would have known whether Starburn died in Cathar, wouldn't she? If they were really having an affair, she would have seen him after he died there. No one else would. And if she had guessed that Maze was carrying out the cover-ups, she would have known it was safe to kill him at that point.'

The light was starting to fade, the trees beginning to seem bright against the evening sky, and the ash looking like day-old snow.

Jon said, 'And if she knew him that well, she could well have known about his hydrophobia. And there's something else I need to tell you, Chrye.' He caught his breath and looked away from her. 'It's about Lapis,' he said quickly. 'In Cathar. I slept with her.'

'Oh.' Chrye scythed her foot through the ash. That was what Jon hadn't been saying. There were hot tears in her eyes. She knelt down, feeling the muscles in her legs begin to go, and slid her fingers through the fine silt on the ground. I asked for it, she thought. I wanted to know whether he felt anything for me and I've had my answer. He's slept with a murderer in a world that may not exist. And she kills the men she sleeps with, and what I feel is jealousy. What sense does that make? What hope could there be?

She wanted to be angry, but there was only despair. She wiped her tears away to see Jon crouched calmly on the ground a few metres away, sifting his fingers carefully through the ash.

'What are you doing?' she yelled at him. She could feel her voice breaking as the anger came out. 'What the hell do you think you're doing?'

'We've come in a circle.' He pointed at the start of their trail and then began to cast about the trees around them. Chrye could see nothing but a few faint lines scored in the smooth ash where the wind had blown brittle leaves around. Jon said, 'I thought I might have been followed. I've been feeling as if someone's following me.'

Chrye ran at him, kicking furiously at the ash, watching it fill the air around them. She stood in the centre of it all and screamed, 'That's what this is all about, isn't it, Jon? It's all about you. It's always been all about you. About *your* guilt, about . . .'

Jon came to her through the cloud of ash and held her until all the breath was gone from her. 'I slept with her in Cathar. All I could think of was you,' he said.

'Hickey Sill wants to hurt you more than you know, Jon,' Chrye said carefully, passing him the mug of coffee. She remembered the first time they had passed it between them, when all the possibilities had seemed good. It seemed like years had passed since then. She felt years older, as damaged as the world. 'He wants to do it through me. He came to my room and tried to rape me.' She added quickly, seeing Jon's face start to crumple, 'Nothing happened, he was high on moonbeam. I got rid of him. But he'll be back.' A silent shudder went through her. 'We have to do something, Jon.'

Jon said, 'You're sure nothing happened? You're okay?' When she nodded he said, 'He was following me too for a while, but then he stopped. I wondered why.' He rested his hand tentatively on Chrye's and she thought, That's as close as you can get to saying you care about me. Each time you come near, you pull away again.

It felt good, though, his uncertain touch.

'It won't be any use making a complaint to the 'fists about Hickey,' she said. 'I checked that out with Madsen. Hickey's one of their stars. I guess he solves more crime than he's responsible for. Though that's either a fine balance or else they don't realise the extent of Hickey's nightlife. And you can't do anything to hurt him directly, Jon. Like you told me, that's exactly what he wants.'

'So where does that leave us?'

Chrye said, 'Hickey has to be in control. When I got rid of him last time he'd lost it. I've got a psychological advantage over him for the moment, and I have to follow it up before that's gone. I've thought about this, Jon. I'm going to arrange to see him. That's the last thing he'll be expecting. It'll throw him right off. And I'll make sure I'm as prepared as possible.'

She wondered if that sounded as crazy to Jon as it did to her. She took the remains of the lukewarm coffee from him and drained it, tasting the bitter grit of the lees on her tongue. She had another flashback to Hickey lying heavily on top of her, his drugged eyes staring and the grimy black stubble of his chin in sharp focus, and she didn't feel like she had any advantage at all.

'That's a plan, is it?' Jon said. He stood up to put more coffee on, the sheet falling from his shoulder as he crossed the room. The tracery of Father Fury's whip marks was hardly visible now, but the deep white stigmata across his shoulders were still a reminder to Chrye of his past. Even when they had been in bed together, half an hour ago, she had been suddenly aware of her fingers unconsciously exploring the scar. At least there were no new scars, no physical ones anyway. He'd been telling the truth about Father Fury. But what did the birds mean to him? She closed her eyes and imagined the rest of his body against her again, but the memory of Hickey wouldn't go.

'I saw my tutor, Jon,' she said when he put the fresh mug in front of her. She waited for him to sit down. She could just see the tip of the scar on the backward curve of his shoulder, the raised white weal like a finger inching up his back.

'Maze has got to her. But I think it goes further back than that. I think it goes back a long time. She denied showing Starburn's journal to anyone.'

'So?'

'The day I gave her the book we had a long talk. Ms Schaefer doesn't like the games industry at all. And she also mentioned that all the games companies employ psychologists. Well, of course they do, Jon. They employ whole university departments. They finance a team at Middlesex University. I *knew* that. I just wasn't thinking. But I made some checks afterwards. Maze finances her post, Jon.' She sat back in the chair, still not believing it. 'I've been feeding her all my research on you, and it's been going straight back to Maze. Whatever you don't tell Dr Locke, she gets from me instead.'

'Oh. God.' Jon closed his eyes and groaned.

'Yes. I imagine Ms Schaefer accepted releasing my stuff about you to Maze until she read Starburn's journal, but she would have seen the journal as a bomb rolled under them. It would have changed everything for her. She would have gone straight to them as soon as she'd finished it. She must have been furious. But whatever they did to her or told her turned her right around.' Chrye looked at Jon and added, 'They must have some influence to do that.'

'Where do we go from here, then?'

'Well, we still don't know any more about the murders, but we're further on than we were yesterday with whatever Maze is doing. I've been thinking – Cathedral's the key. That's what really excited them, nothing else. Not Lile, even. We have to find out about Cathedral.' She toyed with the mug. 'I never got to ask Ms Schaefer about that. So Maze doesn't know we know anything about it. And another thing, Jon. You remember PI?'

'Yes.'

'Before she was warned off, Ms Schaefer gave me a few ideas. Of course she never got to follow them up, but I did. I cross-referenced the names of psychologists who worked on the Dirangesept project with those who ever worked with games companies.'

'And?'

'And I came up with one name. Anton Stuber. Guess which company he worked for?' She reached out and took Jon's hand. 'Are we still getting nowhere? Now, Anton Stuber is a dying man. He's had cancer of the colon for the last five years, and he spends one week in two having treatment while his body's in CrySis. Today's day five of his treatment cycle, so we've got two days to wait. Then maybe we can find out about PI.'

'Good.' Jon squeezed her hand. Chrye liked the clear look on his face. She felt that for the first time they were ahead of the game. She felt that Jon was with her.

'There's something else we can do in the meantime,' he said. 'Kerz may not know who killed Starburn, but he knows what happened to Starburn on Calban's island.'

'Yes. And?'

'You remember when he called from his home to tell me about the bus station gamezone? I saw a cabinet behind him, just like Dr Locke's. I think he's got the record of Starburn's last visits to Cathar at his home.'

211

'And you're just going to go round there and ask Kerz if you can borrow them, are you?'

'Well, it's about as good a plan as yours for a night out with Hickey Sill.'

TWENTY

Jon opened his eyes in Jhalouk's house, shivering with cold. The sheets were dank and sticky under him. Without thinking he reached out for Chrye, and when she wasn't there he thought for a moment he'd only dreamed about her in Cathar.

The bedroom was in shade. It must be noon already. Whoever had brought him back here and put him to bed had draped his clothes over the back of a chair facing the embers of the fire in the corner. Where they weren't damp from the thunderstorm they were scorched, and a stench of fire and mould clung to them. He pulled them on anyway. The clammy leather boots were like the flesh of something cold and dead against his skin and they flapped on his feet and left glistening black prints on the stone floor. Jon felt clothed in death as he walked into the open air.

On the verandah Janus was sitting alone at the table, and Pibald was leaning on the wall looking out over the sea, his shoulders slumped.

'Where's Footfall?' Jon said.

Janus lifted his head. 'Well, look who's woken up at last. You took your fucking time, Sciler. We thought perhaps you'd decided not to come back. We could all have been dead waiting for you. Game down.'

'Don't give me that game shit. Where is he?'

Janus let his voice trail away, murmuring, 'Am I my brother's . . .?'

Jon turned around at the weight of a hand on his arm. Pibald said, 'We couldn't find him, Sciler. Calban might have taken him, but we don't know.'

Jon looked back at Janus. 'What happened?'

Janus shrugged lightly. 'Nothing happened. Nothing at all. We tried to go after him but it was impossible in that rain. The ground turned to mud and we were sliding all over the place. We saw Calban heading down through the fields towards the bay west of the village and then we lost him. Footfall was with me at first, but we got separated. I figured it wasn't such a great idea being alone if I did find Calban, so I came back. I guessed Footfall would do the same thing.'

Jhalouk came out of the house, chewing something, her cheeks bulging. Seeing Pibald, she swallowed quickly and reddened. She said, 'Pibald?' in a quiet voice, swaying slightly and reaching out towards him. 'I didn't know you were back. I was worried about you.' Jon saw flecks of crimson glinting on her tongue and at the corners of her lips.

Pibald frowned at her. 'Jhalouk, I thought you'd stopped taking that stuff.'

Her head drooped. She picked at the hem of her shirt. 'I'm sorry. I just needed it. When you didn't come back . . .'

Pibald went over and embraced her, saying quietly, 'I don't want you taking it any more, Jhalouk. Not now.' He brought her to the table and sat down heavily, rubbing his eyes.

'Tell me what happened, Pibald,' Jon said.

'After Janus came back alone, a few of us went out at first light to check the hillside. It must have rained all night, most of the crop was washed away. There was no way we could make out anything like a trail. No sign anywhere of Footfall or Calban. We went down to the water and checked along the shoreline. There was nothing until we got to the inlet where Lile lives.'

Jon felt his heart thudding. 'And?'

'Lile's boat wasn't there, and nor was Lile.'

'Maybe he's out fishing,' Jhalouk said.

'I don't think so. His turtle's swimming around the jetty.'

'What about Lapis? Where's she?' Jon said.

Janus snorted. 'After you fucked off so conveniently, Calban's thunder-storm snuffed out your little bonfire and it seems wondergirl took it as a sign. She's still up there with what's left of her twin. No one knows if she's even exited Cathar.' He stood up and said, 'Everything's turned shit-coloured right now. Not that wondergirl's any loss to us.'

Jon said, 'She saved my life, Janus, and you know it. I don't know if this place is real or not, but Lapis thinks it is, and she thinks she's lost a big part of herself. Maybe she's right, maybe not, but that's what she thinks, and we owe her something.'

Janus had already turned his back on Jon and was walking down the steps. As Jon began furiously to follow him, Pibald said, 'No, Sciler. Leave him.'

'No. Not this time. He can't keep walking away.'

He caught up with Janus halfway down the steep path beyond the trees and spun him round, silhouetting him against the pale blue sky and holding him by the shoulders.

'Janus, I don't know what the fuck you're doing, but if I find out that you let Footfall die like you let Starburn, then I swear . . .'

Janus was stronger than Jon expected, shaking him off and sending him sprawling into a thick bush at the path's edge.

'Who the fuck do you think you are?' Janus hissed. 'I'm not answerable to you or to anyone else here. This isn't a goddamn army and I'm not a fucking soldier in any private war of yours. I'm not here in Cathar for you, and I'll tell you something else that may come as a surprise. No one else is either. Lapis had her software hacked from here to fuck at birth, you may have noticed, and I didn't tell Footfall or Starburn to go and be heroes. And you think Pibald's a team player, do you? Well, he'll help out where he can, but he isn't going to be a martyr for you any more than I am. He's more like me than you think, Sciler. He's finally got Jhalouk pregnant. In about eight months we'll know if it's possible to have kids here. Pibald's going to want to be around for that, so don't expect him to throw himself on to Calban's sword for you.'

Jon stood up slowly, brushing dirt and leaves from his clothes. A dizzy mist of red butterflies spun up and away from the bush. There was a scent of lemon in the air from the groves behind them. 'Janus, is it real? Is all of this real?'

Janus laughed. 'You're a fool, Sciler. I knew you were a fool the first time I saw you. It doesn't *matter* if it's real, don't you realise that?' He gestured back up the hillside. 'Listen to me. You know what Jhalouk was chewing? It's called mesra. It's a sort of tranquilliser and it's addictive. Not everything in Cathar is perfect. There are other drugs too. There's something called takka. Takka boosts your strength, it's supposed to speed your reactions. Rumour is, that's what Calban's shades are on, along with whatever else he does to them. Takka's readily available and it isn't addictive. No immediate side-effects. Now, I was one of the first wakers out of Maze, Sciler, and since I've been here none of us has taken takka or any of the other drugs available. Why do you think that is?'

'You tell me.'

'Takka kills you. But it only starts to kill you after six years or so of use. You get that long with no symptoms at all. Now do you see?'

Jon nodded slowly. 'If Cathar's a game, it's so real you want to stay here. You don't want to die early. It's deep enough to spend your whole life playing it.'

'No. Fuck it, Sciler, you still don't get it, do you? Cathar might be real, and that's enough. It *might* be real.'

Jon stared across the water towards Calban's rock, wondering whether Footfall was there now. Maybe they were both lying dead or injured somewhere near Lile's bay. Maybe Calban was dead. Jon doubted that, though.

'Why are you telling me this? You mentioned Maze. We aren't supposed to talk about outworld life here.'

'Listen, Sciler, some time soon everyone on Earth's going to know about Cathar, and when that happens there aren't going to be any more rules. They're going to have to get used to it here, this talk about Earth.'

'You're talking as though Cathar *is* real.' Jon felt lost again.

Janus raised his eyes and said, 'Look, Sciler, get this into your head – I don't give a fuck if it's real. All I know is, it's better than the alternative. And I know what the alternative is, I live half my life in it. So I just want to *be* here in Cathar. It doesn't matter to me who wins this little war either. Calban? Sure, he'll do. I'd rather be Calban's slave in Cathar than rot and die in Notting Hill. Do you understand me? I just want to be here to see it happen.' He showed his teeth in a grin. 'And, anyway, if Cathar's going to be invaded by a world of wakers then maybe someone like Calban isn't such a bad thing, keep the numbers down. Oh, yes, things are going to change here. Calban may turn out to be Cathar's first freedom fighter.'

'But what if you die here? You can just come back, can't you? Start again in another body?'

'Oh, no. Didn't anybody tell you? Death's death, Sciler. No one ever comes back.'

Jon said, 'So why do you stay with the rest of us if you don't give a damn about anyone except yourself?'

'Because Calban might end up killing me along with everyone else. So if we can beat him, I'll help. But like I just said, I'm not going to be anyone's martyr. You've got some idea of Calban now. Calban's something else. He's the next level. Starburn was good, maybe you are too, but if you want the truth, Sciler, my bet's on Calban. That's not to say I'd rather he wins, he's a sadistic bastard. Right now I'm on your side, but if Calban starts to turn you over, I'm not going to die for you. Now, are we clear?' Janus shook his head at Jon and disappeared down the path, leaving Jon to stare out at the perfect blue sky.

There was no sign of Lile in the clearing. The door of his hut was ajar and inside was a mess. Lile's axe wasn't leaning against the door. And there was a lingering smell of magic.

Jon headed down through the trees to the stream, making towards his sleep-pit. It was all he could think of. Pibald would have checked everywhere else. When he got there he saw a blunt-ended club handle protruding at an angle from the camouflaged shelter. Jon waited awhile in the shade of a tall tree and listened, sniffing the air. There was nothing, so he went out and wrenched the club free. It resisted, then came loose suddenly, ripping the shelter apart in a welter of branches and leaves. Jon realised that it wasn't a club at all. It was Lile's axe.

That made no sense. Lile couldn't have known the shelter was here. No one should have known it. Jon ran the palm of his hand down the flat blade, seeing rust faintly starting to brown the metal. The axe must have been wet before the blade was smashed into the shelter, so it had to have happened last night during the thunderstorm. Even if Lile had tried to kill Jon, he wouldn't have left his axe behind. Which meant it wasn't Lile who did this, which in turn confirmed that Lile was in trouble.

Calban had done this, Jon thought. Calban had lured Footfall here, and he had done something to Lile too. Jon hurled the axe into the trees and listened to it crack and crash through the foliage. It was all a message for him. He waited until his breathing was even and walked along the rain-swollen stream towards the sea. Whether Calban was a player or a waker, whether Cathar was real or not, someone at Maze who had access to Jon's tapes was feeding him with information. Cathar was fixed.

The jetty still moved under his feet, and the sea was as blue as ever. The rock was out there squatting on the water like everything bad in the world made solid. In either world. Jon sat down cross-legged to wait, knowing that this was Cathar and something would happen.

After a few minutes he noticed what looked like a stain on the water a few metres away. He stood up as the stain drifted closer to the jetty and became a dark shadow that knuckled up half out of the water. Lile's turtle surfaced in front of Jon like something not quite of any of the elements, of land, sea or air, and raised a big-eyed, high-domed leathery head. It seemed to register Jon as other than Lile and subsided quickly again, resuming its steady circling of the jetty's end.

After a while the turtle dived beneath the water's surface and paddled away. Jon hooded his eyes and finally made out a vessel bobbing in the far distance. As he watched, it began to move purposefully towards the jetty. Jon guessed the turtle had hitched itself into the harness. Calban must have used magic to direct the boat, not bothering to cut the turtle's rig.

Jon stood up, trying to see if there was anyone still in the vessel as it approached the jetty. It wasn't until the boat was a few metres away that he made out Lile slumped against the mast. There was no sign of Footfall. Jon jumped down into the boat to throw the rope around the stanchion, then he hauled Lile's dead weight on to the jetty. Lile was cold, pale and barely conscious. Jon propped him up against the stanchion and waited until the light returned to his eyes. It was hardly there at all. Lile had only a faint pulse. He was dying. There was nothing to be done for him.

'Where's Footfall?' Jon said gently. 'Did you see him?'

Lile shook his head and murmured something. Jon bent his head and heard Lile breathe, 'Too late.'

'What happened?' Jon whispered.

Lile's lips moved a fraction, but no more words formed. Jon reached out to Lile's chest, realising that the medallion was gone. 'Who took the coin?' Jon asked him. So many questions, he thought helplessly. It's always too late.

Lile's eyes clouded. Jon could almost see the life going from him. The jetty seemed to be moving more, the creaking becoming more exaggerated and insistent. 'Lile,' Jon said. 'Tell me.'

The air far away over the sea was punctuated by a speck of movement, a bird carving across the sky. Lile tried to turn his head and he raised his arm as if to try and point somewhere behind him, at the island maybe. Then he sighed once, long and slow, and with the sigh his eyelids slid gently shut and all the wrinkles of his face seemed to smooth themselves away. Jon felt tears come into his eyes and he squeezed them closed. 'Lile,' he murmured. The sea moved quietly against the jetty and the sun was warm. It didn't seem right.

Sciler.

Jon heard it soft as a whisper. He leaned forward again to Lile, but Lile's lips were closed. Lile was dead. Beneath the jetty the turtle was growing agitated, bumping against the wooden pilings and stirring the water up.

Listen.

The same voice. It was in his head.

Remember when we played Death-Heart that time in Essler's arcade down in Wood Green? Remember how we played up through the levels for two straight days and nights while the kids kept us going with soyrolls and vitajuice? Never seen the game before and we never lost a life?

Over a hundred and seventy levels, Jon thought. I remember. But we didn't . . .

Ever finish it. No.

That laugh. Jon could almost see his face, the cheeks blowing out and the watery green eyes, small and shining. Starburn. His wide, broken-toothed smile, the break of excitement in his voice.

Every other game in the place closed down as we sucked out the power. Not that anyone was interested in them. And remember Essler finally ripping out our plug and the kids going crazy and smashing the place up? Remember that, Jon?

'I remember.' Jon stared at Lile's dead body. The voice couldn't be coming from Lile. The turtle was thrashing about now, pushing hard against the pilings. Jon felt unsteady. He looked up and saw the bird straight ahead, high but diving down in a swift parabola. It was coming fast, claws stretched out so that its head was the point of a tight triangle whose base was formed by the curved blades of its talons.

The voice was still in his head as the eagle came down towards Lile's skull. Jon could make out the bird's eyes, brilliant yellow with black diamonds, as he shoved Lile's body aside. He looked round suddenly, not knowing quite why, and saw some kind of animal streaking away down the jetty and leaping on to the sand. Then he turned back, diving for the water as the bird was at him. A claw tore across the top of his shoulder, the powerful rip lifting and twisting him round in the air. He caught a glimpse just before the water hit him of the huge bird skimming along the length of the walkway, less than a metre from the boards, its wings overhanging the jetty at either side.

Then he was in the sea, below the surface and rising again, breaking into the air. He coughed water. His shoulder was stinging and there was blood welling out from the wound. He felt disorientated and the salt in his eyes blinded him. He wiped his eyes with the backs of his hands, but the blood in the water let him see only a mist of red. After a moment he was aware of his good shoulder nudging a floating piling that must have been knocked free by the turtle. He was still out his depth and he stretched his hand out blindly to grab the piling, then realised it was the turtle's broad back that he was clutching. He held on and the turtle's front flipper swept him effortlessly up on to the curve of its shell. It was warm and felt like leather beneath him. The turtle moved steadily through the water for a minute or two, then lurched sideways and Jon slid down on to the sand.

He cleared his eyes. The turtle was in the water again and drifting away as Jon looked into the trees, putting a hand to his throbbing shoulder. He glanced at the jetty which was moving more than ever with the swell, and saw the turtle driving itself steadily into the pilings at the jetty's end. Boards were splintering and falling into the sea. Lile's body was still lying there, but the turtle continued to demolish the jetty until in a cascade of cracked wood the body slipped into the water. The turtle dived under it and came up with Lile sprawled on its back. Jon hadn't quite appreciated how big the turtle was. Neither Lile's hand nor his feet reached the shell's rim. He seemed at rest there. The turtle seemed to shrug Lile's body once to centre it, then headed slowly out to sea with him, waves breaking over the prow of the shell. Jon watched until the turtle was almost out of sight, then just as he was about to turn away he saw the animal dip to slide Lile's body gently into the water and raise a flipper high as if in a slow forlorn farewell, then drop the flipper over Lile to clasp him beneath its ventral shell. The turtle raised its blunt head once and then dived down and vanished completely with its burden. Jon waited for a while and waited, then walked away.

There was still blood in his eyes as he made for the clearing, thinking of Starburn and Lile, and there was salt too. The bird was still high in the sky, sweeping effortlessly along the coast, apparently as uninterested in him as it was in the turtle. Remember, Jon thought. Remember. He saw the bird flashing down the jetty and the other animal fleeing before it and there was red in his mind, but he couldn't tell if the red was in the animal's fur, the bird's feathers or just the blood in his eyes.

'I thought I'd debrief you myself this time,' Kerz said. 'Dr Locke seems to think you've lost confidence in her.'

'Not just in her, Kerz. I don't know whether Cathar's real or not, and I don't want you telling me it's just a game any more. Frankly I don't care.

Janus is right, it doesn't matter a damn. I don't know where you get your information about me and that doesn't matter either. But if I'm going to be in Cathar for you I want to know I've got a straight run at it.'

Kerz inclined his head. 'I don't think you quite understand the situation, Mr Sciler. You're getting very involved in the game, which is, of course, our intention. But you're not playing it. This isn't for your pleasure, Mr Sciler, and it never was. You're testing it for us. You're a rat in a maze, if you like, and it's the maze we're testing.' His forehead creased in a frown and he said, 'Maybe this isn't a good analogy. We're not trying to see how quickly you can get out of the maze. We want to see how lost you can get.'

'And how crazy you can make the rat,' Jon said as calmly as he could. 'Lapis wasn't exactly a good subject, was she?'

'I said it wasn't a good analogy,' Kerz said smoothly. 'Lapis was unfortunate. And as for your straight run, well, there are no straight runs in a maze. I take it you mean your little sleeping shelter being discovered. I'm not going to apologise to you, Mr Sciler. Cathar is what we make it. Your contract requires you to encounter whatever there is to be encountered – nothing more, nothing less.'

His voice softened slightly. 'I think, having said that, that we will shortly be in a position to fill you in on some of the background, but until then you'll have to bear with us. You have to get just a little further. Now, today's excursion was clearly tiring for you, so I think we can probably limit the debriefing to a review of the scene on the jetty. Most of it we got, but when Lile died we had a bit of interference, a power surge or something. You were speaking – something about remembering, I think – but we couldn't hear either you or what was said in response.' Kerz waited.

'It was nothing,' Jon said. 'I was just remembering Mr Lile. The real one. Lile died, the Lile in Cathar, and I was remembering the real Mr Lile. But, of course, you already know all about him, don't you? You put him there.'

Kerz hesitated. Jon could see he wanted to push it, but there was nowhere he could take it right now without letting out a lot more than he was ready to. Jon grinned at him, thinking, You don't know what was said to me, Kerz, do you? I bet you don't even know who said it. You just know I responded to something and you want to know what that was. You don't know as much about Cathar as you make out.

'Then that's all,' Kerz said, standing up and forcing his own grin.

Jon closed the door behind him. The question was, who *had* he been talking to about Death-Heart?

TWENTY-ONE

Piccadilly Circus had been the hub of the tech market for the last few weeks. Jon rode down there on the fat-wheeled half-kilogram midnight blue metabike he'd bought with the first salary payment from Maze, unhinging it and slinging it over his shoulder at cracks the chunky tyres couldn't straddle. At Leicester Square he packed it down into the backsack and pushed his way through the tents and sleeping bags of the market's hangers-on and into the hard, glittering core of the market.

The tech market was never long in one place and the tech market had never been quaked. Its stall holders had too much to lose and usually also the tech to let them move on in time, so its groupies lived in an aura of security. Most of them had already lost everything to the Earth. All they had left was what they could carry on their backs and a deep and urgent need to be able to close their eyes and sleep in safety.

Jon hadn't told Chrye where he was going, and he felt bad about it. It was the keeping of secrets. He got himself lost in the gaudy labyrinth of stalls and tarpaulin screens before asking a masked achondroplast where he could get security hardware, and followed the dwarf's directions to a teepee of mirrors squatting in the shade of Eros. It took him three circuits of the teepee before he found the entrance flap. He guessed he'd been scanned and judged safe by then.

The woman inside avoided eye contact with him, playing with the silver braiding in her jet-black hair, her eyes darting everywhere but at Jon. He browsed for a minute among the cabinets of wireware, catching her staring at his reflection in shards of mirror chrome scattered over the shelves. After a while he bought a palm stop from her, not bothering to haggle with her, and then he asked her where he might take it to have it set.

She put the palm stop on the counter in front of him. It shimmered there like a bronze mango stone. 'Try Ghillie,' she said. 'South of Sundown. He's okay.'

'What about Blind Jacob?' Jon asked casually. 'He still work the market?'

Her face was suddenly blank. She flicked the palm stop with a long thumbnail and set it spinning. Light flew around the tent. 'No. Jacob moved on.'

Jon covered the palm stop with his hand. 'Pity. I'd have liked to put a bit of work his way.'

'You used to know the blind man?' She glanced away and he looked sharply at the tiny mirror she was bouncing off, propped delicately on a shelf amongst a pyramid of trigger springs. He caught her glance there and she held the eye contact briefly. He looked straight back at her and this time she met his eye directly.

'Jacob and I, we worked together once,' Jon said. 'Far away.'

The woman's eyes narrowed and left him again. 'Blind Jacob. You knew him when he could see?'

Jon rolled a thumb over the palm stop's curves. He said, 'I knew Blind Jacob before he got stars in his eyes.'

'Too bad.' She shrugged. 'If Ghillie's no good, try the Greek quarter. Ask for Bez's microbazaar. You can get the stop set there.'

Bez's microbazaar looked like it had closed down years ago following a thorough looting. The streetcom hung from its housing by a single grimy wire, its black plastic sheath eaten away, and the door didn't give when Jon pushed it. The windows were boarded over and the boarding was rotten. He bent to the swinging speech grille and pressed the announce button, not knowing if it would work. 'Jacob? It's Jon Sciler. Remember me? We went Far together.'

There was no response, but the door opened when he pushed it again. He slid inside and let the door swing back behind him. The click of its closing was solid and sure.

The room was pitch black and it took Jon a few moments to get his bearings. He could hardly hear the air filter, but the air was as good as the air at Maze. A wall to his left faded darkly into view, and then off to the right a table and chair. And he began to make out the shadow of a figure seated behind the table. He groped his way hesitantly forward, his eyes starting to draw details as his pupils flared.

He was almost at the table when the room lights snapped on with a momentary magnesium flash that made him swear aloud and screw his eyes closed. He stood dizzily before opening his eyes a crack in the renewed darkness. The figure behind the table was a silhouette against the glare of his flash-blindness. He stumbled to the table and cautiously let his eyes open fully again as he sat opposite the figure.

The silhouette was beginning to harden and his retinas were eliminating the flare spots when the light hammered into his eyes again.

'Enough, Jacob,' Jon said, reeling back in the chair. 'I'll keep my eyes closed, if that's what you want.'

There was a silence, then the familiar growling voice. That hadn't changed. 'No, I'm done checking now. Monika wasn't too sure about you. She thought you could have been a 'fist. So where's this palm stop you paid her too much for?'

Jon opened his eyes slowly.

Blind Jacob sat facing him, his head tilted slightly, the ball of his index finger comfortably lodged well within the upper rim of his sunken left eye socket. The eye was open, its white the colour of mouldy cheese. The right orbit was covered by a glittering scarlet bug-eye. That was where Jacob kept the bio-ware that gave him what passed for sight. On Dirangesept his autoid had been speared through its visual receptors, and Jacob in his shipboard cell had screamed and screamed and ripped the bLinkers straight out of his eyes, blinding himself. So Jacob's stigmata were considered by the compensation board to have been partly self-inflicted. They'd paid for the right eye but left him to live with the other, and now he spent his time in vicarious vengeance, a silicon-fixer making small devices for breaking big laws. Even if he'd wanted to, he couldn't have got a legitimate job anywhere worthwhile without a retinal display for security clearance.

Jon slid the palm stop over the desk. Jacob let it lie there beneath the blank gaze of the scarlet bug-eye, moving his head over it in slow rhythm. Jon wondered how he saw the smooth shape, whether somehow he was looking right into it. There was a story that someone had once asked Blind Jacob what exactly he could see and Jacob had answered softly, 'I can see the future, and the future, my friend, is best seen only by the blind.' Now he muttered a few syllables to himself and scratched his finger around in the socket of his left eye, probing ruminatively at the soft, lifeless eyeball. Jon looked away, wondering whether Blind Jacob was able to enjoy his reaction.

Eventually Jacob picked up the palm stop and snapped it open. He held it up close to the bug-eye and then reached under the table and brought out a handful of tiny yellowing scab-packs. He ran his thumb over their braille codings, selected one and popped the packaging with his thumbnail, tipping the bright chip carefully into the palm of his hand.

As Jacob worked, Jon watched the iris swerve aimlessly across his eyeball, its nucleus a smudge of brilliance far brighter than the sour white. For an instant the dead eye fixed on Jon, snatching up the room's neon glow and holding it there, gleaming like a dying bulb, misty and faint as a remote constellation. Jon stared at the useless orbit and thought, A distant galaxy in a blind man's eye. Jacob clenches it there, Dirangesept, the cause of his blindness, as we all cling tight to the moment of our doom.

'It's done,' Jacob said. He clicked the palm stop shut and held it out towards Jon. 'Okay. It's a bit unusual now. But don't try to open it, it'll burn out. Can't recharge it either.'

'What do you mean, unusual?' Jon asked. A palm stop was a personal defence device, a sophisticated synaptic disrupter. Held loosely in the hand, it was as dead as rock. But when you folded your fist hard around it and squeezed, a cluster of metal-edged plastic vanes eased their way out between your fingers and initiated an electromagnetic field. Used passively it would deflect metal. Used actively a glancing blow would knock out an attacker for several minutes.

'Well?' Jon said. 'How unusual?'

'Just don't use it till you mean it.' Jacob grinned. 'Now, you didn't come to see Blind Jacob for a knuckle-duster, Jon.'

Jon pocketed the palm stop. 'No. I've got a list. I want to do some breaking and entering, and I think the place will be razored.'

'Can't get yourself a proper job, huh?'

'I've got a job. I'm at Maze, game-testing.'

Blind Jacob's face clouded. 'Uh-huh. Uh-huh. Be careful there, Jon. That has to be one sweet game they're playing at Maze. People walk inside there, they don't seem to want to come out again. Kill themselves sooner. I know two vets, same thing. Some large coincidence.'

Jon took that in. He said, 'Was Starburn one of them?'

Jacob stretched his lips thin. 'Now I know three.' He snapped off the smile. 'Breaking and entering sounds a whole lot safer to me. Okay. Stay right there.'

Blind Jacob stood up and went through to the rear of the shop, coming back a few moments later with a wire basket that he set on the table. 'Okay,' he said. 'Christmas is early this year.'

He brought out a grey sliver of plastic and held it in his hand. 'Take a look at this. Isn't it beautiful?'

Jon glanced at Blind Jacob, wondering what Jacob could see there that was so beautiful.

'Now,' Jacob said, 'there's breaking and there's entering. Breaking's easy as shit. Any zipwit with a hammer can break.' He tilted his head. 'I take it you haven't come here for a hammer.'

Jon shook his head. 'No.'

'Good. Before we go on, I take it we're not looking at voice or flesh print recognition devices?'

'I don't know.'

Jacob rocked in his chair. 'Assume not. Very few left any more, too easy to shit on.' He made a face. 'I never liked them, no challenge. Like hanging your keys on the end of your nose – all you needed was a mike and a camera and you were inside. Even do you a retinal copy from ten metres, cameras you got now.' He chuckled to himself at that, rubbing his eye hard, then flipped the plastic into the air and caught it again. 'Okay, now this is a real slinkythink piece of silicon. This is an eel. It's your access key, just slips in smooth as thought. When it's rejected it alters and re-presents itself. Of course, you can't spend all day doing that – the reader screams rape if more than one false application is made within twenty-four hours. But they always allow one error because there's always one dumb shit.'

He grinned and settled himself back in the chair. 'And it's the dumb shits who make life so very very sweet. Okay, this particular eel resets the reader's timeclock, puts it a nanosecond back. The timeclock's a weak link in the fence, see? Zipwits spend a fortune on the fence and nix on the timer. So you try the eel again and get it wrong and the first error has become the second. But the machine's already accepted it and so it assumes the alarm's already been sounded, so it doesn't bother to set it off again. Dumbshit machine. That's phase one.'

Blind Jacob tapped the eel on the table. 'Okay, phase two. Now, this eel's a smart little critter,' he said. He turned it over fondly in his hand, crooning, 'One sweet piece of slimeware. It measures the rejection time of each attempt and compares it with the previous rejection. The slower the rejection – and we're talking fracs of nanos – the closer it is to penetration. Of course, each try throws the clock out a bit more. Time you're in, it'll be off by, well, a ten-to-the-three of a second at most. Next system check they'll be suspicious. You'll get away with it on the one-error rule, but you can't repeat it. You've got one shot.'

He put the eel down and reached for the basket. 'Okay, you're through the gate and into the park. Now, there are two things you need to think about. What spots you and what stops you.' He tipped the basket out over the table, picking and discarding as he talked. 'I can give you e-mag monitors, ir and uv eyes, beam screens, the whole damn jump. And they'll be as much use to you as heat sensors in hell. You'll be standing in the eye of a storm of information and you won't even know if it's safe to blink.'

He brushed almost everything aside and picked out a single item, a fat fist-sized convex hub on a long nodular stalk, turning it over a few times and then setting it back down on the table. The device looked like a fibreglass and carbon toadstool. 'But I know someone, lucky for you,' Jacob said. 'Guy's a specialist. This is batOwl. This'll filter it all for you, interpret and inform. It'll tell you what you need to deal with, what you can ignore. It'll point out bumps in the rugs, tripwires, walls and falls, locate them all.'

He held it out to Jon. 'Okay, you're running all over the park now. I guess you'll want to play on the rides?'

'Just one,' Jon said. 'It may be a problem, though. I think it has a copy-protected display. Can I get around that?'

Blind Jacob started to transfer the unwanted stuff back into the basket, saying, 'Get around anything, Jon. But it'll take time. And maybe you'll leave spoor. These things matter?' He chuckled darkly. 'They matter, don't they? Jon, I don't know and I don't want to know exactly where you're going, but I hear you telling me there's more between you and the chest of gold than moats and burning oil. This copy-protection isn't just a "Please Keep Out" sign, is it?' He put the basket on the floor beside his chair. 'Look, break it down. One, the screen's been fixed, that's a hardware thing. You'd need to disconnect it, patch in your own screen. Two, the copy function will have been disabled. You'd have to reprogram.'

The blind man sat back. 'Even with batOwl and the eel you'll be spotted, and there's no way you're going to have more than three and a half minutes before the 'fists get there hard and sharp. Break it down, Jon. Even if you know where the machine is, it'll take you half a minute to reach it. Screen patch, reprogram, take *me* two minutes. Then you got to copy, how long for that? Then detach and restore, *no* way. And even *if*, you think they're going to let you dance out of the magic castle with your copy? I don't think so. My advice, forget it. Can't be done.'

He weighed batOwl and eel in his hands. 'Okay. You still want these, Jon, or have we just been playing make-believe?'

'Getting used to the chair, then,' Chrye said.

Kei grinned. 'Better than legs.' He swung it through a circle. 'And look.' The chair rose unsteadily until it was almost a metre clear of the ground. 'Drains the power, though,' he added.

Chrye walked around the chair, passing her hand underneath it. The chair destabilised slightly and corrected itself. Kei dropped it back down.

'So how's it going?' he said.

'That depends who's asking.'

'What do you mean?'

She pointed at the chair. 'Vets gave you that, did they? What makes you so special, Kei? There are vets who are paralysed, paraplegic, who get a card and a can of soup at Christmas, and you get a float chair. Why?'

'It was a special award,' Kei said defensively, swinging the chair away from her and heading for the ramp. 'I don't know what it is with you tonight, but I'm going to bed, Chrye. We'll talk tomorrow.'

He was at the corner of the room where the ramp began to rise. The chandelier was oscillating gently, agitated by the wash of the float chair, troubling the walls with light and dark.

Chrye went after him. 'Tell me about Jon Sciler, Kei. Tell me about Maze. Tell me the truth.'

She overtook him and stood on the ramp blocking his way. The chair stalled on the slope in front of her, slipping and kicking, jerking Kei's body until he was forced to back down to the lower level. He sat there, harried by shadows.

'I don't know what you're talking about,' he said.

'I never made the connection before. You never even mentioned to me that you knew Jon until I started my thesis. Then my tutor suggested the subject and told me she could get the funding for it, and suddenly you came to me and said you knew Jon Sciler. But you'd never mentioned him before that. Why was that?'

'He didn't like talking about it, Dirangesept or the poems. He was my friend, I respected that.'

'But then suddenly you changed your mind. That's what I don't understand, Kei. You asked him to talk to me about my thesis. And that was sure to be harder for him than any of the other stuff.' She waited but he didn't answer her. 'So why did you do that?'

'I thought it might do him some good. I'm tired, Chrye. Let me go to bed.'

'Maze approached you, didn't they? They said they'd appreciate it if when you next saw him you'd ask him to cooperate with me.'

He slammed his fist down on the arm of the chair. 'All right, yes. What was wrong with that? You wanted it too, didn't you? But you shouldn't have got involved with him, Chrye. I *told* you. You know about Far Warriors, don't you? You should know enough to keep away.' He covered his face with his hands. Light from the chandelier scratched at them until he took them away again. He said, his voice dull, 'I knew this would happen.'

She sighed. 'Didn't you wonder how Maze knew he'd listen to you? You know Jon, Kei. You must have known it wasn't likely. Didn't you even wonder why they were so sure he'd come to you in the first place? Didn't it bother you?'

'They said he'd want to talk to me about games. They said he'd agree to see you, sooner or later. I just didn't think you'd get involved.'

She shook her head. Maze had known it. They'd set her up with the thesis, and they'd made sure Jon had Starburn's journal. Maze hadn't known she knew anything about Jon beforehand, but they'd done everything possible to set them up together.

Kei shifted himself in the chair. 'They told me I'd never sell anything by Maze again if I didn't help them. What was I going to do? Jon can look after himself, Chrye. No one forced him into anything. And so they gave me this chair – what's wrong with that? I didn't do any harm, did I? Nothing's wrong?'

'No, Kei,' she said. 'You didn't do anything wrong. Tell me one thing, though. Does Maze know you sent MaryAnn to me? I need to know whether I can believe anything she told me.'

Kei said, 'You can believe her. MaryAnn's my engineer after school, nothing to do with Maze. I think she part-times for Id/Entity too. Though I haven't seen her for a while.' He frowned. 'Not since I sent her over to you, Chrye.'

The sky was the colour of old rust. A microflite sliced low across it and banked hard towards Marble Arch, the muffled flare of its jets drawn out into a keening whine. For a moment the twin vapour trails were pure white threads, but almost immediately they began to stain and unravel. In the distance the microflite started to climb on the drifting reins of its trails and Jon lost interest. If he was being followed it wasn't by microflite.

In Covent Garden most of the shops were boarded up. At the shuttered-down Underground station someone had sprayed ARE YOU HERE? over the route map. Jon walked on, seeing no one at all until a movement in a doorway caught his eye, an open hand thrust up and out at him.

He peered and saw it was a man in there, or else a woman. There was no way of telling. The head was bound round with grimy cloth in place of a respirator. He could make out the eyes through a slit in the cloth and there was no life in them. There was hopelessness in the half-open hand too, the callouses and the deep lines etched in grime. Jon pulled an ecu from his pocket and placed the coin in the hand. The fist closed and drew back and became part of the shapeless mound again. The figure might have just been a pile of windblown trash in the doorway now. Jon hunched into his jacket. There had always been homeless in London, he knew that, but he seemed to remember that before Dirangesept they had been visible. They had always lived desperate lives on the streets with their hopelessness and hunger, the rags of their clothes. Now their environment had changed to blend in with them. They were the future.

It took nearly an hour to find her, but Mira's booth was still there, sandwiched between the stalls of astrologers and tarot readers. The door had a veneer of real wood through which the metal was beginning to gleam. There were no filters. Mira relied on an ancient airlock disguised as an antechamber. It worked as a step down-century before the seeker entered her sanctum.

Jon peeled off his respirator and opened the inner door. The instant stench of shit veiled by aerosol sweetness made him gag. Around the room Mira's supplicants sat clutching their bottles of urine and their cartons of excrement. They were thin and pale, or else they sat with thin and pale children. Many held scented rags to their faces. They all, at his entrance, stared at Jon.

He was the only outsider. After a few minutes the small far door opened and a man stumbled out coughing, clutching a shard of green crystal and a small dark bottle that rattled as his body jerked. Jon shifted in his chair and caught Mira's eye. She said, 'Would the outsider enter now? I sense the slipping of his time. You who grant him this will be rewarded.'

He slipped past her and she closed the door behind him. Her room was odourless except for the clean scent of candles and Jon took a deep breath, letting the air out in a long sigh. At her gesture he sat cross-legged, facing her over a low hexagonal oak table carved with runes and zodiacal signs. In the table's centre an iron crucible squatted on a tripod like a fat black spider.

Mira smiled at him. 'Jon Sciler.' She said his name as though she could taste the words in her mouth and liked the taste of them.

'How are you, Mira? Still reading the future from shit, then.'

She rebuked him gently. 'The future has always been for us to read in the past, Jon. They don't come to me to tell them the colour of their true love's eyes, or to put a hex on a rival. They're beyond that. They show me yesterday's shit and I tell them how they'll die tomorrow.'

She ran a finger over the table and cleared her throat, erasing the edge of bitterness in her voice. 'I have a reputation now, so perhaps they come a bit earlier. Or maybe it's just the attraction of my own affliction. The crippled wise-woman.'

She reached beneath the table. 'I have a PathSlab now. Look.'

The oak shimmered away and the table was bronze glass. Beneath the crucible a web of pipettes and tubes ran down to the floor and away. She brought up her hand and the illusion returned.

'It's a great diagnostic tool. And sometimes they'll let me take their blood too, as long as it's with this.' She showed him a dagger rough with rust. Only because he was watching for it, he noticed the slight tremor of her hand. 'Twice as expensive as surgical steel to have it look like this,' she said, 'but if I showed them a syringe I'd never see them again.'

'You're doing well, then.' He bit that off, overtaken by her expansiveness, but she nodded.

'I'm in semi-remission. I don't know how long for, and they won't let me practise legally, of course, but who's to practise on these days? I probably see more patients here than any medic at Health. And it's not only pathology. I treat who I can, on the side, and Health turns a blind eye. All this equipment was given to me by the friends I still have there. I don't make any money. Even if these people trusted the medics, they don't have the plastic to pay for treatment.'

She stopped herself and forced a wry smile. 'I'm sorry, Jon. I haven't anyone to moan to, that's all it is. What can I do for you, then? No entrails for me to divine?'

'No. Well, I don't think so. You said the future's always in the past. It's the past I'm interested in. Dirangesept.'

Mira leaned back and sighed. 'You're right. That is the past. Dirangesept stinks of shit more than anything out there.' She gestured towards the waiting room.

'I know that, Mira. But I have to ask you something. About the first colony.'

'You know I can't tell you much,' she said. 'I was never down there. I was a shipboard medic.'

The fingers of her left hand were beginning to twitch. He wondered how far down the track she was with the stonevirus. He hadn't even been sure she'd still be alive. The disease came and went capriciously. Last time he'd seen her she'd been bedridden.

'Are you in touch with anyone else?'

She shook her head. 'No.'

'I remember you once telling me about someone on the project with you. He was a game-player, supposed to be a genius. They say it was because of him that a few of the ground-based colonists did survive.'

'You mean Daedalus.'

Jon leaned forward. 'Yes, that's him, Mira. Tell me about Daedalus.'

'Daedalus was the nearest thing we had to a hero. But Dirangesept was nothing more than a game to him. Plasm-bombing the forest, all that death meant nothing to him. He killed more colonists than he saved, and maybe he even killed a few beasts. I knew it was unavoidable, but he never showed any relief, any remorse, any feeling at all. It was an equation. Maybe that's the nature of heroism. Utter certainty. I found it frightening.'

'Do you know if he's still alive, Mira? His name's on the original crew list, but I can't trace him. And there's no record of his death. The roster just records him as Daedalus. No first name. And he's not in any of the directories.'

'Daedalus was his only name, as far as I know. He never used anything else. If he had any other name, no one ever knew it. That was part of his arrogance. Why are you interested in him, Jon?'

He ran a finger along the lines of a pentagram on the table, then cupped the crucible in his hands. It was blood-warm. 'I'm interested in games,

233

Mira. A friend of mine was murdered, and he was working for Maze when he died. I need some help, and I'm running dry on ideas. I thought that if I could locate Daedalus . . .'

'Forget it, Jon. Daedalus vanished as soon as we got back to Earth. Before you even arrived on Dirangesept. He didn't want to be dead news. I guess he preferred to be dead. He probably is now. And better that way, Jon.'

Jon saw he'd get no further with her. He was sure she was telling him all she knew. She didn't know anything.

'Are you still treating that guy with the weird memory?' he asked her. 'What's his name?'

Mira relaxed visibly. 'Irfan Culchic. Yes, I am.'

Irfan Culchic was an idiot-savant with an odd gift. He had a perfect video memory. You could point him at anything, then hook him up and play it back like it was on tape. It wasn't much good to Irfan, who had an IQ of fifty-eight and who loved only sweet things and the colour orange, and it wasn't much good to anyone else, since cameras were smaller and a lot easier to handle. But Jon had always liked Irfan, and Irfan for some reason had instantly taken to Jon.

'Does he still live in the shelter, Mira? Maybe I could drop by and see him.'

Mira's hand was trembling like an idling motor. She tried to cover it with the other, but the fluttering wouldn't be controlled. 'He'd like that,' she said. 'They don't treat him so well there any more. There was a change of management. He asks after you. Do you believe that? He doesn't remember me, and I see him every week, but he asks after you.'

Jon grinned. 'There's no justice.'

Mira's forearm jerked, cracking her hand against the table's edge. 'No, there isn't.' She winced, then smiled weakly. 'At least I can still feel it,' she said.

Jon felt awkward. Mira appeared old and fading. He'd never known her like this before, even when the illness had been worse. She was making herself seem strong for him.

'One last thing about Daedalus,' Jon said, getting up. 'Was he ever down on Dirangesept, bLinkered?'

'Yes. Just once. He didn't like it at all.'

'Why? Do you know what happened?'

Mira rubbed her arm wearily. 'His autoid malfunctioned. He had a partial system failure. He was trapped down there with fully operative sensory functions but no motor function at all. His communications were working normally but the voicelink went out with the motor failure, so he couldn't transmit. His shipboard failsafes went out with the voicelink. It was some design fault, I think. No one knew anything was wrong. It was like narcolepsy, as if he was paralysed but still totally conscious. No one guessed he had a problem for twelve hours. With the voicelink gone he couldn't even exit.'

'Was that it?'

'No. He was deep in the jungle at the time, flat on his back. Something got into a couple of his major joints, his pelvis just by the groin and his neck. You know how fast everything grows on Dirangesept, well, this creature, whatever it was – it wasn't one of the beasts, I know that because Daedalus saw them as some kind of ape – this creature laid its eggs in the joints. After a short while they hatched out and started to eat their way through some of the wiring and into his circuits. I think he had a lot of pain. A lot of it. He didn't care too much for Dirangesept after that. He never bLinked again. Everything he did after that was by remote. I think he would have been happy to destroy everything down there and start all over. Perhaps that's what he was trying to do at the end. I'd never really thought about it until now.'

She seemed to draw into herself for a moment, troubled by the memory. 'Is that any good to you, Jon?'

'Maybe. Who knows?' He reached over and kissed her cheek. 'I have to go, Mira. It was good to see you. I won't leave it so long next time.' Without intending to, he glanced at her hand. The palsy was almost at her elbow.

She caught his unvoiced thought. 'I'm as sick as the Earth, Jon. Maybe I've got two years, maybe the Earth's got less. There isn't any hope. Forget your friend. Forget Dirangesept. It's less than yesterday's shit. All that matters now is pain.'

Staring at her distorted image through the security lens, Jon didn't immediately recognise Lapis battering at the door with her fists. He could hear her crying out, 'Let me in, Jon. I know you're there. You have to let me in.'

He was late leaving for Maze already. There was no point trying to wait her out, and he had to talk to her some time, so it might as well be now.

And he was probably safe from her at the moment unless Calban had taken him in his absence.

When she was inside he sat her down and waited for her to stop crying. Her eyes were red and puffy. She was wearing a short red skirt and a shirt open to show the curves of her breasts. He thought of her body moving beneath his on the reef, then thought of Chrye and held that in his mind. He said, 'How did you know where I lived?'

She wiped her nose with her sleeve. 'Starburn used to talk about you. And I followed you after the scattering.'

'Have you been following me since then?'

She looked at him curiously, then let out a small laugh that made him uncomfortable. She said, 'I'm thirsty, Jon. I forgot to wear my respirator. My throat hurts. Won't you give me a drink?'

He quickly sluiced tap water into a glass and turned around, uneasy with his back to her. She was staring at him but she hadn't moved. 'What happened to Starburn, Lapis?' he asked her, putting the glass in front of her. The water was cloudy and faintly brown. She swirled it round once and gulped it down, the drink leaving her lips stained with rust.

'After he was taken by Calban, I went to see him. He wouldn't tell me what had happened on the island. You know we're not allowed to talk about it, but I thought . . .' She played with the empty glass, rolling it over in her hands. 'He said he wasn't safe, he was being followed all the time. He just pushed me out of his room and locked the door behind me.'

She put the glass down and looked hard at Jon. 'He didn't care about me at all. Do you believe that, Jon? He didn't understand. He didn't know how terrible it is to be alone.' Her voice rose sharply and she began to scratch a fingernail on the table. Without thought Jon put his hand over hers to stop her, and realised immediately that he'd done the wrong thing. She clutched at his hand, pulling it towards her and staring desperately at him.

'You understand, Jon, don't you? In Cathar at least I had Lazuli. Now there's only you, Jon.' Her eyes were wide, crazy and perfect, perfect blue.

Jon tried to pull away but her fingers pinched at his. He said, 'Did Starburn say anything to you about Calban?'

She looked at him blankly. 'What do you mean?'

'Did he tell you what Calban looked like?'

There was no reaction at all and he reluctantly let it go for the moment. He was thinking that perhaps it hadn't been Calban at all up there on the hillside above Lazuli's funeral pyre. It could have been just one of his shades bolstered with magic, a misdirection and a lure for Janus and Footfall.

Or just for Footfall. It struck Jon that until Janus first woke in Cathar, Calban had been just a legend to scare the children. Perhaps Calban had died there a long time ago. Perhaps Janus was trying to carve out a kingdom.

'Calban didn't look or act anything like Janus, did he?'

She started instinctively to laugh but then her face froze abruptly, the expression only half-formed. 'No,' she said, then once more, more quietly, 'No.' Everything seemed to drain from her face at the same time. The muscles slackened and even her eyes went dull and pale. Jon wished he hadn't said anything. She was silent for a long moment and Jon wondered what was going through her mind.

'Tell me about Starburn, Teomera,' he said at last, trying to re-engage her.

She blinked hard and was with him again. 'My name is Lapis,' she said. 'That's who I am.' Her head jerked up as a thought struck her. 'Maybe you can bring her back, Jon? You can do magic, can't you? Footfall thinks you're the most powerful of all of us.'

'Lazuli is dead. And your name is not Lapis. Your name is Teomera. Now, I want you to tell me about Starburn. It's important.'

'I don't know any more. Something awful happened when Calban took him away and it changed him, Jon.' She was crying again. 'And then he killed himself, he killed himself just to show me he didn't care about me. I didn't matter. I was nothing.'

She pushed her chair away and stood up suddenly, throwing herself towards Jon. He got to his feet as she reached him and she was immediately pushing against him, backing him towards the bed. Her voice was thick and breaking. 'Am I real, Jon? Show me I'm real. Show me I matter. You showed me once, Jon. Show me again. Please, Jon.'

He managed to hold her off. 'You're real, but your name isn't Lapis. Your name is Teomera Sequiera. You don't need me.'

She swept her arms away suddenly, as if it had been Jon attacking her, then raised a hand and pointed at him. 'You'll die, Jon. You'll die like Starburn and you'll never go back to Cathar.'

Jon eased a pace back. 'Did you kill Starburn?'

She laughed again. 'They're following you, Jon, aren't they?'

'Are they following you?'

She opened the door and stood there. 'Oh, I haven't been chosen. They don't care about me. They don't care if I exist. Maybe I don't exist, or they would be following me, Jo . . .'

She was insane. Jon took a sharp step towards her and slammed the door shut, falling against it in relief. Her fists thudded on the door, the door thumping against his back. Jon waited until eventually she gave up. He listened to her sobbing for a while longer, and then at last there was silence. Jon pushed himself upright, but he was still within earshot when she whispered, 'You can watch out for them, Jon, but you'll never see them.' She was breathing loudly, the air eating at her lungs as she added, 'You do need me, Jon. You'll see. I'll be waiting for you in Cathar.'

He went to the window and watched her weaving down the street. As soon as she was out of sight he left for Maze. He wondered suddenly about Footfall. All the others had been killed after Calban had taken them to his island, and now Footfall had vanished in Cathar.

TWENTY-TWO

Jon woke up in Lile's bed. That was how he thought of it now, just waking up. There had to be time. Footfall wasn't dead yet, and as long as he wasn't dead in Cathar he ought to be safe from Lapis in the real world. And while Footfall was still alive on the rock, even if Calban was getting ready to kill him, Calban's attention had to be on Footfall. Which meant that there was time.

The villagers were starting to clear the shore road of all the mud and slurry that the rain had washed down from the hillside, brushing it laboriously to the side of the track with brooms and spades. It would take them weeks. What remained of the hillside was just brown mud and clay. Even the trees had been swept down the slopes. The devastation reminded him for the first time in Cathar of the Earth, of hopeless attempts to uncover order from accelerating chaos, and the thought of Earth brought him an image of Chrye. He looked up at the blue sky, blinking away water, and began to run. He had been here for at least half an hour already. Lapis would be in Cathar and awake by now.

There was someone Jon didn't recognise at the table, a woman who stood up as Jon's boots chimed on the stones of the verandah. For an instant Jon thought it was Lapis, but the woman was built too stockily and moved without Lapis's grace. Jon knew immediately that she was a Far Warrior.

'She's just awoken,' Jhalouk said, her hand on the woman's shoulder. 'Her name's . . .'

'Herta,' the woman said, staring at Jon. She was Jhalouk's height but her body was taut with muscle and tension and there were deep lines of worry fanning out from the corners of her eyes. Her hair was wild and brown. She was pressing her palms on the table as if it might disappear at any moment. Which was probably exactly what Herta's brain was telling her right now.

Janus chuckled. 'Lapis wasn't too happy.'

'What do you mean by that?' Jon said. But, looking at Janus, he knew. Lapis had lost her twin, and Footfall had been taken by Calban, and Jon had rejected her too, so Lapis would be needing a new crutch for her problems.

It nagged at him that Herta was a Far Warrior, and he wondered for a moment why that seemed so important. Then he saw it. Lapis only went for Far Warriors. That was why she and Janus despised each other – Janus hadn't rejected her, or she would have killed him. He must have been rejected by Lapis. That explained Janus's hatred of her. But Lapis liked men so the arrival of a female Far Warrior left her more alone now than ever.

Something more struck him. Footfall had been here when Jon arrived, and Starburn had just gone. Then Jon had come and Footfall was about to die. Now someone new had arrived. Cathar was a death line, and Jon had to be next.

Jhalouk and Pibald were pointing Calban's rock out to Herta. Jon looked at them all, working it out. The others, Janus, Pibald – although Lapis didn't quite fit the mould – were not Far Warriors and they were allowed to survive. Calban didn't care about them. Jon slipped from the verandah and headed round the back of the house.

'What are you doing?' Lapis said.

Jon hadn't heard her coming through the trees and he realised that the sound of the wind in the trees had been muted for a while now. He kept his voice as neutral as possible. 'How did you find me?'

'I can't do magic, but sometimes I can smell it. You've been casting spells here.' She sniffed. 'Strong magic.' She came up behind him and put her arms around his waist, kissing him on the nape of his neck before he could pull away. He could feel the slowness of his reactions and knew it was the magic doing that, just as it had been the magic dulling his senses enough that he hadn't heard Lapis approach. It was as if the computer wasn't powerful enough to do both, that it was pulling power from elsewhere, shutting down other functions.

He unbuckled her hands with difficulty and stepped away from her.

She looked at her feet, then up at him again. 'Why are you doing it out

240

here?' she said in a hurt little voice. 'I almost didn't find you. You should have told me. I was worried about you.'

He said, 'Lapis, I told you yesterday . . .' But he saw she had no idea what he was talking about. What happened on Earth no longer existed for her. He changed tack. 'I can't be distracted right now, Lapis. Calban has Footfall and I need to be strong enough to fight him. I need to know what magic I can do and I need to know how much it weakens me to use it. If I hadn't used so much power lighting Lazuli's pyre, maybe Footfall . . .'

'Lazuli knows that,' Lapis said.

Jon couldn't read the look in her eyes. She stepped towards him again. 'She's dead, Jon. I've been thinking about it. She died to save you. And, as you say, Footfall was taken by Calban. You owe me a debt, Jon.'

'I owe you nothing, Lapis. If I owe anything to anyone, I owe it to Lazuli. And what she did was selfless. You know her as well as you know yourself, and she would have expected nothing in return. Let her be generous in death, Lapis. Leave it.'

'You took my sister from me. You owe me half a life.' She sat down against a tree and folded her arms, her face set hard, staring at him with that unreadable look.

It was pointless, he realised. He turned away and tried to clear his mind of her, focussing on the hillside across the valley where a cart was winding along a white chalk track between the blades of two hills, leaving a floury trail. He pulled pictograms together and began to mutter the spell, letting his gaze drift over the pockets of trees scattered among fields, the fields ploughed in lines like the deep grain of the land exposed.

Preparing the magic like this, he felt like as though he was making its background somehow more real, as though he was cementing Cathar more firmly together. He felt as if the place existed more certainly for being in his memory in all of its detail. It was as if he were creating as much as experiencing it. He examined the fields, the combed appearance of long, dark, even furrows separating rows of yellow crops, other fields more roughly blocked out, their dark earth speckled with bright lilac flower heads. Jon let the spell surge forward in his head, all the time observing the farmhouses, hedges, streams and neat orchards of inland Cathar. The haze he wanted was rising slowly from the valley floor as the wind came at him, filling his mouth and blowing the pictograms together in his head, and he noticed that the leaves all around him were

241

undisturbed by it. He finished the spell and watched the heavy haze settle over the land.

It was improving all the time now. Exercise and practice seemed to make the whole process easier and smoother. Maybe he wasn't ready for Calban yet, but he was getting there. He could carry through a major spell now without losing it halfway or collapsing afterwards.

'Did you do that?'

John turned round and saw Herta beside him looking out over the valley. The haze was already lifting. Her hair was tidy now, cut short and swept behind her ears, and she kept touching her earlobe. She was a little more relaxed, but only that.

'Yes,' he said. 'It won't stay there, conditions aren't right for haze. The environment corrects itself pretty quickly. Magic's just there and gone. Change only stays done if it's totally compatible with the environment.' He could see Herta thinking about that, the fact that he'd said the environment instead of the program.

Jon glanced above her, saying, 'Watch.' Up here the trees had almost completely recovered from the rainstorm, their leaves washed and dried in the warm breezes of Cathar. He focussed his eyes and said words to crack a high twisted branch, and watched it tumble down with its single leaf like a slow pennant of defeat.

Herta said, 'You just broke it. Gravity brought it down. The environment.'

She was waiting but Jon said nothing else, thinking, Don't ask me if it's real.

Lapis stepped around the tree and stood with her hands on her hips. Jon hadn't even realised she was still there. She picked up the branch and glared at Herta and then at Jon. 'It's not the environment you need to worry about. Why don't you tell her that, Jon?' She jabbed a finger at Herta. 'Don't waste your time with him. He's marked. And you'll be next.' She snapped the branch in her hands, then walked away until Jon lost her in the trees.

It was still dark. The sun would be rising in an hour, but now it was cold and dark and the rain was coming down like it was on tracks. Jon looked at Footfall. Maze was a black silhouette behind them, ringed by the blossoming security cordon and framed by the glimmering rain. Far away there was a faint truncated screech like a tyre skidding on wet road and a brief pale flare through the rain like a light bulb shattered. A scattering on Primrose Hill, Jon realised, the end of someone's life marked by that forlorn stab at the shifting belly of the night. The flare seemed to hang in the lenses of Footfall's mask and the rocket's shrill scream echoed in Jon's ears.

'Okay,' Jon said. 'You don't have to say anything. Nothing at all.' This time he was sure Footfall was different outside Cathar. Last time he'd confronted him, Footfall might just have been taken by surprise and panicked, or else he was frightened by the secrecy rules of Maze, but this behaviour was something else again. Now Footfall didn't seem to care.

'We're going to go back to where you live and we're going to talk,' Jon said. 'I'll follow you all day if I have to, but you're going to talk to me.'

He hadn't expected Footfall to accept it this quickly. Footfall just shrugged listlessly and walked away, letting Jon catch up.

He walked Jon to the ruins of the Barbican and began to climb up through the rubble. Jon followed him, wondering where the hell Footfall lived in this wreckage. Huddles of people in concrete and tarpaulin shelters ignored Footfall as he passed but shrank away from Jon, and small animals slid like oil into the crevices between slabs of concrete. Footfall slipped once, dislodging a rock with his boot, and a brief crackle of scree uncovered the red metal phi of a London Underground sign. Footfall eventually slowed down at a skewed door that had somehow remained unblemished in a listing flat slab of wall and keyed the door open. He held it for Jon to follow, then closed and bolted it behind them. There was a border of orange visgel around the steel doorframe, and the door was a perfect fit. Jon heard a faint hiss as it closed. An airseal in this wreck of a place, he thought. Insane. Then he turned around to see the place where Footfall lived.

He didn't believe it. The place had slipped about twenty degrees from the horizontal, but it was still just about intact. The walls were cracked and Footfall had plugged the cracks with visgel, and the windows were taped over with layers of visthene. The visthene had discoloured and distorted until the rubble and sky outside looked like they'd been scrawled there by a kid. There were face masks everywhere and boxes of spare filters, and about a dozen rusty red oxygen tanks rolled and stacked against the bottom corner of the room. Footfall had tried to level off the tables and everything else he could with timber and saw, but the place must keep shifting all the time.

Footfall walked over the sagging floor to a huge old airfilter unit screwed against the wall in the room's top corner and activated it. The unit shuddered once and the grille began to shake, and then with no warning a deafening noise slammed across the room into Jon's ears.

Footfall waited patiently for a few minutes until the filter stopped. Then he peeled off his mask and muttered, 'It's all right now.' He took a bucket of visgel from a cupboard and went to the wall, checking for fresh cracks and feeling along the visgel wadding, adding to it. The filter burst on and off every couple of minutes, pounding the air. Jon waited a while for Footfall to finish checking the walls before realising that it would never end. Footfall would never finish repairing the walls. He would go over them until it was time to go back to Maze, to Cathar.

Unless he was never going back.

The filter came on and went off. Jon said into the brittle silence, 'What happened to you, Footfall? Did Calban take you? Tell me, I want to help you. Where are you in Cathar?'

He wasn't even sure Footfall knew where he was in this world. Jon walked awkwardly over to the filter while it was quiet and read the manufacturer's plate. FILTRATION SUITABLE FOR VOLUMES 150000–250000 CUBIC METRES. It was an industrial filter and Footfall had it set to maximum output.

Footfall was smoothing visgel rhythmically into the walls. 'Cathar's real, Jon. You know it is, don't you? I had my chance there and I failed. You can't go back there once you're dead. It isn't a game. I know that. Don't think it's a game. You can't go back. Calban doesn't want us there.'

Jon retreated from the filter and said, 'Okay, let's forget about what happened to you. What happened to Starburn when he was taken to Calban's rock? Did he tell you?'

Footfall shook his head, appearing for a moment to gather his wits. He stood up and began to wander around the room, picking a small bronze medal from its hook on the wall and staring at it as though he'd never seen it before. After a second he sighed as if he couldn't even read the words engraved there. The gleaming star looked familiar to Jon, and he realised that it was Footfall's Dirangesept Service Medal. Jon didn't know where his own was, but he recalled the weaselly script in raised italics. *None shall know thy Valour.* The medals were worth less than the core value of the metal. It must have meant something once to Footfall, though, to have hung it there. Although he kept it burnished out of mere habit now.

244

'I don't know what happened to Starburn,' Footfall muttered, replacing the medal on the wall where it hung straight and looked crooked. The filter roared into life again and Jon watched Footfall's lips move until the unit closed down again. ' . . . left Maze once he was killed in Cathar. I never saw him again. Maybe Lapis saw him, she was in love with him. I heard a rumour that he's dead. She's crazy, Sciler. I slept with her. That was a mistake.' Footfall jerked his head around and sweat sprayed from his forehead. He picked up the nearest respirator and held it tight against his face, then let it drop for a moment. Jon could see a pressure line curling fine and white over his cheeks and cutting across the bridge of his nose. Footfall brought the mask up again and inhaled hard.

'Look, we can't talk. I'm being followed. They've been following me ever since I started going to Cathar. Listen to me. The world's dying, Sciler. Cathar's the only hope. It didn't end with Dirangesept. Kerz knows. Maybe we can start again in Cathar, but it's too late for me.' His eyes were wild, dancing around like if they tried hard enough they could jump out of his skull. The airfilter came on and off again in the room, pounding in Jon's head until he wanted to dive out through the visthene window into the child's scrawl of a world outside. 'Calban,' Footfall said suddenly, his voice trembling. 'You have to kill Calban. He's insane. Don't let him take you to the rock. And the bird, Sciler, watch out for the bird.'

'What happened to you, Footfall? What happened on the rock? Has he killed you?'

'He . . .' Footfall shook his head and brought up the respirator again. He was breathing faster and veins were standing out on his forehead.

'Just nod. You're on the rock, aren't you? But has he killed you yet?'

The unit came on as Footfall shook his head. Jon wiped a film of sweat from his forehead, wondering whether Footfall had slept with Lapis in Cathar or on Earth, or both. The over-cleaned air smelt of acid-scoured metal. He could even taste it on his tongue. The resumed silence was like a vacuum.

'Footfall,' Jon said, 'this is important. You've seen Calban now. Do you think Janus could be Calban too?'

Footfall was just muttering urgently to himself.

'Okay, listen to me,' Jon said, giving it up. 'I've got a friend who does psych. I want you to talk to her. I don't want you to go back to Cathar.'

'I have to.' Footfall's face was set, and Jon knew there was no point arguing it.

'Okay,' Jon said, giving up on that. 'Okay. I think you're safe unless he kills you there.'

Footfall nodded, his face still set hard.

'If that happens they'll debrief you at Maze, and then I want you to come straight back here and stay here. I want you to lock the door behind you and I don't want you to let anybody in. Anybody at all. Just like in a 'fist vid, except you're not going to be stupid and let the bad guys in. Do you understand me? I think they did something to you in Cathar. Or maybe Maze did something to you while you were bLinkered, so you can't talk about it. But you're not well.'

Footfall seemed to calm down. 'They did something to me, yes. Kerz told me.' He brought the respirator up to his face again, holding it there. His chest rose and fell. 'But they're here already. It's no use locking the door.'

Feeling suddenly nervous, Jon said, 'Kerz did something to you? Tell me.' But Footfall was back at the wall.

'Footfall, tell me.'

Footfall muttered, facing the wall so that Jon could barely hear him, 'Kerz didn't do anything, Sciler. *They* did. He *told* me. They're still here. He's trying . . .' The unit went on again and Jon swore. When it cut off Footfall was at the wall again, creaming visgel into it, pretending he couldn't hear Jon.

Jon went through into the toilet. It stank of shit and mould. The walls were cobwebbed with visgel and beaded with condensation. There was no window and Footfall had sealed up the ventilation grille like everything else. Jon came out leaving the door ajar so that the airfilter could sweep it. The tiny kitchen stank too, but it was as empty as the bathroom. The only other door was completely covered by a steel plate bolted to the wall, the whole thing sealed up with visgel. Jon came back into the main room and said, 'What's behind that door, Footfall?'

'Nothing,' Footfall said, then chuckled. 'The world. The rest of the place fell off a month ago. I didn't need it anyway. It makes things a lot easier.'

'Well, there's no one here, Footfall. You've got this place sealed up like an egg. Your only window's sitting twenty metres over concrete scree and the only other way in apart from the front door is through the airfilter. And no one's going to crawl through that. So no one's going to get in unless you let them in. And you're not going to do that, are you?'

Footfall shook his head and went back to the walls with his bucket of visgel.

Jon turned around in the doorway and said, 'You don't have to go back to Maze, Footfall. Why go back if you know he's going to kill you?'

Footfall had his mask up to his face, waving Jon away. That crazy look was in his eyes again. He said through the mask, as the door was closing, 'It isn't over. Cathar's going to save us, Sciler. Cathar's going to save us all.'

Jon waited while the warden worked his keys in the door. He said, 'There was another warden here last time I came. They called him Smoke. What happened to him?'

'Got sacked. Bringing stuff in for the zoms, getting them excited. They were making too much noise.' The warden stretched to unlock the top lock, breathing hard with the effort. His too-small jacket rode up over his too-tight trousers, giving Jon a sight of rolls of pale fat around his waist.

'And since when were the rooms kept locked? And no one out in the garden. Why's that?'

The warden bent to the final lock, set down by the floor. 'Same thing. They get over-excited and that screws up staffing levels.' He straightened, wheezing, and pushed the door open.

'Irfan,' Jon said.

Irfan must have smelt it. He was standing there, his eyes bright with anticipation. 'Orange,' Irfan said reverently.

'You want me to stay with you?' said the warden. He raised his hand and swung the hank of keys vigorously in Irfan's face. Irfan flinched and put his hands up to muffle his ears.

'When was Irfan ever violent?' Jon said to the warden.

'Always a first time. Knock on the door when you're done.'

Jon waited until the door was closed, then he brought the orange out of his pocket and gave it to Irfan. It had cost Jon almost a week's credit, but it was worth it for the look on Irfan's face. Irfan held the orange in his hand and stared at it as if he could read the future there, then put it up to his nose and breathed it in long and slow.

'Orange,' he repeated in awe.

'That's right. And who am I?' Jon asked him.

Irfan's face crunched up in thought. 'My friend Jon. I saw you yesterday.'

Jon smiled. Irfan's yesterday was as likely to have been ten minutes ago as ten years. Yesterday was the past. Yesterday was before Irfan last looked away. Everything else was today. There was no tomorrow in Irfan's life. It seemed a good philosophy to Jon.

'Irfan, you remember we used to go out walking, we used to play cameras?'

Irfan slowly pushed his fingers into the orange until the pith gave and the pulp began to swell out around his knuckles. His eyes closed with joy. 'Yesterday,' he murmured dreamily. 'I remember.'

They'd gone out together and when they'd returned Jon had bLinkered Irfan and been able to replay everything on to a monitor. Every time the walks were the same for Irfan, sequences of lingering glances from one orange object to another. Street lights, tram lights, clothes, microflite tail jets, anything orange.

Irfan had the orange up to his nose, clawing into it with both hands, breathing it in and lapping up the juices as they ran down into his mouth. The orange crumpled. He broke off to repeat, 'Yesterday.'

'They told me you don't get let out any more,' Jon said. 'Would you like to come with me again?'

Irfan licked his lips and nodded enthusiastically. 'Today.'

'Well, some time today.' Jon fished in his pockets and brought out the tiny diamond pen and the tightly rolled sheets of glassite. 'You saw the nurse's keys, didn't you?'

'Keys.' Irfan held up his hand like the warden had and shook it, wincing at the imagined sound of clattering keys.

'That's it. Now, I don't know which are the ones we need, so I want you to draw them all for me. Can you do that, Irf?'

Irfan put the crushed orange carefully on the table by his narrow bed and licked his fingers clean. He took the pen from Jon and smoothed the first sheet of glassite on the table. Jon watched Irfan begin to draw, one at a time, twenty-one keys, each from three views, each to exact scale. He drew them at odd angles slewed over the glassite, as if at random. Jon watched him and it was as if Irfan was simply using the pen to trace around what was already there. He hesitated before starting each outline, but once he got going he was quick and sure. Jon realised that Irfan wasn't ordering the images at all, just snatching the best image from the perfect scan in his head of the warden rattling the bunch and transcribing it directly. There wouldn't be any trouble getting the keys cut now.

When Irfan was done Jon rolled the glassite sheets up and slid them into his pocket with the pen. He rapped on the door, saying to Irfan, 'I'll come back, well, later today, and I'll bring the keys. And maybe I'll get hold of another orange for you too.'

Irfan beamed.

TWENTY-THREE

Chrye peeled the plastic shield off the SiliCote-Pro contraceptive cone and spread her legs to ease the barrier into place, wondering what sort of people needed this degree of protection on a routine basis. Then she thought of Hickey Sill and wondered if it would be enough. Maybe this whole idea wasn't so good after all.

She checked her watch, beginning to feel tense about the prospect of the evening to come. It was too late to back down now, anyway. She had three hours before the membrane began to disintegrate, if she didn't remove it before that. With luck Hickey would never know she was shielded, never even guess there was anything there. She could hardly tell herself. Although Hickey Sill probably wouldn't know the inside of a vagina any better than he knew the right end of a toothbrush. She wasn't going to get pregnant by Hickey, and if the worst happened, he could assault her with anything short of a laser and the SiliCote would ensure she'd survive it.

She rolled lethargically off the bed and considered Hickey again as she dressed herself for him. She figured that as long as she started the evening in control she had at least a good chance of finishing it that way too. Hickey was a nasty little bastard but a straightforward one. Her reading of him was that the possibility of real sex with a willing partner would probably terrify him, so she'd come over like a predatory female. She'd turn up like Hickey Sill's worst nightmare, looking like a sex doll and acting like vagina dentata. If she got it right he'd be backing off from the moment he opened the door to see her there.

Chrye put her hair up and spun it into a soft peak that twisted as she moved, then eased herself into the red corset-dress. The tight sheath shunted her breasts up and descended to flare sharply from her waist, exhausting itself barely below her crotch. She hated herself in it but it was perfect for Hickey.

The shoes were even less comfortable than the dress, but their function was the same. The titanium pin heels were thin enough to be all but invisible, and the mirror polish on them took them the rest of the way. Chrye wanted Hickey to be seeing her jerked up on tiptoe for him like a puppet, her availability not even in question, not one of the evening's variables.

She stared at herself in the mirror, unable to meet her own eyes, and noticed a white tag at the hem of the dress. She tore it off and scanned it. HANDWASH. COLOURS MAY RUN. She tossed the instructions into the waste. She wouldn't be wearing the dress again.

It was nearly time. She calmed her nerves by going into the kitchen and scouring the surfaces and washing up the day-old pile of dirty crockery. She thought back, remembering doing the same thing before going to Nearvana to meet Jon for the first time. She'd been nervous then for different reasons. That had worked out pretty much as she'd expected, and she'd only had guesswork and a book of poems as preparation. Although she hadn't expected to be bringing him back at the end of the evening.

But it wasn't going so smoothly any more, and Hickey Sill wasn't Jon Sciler. Nothing any more seemed to be turning out how she expected it to. Jon and Lapis, for example. She wondered where Jon was now. Although she'd told him what she was intending to do with Hickey, she wasn't sure how much he'd taken in. Everything depended on him.

The water in the sink spun away down the drain. Chrye wiped the last plate dry and reached up to the cupboard to put it away, her heel sliding on the tile as she stretched. Then she took out a small glass bottle of chilli powder and cocooned it thickly in plaswrap, picked up a heavy pestle and began to smash the bundle with it. The crack of glass sounded like bone splintering. When the plaswrap was quite soft she pulled it carefully apart, then pulled on a thick pair of rubber gloves and started to scoop up the mess of chilli and glass. The chilli was exactly the same shade of red as her dress.

Chrye checked that the time-light in the hall was at the start of its two-minute span, then took as much of a deep breath as the dress would let her. She stood well back from the door as Hickey opened it.

All Hickey could manage was, 'Fuck,' which was the best beginning to the evening Chrye could have wanted. His eyes skidded all over her. He didn't know where to start.

She stepped back another pace, feeling sullied by his stare already. She wondered again where Jon was, not daring to let her eyes slide towards the stairs. The dress pulled at her as she moved, forcing her hips into a swing, and the skirt's mirrored lining focussed Hickey's eyes instantly on the scattered reflections of her thighs.

Good, she made herself think. Images of Jon with Lapis, images of him with her in Cathar, flooded her mind as Hickey faced her, gaping, and she tried to dismiss them. Hickey stared at her longer than was comfortable, although there was nothing ever comfortable about Hickey's attention.

She moved a fraction on the titanium pin-heels, bringing Hickey's eyes down her legs. This was easy.

'Late, though,' Hickey added eventually. 'Another five minutes and I was gonna come for you.'

'No, you weren't, Hickey,' she said, trying to keep her voice level. She stood there a bit longer for him, checking his eyes were all over her, skimming everywhere except for her wrists with the fat bangles that his subconscious should be interpreting as manacles. She fought back a sudden wish that she wasn't doing this, but there was no other way. Hickey Sill wouldn't ever go away like a bad dream.

Hickey gestured behind him. 'I tidied the place up special. You want a drink first?'

'I don't think so, Hickey. We'll come back later, won't we?'

He nodded and grinned at her. 'Oh, yeah. We'll be doing that.'

That wasn't quite the reaction she'd anticipated. She couldn't work out what it was about him that had changed, but something had. He went back and dragged a cracked black leather jacket from the couch and slung it over his shoulder. Chrye glanced past him. His room looked different. He'd cleared the bed. Beside the stove was something new that she took at first glance for an ancient bean bag, but then she saw it was his bed sheet knotted up with a cargo of food waste. That was what Hickey called tidying up. The cuckoo was still sitting on the table in the corner, its widescreen dark and empty. Chrye imagined the trig motionless on some street corner, waiting to rise and move at the cuckoo's command.

'Yeah, we'll go out first,' Hickey said, pulling the door closed behind him. He nudged Chrye down the stairs ahead of him, and she realised that Hickey was walking and talking straight. That worried her as she negotiated the worn steps in her pin heels with Hickey's breath at her back, but then she thought maybe it was fine. It must have taken a lot for him to resist stuffing his system with drugs. He still couldn't have worked out what had happened last time. He didn't know whether he was a virgin or a stud, and he wanted to find that out as much as he wanted to hurt Jon. Chrye allowed herself to relax a fraction. Hickey Sill was confused, which he wasn't used to being, and he was totally undrugged, which he also wasn't used to being. And despite his intimidatory tactics he hadn't expected Chrye to accept his demand for a date so eagerly, and he certainly hadn't expected her to turn up looking like she did. No, Hickey didn't feel at all in control.

'Where are you taking me, then, Hickey?'

'It's a surprise.'

'Okay. I like surprises.' She pushed it a bit. 'But you promise me we'll come back here afterwards?'

'I said, didn' I?'

Too much confidence. She didn't like that at all. But maybe she was over-anxious. His answer was the right one. This time Hickey would want to be on his home ground to rape her. Especially when his home ground was so close to Jon Sciler. She wondered anxiously where Jon was now.

Jon double-checked batOwl's heat sensor, running it over the house front and then checking it against Irfan to be sure Blind Jacob hadn't given him a blank.

It was fine. If there was anyone inside the place they had to be either in CrySis or terminal fever. Jon reached up to punch out the security vid before feeding the eel into the maintenance slide beneath the entrycode panel. His knuckles tingled as the glass shattered, but the pain he'd half expected never developed. Too used to the bLinkers, he thought. He felt the adrenaline coursing through him and turned to glance at Irfan. 'Here we go, Irf. Just you and me. Big adventure.'

Irfan was simply standing there by the door, his jaws working at a mouthful of sweets.

'That's fine,' Jon told him. 'Just remember not to wander off. Stay close by me and do exactly like I do.' Jon reached out and touched Irfan's hand, waiting while Blind Jacob's eel told the security chip it needed to access the vid camera from within the building in order to fix it. Then he pushed the door open.

'Okay, Irf. Concentrate now.'

He closed the door behind them and saw the second door, just like Jacob had guessed. The screen beside it was speaking to him. 'You are authorised to proceed no further. All maintenance systems are located within the console indicated. Please complete your task and enter your invoice code before leaving.'

The maintenance console was flashing. 'Replacement of video illuminator unit Bs 986R. Press YES to expel failed unit.'

Jon pressed YES, then turned his attention to the inner door. Jacob had told him that once the outer door had been compromised, the inner door would automatically be failsafed. There was no way of getting through that without time or a lot of damage.

'Okay, Irf, what do you think? Time or damage? I think we'll go for damage. Back off a moment and cover your eyes.'

Behind him the maintenance console was flashing again. 'Failed unit expelled. Now insert replacement video illuminator unit Bs 986R.'

Jon let the dust settle in the doorway and onlined batOwl. His view swam, then stabilised into a coloured grid superimposed over the entrance to Kerz's house. The hallway was long and narrow and the walls were lined with pictures, each with its own hooded toplight. They were oil paintings, the colours muted, the paint brittle and cracked with age. Jon walked carefully beneath the supercilious glare of a long-dead man in a greying wig and a ruff, and stopped. The toplight was also an infrared tripbeam, slanted down to a concealed receptor by the skirting. That wasn't security for the paintings. Kerz didn't care about the paintings. The paintings were throwaways for anyone who got this far. Jon backed against the wall and high-stepped carefully over the angled beam, watching Irfan follow him, then moved through into the kitchen. 'Just keep doing like me, Irf.'

Irfan pointed. 'Pretty things, Jon.'

'Very nice, Irf. A whole rack of orange saucepans. Something of a chef, Mr Kerz. Probably a cannibal. But we're not interested in cooking right now.'

Jon headed out of the kitchen. There was nothing there. He could see the pressure pads on the stairs as yellow blisters on batOwl's grid.

Cameras were green beads and he blew them away as they came into sight. The house was alive with security.

He was wishing he could be bLinkered now. He was feeling rocky and vulnerable, and batOwl didn't help that. He stood uncertainly at the bottom of the stairs, conscious of the seconds passing.

There were two more rooms down here, both with their doors closed. BatOwl gave them vivid purple frames and scarlet hinges. He decided to leave them for now.

'Okay, Irf, I'm moving on. Stay with me.' He checked Irfan's mouth was still full of sweets, then headed for the stairs. BatOwl whined as he approached the pressure pads and registered their activation as swift blue ripples. Shit. He climbed carefully up the stairs, dizzy with the lights and colours of the readout.

He stopped on the landing. To the left there were two doorways, and to the right just one. The left doors were open and unprotected. One was a bedroom and he peered in to see the bed unmade, a red and white striped duvet balled up on the mattress. The other was a bathroom. Wet towels on a tiled floor.

The door on the right was closed. Jon checked the batOwl display and saw that the door was triggered to a screecher. This would be it.

There wasn't much margin. He lasered through the door and disabled the screecher.

'Pretty lights,' Irfan said.

'Enjoying it now, are you?' Jon pushed the door in.

Irfan took another sweet from his pocket and unwrapped it, nodding happily.

There was a monitor and the cabinet of cassettes that Jon recognised from Kerz's call to him. He ran batOwl over it. The cabinet was wired. He skimmed round the rest of the room and stopped at a filing cabinet in the corner that crackled with tampersafe apparatus.

'Okay, Irf,' he muttered, 'that's our baby.'

He spent more time than he wanted to disabling the locks, then yanked the door open and saw them. Starburn's tape was there, labelled and cased in a clear plastic sleeve.

He pulled the case out and checked his watch. A minute twenty-five. Too long. Far too long. His neck was tense. He stretched out his arms and locked his fingers, then massaged the back of his neck. Then he took the cassette from its case.

'Your turn now, Irfan. You still got those bLinkers I gave you?'

Irfan tipped back his head and fed the bright orange tendrils into the corners of his eyes. Jon snapped the cassette into the dropslot and selected speedplay. Irfan's jaws were working. Jon bLinked him directly into the processor unit and waited.

Shit, Jon thought, it's not going to work. Then Irfan stiffened. For a moment he stopped chewing, then his jaws were moving again.

'Got you,' Jon murmured. 'I've got you, Kerz.' He checked his watch once more. 'Okay, do your stuff, Irfan.'

The screen was record-protected and there was protection too on the processor's copy function just as Blind Jacob had predicted, but the unit was happy to play with the screen off. It was happening. Jon tapped Irfan's shoulder and Irfan nodded fractionally, setting the bLinker cable swinging between his face and the machine.

Jon left Irfan to it and went out into the hall. It didn't matter any more that he was tripping alarms. He used a titanium detector to locate the safe and made a mess of the lock and the wall around it until he was happy that it looked convincing.

He checked the time again. Two minutes twenty-five. The 'fists would be here any time now. Jon wondered what was happening in Irfan's head.

That was it, he thought, hearing sounds downstairs. They were at the door now. They wouldn't be too fast after him, they would have seen the damage and they'd have a pretty good idea what they were up against. Jon returned to Irfan, prowling anxiously around the room. It should be done by now. Irfan was still chewing rhythmically, his head ticking from side to side. Hurry it up, thought Jon.

He looked around, heart thudding, thinking suddenly of Irfan's bLinker. There was an organics shredder by the workstation, but Kerz must have a shredder for hards too somewhere.

Yes. It was in the wall beneath a flipdown mirror. Perfect.

Two minutes forty-eight. They were on the stairs, the old Georgian timbers creaking under the weight of all that metal.

Irfan removed the bLinkers.

'All done?' said Jon, taking the tape from the slot and replacing it carefully in the cabinet. He reset its security lock.

Irfan nodded.

'Okay, Irf. We're going to be quick now.' Jon took the bLinkers from him, hearing noises from the landing. They were being cautious. Jon threw the bLinkers into the jaws of the shredder and listened to it whine briefly. He tossed batOwl after it, then flicked the mirror back down. The dull gleam and symmetry of his reflection startled him for a moment. He was too into it. He took a quick glance around the room. Irfan was twitchy and Jon threw him a sweet, tossing the wrapper into the organics shredder. He checked they'd left nothing in the room.

'Okay, Irf, let's move.'

He went on to the landing. All the alarms were screaming now. Three minutes ten. He couldn't see the 'fists. He went back into the bedroom and raised a chair to heave through the window.

He heard them behind him but let the chair go anyway. He turned around. There were two of them and they both had their hardhands swinging, sharplights blinking. Then they hesitated, as Jon had known they would, and one of them said, 'What the fuck are *you* doing here, Hickey?'

TWENTY-FOUR

'I booked us a table at M-phasis,' Hickey said. 'You been there?' He didn't wait for her to answer and there was nothing for her to read in his voice. She wasn't feeling at all certain any more that Hickey Sill would be manageable.

'They owe me there,' he went on. 'They offer a special menu, I get them some rare ingredients they need. Volatile ingredients.' His breath clouded the screen as he spun the microflite round the jagged summit of Centre Point, close enough to wing-tip the masonry, and dipped down to twenty metres to head over Oxford Street.

'Hickey, do you mind if we don't go there?'

Hickey turned to stare at her. 'What? You know how much it costs to eat their fucking shit food if you're paying?' He stabbed his foot down and the microflite surged forward and screamed sharply left, juddering towards a pyramid of scaffolding. Hickey swore and pulled the microflite straight again. 'Fucking machine needs fixing. Who owns this pile of shit? I'll fucking report them. Pull out the logbook . . .' He jabbed a finger at the document box.

'Hickey, you stole this 'flite,' Chrye said. 'Perhaps we should just land it and walk.' She didn't like this at all. Maybe it was the sense of power he had in a microflite, she thought. Maybe it was just that.

'We're not fucking walking. What's wrong with M-phasis?'

'Why don't you put us down in the Mall? We can go to Buckingham Market, eat at the stalls. I'd like that.' She rested her hand on his knee for a second, trying to calm him down. His trousers felt faintly greasy and she pushed her fingers through a rip in the plastic seat cover to wipe them dry on the foam wadding. 'Then we can go back to your place.'

There was no reaction to that from Hickey. 'I booked us a fucking table,' he repeated.

'I don't want to spend the whole evening at some restaurant, Hickey,' she tried. 'I want us to eat and go back to your place.' She leaned toward him and whispered, 'Jon might be there, Hickey. He might see me with you. Maybe that's what I want, Hickey.'

She waited a moment then gently touched his hand on the joystick, tilting the microflite south. Hickey didn't correct it, letting the microflite drift down Regent Street until the Mall's ragged lake of lights came into view.

Wondering whether she was pushing it too far, Chrye said, 'Maybe we can both hurt him, Hickey. Huh?'

'Yeah,' he muttered eventually, as if to himself. 'Okay. Fucking yeah.' He spun them down and dropped the microflite behind the ICA. Chrye bent low as she went through the doorflap and let Hickey see her cleavage. He threw the microflite keys towards a huddle of beggars in the shadows of the building.

'Okay,' Hickey said. He jerked his head down the Mall's glittering ghetto of cheap food and sex.

Chrye took his arm. Her heels were sinking into the mud and she felt unstable. She made him lead her to a concrete path under a sine wave of strung bulbs. The harsh downlighting made her exposed flesh hot and uncomfortable. She could see prostitutes eyeing her and Hickey, and she could see their pimps drifting through the crowds like they were really somewhere else altogether.

'We could have been at fucking M-phasis,' Hickey muttered.

Chrye was thinking the same thing, but she felt safer here with Hickey where there were so many people around them. She told him, 'I feel safe with you here, Hickey. Why don't we get a drink?'

'Yeah,' he said. 'Wait. Let me think. Okay. I know where.' He led her quickly off the main walkway, leaving her trailing on her needle heels. She saw him stop at a stall and hand over a fist of notes, then as she caught up he turned quickly back to her with a pair of rough red clay cups in his hands. He gave her one and then threw back his head and drained his. He dropped the cup to the concrete and ground it into dust, and nudged the other cup up towards her lips. 'It's unstable,' he told her sharply. 'You gotta drink it before it evaporates.'

Chrye hesitated. She glanced at the stall but there was no clue to what the drink might be. The stallholder was stirring a tub of thick fluorescent green gel. Chrye watched him draw up the ladle from deep in the tub and tip it enough to let the head of gel slide back into the tub before pouring the clear liquid that was left into a clay cup. He handed it to the next customer in a swift movement. The customer drank it instantly. Whatever the man was selling, it didn't like the Earth's air. But, then, no one did any more, and as far as Chrye could tell, Hickey had drunk the same thing.

Hickey was looking at her, his mouth twisting out of its smile. 'Shit, girl,' he said. 'You don't trust me? You're the one suggested it.'

It had to be safe. Hickey wasn't going to try anything this early in the evening. She said, 'To tonight, Hickey,' and poured the liquid down her throat. It was blood-warm and it felt somehow thinner than water. It tasted vaguely of mint. Her mouth felt very dry and then numb. Hickey took her cup and crunched it under his foot.

She glanced back as Hickey walked her on. They were all couples buying from the stall, and the women were all prostitutes, pumped up and pierced, watching their johns drink and leading them off. Some kind of aphrodisiac, she thought. She wondered whether it was her that Hickey didn't trust, or himself.

He walked her further into the market and she felt she'd already lost control of the situation. The dryness in her mouth was replaced by a flood of saliva. All she could do was swallow. She felt thirsty and hungry, and all her senses seemed to catch fire at the same time. The market was clutching at her with its smells of burnt cooking oil and adulterated spices, of sweat and rot and cheap perfume. Chrye felt herself ridiculously alive, every-thing tingling, and Hickey's hand openly pushing up her skirt from behind heightened that feeling. The idea of his touch revolted her and she tried to pull away but it was suddenly impossible. She couldn't resist easing her buttocks against the palm of his hand. It was getting stronger, becoming a need. She was aware of an itching that needed to be dealt with, and even the touch of her clothes was teasing her, making her almost moan in frustration as she walked unsteadily along in her titanium heels.

Hickey whispered in her ear, 'How do you feel?' His voice was a rasp that made her shiver as if he was goosing her with it.

She swallowed and said, 'Itchy. Oh, God . . .' As soon as she stopped swallowing to talk, her mouth filled with saliva and she couldn't get any more words out. Hickey was grinning at her and she felt something wasn't right about him. He was full of confidence. 'The drink . . .'

His face changed abruptly and she knew immediately that she was lost. He put his face right up to hers and said, 'There's *nowhere* I don't know someone, girl. Nowhere. You think I had something set up at that shit-and-champagne restaurant that I couldn't make happen anywhere else? Huh? I don't know what you did to me last time, but it ain't fucking happening twice. Toby back there services the Buckingham whores, makes sure everyone has a good time and doesn't mind paying for it, and he's just done that for me. This time I'm keeping my head crystal fucking clear.'

He jabbed his finger at her, grinning crazily. 'You can't say too much, girl, you can't think too much either, but you can *feel*. Whether you like it or not is up to you. You can enjoy the ride or you can fling yourself around in the seat as much as you fucking like. But you've had a bellyful of Toby's joyjuice, girl, and a few extra drops of neurosensory potentiator, and you're strapped in tight until the ride's over.'

Hickey was right. Chrye couldn't say anything. She felt hot and she wanted to be touched everywhere, for the itching to go away. Her hands itched and she wanted to touch Hickey to relieve it, but she made herself hold back from him. She wanted to touch herself too, and forced her hands together instead, kneading them convulsively, trembling even with the sensation of her thighs brushing against each other.

Hickey smiled and said, 'Now I'm hungry, and I can see you are too. Side-effect. Can't stop drooling, can you? Or maybe you're thinking of later, eh?' He squeezed her thigh again and she felt faint with the relief of it. It wasn't pleasure, it was like an addiction being fed. It was like the need constantly to swallow. She couldn't help it. Her legs began to buckle and he took his hand away. No one around them in the market even glanced at them. This was the wrong place to be dressed like this, the wrong place to feel like this. This was the wrong place to have come with Hickey Sill.

She could hardly stand for the itching. Hickey took her arm and it was like voltage passing. She'd got Hickey completely wrong, she realised. She'd read him all wrong, misinterpreted his walls bare of women. Hickey knew about sex, knew all about it. He knew how to use it. He just didn't need it.

'Shit, girl, you know what, I think old Toby's overdone it. We better get some food inside you, take the edge off this or you're gonna die of a phantom fuck before we even get back to my place.' He grinned happily.

'Hell, this is a good evening. I can't remember having this much jump and thinking straight too. You enjoying it, Chrye? Sure look like it, goosebumps all over.' He ran a slow finger down her arm. 'You were right, girl, this is way better than shit 'n' champagne. Now, you want Italian, Chinese, Indian, French . . . ?'

She let the idea of food take over, finding it reducing the terrible itching a little, the weakness in her limbs and the terrible desire to have Hickey touch her. She concentrated on the smell of food around her, on all senses except the sense of touch.

'Thai,' she said, thinking of lemongrass and coriander, anything but the desperation of her flesh. Even with the single word she couldn't help the saliva tumbling down her chin. Hickey wiped it away with his finger, then wiped the moisture slowly down her cleavage. She leaned towards him involuntarily, needing it and hating Hickey for it.

'Yeah, we can do that, Chrye,' Hickey snickered. 'We can do it any way you like. But we'll eat first.'

He led her through the crowds to the tables of Thai Chi and she sat squirming in the rough rattan seat of a chair until he came back to her with a tray of fake Tiger beer and fake Thai food. 'I ain't hungry,' Hickey said, ''cos I just saw them cooking it. But I don't imagine that's going to bother you, the way you're feeling. Am I right?'

Chrye picked up the red plastic chopsticks and began to shovel food into her mouth. It tasted worse than the takeaway MaryAnn had brought with her, but that didn't matter. It only mattered to be swallowing something, to feel the texture of something in her mouth. Hickey drank his beer slowly, watching her.

'You know, I could tell you you're eating stir-fried rat turds and you couldn't stop now, girl,' he told her, and she knew it was true. She was beginning to feel bloated but she couldn't stop, she needed the feeling of the food in her mouth so much.

'It's gonna be the same when we go back to my place,' Hickey said. 'I'm gonna have myself a real good time and it ain't gonna matter what I do, you're gonna love it and you're gonna want more.' He laughed and drained his beer. 'Well, maybe that's not strictly true. Maybe you won't like it, won't like it at all, but you're gonna let me do it, girl, gonna *need* me to do it.' He leaned over and almost touched her breast, watching her quiver towards his hand before he drew away, and then he chuckled. 'You eat up now, gonna need your energy soon enough.'

His voice changed, becoming softer. 'You know, I once saw a vid,' he told her, almost dreamily. 'A snuffer. It wasn't meant to be a snuffer, but the girl was on Touch, which is by the way what you're on, maybe not quite as high as you but pretty high, and the guy put his cock in her mouth. Didn't know any better. Must 've seen all that sweet sticky spit and thought he wanted some of it. You guessed what happened? Yeah, you guessed, but you still can't stop eating, can you? She probably didn't want to do what she did, but she couldn't help it either.' Hickey drew back his lips and clacked his teeth together and then giggled to himself. 'Involuntary manslaughter. Never was a truer verdict, girl. Kept right on eating, she did. And you know what? When it was down to the stump she just put her face to the place and she sluiced it on down with the spurting red stuff. Shit, you should have seen the jury.'

He pushed a beer over to Chrye and she washed the whole bottle down her throat, trying to blank out everything but the food.

Hickey stood up and pulled her to her feet. 'So don't get any clever ideas this time, girl, 'cos I've already had them all. Understand me?' He ran his knuckles down her spine and she groaned, arching herself against him like a cat. There was nothing else she could do. She shivered as he slid the black bangle off her wrist and ran his fingers over its curves until the charge crackled into the air.

'You thought this was going to fool me?' He ran it under Chrye's chin and she trembled but couldn't draw away from it. She could imagine the pain to come but she couldn't escape it. Her mouth opened but there was still too much saliva.

'You think this would hurt?' Hickey said.

She nodded helplessly, leaving her jaw against the bangle, nuzzling it into her neck as he pulled it towards him. She wanted the feeling of it. She couldn't think of anything else.

'It'd kill you right now. Sensed up like that, this would kill you dead, heart attack. You still want it?' He pushed it hard against her cheek. She felt herself quivering. She put her hand up to it and tried to push the bracelet away, but instead her hand pressed against Hickey's, pressed the bangle against her cheek.

'Let's see how much you want it, Chrye. I'm going to discharge it on three. One, two . . .'

There was nothing at all she could do.

'Three.'

His finger shifted under her hand, but nothing happened. He hadn't clicked it.

Hickey giggled. 'That was good,' he said. 'I enjoyed that. Did you? Like one of those games of trust new lovers play with each other. Have we established a sense of trust between us, Chrye? I feel you know what to expect of me now, and I know what I can expect of you.' He took her face between his hands and held her still, kissing her carefully on the lips. Holding her there, he whispered, 'There are whores who have all their teeth taken out. They say there's nothing in the world like a toothless whore on Touch. But I think that's going a bit far. We'll think of something else.'

He let her go, and Chrye stared around. A few people caught her eye and looked away, seeing just a whore with her pimp. There was nothing she could do about it, nothing anybody would do for her. Hickey waited until she turned back to him and then he said, 'I don't think we need the other bracelet either, whatever it does.' He stripped her of it and left both bangles on the table.

'Now, let's get us another 'flite and we'll go back and this time we'll have some fun we can both remember. And then when you're all sweated out we'll drop you back at your boyfriend's to sleep it off. Along with a vid of the whole thing as a souvenir for you both.'

Hickey was behind her climbing the stairs, his hands on her thighs, guiding her, giggling, and she was trying to back up against him all the way, desperate to relieve the uncontrollable itching. She couldn't think and she could hardly breathe for the feel of it. The idea of food still seemed to ease it fractionally and she tried to think of turmeric and cardamoms, chilli and ginger, but Hickey's hands were all over her and she wriggled against him, needing more. At his door Hickey brought his hand up and inspected it. His fingers were red.

'Hey, girl,' he said, 'either your dress is running or it's the wrong time of the month for you.' He giggled again. 'It certainly is that, girl. Wrong time altogether.'

He fed his keycard into the doorslot and pushed. The lock clicked twice before it opened. Hickey frowned and held back for a second, glancing at the mechanism and his card. Chrye rubbed herself against him. She looked up to the next landing, trying to gather her thoughts. There was no sign of Jon. Where was he?

'Okay, let's have fun,' Hickey said, closing the door behind them. He crossed the room and knelt at the skirting by the far wall, bringing out a camera from a hole under a floorboard. Chrye stood beside the couch, scratching her nails into her palms, trembling, unable to do anything else except watch Hickey as he stood up and set the camera on a slender tripod in the corner of the room. She couldn't think to resist and stood shuddering as he stripped her, letting everything drop to the floor until she was naked. The feel of the fabric moving against her skin made her moan, but then the abrupt absence of sensation was intolerable. She didn't care about anything else. Suddenly nothing was touching her and the whole of her body demanded to be touched. It was worse than hunger and thirst. She felt dizzy. She opened her mouth and saliva cascaded down her chin and on to her breasts. A tiny voice inside her cried out to run from Hickey but she was shivering from need. Chilli, she thought from somewhere, and she held on to the thought of the sharp taste.

Hickey was holding something out to her. The need to be touched was terrible and mounting. Her hands were wet and sticky where her fingernails had convulsively scoured the skin from her palms. Hickey was saying, 'I want you to put this in your mouth, Chrye. I want you to put it on yourself, so Jon knows you want to wear it for me.'

She managed to shake her head but Hickey was between her and the camera. He came up to her and let the leather straps of the muzzle roll against her cheek. The sensation was agonisingly good. She took it from him and he went behind her, his hands all over her. She tried to let the muzzle go but Hickey took his hands away and that was worse. 'Put it on,' he whispered in her ear.

She strapped it on behind her head, feeling the tears fall down her face. There was a small hard leather ball between her teeth that she couldn't resist chewing. She was quite free inside it, able to talk as much as the flood of saliva allowed, but the saliva was still coming almost as fast as it had at the market and anyway her thoughts were too confused to put into words. She kept trying to think of chilli, though she no longer knew why.

'Now, Hickey,' she managed to say through the spit and webbing of leather, hearing the pleading in her voice. 'Do it to me now. Please.'

'Say it louder, Chrye,' Hickey said. 'For the camera. For Jon.' He pushed her on to the couch. The feel of the cold, cracked leather against her back made her gasp.

'Do it Hickey,' she drooled desperately. She thought of chilli and readied herself for him, sobbing.

Hickey looked at her and then at the camera, and then she felt him pushing into her. The SiliCote membrane dulled it slightly but the drug cranked the sensation right up again. She wanted to push him away but the drug was coursing through her veins and there was no control, her hands were locked around him holding him inside her. His head was back so that he could see her eyes.

He hissed, 'You don't want me at all, Chrye. I know that. You never fooled me. But when Jon . . .'

There was a sudden look of concern on his face as his hips jerked abruptly. He was quite motionless inside her and there was absolute silence between them. Chrye bit hard on the leather knot in her mouth and held Hickey tight. She ground her hips into his.

He winced uncertainly, a look of total concentration in his eyes. She saw a vein throbbing in his forehead. He smelt suddenly of acrid sweat.

'What . . . ?'

He moved a fraction, trying to withdraw from her, and she felt the spasm of pain that whipped through him. She held on to him with her hands and locked her legs round him, feeling what there was of him inside her diminish almost altogether. He began to move again, urgently now, yelping and trying to pull away from her, but for the moment her drugged need was still greater and she closed him in.

'What the fuck . . . ?' he said tautly, and then he screamed and pulled out and there was nothing she could do to stop him.

There was blood on her thighs and where he was sitting over in the far corner of the room she could see that his penis was a tiny curled clot of blood. But his shrivelled flesh glittered too as the embedded shards of glass caught the light.

Chilli, she thought. The drug's effects were starting to wear off. She began half-consciously to pick fragments of glass out of her pubic hair, but Hickey had taken most of it with him. He was still screaming, staring at his bloody crotch and screeching into his own echo.

Hickey was making so much noise that Chrye didn't hear the door breaking down at first. She saw the pair of trigs standing there, and then one of them was striding over to the desk where Hickey's cuckoo sat. The trig delicately stretched out a claw to pick up the cuckoo and brandished it at Hickey, who was whimpering now, too hoarse to scream any more.

'Fuck it, Hickey,' the trig said. 'I always thought you were weird, but this time you've gone too far.'

Chrye managed to peel the muzzle away and crawled over to her dress, pulling it on while the trigs watched her. She croaked through her spit, 'Please can I go?'

The trig at the door didn't move, but the one holding the cuckoo said, 'Yeah. Let her go. Hickey's foreplay's already drowned him in shit. He doesn't need this too.'

She made it to the door on her hands and knees and looked up the stairs.

Jon was there. He took the whole flight in two long steps and picked her up. Her body tingled at his touch, and for the first time tonight it felt good. She wondered if she looked as bad as his face told her she did.

'Oh, God, Chrye. What did he do to you? I wanted to come down . . .'

She shook her head, barely managing to say, 'We agreed. It's okay.'

As he took her up the stairs, Chrye heard the trig's voice say, 'Time they've finished with you, Hickey, you're gonna wish you'd asked her to cut it right off.'

Chrye didn't know how long she spent lying in Jon's bath, but at last the water began to feel just like water against her skin and she didn't need to swallow her own spit any more. Jon had teased out the SiliCote sheath together with what Hickey hadn't removed of the glass and chilli powder and she was okay except for a few minor cuts and bruises and a thudding ache in her jaws from the hours of chewing.

She stepped stiffly out of the cold water and let Jon dry her. He wouldn't meet her eyes, rubbing the fibres of the worn towel over her until her skin began to chafe and she had to tell him to stop. 'Jon,' she told him, 'it's all right. He didn't hurt me. It was my choice, remember? And they've taken him away, just like we planned it. Everything's all right.'

But she could see he wasn't hearing what she said and she knew she couldn't stop him feeling responsible for the way she had looked, crawling from Hickey's room.

'Jon,' she tried again, pulling him towards the bed, but he still wouldn't answer. It was his guilt that told her how he really felt about her. She wondered if he knew it himself, if he knew how she loved him. She wanted to tell him she had done this for him, but knew how it would make him feel. So she lay with him and said nothing else.

Once she woke up in the night and saw him silhouetted against the window, naked, staring out. She called him and he came silently back to her, folding himself into the curves of her back just like she had folded herself into him that first time. But when she turned towards him, needing him to take away the memories of Hickey's hands touching her and of wanting that, he rolled away. She was left empty, staring at the blank screen against which Jon practised magic, and in the moonlight she was certain she saw a great dark insect crawling over it. When she rubbed her eyes to be sure, there was only the screenscribe squatting in the corner of the screen, and Jon was sleeping. Half-asleep herself, she moved her fingers over the battlefield of his back as if the scars there were his soul revealed in braille. But their message eluded her and she slept, unable to comprehend him.

When she woke again it was hours later with her fingers knotted in the warm sheets that smelt of his sweat, and this time he wasn't at the window. She knew she had lost him to Cathar.

TWENTY-FIVE

He should have left earlier for Cathar. The sun was already high. Jon's spine was tingling as he woke up and he remembered bLinking down to Dirangesept with exactly the same anxiety over what might have happened to his body in his absent time.

But nothing had happened. He pushed off the covering of foliage and got stiffly to his feet, stretching his arms and rubbing sleep from his eyes, reflecting that Cathar's reality had lost its wonder for him and become simply mundane.

He started to walk into the village, looking out over the gentle sea at the rock, wondering what was happening there, thinking of Footfall. It was hot and heavy and nothing was moving. The sea was as dead as the dark rock. A few fishing boats sat listlessly out there, their sails furled in the windless hours, their masts weakly stirring the sky.

Everything was going wrong now, he thought. He had failed Chrye. He had failed Starburn. There seemed nothing left but to go on.

Before the village he slipped off the track to climb the hillside through the still muddy groves of what he thought of as lemon trees. The scent of the fruit was strong, like heady perfume, and somehow it lightened his mood.

Herta was already on the balcony with Pibald and Jhalouk. She was the first to notice Jon. 'Lapis and Janus have disappeared,' she said, standing up. She was almost twitching with energy. 'There's no sign of them. I don't understand.'

Jon went over to stare out at the rock again. It was holding to itself what remained of the night, holding all the secrets of Cathar.

'We should check if there are boats missing,' he said. 'Lapis might have . . .'

'No,' Jhalouk said, her voice full of exhaustion. 'The boats go out before dawn. We'd already know if she'd taken one. She argued with Janus last night. We heard them. Something happened."

She stopped and Pibald took over. 'He went to her room and she threw him out. That wasn't going to be the end of it, though. Not with Janus.' He made a face. 'It's been a long time coming, but it had to happen. I warned her. He raped Lazuli a long time ago. Lapis suspected, but Lazuli never admitted it. This morning Lapis's room was empty, the bed was hours cold.'

'Where does Janus sleep?' Jon said.

'No one knows. He's like you, Sciler, he trusts no one. He's never slept here.'

Of course not, Jon thought. Not if he has to go and be Calban. He probably sleeps on the rock.

'What's that?' Herta said, so sharply that Jon pulled out of his thoughts and looked off towards the rock. A thin plume of smoke was unthreading over it, lifting steadily into the blue morning. There wasn't a breath of wind until the smoke had grown tall, and then its peak began to twist and coil and the plume's stalk became thick and black.

'Footfall. He's dead,' Pibald said bleakly. 'This happened before. Calban's telling us.'

Of course, Jon thought. That would have been Lapis's signal each time. That was how she knew it was time to kill them, that it was safe, that Cathar was finished with them. Now it could be Footfall's death knell if Janus hadn't killed her and she was still alive to see it.

Herta looked around, waiting for someone to tell her what was going on, but no one said anything else. Jon thought, No one's saying that Footfall's weary no more.

Jhalouk was weeping into Pibald's sleeve. Jon stared at the smoke and thought of Footfall, of Starburn and of Chrye. The smoke continued to peel away into the sky, and all movement slowly died in the village below. The few boats out of the harbour that had raised their sails in the early morning breeze were lowering them again to bob gently in the water.

The smoke from the rock was just a grey column of air now.

'That's odd,' Herta muttered behind Jon. She was looking in the other direction. Jon turned to see another faint skein of smoke rising.

'That's Lazuli's pyre,' Jhalouk said.

Lapis, Jon thought. That's where she is, if she's alive.

270

'Sciler?' Pibald said, but Jon was already running.

From the crest of the cliff he could see what remained of the pyre. It shouldn't have been smoking any more, not after all the rain that had fallen. And there was a body lying by it, but it wasn't the body of Lapis.

He carried on down, tripping and sliding on the mud and rocks until he reached the pyre.

It was Janus lying there dead, the handle of Lapis's knife jutting from his chest. His ribs had cracked and caved in with the force of her blow. Jon knelt to feel Janus's cheek. He must have been dead for hours. His fist was closed tight around a long, thick wave of Lapis's hair. Jon forced the cold hand open, snapping the rigid joints, and let the wind of Cathar carry her hair away. Janus must have followed Lapis here after they'd argued, and tried to rape her, not realising the strength of her madness, and she'd killed him. He hadn't been Calban at all. He'd just been a little shit and a rapist.

So where was Lapis?

The pyre crackled behind him. The smoke had barely started up again, so it must have only just been relit. The stack had fallen in on one side and Jon peered in, squinting in the heat. Through the crumpled wood he made out what looked like a hank of barely charred cloth. The fire was hot and its core fuzzy with smoke. Jon walked around it until he found a straight, strong unburnt branch that he could use to poke out a clear hole to see what it was in there.

It was Lapis. For an instant he thought she was still alive, staring at him and writhing to free herself, but it was just the swimming heat making that seem so. Her body was lying beside the bones of her twin's. The white bones of her fist were poking through her charred skin where a tiny nucleus of fire had burned fiercely, but the rest of her was relatively untouched. Jon carefully withdrew his stick and the fragile fire collapsed into itself in a hissing breath of ash, burying the twins completely. He turned away from it and noticed the dull gleam of a puddle of wax still cooling on the ground. Lapis must have crawled into the ruined pyre with a candle to be with Lazuli and tried to reignite the pyre to join her in death, but the wet wood hadn't properly taken flame and the fire had fallen in around her. She would have lain in helpless agony until she suffocated, her lungs filling with smoke and her hand on fire.

Jon looked up into the sky, following the diminishing plume of smoke,

271

and saw a curl of ash spinning high in the tower of warm air. The scrap seemed to shake itself and spin away, and Jon realised it was the bird again, the eagle that was with him almost all the time now. He watched it glide out of sight, then headed for the woods beyond the pyre.

Deep in the trees, he said enough words into the resisting wind to make a long, sheltered shallow hole that he could ease himself down into, and covered himself with leaves. His body was as safe there as anywhere else in Cathar. That was all there was time for, in any case. Janus's corpse had been lying there most of the night but, judging by the wax, Lapis had only just died. She would have been alive to see the plume of smoke from Calban's rock. She had probably been waiting for it.

'Chrysanthemum,' Jon said.

It was too late, though. Jon knew Footfall was dead as soon as he saw the pair of 'fist trigs set like black beacons in the rubble outside Footfall's skewed home. The airfilter was pounding the air and Jon could feel the rubble shivering under his feet like the bow wave of a quake.

After a while the filter switched off, leaving the air empty and silent. Footfall's home looked like something that had crashlanded from another world with no survivors. Jon stood until his breath came back, and then he turned around and walked away. Ahead of him a couple of men carrying a fat black nylon holdall between them climbed into a microflite that rose away from the ruins, banking north and sweeping high until the choking brown fog claimed them.

Madsen was pulling at his hair again. Chrye wondered whether he ever stopped, whether he lay in bed and pulled out his hair, whether he pulled it out in his sleep. He stood up as she came through the door of the café, and she thought it was to show her where he was, though that was unnecessary. The Has Bean was almost empty.

Madsen was standing at a round wooden table in the corner, looking conspicuous and uncomfortable. At least he wasn't wearing his uniform. The pale blue casual jacket he had on was stretched tight across his shoulders and upper arms, and a brown shirt showed like mud through the jacket's exhausted weave.

He didn't sit down until Chrye had, and she felt oddly touched by that. Somehow she didn't think he was just handling her.

'Colombian,' he said to her by way of greeting. He brought his hand away from his scalp and waved to the waitress. 'There's been a cargo from South America. Ten tons. It was a close thing. The ship was nearly lost in the Atlantic storm tides.' He made a gesture of disbelief. 'Amazing how people go on, isn't it? How many left alive over there, no one knows, but they still grow the coffee, we still sail the ships. You can still get almost anything, you know where to look, you can pay. You'd think we'd all just pull in, wouldn't you? Become tribal, look inward, shrink.'

'It isn't like that, Madsen,' Chrye said, liking him. 'Man isn't like that. We don't give in. The survival instinct is strong. We don't ever give in, we fight. Sure we don't need coffee, just like we don't need bananas, tea, all that stuff. But coffee from South America gives us hope. It gives us hope when ships can still make it that the world hasn't beaten us yet. And the routine comforts us too, the sense of order. Doing your job, carrying on. Every time a ship returns, it's like maybe this turmoil is all going to grind to a halt and the world will get back again to how it was. Even though we know it won't.'

She stopped. The waitress was at her shoulder. She looked about eighteen, with brown hair in a ponytail. 'Two of us, Ursie,' Madsen told her. 'No milk. And a couple of bars of that chocolate. That okay?'

'Fine, Captain Madsen. I'll have to check about the chocolate. You like the high roast, don't you?'

He smiled at her. 'Always have.'

Chrye noticed he wasn't pulling his hair any more.

'We don't shrink,' she said when the girl had gone. 'A starving man doesn't get shorter. He gets thinner, yes, but the organs keep working together for a while. As long as there are people driven enough to pick the beans, there will be others prepared to risk everything to haul them back over the Atlantic.'

Madsen said, 'Time'll come when we can't get over the Atlantic, can't go anywhere.'

'Yes. But a few people will survive on what we can grow and synthesise here. There will be pockets of survivors everywhere. Maybe we can adapt fast enough, maybe it will all go into reverse eventually, the new beginning,' Chrye said. 'You understand that I'm not saying what I believe. Just what we all hope. And there's always going to be rumours, stories of another Dirangesept.'

Madsen started to raise his hand to his hair, but instead he brought it back to the table, staring at his short calloused fingers with their nails chewed down to the quick. 'And in the meantime all we can do is drink the coffee,' he said.

'That's right.' Chrye could smell it now. She wondered how much it was going to cost. She'd never drunk coffee that smelled like this from the cup's rim, let alone across the room.

Madsen was saying, 'You know, I've started to wonder if CMS isn't an evolutionary imperative. A sort of Darwinian self-sacrifice, leaving behind fewer mouths to feed. And they usually feel they're going to a better place. Who knows, perhaps they are and we should just let them get on with it.'

'Here we go, Captain Madsen, coffee's up.'

Ursie lowered the tray to the table and unloaded two small white cups with thick rounded rims, sliding them in front of Madsen and Chrye. She filled them halfway with coffee from a fat white jug and left the jug on the table. She put a slim bar of paper-wrapped chocolate beside each cup, then stepped back to inspect the table.

'Thanks, Ursie, that looks great.'

'Chocolate's from Belgium,' she said. 'Seventy-two per cent. Dad said to tell you.'

Madsen dipped his head to smell the coffee. 'Tell him I appreciate it. How are you doing yourself, Ursie?'

'Oh, it's okay.' She coloured and smiled shyly, then left. Chrye noticed she had a limp, walking away.

When she'd gone, Madsen said, 'The café was broken into when Ursie was a kid. They thought her dad was dealing in something else from Colombia as well as the coffee. They wanted a cut and they shot Ursie in the knee to encourage him. I was just coming through the door.'

He unwrapped the chocolate and cracked off a square.

'Talking of CMS,' Chrye said.

Madsen washed the chocolate down with a sip of coffee. 'If you wanted to talk to me about CMS you would have come to my office. So?'

'There's been another death at Maze,' Chrye said. 'His name was Anders Sosa. He also called himself Footfall. You know about it, don't you?'

He didn't say anything, sipping his coffee, peering at her over the cup through the fronds of steam. He isn't making it easy, Chrye thought. Though why should he? She said, 'Your computer, Anal, referred it to you, and you referred it straight back, just like before.'

'Go on.'

'It was in the news. He was found asphyxiated, a plastic bag tied tightly round his neck, hands cuffed behind his back.'

Madsen was holding the coffee cup between his hands like a priest with a chalice, drawing in the aroma. He breathed out and said, 'What's the problem with that? You tie the bag on but you don't trust yourself not to rip it off, so while there's oxygen you cuff yourself.'

Chrye took a first gulp of her coffee and what she'd been thinking left her. For a moment she couldn't speak. She couldn't remember drinking anything this good. She closed her eyes. When she opened them Madsen was grinning at her. She thought, He's on my side now. I don't need to say anything else.

'Good, huh?' he said.

She nodded and he poured more, carefully filling her cup to the halfway mark, then his own.

'Go on,' he said again.

He knew it already, she realised. He just wanted to hear it from her. 'All right,' she said. 'Forget for a moment that there are easier ways to kill yourself. Sosa was asthmatic. He knew what it was like to be short of breath. It's . . .'

'It's more or less a phobic situation,' Madsen said. 'Yes.'

'But it wasn't CMS, was it? Just like the others. You had to send it back. Let me guess. The wrists weren't bruised, so he hadn't struggled. It was a cover-up. He was murdered, just like they all were. Serial murder. And, just like before, nothing's going to be done about it.'

The door opened and closed as someone came in, and a corrosive whiff of the street stung Chrye's nose for a second before the coffee overrode it. A man and a woman, chattering. They passed out of Chrye's vision, and she heard chairs scraping against the wooden floor as they sat down. She watched Madsen observing them. Ursie went and took their order, then trotted back to the kitchen, her feet ker-ticking across the polished wood. The couple went quiet watching her, then started talking again. Chrye unwrapped her chocolate.

'Okay,' Madsen said eventually. 'My turn. Here's a few scraps. Sosa worked for Maze. The director of Maze had his house broken into by Hickey Sill yesterday, using Hickey's autoid controlled by an illegal device, and Hickey tried to use you as his alibi, which you denied. You said you were with a Jon Sciler, and Sciler confirmed that. Jon Sciler works for Maze and he lives in the same block as Hickey Sill.'

He sat back. 'I don't think the jigsaw's got too many pieces, Ms Roffe.'

'But Kerz isn't pressing charges, is he? Am I right? Nothing was stolen, the safe's intact, it was botched.'

Madsen nodded. 'There's not even going to be an investigation. Maze has total immunity. I don't know how or why. There's a government order. The only information I could get was that the blocking order came from the Department of Information. Maze might be another planet for all the access we can get to it.'

'So what's going to happen to Hickey?'

'Hickey's being charged with possession of the cuckoo. You don't need to worry about him for a long while. I wouldn't be around when he gets out, though. Or your friend Sciler.'

Madsen didn't say anything else, so Chrye had to say it. 'There was someone else in Kerz's house when Hickey was found.'

Madsen said, 'Yes,' slowly, looking at her. He even put down his coffee cup, settling it carefully in its saucer. 'I haven't figured that out. Irfan Culchic. Mentally retarded, broke out of his home along with all the other residents just a few hours before the break-in at Kerz's. They all had keys, God knows how. The 'fists found Culchic wandering around Kerz's house, trailing after Hickey's trig. Couldn't get any sense out of him. They figured there probably wasn't any in there in the first place.' Madsen put a chunk of chocolate in his mouth and started to chew it.

Chrye waited.

'He'll be released,' Madsen added. 'Kerz's not pressing charges, like I said. Hickey, of course, has no idea about Culchic. He could be done for kidnap, but what's the point? No, Culchic'll be released.'

The chocolate was sweet and bitter in Chrye's mouth, and the coffee was starting to make her buzz.

'So, are you going to tell me?' Madsen said.

'Are you interested?'

He sipped some coffee. 'Something's happening at Maze and no one's following it up. There's nothing I can do officially, but if you've got something I might know what to do with it.'

'The murders, I think they were committed by a woman who works at Maze. Her name is Teomera Sequeira.'

Madsen sat back. He nodded. His hand went to his hair.

'You've heard of her?' Chrye said.

'Oh, yes. I've heard of her.' He chuckled. It wasn't something that sounded right coming from Madsen. 'You know, I was starting to think you had inside information here. Teomera Sequeira's dead, Ms Roffe. We found her dead yesterday too. She killed herself.'

Chrye couldn't say anything for a moment. Then she just repeated, 'Killed herself?'

'That's right. She swallowed everything she had in the med cupboard. And that was a three-course meal, believe me. Washed it down with a cocktail of bleach and blackcurrant vodka. But this wasn't like the others, Ms Roffe. There's no suspicion about it. It was suicide, pure and dirty as they come. She even left a note, three words. "This Proves It." Her death didn't get on the news, though. Too ordinary.'

Chrye began to sort it out in her head. She hadn't been expecting that, but it had its logic. The woman was sure to have done it eventually. She just hadn't been caught in time. The death of her imaginary twin would have tipped her over the edge. She'd killed Footfall, then herself. 'Proves I don't exist,' Chrye murmured.

'I figured,' Madsen said.

Chrye gave him a small smile, thinking one last time of the woman Jon had slept with in Cathar, dead now. Jon was safe. It was okay. She felt a little bad about thinking it, but not much. 'That's it, then,' she said. She put a small velvety square of chocolate into her mouth, relaxing at last. 'Except that we'll never know quite how she killed them all.'

'Well, not exactly,' Madsen said. 'She was dead at least three hours before Anders Sosa died.' He took a sip of coffee and waited a moment before saying, 'Now, Ms Roffe, let's talk about Irfan Culchic.'

'Irf, this is my friend Chrye. Chrye, this is Irfan.'

Irfan took Chrye's hand and lifted it to his lips to kiss it. Chrye laughed at the chocolatey kiss. 'Thank you, Irfan. Nice to meet you.'

'Pretty lady,' Irfan said. 'Lucky Jon.'

'Yes,' Jon said, without thinking. Yes, he thought. He glanced at Chrye and she smiled back at him. He'd never noticed her smile before. There hadn't been any reason to smile. It seemed to make fire dance in her eyes. He thought what it meant to him that his look could make her smile. It meant a lot. Perhaps, if it hadn't been for Cathar and the memory of Starburn, it would have meant everything.

'Lucky Jon Sciler, eh?' the man with Irfan said, his eyes examining Jon. Jon wasn't sure how to read either him or his tone. Whatever Chrye had said, Madsen was a 'fist. He'd got Irfan out of custody and made sure the management of Irfan's hostel was changed, and he'd got Lindt orange chocolate all over Irfan's face, but he was still a 'fist to Jon.

'Sit down,' Chrye told Madsen. 'I'd give you coffee, but it wouldn't . . .'

Madsen was fishing in his pocket. He brought out a small, glittering foil bundle and handed it to her. 'Courtesy of Ursie's dad,' he said. Jon didn't like the way he gave it to Chrye, the assumed intimacy of the exchange, but Chrye's smile as she broke the VacWrap seal to draw in the aroma jumped straight from Madsen to Jon, and she immediately held the ground coffee under Jon's nose for him to breathe.

It was like the coffee in Cathar, John thought. But not quite as perfect, as rich and strong. It made him uneasy that the memory of Cathar could seem more powerful than this present reality. 'Thanks,' Jon said to Madsen as Chrye went to boil water for the coffee.

'Ursie took a shine to Irfan,' Madsen said, sitting down heavily at the table, his eyes still inspecting Jon. 'Irfan liked her a lot too. He told her some things he never told the 'fists.'

Jon glanced over at Irfan helping Chrye make coffee. Madsen didn't say any more. There wasn't any need. Jon said, 'I appreciate what you did for Irfan. Shaking out the management of his home.'

'It was overdue. It just needed something to bring it all out. But, then, you knew that, didn't you? I was just the last link in your chain.' He flicked his head towards Irfan. 'But I was glad to do it.'

Jon smiled at Madsen. Whatever Chrye hadn't told him he'd worked out for himself, and he was telling Jon it was okay.

Madsen lowered his voice and pulled his chair into the table, leaning forward on his elbows. 'Incidentally there was a camera running in Hickey Sill's room when he was picked up. I heard about the film but I never saw it. The film got destroyed somehow. You understand? You take care of her, Mr Sciler. She's done a lot for you. She must think you're worth it and I hope you are. If I were a lot younger I wouldn't be saying this, I'd be trying to give her a hard choice instead. But if you're ever in trouble, either of you – and if you aren't already, I think you're going to be – then call me.'

'What's that?' Chrye asked, putting the coffee on the table. It smelled no different from when Chrye had opened the ground beans under his nose, but with Chrye and Madsen there, and Irfan giggling and still licking his fingers by the lightwall, it was better than it had ever been in Cathar.

'Jon?' Chrye repeated. Madsen was pouring the coffee into four cups.

'Madsen was saying there's still a place in the world and time enough for dignity and honour,' Jon said.

Madsen raised his cup, grinning. 'Hell, did I say that?'

'Irfan,' Jon said, 'we'd like you to remember what you saw yesterday at the house with the orange saucepans. You remember that?'

Irfan nodded, holding out his hand for the bLinkers.

Jon took down the screenscribe and activated the lightwall. It looked like a dazzling white tunnel that he could just step forward and walk into. 'Okay,' he said, feeling dizzy and looking away. 'Ready.' He felt suddenly nervous, thinking of Starburn.

Chrye pressed start and 'PLAY' winked briefly at the top of the big screen before dissolving into the display. Irfan was sitting at the table, bLinkered to the lightwall's input console, nodding his head and murmuring to himself.

The display was divided into three segments. The left of the screen was cut in two, at the top the brain scans he recognised, squirming with red and orange blobs. Irfan must have loved that, Jon thought. Below the brain scans were a series of what he guessed were EEG readouts, two of them active and a third flatlined. On the right was the picture, fading slowly into view.

Chrye pointed at the EEG s. 'The top one's yours, I think, Jon, and the second's probably some sort of register of game activity. The third, I've no idea. It's not active so maybe it's a backup or a spare.'

The picture focussed. Starburn was lying on the deck of a sailing boat, his arms and legs chained, and there was a brown cloth blindfold tight around his head. He looked unconscious, lolling from side to side with the boat's roll. The boat was making its way steadily towards Calban's rock. The rock was as dark as ever.

'It's so real,' Chrye whispered. 'I never imagined . . .'

'I don't even notice it any more,' Jon said.

They watched for several minutes, nothing changing except that the rock came slowly closer, and Chrye told Irfan to fast forward the record. Jon caught a glimpse of red flotsam in the waves once or twice. Madsen got up to make more coffee, managing it without taking his eyes from the screen.

Eventually the boat rounded the rock. The distant shore of Cathar was visible for a few moments before the rock obscured it, and the crew of shades beached the boat in a small rocky bay. Starburn was transferred like a carcass to a waiting party of more shades and carried over the featureless dark rock to a long narrow chamber open to the skies and ringed by high rock walls. The shades climbed down into the chamber with Starburn and chained him to a rock in the bare centre. Jon noticed a trickle of water running between Starburn's feet, the water seeping from beneath a lowered iron shutter at the higher narrow end of the chamber. There was another, raised shutter at the far end where the water was leaving.

'There,' Jon said sharply. 'Calban.'

Madsen squinted at the screen and Chrye said quietly, 'Oh.' The rhythm of Irfan's nodding accelerated.

Calban was standing above Starburn at the top of the chamber's surrounding wall. It was impossible to tell how tall he might be. His eyes were yellow, his cheekbones high and flared beneath the yellow eyes, and the wind was whipping his long brown hair across his face. He stroked the hair back once with the angular fingers of a long hand and it never again came over his face, though still blowing around his head as if trying to escape him. Calban's other arm was stretched out and thickly padded, and there was a heavy black glove on his hand. The eagle perched there, moving restlessly up and down, its thick talons constantly gripping and releasing Calban's forearm. They curled around the bindings almost to meet at front and back. Jon tried to imagine the spread and power of their grip.

'Recognise him, Sciler?' Madsen said.

'No. I thought perhaps I knew who he was until recently.'

'Well, I guess if we ever catch him you'd be able to pick him out of a line-up. Even without the budgerigar.'

The bird was jerking its head around and adjusting its wings. Calban seemed to be whispering to it, and it gradually settled.

Then Calban spoke. His voice boomed down into the chamber, slow and easy, sounding hardly raised at all.

'I know you're here, Starburn. Remember, I know everything. I'd advise you to pay attention.'

Starburn came alive. He stood up carefully and lifted his manacled hands to drag away the blindfold. He rubbed his eyes and gazed around until he found Calban.

'That's better,' Calban said. 'Now, here's a game we can play. A special game I prepared just for you. I know you like games.'

Starburn picked his feet out of the water and spread them as far to either side of the trickle as the chains allowed. His mouth opened and his eyes glazed. Jon could see him starting to hyperventilate.

He knows, Jon thought. Calban knows Starburn's hydrophobic.

Chrye's hand moved to cover his.

'Take your time,' Calban said, waiting in the wind, and eventually Starburn became still, straddling the thread of water.

'What do you want?' Starburn said, his voice on the edge of panic. Jon had never heard him sound quite like that, even on Dirangesept. He held on to Chrye's hand. Starburn said, 'Who are you?'

'I am your saviour. Now, prepare yourself. The game is beginning.'

Calban gestured and mouthed something, and the downstream shutter fell. Water slowly began to pool against it, welling up through the stones and backing towards Starburn's feet.

'It's a simple game,' Calban said. 'We play it with seawater. Don't worry that we'll run dry, though. I created a reservoir especially for today, and it's full to the brim. And this is how we play. That was move one,' Calban said. 'And this is move two.'

The upstream shutter began to rise and from beneath it a torrent of water roared into the chamber, rushing at Starburn's legs. Starburn let out a cry and then dropped his head as the water hit him. It crashed against the far shutter and the shutter rose. The water started to escape and the level dropped.

Jon raised his free hand and clenched his fist. Starburn had used a spell to raise the shutter.

Calban laughed. Starburn had slumped back with the effect of the spell, and Calban dropped the escape shutter back. The water began to rise again, but the rate of its rise slackened almost immediately as Starburn managed to rouse himself to drop the entry shutter.

Chrye looked at Jon and gestured at Irfan to move on. The water level continued to rise and fall as Calban and Starburn competed with each other, but gradually the water rose until it had reached Starburn's waist.

Jon could see Starburn tiring. Only his fear of the water was keeping him on his feet.

Calban suddenly turned to the bird and murmured, 'Anyone coming yet, Arel? Go and see.' And with a brisk movement the great eagle rose in a flurry of wings to shear away out of sight. Calban watched it away and turned his attention back to the game. 'Is someone coming to save you, Starburn?' he shouted.

Both shutters were open now, the chamber in full flood. The water was a deafening roar and it was at the level of Starburn's chest. He was screaming and flailing about wildly, trying to wrench his legs free of the chains. There was blood in the water. Starburn vanished, knocked over by the torrent, and reappeared again coughing.

'Stand up and keep still,' Calban yelled down at him. 'You'll last longer.'

Jon could hardly watch. Starburn was hysterical. He wasn't even trying to move the shutters any more, but the water wasn't rising further. Calban had regulated the shutters to stabilise the level. Jon didn't understand it.

As the eagle returned to Calban's arm, furling its wings, Jon saw a movement on the battlement. Something had leapt up to crouch on the rock's rim. He recognised it immediately, the beast with its teeth bared white and the mane of red hair flattened against its long low skull. Jon leaned forward and said, 'That's Starburn's wolf, Chrye. From the flickbooks.'

Calban had seen it. He cried out and flung the bird from his arm. The eagle dipped and beat its wings against the air, heading for the wolf.

The water was rising again and Starburn had his head bent desperately back to draw breath. Jon watched the eagle rear back as it neared the wolf, talons stretched wide to rake its prey.

Jon looked back at Starburn. Starburn was mouthing a spell with the last of his breath, but the water was closing over him. He dipped down suddenly, then bobbed right up, head high and dragging in air. Even his shoulders were clear of the water.

He's slipped the chains, Jon thought. That was the spell. He's going to make it.

Above Calban the wolf leapt aside as the eagle came at it, but the bird twisted in the air and ripped one set of talons along the animal's flank, then wheeled round to come again.

The water was louder now and as the bird came round the wolf crouched and leapt. The bird's claws met nothing as the wolf fell into the torrent and disappeared.

Calban screamed, 'No!' and Jon realised that Starburn had managed to raise the exit shutter all the way while Calban had been watching the wolf.

The water level was dropping. There was no sign in the water of Starburn or the wolf.

Both shutters dropped instantly at Calban's yell, and the water steadied. When it was almost still, Calban raised the exit shutter a fraction. The water began to drain away.

'He's escaped,' Jon whispered. He felt he was watching it happen. At the periphery of his vision he caught Madsen fractionally shaking his head. Calban didn't react and as the last of the water seeped through the crack beneath the shutter, Jon saw what they had just seen.

Starburn's body was washed up against the iron sheet like a long hank of weed. There was no sign of the wolf, though. The wolf had escaped.

'Arel,' Calban cried out, and Jon saw the bird circling high. It dipped its head and pulled in its wings and began to drop like a black pip through the pale blue sky.

Calban scrambled up to the top of the chamber wall where the wolf had been. The record's viewpoint rose with him.

The red wolf was loping awkwardly away towards the sea, slowed by the wet rock underfoot, slipping. It was obvious that it wouldn't make it. The eagle was hurtling down, coming behind the wolf, bringing out its wings at the last moment to level off.

The wolf must have sensed the bird, turning and baring its teeth, but the eagle smashed into the wolf's flank with its talons, hurling it over, bouncing the wolf over the rocks. The bird recovered quickly and rose immediately to regain height, wings beating hard, while the wolf struggled to its feet, thrown closer to the water's edge by the impact of the bird. It was just metres away now but limping badly, its left forefoot seemingly broken.

'Come on, come on,' Jon murmured.

The bird came down again and this time the wolf didn't turn in time to face it. The bird's talons ripped into the nape of the wolf's neck and held there. The eagle let out a piercing scream that cut through Jon like a blunt saw and then it rose slowly into the air again, the wolf writhing helplessly beneath it. The bird was over the sea with its prey and still rising, starting to circle slowly back towards the land, dipping with every upbeat of its wings but each time pulling up again strongly. It was heading towards the shore when the wolf's head jerked up sharply and its jaws closed in the feathers of the bird's belly. The bird screeched and opened its talons, releasing the wolf and rising abruptly. The wolf fell on its back in the breaking surf and lay there, its neck twisted. The dying waves rolled the animal's limp head to and fro, slowly tugging the body back into the sea.

Calban held out his arms and yelled in fury. The bird turned and swooped down again, tracing lazy figures of eight up and down the shore, but the wolf's body had gone, washed under the waves. At another command from Calban the eagle gained height and extended its search pattern further over the sea, but it found nothing. After a while it glided back to settle on Calban's arm, folding its wings. Blood from its talons dripped from Calban's sleeve to the ground.

Calban seemed to withdraw into himself briefly, and then he looked up again. Smoke was starting to rise from the chamber to form a long plume into the sky.

The lightwall went white again. 'ENDPLAY' flashed up, then vanished against the dead screen. Irfan picked the bLinkers out of his eyes and sighed. 'All gone,' he said.

Chrye checked the console. 'It's taped and filed,' she said. Looking up, she made a face at Jon and went on, 'Well, if it's not real, then Calban's a player. Whoever he is. Otherwise the record would end when Starburn died.'

'The wolf,' Jon said. He felt numb, as if Starburn had died again. For a third time. Only the real death was still a mystery now. 'The wolf's still in Cathar. I've seen it.'

'Or another one,' Chrye said. 'If it's a game – I mean *as* it's a game – they can just program a new wolf into it.'

'The wolf was trying to save him. I think it's helping me.' He went quiet, thinking of Starburn and the wolf of his childhood dream dying for him in Cathar, dying in vain.

Chrye was rewinding the tape and replaying it. 'Look at the EEG,' she said suddenly. 'It's going crazy towards the end.'

Jon watched the tape. 'But Starburn's dead there.'

Chrye shook her head. 'His *character*'s dead. Starburn – Marcus – is still alive, isn't he? The EEG would only flatline if he was really dead. No, what I mean is it's a real mess here. I don't recognise any of these spikes on the scale.'

'That's when the wolf's around, isn't it?' Madsen said.

'Yes.'

Madsen leaned forward, tapping his finger in the air. 'Go back, Chrye. Back to where he's still in the boat coming to the island.'

Chrye reversed the tape until Madsen said, 'Stop.'

'What?' Chrye said. 'I don't see anything. Just sea.'

'Run it again. There,' Madsen said. 'That flash of red in the waves.'

Jon nodded slowly at Madsen, saying, 'Yes. I thought it was just a rag or something floating in the water. That was the wolf swimming along with the boat. It was there then.'

Chrye froze the picture, staring at the EEG reading beside it.

'When did you first see the wolf in Cathar, Jon?' she said suddenly.

'I've never seen it properly. But that flicker of red. I saw that in the hall when I first awoke. I didn't tell Dr Locke. She kept saying had I forgotten anything. I didn't tell her because it was so insignificant. I forgot it completely. It was just a glimpse of colour at the corner of my eye, and there was so much else happening at the time.'

'But she knew it was there, didn't she?'

Jon could see Chrye was excited. He couldn't work out why. 'I don't know,' he said.

'I'm telling you, Jon. She knew. Look at the spike again. The wolf spike. Look at the shape of it.'

The spike shot up high and began to slide down at the same angle, but then on the down strike it stopped suddenly and ran in a plateau for a beat before dropping vertically back to the baseline.

'See it, Jon?'

Jon stared at the screen. 'Cathedral,' he said finally. 'That's what she wanted. That's their cathedral, the wolf.'

'Yes.' She paused. 'But it doesn't make sense. They put Lile there, and they put the wolf there, we assume. But Dr Locke got excited about your first cathedral reading, and she wasn't at all concerned about Lile or the medallion, which they *can't* have programmed.'

She was flicking through the record. 'And the brainmaps,' she said. 'I don't know enough about them, but they make no sense to me. The activity's all over the place. Maybe their reader's highly sensitive, or selective and we don't know its criteria, but it seems to me that there's just too much of it.'

'Too much! Jesus, Chrye, Starburn's stuffed full of the game or whatever the hell Cathar is, and he's a hydrophobic being drowned there. And you say there's too much activity?'

'And that's another thing,' she said. 'He's in a phobic situation. Hear him say anything odd any time?'

285

'The spells, I suppose, though they meant nothing to me. Why?'

'His exitline. Don't you have an exitline that you won't forget?'

Chrysanthemum, Jon thought. My exitline. Something I won't forget.

She said, 'Why didn't he use it? And if he did, why didn't it work?'

Jon said, 'Program error?' But he knew it wasn't that. There was no program error at Maze.

She ignored him. 'And there,' she said. 'When the bird first appears, the other line activates for the first time. The one we thought was just a backup. That was the eagle's readout.'

'So?'

'This is Starburn's record, Jon. Calban's a player, but the bird, Arel, and the wolf must both be part of the program.' She pointed at the lightwall. 'And yet the wolf's on Starburn's EEG, and the eagle's got its own readout. It doesn't make sense.'

Jon said, 'There's something else in Cathar, Chrye. Apart from the wakers and the Catharians. There has to be. There's something else, and I think it can cross from Cathar to the player.'

'What do you mean?'

'The wolf, the follower. This sounds crazy, but you know how I've been feeling as if there's something following me, like Starburn wrote in his journal? Well, in the zone it was the wolf, but what is it out here?' He went to the window and gazed out. 'Before he was killed, Footfall told me, "They're here already," and that's just how I feel.'

His cheek was itching for some reason, and he rubbed it with the palm of his hand. He was wasting time now. He should be back in Cathar.

'It could be Maze keeping an eye on you,' Madsen said.

'No. It isn't Maze. It isn't like that. It's more than something physical. It's . . .' He tapped his head, not knowing how to explain it better.

'You're not going to Cathar again, Jon,' Chrye said. 'Everyone dies. I don't want you to go back.'

He took her hand. 'How else are we going to find out what's going on? I'm not letting this go, Chrye. I can't. And if it is with me now, like it was with Footfall and Starburn, then it's with me whether I'm here or in Cathar. It isn't something I can run away from.'

Chrye looked at Madsen who just said, 'This isn't my argument. But, Jon, you remember what I told you.' He stood up and pulled on his coat, saying, 'Irfan, you want a ride home? Maybe we'll drop in on Ursie on the way.'

TWENTY-SIX

The wind was bitter, hurling itself at Jon as he walked towards Maze, and his face felt unusually sensitive to it. His cheeks were as tender as if they had been scratched or scraped.

The work around Maze had nearly finished now, but the security fence was still there, as solid as Maze, and a wall was going up behind it. Maze wasn't concerned about safety at all. The building looked like a prison now. A further area was cut off from the street beyond the building, and there was new excavation. The security guards there were wearing Information Ministry flashes. Jon started over there, but the wind was stinging his face viciously and he turned back to Maze. He showed his pass and was let straight through, wondering whether there had ever been a tremor here, whether it had all just been an excuse to isolate Maze from the surrounding streets.

He walked past Kerz's office, realising suddenly that he had never had to wait to be debriefed after exiting from Cathar. Forgetting Calban, there seemed to be just two wakers at any one time who were Far Warriors. Starburn and Footfall, Footfall and Jon, Jon and Herta. Dr Locke would debrief one, Kerz the other. No one else in Cathar was as important. They could be debriefed at any time by whoever else was part of the project.

Jon stopped dead in the corridor. The whole Cathar project was concerned with Far Warriors. Everyone else was just part of the setup.

'Everything okay, Mr Sciler?'

Jon whirled round. Kerz was standing at the door of his office. Jon couldn't tell whether he was going in or had just come out.

'Why shouldn't it be?' Jon said.

'No reason at all,' Kerz said lightly. 'You seemed a little disturbed last time, and then you rushed off without completing your debriefing. And while we don't tell you when to enter and leave Cathar, we expect you to take it seriously. You have been arriving late.'

'I take it seriously,' Jon said, massaging his cheek. Maybe he was developing a rash.

'You have been curtailing your debriefings too. They are a contractual requirement, Mr Sciler.'

'And what else is in the contract, Kerz? Why don't you tell me what else is in the small print?'

Kerz's eyebrows arched. 'There's no small print, Mr Sciler.' He stretched out his open hands and pulled his cuffs high up his skinny forearms. 'I have nothing up my sleeve.'

Jon turned his back on Kerz's grin and headed for the CrySis chamber. There wasn't time for this.

The voice seemed to be in his head even before the lid of the CrySis pod closed. For some reason his cheek was still stinging. That shouldn't be happening at all. There shouldn't be any sensory carryover.

Don't speak out loud, Jon, they can hear you if you do.

Who are you?

Wake up now, you have to wake up. You're in danger. I've been trying to wake you for hours. We have to talk while there's time. Remember when Mr Lile took us to Brighton, to the sea?

Starburn, is that you?

Jon kept his eyes shut, thinking that maybe it was a dream and he didn't want to wake up and lose it, lose Starburn again, but his cheeks were burning. Someone was blowing hot air at him and rubbing his face with a rough wet cloth.

Jon squeezed his eyes closed, trying to ignore the sensory stimulus. He thought, We played Dark Sword in Brighton and we never lost a single life. But now you've lost yours, and this isn't a game, is it? That's what you're telling me. So how are you alive? How are you talking to me?

The cloth had gone from his face and the warmth too. There was no answer to his questions and he opened his eyes.

There was no one there, just a blistering glare of colour all around him as he pulled himself out of the sleep hole and stood up. Everything had changed overnight. The leaves had turned brilliant colours while he had been asleep and dropped from the branches. Above him the trees were sharp bones bent against the sky, flagged with a few last stubborn handfuls of foliage. Everything else around him was gold, red, orange and yellow.

Whatever you do, Jon, don't say anything aloud. They mustn't know about me.

Jon rubbed his face. The voice in his head was fainter. There was someone nearby, standing just out of sight. The foliage moved at the edge of his vision, flashes of colour over colour like blinding camouflage. A tongue, he thought. A tongue and hot, panting breath.

What are you? Jon thought. *Who are you?*

Beyond the trees there was sudden broad noise as if a wind was building, but then it became sharper, condensing into the sound of something crashing towards him.

No time, Jon.

The two shades seemed to come from nowhere, bursting at him through the trees. Jon turned and fled, his feet sliding on the loose patchwork of leaves as he bounced off tree trunks and carried on running. Turning too fast, he hit a slope with the side of his foot and tumbled down, glancing behind as he stood up again to see how far behind him the shades were and registering the dull scar of mud his fall had left across the brilliant matting. They were close. He kept on running.

Behind him a scream shook the air and he knew one of the shades was somehow gone. Ahead of him the forest light was brighter. He was nearly at the edge of the trees, and something made him feel that he'd be safe once he was out in the open. The remaining shade was closing on him, though. Still running, he formed words into a spell and set his eyes on a great tree ahead, starting the spell twenty paces before it, timing it for the sound of the crashing feet behind him. He passed the tree just right, his eyes locked on its base, only hoping he wouldn't trip on the ground. The spell's end took the last of his breath and left him gasping, doubled over at the edge of the wood as the fractured tree came down on to the shade.

He stood straight, his breath gradually returning, watching the shade try to push and kick the tree off with its broken arms and legs.

Something moved close behind him and he turned around, still wheezing.

Calban was standing there, tall and grinning. He'd been waiting for Jon. The shades were just his shepherds, his beaters. Jon hadn't been running at all.

He had no strength to resist as Calban took him by the neck with both hands and held him high, cutting off his breath with long, bony thumbs until Jon felt he was going to faint. He was aware of the bird swooping down behind him towards the bank of trees. An animal howl came from the woods, followed by the bird's long, keening cry echoing through the air as it soared up again.

Calban's face was fading away as Jon started to lose consciousness, those yellow eyes piercing him through the lowering grey mist of unconsciousness. Jon tried to speak, and the pressure lifted a fraction.

'You want to say something?' Calban said, far away.

'Yes,' Jon managed. He exited.

'He isn't strong. You can have ten minutes with him and no more than that,' the nurse said, standing before the door. She looked hard at Jon and then at Chrye. 'I'll come back.' She knocked once sharply and pushed the door open.

The first thing Jon saw was the CrySis pod that dominated the room. It looked no different from the pods at Maze except that this one was white, the colour of healing. At Maze they were silver, like they had been on the ships that had taken the Far Warriors to Dirangesept. Silver implied cuspal technology, Jon assumed, what they do being more important than what they look like.

The reedy, cracking voice seemed to intercept his thoughts. 'Like a sarcophagus, I always think. The ancient Egyptians used to imagine they were being ferried between worlds, from this world of ruin and woe to the next world in which they'd be gods. My name's Anton Stuber.'

Jon turned round. Anton Stuber was sitting in a chair backed up against a wall shelved with data screens and drug delivery systems. He made a gesture to welcome them in and moved his hand on the chair's arm. The chair came forward from the wall and a segment of the wall detached and followed the chair, maintaining a discreet distance and linked to Anton Stuber by hanks of conduit and wire.

Stuber reached out a trembling hand to stroke the white casing of the pod. There appeared to be no muscle to his arms. The plastic conduits from his wrist and the crook of his elbow jerked with his action like puppet strings. Jon wasn't sure whether they were following him or leading. Anton's scalp was hairless and mottled with chloasma and there was a brittle tremor in the movement of his head that made him seem slightly out of focus.

He said, 'It's a shame we don't use coffins to bury our dead any more, don't you think? Just because the earth won't guarantee not to throw them straight back up again. But such a potent symbol in an age that rejects symbols.' He moved around the pod, the treatment wall with its wires and tubes gliding in his wake.

'It prolongs my life, this coffin, keeps me from the next world. Anchors a dying man on a dying planet. What would Tutankhamun have made of that, do you think? Would he have approved? Hmm?'

Jon said, 'One of those took me to Dirangesept and brought me back.'

'Another world again,' Anton noted with approval. 'A Far Warrior, then. Of course. It's why you're here.'

Jon thought of Cathar, of lying in the CrySis pod and waking in Cathar. He glanced at Chrye and she was already looking at him, thinking the same thing, he knew. Worlds within worlds.

'More than a symbol, then,' Anton said. He wheeled himself around to face Jon and Chrye. 'I don't get visitors much any more, just medics and maintenance workers. Not that there's a difference. They're all just interested in the machinery.' He raised his arms with difficulty, setting wires swinging like the rigging of his delicate frame. 'I'm the only weak link in it all. They'll be so disappointed when I die. They'll have to take it all down again.'

He patted the white metal of the pod once more and gestured to a stack of metal and plastic chairs. 'Sit down, please. I forget. I sit, and at night I lie down, but I never stand. I take pleasure from seeing people standing, walking around. My dreams are of running, endlessly running.'

'We're happy to stand,' Chrye said. 'Whatever you want.'

Anton chuckled. 'Perhaps you'd dance for me. A tarantella, maybe. Around my chair.' He rubbed his hands together. They made a sound like the rustling of dry paper far away. 'I'm rambling. You haven't got long, have you? Longer than me, of course, but all the same. Hmm? Your note said you were interested in PI.'

'That's right,' Chrye said.

'Fine. Now I'm going to backtrack first. I'm going to tell you something about virtual reality, as it was called. Is that all right with you?'

Jon said, 'Yes.'

'Good. You need to understand this about virtual reality, that for a long time we were confronted by two big problems. The first was the fractional motor time lag. You move just before the scene does, hmm? Are you with me? Like long-distance face-to-face communication even now. That microsecond throws you, doesn't it? We dealt with that partially with sensory suppression, but it hadn't been really solved in my time.'

He paused. 'The second and greater problem was the complexity of the virtual image. The computing requirements even for a simple interactive scenario with limited participant choice are almost unimaginable.' He tilted his head and added. 'But not quite. Real-time image generation was the objective, and we solved it in two ways. Firstly with seventh-generation free-state ultra-computers, and secondly by using participant fill-in.'

His voice went up a notch there, and Jon held up his hand. 'Participant fill-in. Explain that.'

'Yes. What isn't vital to the program is recall-facilitated from the subject's own memories. In this way the program could be freed for the essential work.'

'Wait a minute. Where are the memories trawled from?' asked Chrye. 'Conscious or subconscious?'

Anton nodded approvingly. 'Good question. They're usually limbo memories, quite beyond conscious access. When we surfaced them, interestingly, the subjects frequently reported feelings of *déjà vu*. We were initially a bit concerned about that at first, but it did seem to anchor the scenario very well.'

'What do you mean, anchor?' said Jon.

'They said it was quite real.'

Chrye broke in. 'Did you investigate image sources in any detail?'

'Oh, yes, naturally. Subject input was usually from appropriate indirect sources. Films, vids. Books even, surprisingly enough.'

'Not necessarily visual memory, then?' Jon said.

'That's right.'

'That's not really so surprising,' Chrye told Jon. 'Some people can store heard or read stimuli as visual memory. After a passage of time they can be convinced they've been places only described to them. They process what they've been told and can see it in their minds. That's nothing new. Remember false memory syndrome?' She glanced at the old man. 'People like that made your best subjects, I bet. Imaginative people.'

He gave her a flat smile and his cheeks coloured. Chrye thought, I hit something there. What the hell was it?

'In other words,' Jon murmured to him, 'the more you put into the game, the more you get out.'

'Exactly so.'

Jon leaned towards Chrye. He said, 'Dirangesept must be a hell of a source.'

Anton interrupted excitedly, moving forward to touch Jon's arm. 'Exactly! Exactly! But listen to this. We found that a few people provided such powerful input that the fringes of the program, designed to seam into the participant's input, actually changed to fit the input better. They actually changed! And the astonishing thing was that with an even smaller sample the program *retained* those changes.' He pulled back. 'Minor changes, of course.'

'Oh, Christ,' said Chrye.

'Yes. It was quite a problem. Obviously it was no good if the software was too soft, hmm? But by this time we had other priorities. The Dirangesept project, the second one, was beginning, and most of our research was channelled into military bLinker and autoid hardware.'

'We're not interested in that,' said Chrye.

'Wait,' said Jon, touching her hand. 'Go on.'

'Yes. On Dirangesept we began losing autoids, and the operators – who, remember, were selected for their gaming skills and experience – suffered from what we later called Dirangesept stigmata. Back on Earth we developed a process by trial and error as a rough means of quantifying susceptibility to stigmata. It was called SS, stigmata susceptibility.'

Chrye nodded. 'I've heard of that. It was just a rough measure, though, and it was too late to be of any use to the project, wasn't it?'

'That's right. We found quite incidentally that the subjects with the lowest SS scores were the best autoid operators and games players, too.'

Jon looked at Chrye, but her attention was fixed on Anton.

'When the Dirangesept project was aborted,' Anton said, 'our research was discontinued. Most of us joined games companies. Maze, Dimension Seven, Id/Entity. At Maze, where I was working, research into SS measurement was prioritised, just because of the correlation between gaming and autoid operating. We were intending to use SS simply to select good games players as testers. But, to our surprise, it turned out to link with other observations. Remember I told you that input sources for zone background could be written material as well as visual, that in some people, as you said, vivid written or auditory material is stored as visual imagery?' He nodded at Chrye. 'Your highly imaginative people, hmm?'

Chrye nodded. Bull's-eye. Here it comes now. She glanced at Jon.

The man said, 'The degree to which people had this ability was SS-linked. High visual transfer, low SS.'

He paused and took a long breath. His throat rattled. 'It goes further. We found by chance that a low SS was in some cases associated with a greater likelihood that a player's input would alter the program, and so we used SS to find players to help us discover how to protect our software.' He gestured at Chrye. 'Are you with me? Hmm?'

Chrye said slowly, 'So you honed the tests a bit and renamed the aptitude PI.'

Anton smiled. 'Exactly. Psychic Inertia. I'm afraid I'm getting a bit tired now.'

'We're nearly there,' Chrye said. 'Tell me about Psychic Inertia.'

'Well, we found that the best way to test the programs was to use threatening situations – the greater the threat, the more likely a player with low PI was to change it, make it safer for himself.'

'So you used fears and phobias in these situations.'

'Yes. But we succeeded. We *did* harden the programs. We tested them to death. We killed the players. But in the game, only in the game.'

Something in Anton's eyes told Chrye to push it further. She paused a second and then took the leap. 'But a few of the players died later, didn't they?'

Anton wasn't reacting at all, and that was enough. Chrye said, 'They were murdered and you never found out who killed them.'

Anton dropped his gaze. 'There were rumours that the government was involved in the research and they didn't want it all ripped open. The project was closed.'

Chrye felt Jon's eyes on her as she said to Anton, 'When was that?'

'Years ago.'

The door opened behind them and the nurse's shoes clicked on the floor. She looked at Anton, then at Jon and Chrye. 'You've had more time than I should have let you. Off you go now.' She started to shepherd Jon and Chrye out of Anton's room.

'It's started again, hasn't it? And you're involved,' Anton said suddenly to Jon.

'Yes,' Jon said.

Anton nodded. 'And you're a Far Warrior, of course you are, you said so.'

Jon waited for something else, but Anton seemed to lose his focus. He sighed wearily, backing himself towards the main wall. The detached unit docked into it first, all the main screens progressively reactivating. Jon had a sense of the whole meeting rewinding, going into reverse.

Chrye stopped at the door and turned round. She said, 'Anton, who else was at Maze when you were there?'

Anton shrugged while lights winked on around him like an aura. 'People came and went all the time, but Kerz was the head of the research team. I think he's still there. You could check. Daedalus Kerz.'

As they walked away from the building, Chrye said, 'The research was never stopped, Jon. And the murderer was never found. They simply started to cover up the traces and trimmed the team, took out people like Anton Stuber. And they're still doing it now. Whatever's going on is important enough for them to consider it worth it.'

'Unless the deaths are a part of it,' Jon said. 'Unless the players can't be allowed to live once they've been killed in the zone, maybe. Maybe it's that important.'

'It's only a game, Jon. We know that for sure now. We know it's a game and we know Kerz is playing Calban. It's just business. Maze just wants to keep it quiet until they're ready to put it on the streets, even if it means shielding the killer.'

Jon said, 'You're wrong. It's something more than that. I know it is.'

Chrye shook her head. 'Whatever, that's how Starburn and Footfall died, Jon. In the zone and then for real. And if you go back, you're going to be next. Look, maybe we've taken this far enough. Maybe Madsen can do something now.'

Jon wouldn't meet her eyes. 'You know how much Madsen can do. He can pull out his hair until there isn't any more. There's no one else any more, Chrye. There's just you and me. And I want to know what's going on at Maze, what could be this important.' He reached out and stroked the curve of her neck, saying, 'We still don't know about the follower, Chrye. Starburn is dead, but what about the wolf with his memories? Kerz hasn't killed the wolf and he doesn't seem to know much about it. That's what this is all about. The wolf. Cathedral. The wolf wants me to go back, Chrye. I think that the wolf could somehow be Starburn.'

She shook his hand away. 'Jon, you don't know the wolf said anything at all to you. Even in the zone, it was in your head. It didn't exist.' She heard her own voice rising, becoming shrill. 'Maybe you put it there, like

295

Anton was saying. It could have been your own unconscious just projecting it, refusing to accept his death. Like you said, Kerz had no record of anything.'

She waited, but Jon wasn't interested. It was futile trying to argue with him. She knew what he'd say anyway.

'I'm not going to desert him again, Chrye.'

'Jon, you never deserted him,' Chrye said, knowing it was just a waste of the words. She bit the rest of it off but it still looped through her head. It's too late to save Starburn now. It's too late to save the world. And I think now that it's even too late to save yourself.

'Okay,' she said. 'Your phobia or whatever it is that they'll use to kill you in the zone. Maybe we can do something about that.'

'I haven't got one. We've been over this. It's safe. Believe me.'

She sighed unhappily. 'No anxieties, no fears? There must be something. It just isn't there on a conscious level. I don't . . .'

He took her hand and held it. Her eyes were bright and wet. 'You won't lose me, Chrye,' he said. 'There's nothing, I promise you. Nothing worries me enough that I can't deal with it.' He grinned and leaned forward to kiss her. 'I'm Cathar-proof.'

TWENTY-SEVEN

The pavement was slimy where a drizzle of rain had combined with the ash to create an uncomfortable pulpiness underfoot. Today the ground might have been melting.

The security wall around Maze was complete now. From the edge of the cleared area the roof of the building was just visible. Dark pillars jutted straight up from the corners of the roof, and the oblong of sky trapped between the pillars seemed viscous and murky. As he came closer to Maze Jon lost the building behind the security wall.

He had to show his pass twice before being let in, a second security guard stopping him with a gloved hand flat against Jon's chest at an inner gate that hadn't existed the day before.

'Mr Sciler? You're to go up to the roof first. Mr Kerz is swimming. He wants to speak with you.'

The rooftop door opened without the crackle of a vent seal and Jon stood back in the doorframe, his breath catching instinctively until he recognised the solid grey MagNet posts studding the corners of the roof. The MagNet's canopy threw down reflections of light from the pool and blurred the sky beyond. The sky looked almost blue but the MagNet could have been tinted. All Jon could smell was the chlorine of the pool.

He let the door fall closed behind him. In the water Kerz was swimming languid lengths, his arms stroking evenly, his legs shuddering through the water as if he was quelling it as he advanced. His head seemed not to surface as he swam, just to tic sideways every third stroke. He didn't appear to need to breathe. He didn't acknowledge Jon.

The pool was illuminated from beneath and Kerz's shadow, trapped high against the MagNet, caught Jon's attention, giving him the odd feeling of floundering below the swimmer, and the light in the splintered water made Kerz's body indeterminate and illusory.

Jon watched Kerz for a few minutes before calling out to him.

Kerz stopped to tread water in the centre of the pool. His face was pale and his hair was plastered like dead weed against his scalp. His white body, foreshortened in the water, seemed to be dissolving and reforming. 'Mr Sciler,' he said slowly.

Jon shrugged. 'What should I call you? Should I call you Daedalus? Or Calban? I'm not going back to Cathar until you tell me what's going on here at Maze.'

Kerz exhaled and sank down out of sight, then rose up again, shaking a bright crown of water from his head. The water had rearranged his hair and he looked quite different.

'Jon Sciler,' Kerz said. 'Jon Sciler. That's the name everyone knows you by, isn't it? Everywhere. Plain Jon Sciler.' He raised a hand and sliced it cleanly into the water. 'Is that supposed to make you somehow more trustworthy than the rest of us? More certain of yourself? More . . . what, more real? Do you feel more real, Jon Sciler?'

He didn't wait for an answer, taking a sharp breath and diving down in a splash of light to glide smoothly along the floor of the pool. He came up at the pool's edge a few metres from Jon and took a lungful of air. 'Yes, Mr Sciler, in Cathar I am Calban. But does that change anything for you? Tell me what difference it makes. No difference at all. It helped you to think that Calban is pure evil, and now if you like you can think that I am pure evil instead. As long as you play the game . . .'

Jon tried to keep his voice even. 'It is a game, then.'

Kerz put his elbows up on the side of the pool and chuckled. 'What is in those words? Relief? Disappointment? Both? Neither? Really, Mr Sciler, I've never tried to mask the reality from you.' The water had nearly stilled around his chest and he threw himself back and pushed out with his legs, sending sharp waves back into the wall as he back-pedalled to the centre of the pool.

'What do you want to hear? That Cathar is real and we shall be escaping there, all of us, everyone on Earth? Or that this is the cover story for an attempt to rid ourselves of the vast majority of the population so that we who remain can better survive? You like that one? Or that Cathar is the precursor to another even more sophisticated zone called Dirangesept which ditto either of the above? Or how about this? That the Dirangesept to which you went was the precursor to Cathar. That there never *was* a Dirangesept. That the beasts were self-generated figments of your imagination, your id, and that players were selected for the project not for their skills but because the project was a game all along. That the Dirangesept project was all a ploy to keep control while the governments of the world tried desperately to find a *real* Dirangesept. What about that, Mr Sciler?'

Jon said nothing. This wasn't a conversation.

'Of course, none of them is true, but you've considered them, as everyone on Earth either has or will before too long. But, no, Cathar isn't real. As I've always said to you.' Kerz shook his head. 'But nevertheless Cathar is as important to us, to the world, as Dirangesept was. And still is. And you, Mr Sciler, are at this moment crucial to us.'

Kerz pulled himself out of the water in a lithe movement and stood against the haze of the MagNet's field, water dripping from him. The pool began to settle. Kerz held up his hand to stop Jon interrupting. 'Wait, Mr Sciler. Listen to me. I'm going to tell you something that very few people alive know. Back during the first expedition, a few of us had an inkling that, for want of a better word, magic was possible on the planet. Of course it isn't magic; magic's just what we can't yet explain. We came back, our frozen tails between our legs, and you went off, really no better equipped to deal with the beasts than we were. I knew that but, of course, some time after I climbed out of my CrySis pod, a bLink of the eye later, you were accumulating stigmata and dying up there.'

Kerz walked around the pool, his footprints drying and fading as he passed. He picked up a large white towel from a low slatted metal bench and shook it out before spreading it over his shoulders like a cape.

'I joined Maze, and at the same time I was working for a government-funded research foundation. I believe you've spoken to my old friend Anton. Anton had a fairly low level of clearance. He knew a little, guessed some more. He developed a conscience along with a cancer. I always thought there was a connection there.

'Back then in game research we started to develop software for magic abilities for players in zones. We found creating the ability in players easier than controlling it – that's why we called the quotient Psychic Inertia; hard to set off but even harder to stop.'

There was hardly any movement in the water now. The sky was reflected darkly there, blurred more by the MagNet field than by the water's faintest motion. Jon felt weighed down, trapped in the pressing air of a killing jar.

Kerz was saying, 'We found, when we started to develop magic within the gamescape, that low PI reflected a greater ability, and vice versa. It was a very deep, basic block. Some people simply couldn't do magic in a zone while others, as I'm sure Anton told you, were changing the zone.' He waved a hand towards Jon. 'Like Starburn bringing in Lile, and you changing him. From a commercial point of view, a disastrous ability.'

'Nearly as disastrous as your testers being murdered. Or were you killing them?'

Kerz smiled evenly. 'You have no idea, Mr Sciler. There was no murderer in the sense that you have of it. Within hours or sometimes days of being killed in the zone they were simply found dead in rather odd circumstances, in manners duplicating the virtual deaths. We aren't killing them. Oh, no.'

'But why did you continue with the research, Kerz? At one end of the scale you had a useless gimmick, at the other people dying. Why bother?'

The water in the pool was completely still. It was like a mirror. Jon wondered how much visgel it took to do that, to iron out the planet's fever so totally. He wondered how important a place had to be to justify that. As well as all the security outside.

'You don't understand,' Kerz said. 'The circumstances of these deaths were not merely strange. They were quite bizarre. We were curious. Eventually we worked out that the victims were dying as a result of a sudden and deadly manifestation of some form of telekinetic power. And then as we backtracked from the death of each tester we started to see a pattern. Prior to their deaths they had begun to exhibit what you might call a *real* magic ability. It was difficult to verify, which was why it went unnoticed for so long. They'd get drawn into the zone scenario and preoccupied, become absent-minded and thus accident-prone, and yet accidents would be deflected without explanation. They might walk into the road and a vehicle would swerve impossibly to miss them.'

Jon said, 'I suppose it helped if you encouraged them to believe the zone scenarios were real.'

'Yes. We did that. And what we began to conclude, incredibly, was that it was the program drawing out a true magic ability. Unfortunately the ability was quite uncontrollable. But we carried on with our research – Anton had left by then – and we made our breakthrough. I knew all along there had to be something else. You see there was a further link between the testers who died that we hadn't realised. Not all of the low PI testers died. Some of the mortalities were relatively high PIs. It wasn't logical.'

Jon suddenly saw what was coming. 'Dirangesept,' he said.

Kerz looked pleased. 'Exactly, Mr Sciler. Very good. Most of our initial tranche of subjects were from my group of so-called first colonists. As they decreased in numbers we replaced them with civilians who tested low for PI, and our results became confused and unreliable. This was when the research was officially discontinued. But I carried on with it here at Maze. Then when your ships returned I went back to the government with my data and requested funding to continue, which they granted. Dirangesept was, of course, the missing link.'

Kerz knelt at the side of the pool and dipped his cupped hands into the water. He said to Jon, 'Look here, Jon. The water looks blue because the sides and base of the pool are blue, but, of course, the water isn't blue. Why do we want it to be blue, though? Have you ever wondered that?'

Jon could see Kerz wasn't interested in an answer. He just stood and waited for Kerz to go on.

'I'll tell you, Mr Sciler. We like it to look blue because the sea looked blue when the sky used always to look blue, back in our misremembered, never-was childhood. When blue was the colour of a clear, unadulterated, oxygen-rich, pathogen-poor sky. When all was not ill with the world.'

Water was dripping through his fingers. He stood up and walked to the edge of the roof and threw his scooped hands outwards. The water fanned into the MagNet and splintered through it, suddenly dulled, to disappear. 'But the sky was never blue,' Kerz said. 'It's one of the first things you learn in school, isn't it, that blue's simply the only colour of the visible spectrum that reflects back at us? The sky was never blue. Misinterpretation and illusion, Jon.'

'What's the point, Kerz?'

'How did you see the sky over Dirangesept, Jon?'

'It was blue.'

'How did you see the beasts?'

'I saw . . .' Jon stopped, seeing in Kerz's eyes how much he needed Jon's answer. 'It was different for everyone,' he said. He thought of Starburn's voice in Cathar and said, without quite knowing why, 'I saw wolves.'

It seemed to satisfy Kerz. It was like another test that Jon had passed. Maybe the last one.

Cats. Other people saw cats, of course, but Jon's were special to him. He hadn't thought about it for years, but suddenly he had one of the cats in his mind, the colour and sheen of its coat, the fullness of its eyes. He had a vision of it when he'd been a child too, and suddenly the car crash that had killed his parents was playing itself out in his head.

He was on the back seat of the car and opening his eyes out of sleep as his father's cry of shock was overtaken by his mother's scream, and the cat coiled on the seat beside him, his pet, was leaping in front of him and making him duck beneath the imploding windscreen. He saw the cat vividly, its orange fur turned to silver in the sudden stream of fiery light and then instantly to black as the car flipped over and all the light was gone. Black and silver. That's how he remembered the cat now. It was the first time he'd ever recalled the crash. But on Dirangesept he'd seen the beasts as cats with coats of black and silver.

Kerz watched Jon for a moment, waiting. 'They tried to make themselves sympathetic to us, to give themselves an edge. They had that power, Jon. They made themselves whatever they wanted to.'

Jon pushed the memory down, and the tears that tried to surface with it. 'That's been suggested before. So what?'

'Two things, Jon. First thing. You saw blue sky, as everyone else did. But the sky over Dirangesept shouldn't have been seen as blue. Their atmosphere is quite different to ours. We should have seen it as a sort of magenta. But it wasn't the beasts who gave you that. You did it for yourself.'

Jon couldn't think of anything to say.

'The beasts were in your heads. That's how they knew how to appear to you, and that's how they were so fast. They knew what you were going to do as soon as you'd thought of it. They never reacted to your actions, they reacted to the thought that preceded the action.'

Except for Starburn who acted instinctively, Jon thought.

Kerz said, 'But they released the power that made the sky blue for you. Do you see? You did it, but they enabled it. It didn't matter to the beasts, so they let it be. Which was a very big mistake. Jon. It was the clue to the fact that we have the potential for that same power. Something about the atmosphere of the planet Dirangesept potentiates it, but we're working on that, on our own power. We're working to develop it, so that we can return to Dirangesept and this time win.'

He went on, his eyes bright. 'Now, the second thing. The beasts feared we might do that. They sent themselves back with you, just like they had the first time with us, and they provided me with a great new source of infected hosts for my research. And this time I had government funding.'

Jon stared at him, and Kerz seemed to retrench slightly. 'You think that's the only way I see it. It isn't. They killed hundreds of Far Warriors, Jon. All those suicides over the years, the vast majority were murdered by the beasts.'

'And the recent string of murders at Maze?'

'That was the same thing. The beasts were killing their hosts in the way they'd been killed in Cathar. Your friend Starburn was one of them. Of course we've had to keep it quiet, there's enough panic and hysteria on the streets as it is.'

'So Lapis . . .'

'Teomera was our scapegoat, if you like, though we never needed her. Her twin was a psychological experiment of Dr Locke's that had got out of hand. I decided to terminate it. Dr Locke didn't expect her to kill herself. Or your friend Janus. That was unfortunate. We'll have to find another scapegoat now.'

'But what about the phobias? What do they have to do with PI and the questionnaire?'

'Far Warriors' phobias were invariably initiated by bLinkered deaths on Dirangesept. Starburn's hydrophobia was triggered by drowning, for instance. And we used phobic situations in Cathar to accelerate the development of magic abilities.'

'And the beasts then killed your guinea pigs for real with the same phobic situations.'

Kerz looked pained. 'Our volunteers, Jon, please. We have – are – getting somewhere at last. We're closer than ever to an understanding and control of magic now. This is what frightens them. They remain dormant under normal circumstances, but in Cathar they manifest themselves.' He punched a fist into his palm. 'They're pointing us in the right direction, but more than that, if they only realised it. They aren't so goddamn clever.'

He collected himself. 'It's a complex interaction. You know the principle of the observer affecting what is observed, Mr Sciler?'

Jon nodded.

Kerz was visibly burning with emotion, almost twitching. 'It's strange, they seem to exist independently within our brains and yet have no physical presence at all. They use the host brain like we use a computer, familiarising themselves with it, initially using those circuits that we aren't actively using, flicking around the place, avoiding us as much as possible.'

Jon thought of the brainmaps that Chrye couldn't interpret, the apparently meaningless activity. 'Like playing tag around a half-empty house.'

Kerz frowned then smiled. 'I like that. Yes. Occasionally you'll seem to get a faint glimpse of them. The hosts describe it as like being followed. You've had that? And you'll get odd memories turning up. Yes?'

'That's right.'

'All of this is exaggerated in the gamezone, so that we can trace them. And they leave new synaptic linkages in their wake, linkages related to magic ability.'

'The wolf is one of the beasts,' Jon said in a moment of clarity. 'Cathedral.'

'You have been industrious, Mr Sciler. You and Ms Roffe. Yes, Cathedral is the beast's signature brainwave. It took the wolf form for Starburn, trying to make for itself a sort of friendly camouflage. We killed it in the end, though not before it killed Marcus, unfortunately.' Kerz's eyes narrowed as he examined Jon. 'The wolf form worked with you too, didn't it? Be very careful, Mr Sciler. Your beast has been through your speech centre now. It may try to communicate directly with you. Don't believe anything it tells you. It knows precisely how to seduce you. It may pretend to be someone you know. It knows your paranoia just as well as we do, Mr Sciler, and it will feed on that. It will feed on you. It's no exaggeration to say that the beast knows you better than you know yourself.'

Jon hesitated, then said, 'So why did you kill Starburn in Cathar if you knew the beast would then kill him?'

'We had to do that. Unfortunately the beasts only manifest themselves plainly if the hosts are in true danger in the zone. And that's when our beast-killer, Arel, can attack them. Your beast has communicated with you, hasn't it, Mr Sciler? If you don't tell us everything that happens in Cathar, you're preventing us from helping you. You're putting yourself in great danger. What has it told you?'

Jon thought of Starburn, and of Lile dead in his arms on the jetty. He said, 'Arel is the software in your AI, isn't it, Kerz?'

'Arel isn't quite perfect yet. If we could have killed the beast before Starburn died in the zone, we would have. That is always the intention. If we can do that for you, we will. And I think we can, Jon. If you help us.'

'But why would the beast have wanted to keep Starburn alive in the zone if it's just going to kill him once he's out of it? That's crazy.'

'You don't understand, Mr Sciler. When you enter the zone, the beast enters it too. If you die in the zone it fears getting cut off and trapped there, and then it would not be able to fulfil its purpose.'

'Its purpose? What purpose, Kerz? What are they trying to do?' Jon looked out through the MagNet at the blurred sky. Nothing seemed real.

'To kill you,' Kerz said. 'To keep the secret of their power. But unfortunately for us, when you die in the zone your beast doesn't get trapped there at all. It remains with you. And then when it has killed you outside the zone, for real, it disappears. And that's no good to us at all.'

'No,' Jon said sarcastically. 'I can see that.'

'Well, since it has no physical presence, it ceases to live when your brain's dead. But if we can kill it *before* it kills you, and if it's already reprogrammed your brain to do magic, then we've got two things. We've got an effective beast killer here on Earth and we've got ourselves a piece of software that we can take back to Dirangesept for a third time and take that goddamn planet.'

'And you've got a live tester.'

'That too. So, you see, you really have no choice but to carry on. For the sake of Earth.'

'What about you, Kerz? Do you have a beast within your head? What happened to that? Why are you still alive?'

Kerz chuckled. 'It knows me, Sciler, doesn't it? It knows it can't fool me. So it remains dormant. For the moment, we observe each other. I've never been in danger in Cathar, so it's never feared my developing synaptic linkages related to magic. And it knows it risks Arel if it does manifest itself. I'll deal with it later, when there's time.'

'When it's quite safe,' Jon said.

Kerz spread his hands and inspected them. 'If you like. We believe we're far enough along to save you, and you can incidentally help to save the Earth. The Dirangesept project is not dead, not at all. With Arel and with magic we can win this time. We can kill them all.'

Jon looked at Kerz's face and wanted to turn his back on everything at Maze. He felt disgusted. Dirangesept wasn't worth this. He didn't trust

Kerz. But then he thought of Starburn dead and knew he couldn't walk away now. It was too late for that.

Kerz finished rubbing himself dry and tossed the towel back on the bench. 'We'll enter Cathar shortly, Mr Sciler. You have time for a swim first, if you like.'

Jon said, 'I'm not sure I'd float in your water, Kerz.'

TWENTY-EIGHT

'This isn't necessary, Kerz,' Jon said tightly. 'I thought the idea was to hunt the beast.' He could see Calban now as Kerz, despite the yellow eyes of Cathar. His face framed by the cape's hood, Calban had Kerz's sharp cheekbones and the fluid ice of his smile. The hood and cape slapped in the wind and behind Kerz the sky was full of fast scudding cloud. Jon pulled at the rope around his wrists and ankles, feeling the earth's grit rubbing through his shirt and into his back.

'Oh, it is, Sciler. It's very necessary.' He made a gesture and a blindfold was put over Jon's head from behind.

Jon felt himself yanked into the air and slung over someone's shoulder, the rough movement knocking the air from his lungs. After a few paces the carrying movement became jerky. He was being taken up steps. The wind seemed to swell and fade. All Jon could hear past the buffeting of the wind was the shade's thick, even breathing in his ear. He thought of Starburn on the rock before he died here, and wondered how Footfall had met his end in Cathar. But they had been different. They had both had phobias. Jon didn't like heights at all, but he wasn't phobic about them. If that was Kerz's idea, he was making a mistake.

He tried to remember the view of Calban's rock from the replay of Starburn's death as they continued to climb. There were no heights then, except for the wall of the arena of his torture. But Cathar was fixed, of course, and Kerz could create anything he wanted to. The rules of the game didn't apply to him. The steps could be going anywhere. Jon tried to count them, to lose himself in the rhythm of counting, and hit a hundred and eight when the shade carrying him made a few level paces before stopping to lower Jon on to his feet.

They were in the open, the wind stronger now and more consistent. Jon felt dizzy and disorientated. The shade was standing away from him, steadying him with a hard palm against his shoulder. He tried not to think about the height, to turn it into a number, to ease the thought of where he might be. He guessed at about ten steps before he'd started counting them, so he was about thirty metres above the ground.

The hand abruptly left him and the rope around his wrists slid away. Jon sank to the ground. He pulled his hands up to the blindfold and found that he couldn't remove it. There was nothing at all stopping him but he just couldn't do it.

It was the cliff. He suddenly remembered it. Starburn wasn't with him that day. He was on patrol alone in the jungle and he'd come to the end of a track that hadn't seemed right all along. He'd never been this way, it was uncharted, so he was going cautiously. There had been a barrier of packed foliage in front of him and he'd backed off a few metres, suspecting an ambush or a trap.

He'd forgotten it until now. The jungle was dense, so there was no warning. No change in the quality of sound, in the light penetrating the canopy. Going round the condensed wall of foliage and scanning nothing to either side he'd thought stupidly that he was safe and picked up speed to get past the area more swiftly.

There was an instant when he registered clear sky through the vegetation, but it was too late then. The ground had already begun to slip away from him and he was on his back, sliding forward on a chute of mud and slick leaves. He threw out his arms and caught desperately at vines and branches, but the machine's weight was too much for them and they only slowed him a fraction.

He shot completely clear of the foliage and there was nothing at all ahead of him but sky. He dug his feet down and they locked too hard into the sludge, catapulting him forward on to his belly and still sliding on head first. The mud was like oil against his chest and thighs. At the last moment he managed to stretch out both arms and punch the hardhands deep into the mud and kicked his splayed feet into the earth.

He came slowly to a stop, hanging in silence over the edge of a vast ravine. The ground was hundreds of metres below him, and it was all that he could see.

The mud was moving beneath him, warmed into flow by the heat of the machine. As he tried to push the hardhands deeper, one of his ankles abruptly came free. He jerked his leg in panic and the movement flipped him on to his back again. Every movement he made eased him further down. It was impossible to keep still. He started to get cramp in his other locked ankle. When he tipped his head up as far as possible, he could only see sky, and to either side there was the smooth edge of the cliff.

There was nothing he could do except call for assistance, so he did that. The project was winding down now, though, which was the reason Jon had no partner on the patrol, and the nearest backup was a couple of hours away.

'Okay, Sciler, we're on our way. Just follow standing orders. Don't exit. You can take a fall. You could make a good drop and walk right out of there.'

He'd hung in there for an hour and a half, slipping slowly, before the cramp in his foot had become too much and he had fallen.

Now, blindfolded in Cathar and high on Calban's rock, he remembered the whole of the drop. Every second of it, every detail. He remembered the first few metres that hadn't been so bad except for the pain of scraping his back on stones and protruding roots as he'd tried to grab at them and failed, and then just before reaching Dirangesept's extreme terminal velocity he'd slammed against the rock that had agonisingly gouged his shoulder and fractured his spine and bounced him right out into space. He remembered the pain, the sensation of speed and utter helplessness as he'd fallen, turning and turning until the ground and the sky were just an accelerating sequence of colours, of green, then blue, and green, blue, green-blue-green-bluegreen . . .

He'd forgotten it completely until now. That was his nightmare. The agony with the sense of total helplessness and failure, and the pure terror of waiting to hit the ground. Now they were back with him. He knew there was more too, but that still lay out of reach. The thought of what else there had to be made him shudder.

There was pain in his back as he lay on Calban's rock and he knew the true source of his stigmata. They weren't from the tree that had struck him as he'd tried to save Starburn. They were scars from the first part of that terrible fall.

The blindfold was gone and he knew that Kerz had done that. He got ready to open his eyes, thinking that anything would be better than the vision in his head of that endless fall. About thirty metres, he thought. Say forty. Be ready, say fifty.

He looked and sank flat on the tiny circle of stone, pulling his arms and legs into his body, hugging himself. The tower was no more than a metre wide, and it was over seventy metres above the rocks. There was a stairway of projecting stone slabs on its outside, totally exposed, barely the width of two feet side by side. Staring down, his chin hard against the cold stone, Jon could see the top of the shade's head appearing and disappearing round the tower's tight curve as it walked steadily down to the rocks below. The tower was set just in the sea, waves shrieking as they broke grey and silver against its base, almost washing the shade away at the bottom as he scrambled with difficulty on to the dry land.

'There. We're ready.'

The wind distorted Kerz's voice. Jon turned himself around, crablike, to see him.

Kerz was standing about twenty metres away on a wide stone platform on the main body of the rock. He was at the same height as Jon. The huge bird was hovering unsteadily above him, wings not even fully stretched in the harsh wind.

Chrysanthemum, Jon thought, but he didn't say it yet. It was enough to know that the word was there, and that Chrye was there. It gave him a small strength. And then the voice was in his head again.

Jon, I'm here. Don't look down. I'm behind the tower.

Who are you? What are you? You have to help me. I can't . . . can't take this.

You mustn't let him kill you, Jon. If he kills you here, you will really die, like I died.

Starburn? Is that you? Or is it the beast? How do I know?

The bird suddenly left Kerz and rose high to hang in the air just above Jon. He could feel the beating of its wings as it held itself with difficulty against the wind.

It hasn't seen me yet. Listen to me, quickly. I have his memories. I was his beast. Everything Kerz told you was true, except for one thing. If you die, we *are* trapped here. Kerz thought I was dead, but he's wrong. He thinks I'm your beast, but I was Starburn's. Remember that. It's important.

If you were trapped here, how did Starburn die?

The voice cut through the wind. It was Starburn's voice, and somehow it was Starburn speaking to him. But there was a sadness too that wasn't Starburn's. It came from the beast's knowledge of Starburn. Somehow the beast was Starburn. Jon listened to it.

He died like all the others. The phobic murder in this place boosts your power to do magic, but the memory of such a death is too much for you to bear. Starburn remembered his death and he made it happen again. He couldn't help it. Out of here I couldn't help him. Kerz knows. You have to trust me. If you die now, it will happen to you.

Kerz was shouting, 'Where is it, Sciler? It's here, Arel knows it is. Help me and you don't have to die. I can save you.'

Jon hunched down against the wind, feeling dizzy. The sea was crashing against the foot of the tower and the wind seemed to be shaking the stone under him. He didn't know what to think any more, who to believe. Nothing made sense.

He pulled the spell together and lowered the tower, but Kerz drew it up again and Jon didn't dare risk any more magic. This was Kerz's domain, and Jon couldn't leave himself any weaker. He had to climb down the tower.

The wind ripped at him as he backed himself to the steps, feeling for the first slab with his toes. He inched back and round from slab to slab until his feet were flat and his legs straight, then took a long breath and stood up. He wasn't going to fall.

Clutching the tower's rough rim so hard that it scratched blood from his hands, he began to descend. When the flat top came level with his eyes he had to force himself on. Kerz hadn't interfered with him. He must be concentrating on the beast. Jon didn't care, as long as it took his attention away from him.

The wind was unpredictable, battering and deafening him most of the time but occasionally falling away so completely that he could hear the thudding of his heart and the scrape of his feet on the stone. He carried on winding his way down, embracing the tower as far as he could, though the protruding steps above him that gave him something to hold on to jutted into his thighs and chest. He kept edging further on, further down, counting the steps and trying to remain oblivious to everything except the rhythmic sound of numbers in his head.

He'd reached three hundred when he decided to look down, guessing he must be near the bottom. He took his face away from the stone and realised his cheek was split and bleeding where he'd been pressing it against the rough surface all the way. His fingers were blistered and his trousers were worn through at the knees and thighs.

He was still as high as when he'd started. He pushed his cheek back into

311

the rock and sobbed, then drew a long breath and began to inch his way round until he reached the next point in the tower's curve that gave him a full view of Kerz.

Kerz was waiting for him with a savage grin, the cape whipping around him as if he himself was the wind's source. 'There's no way down, Sciler. And there's no way up either. Where's your saviour now? Call him, Sciler, make him come to you.'

The bird was at Jon, swooping close and then swerving away with a hard slap of air. Jon stopped and tried to concentrate on a spell, forcing himself to look down at the rocks, forming a sequence of pictograms into a spell to bring the rocks closer.

It worked, but they receded again almost instantly. Jon could hear Kerz's laughter on the wind.

'There's nothing you can do, Sciler. Nothing at all. I am the master here.'

One of the steps Jon was holding came away in his hand and he nearly fell out into space. He edged round another pace and there was hardly any room on the step for his foot. His heel was hanging out. He pulled back and glanced carefully down. The steps petered gradually away to nothing beneath him. Beyond a few circuits the tower below was perfectly smooth. He looked up and saw the same thing.

For a moment he started to panic, but then he remembered the word nestling in his mind and it was okay. As long as he had the word, he knew it would be okay.

It was cold in the wind and his fingers were growing numb. He was facing Kerz round the curve of the tower, but Kerz seemed to have lost interest in him again, pacing the platform and directing the bird in the sky with his gloved hand.

The wind was getting between Jon and the rock, wedging his body out, and another step cracked and came away in his hand. He let it fall and grabbed at another one further away, but couldn't help watching the dropped slab as it tumbled down to shatter on the shining wet rocks.

There was real fear now. The word, he thought, what was the word? He couldn't remember it, then it was there, it was Chrye, no, not that because that could have been an ordinary word, cry, he felt like crying now, crying with fear and terror.

Chrysanthemum. That was it, and he held the rock tight again. The wind seemed to ease a fraction.

He knew he couldn't last much longer, though. He stared at Kerz, putting pictograms together, and held his gaze still, knowing this was his last chance. The bird was there right above Kerz and it was coming for him again, but he ignored it. The spell went on, and the wind that came with it was bursting at him, shoving at him as hard as the wind around the tower. He kept his eyes on the ground just behind Kerz, bringing on the spell, and didn't even move his head as the bird's wing smashed into his shoulder. Kerz was moving in the wind now, it was even blowing him about, but Jon kept his eyes focussed on the platform, on the exact spot.

It was done.

Kerz stood still, sniffing the air, obviously knowing something had happened, but the wind was too strong for the scent to linger, just as it had been for Jon to have smelt Kerz's magic.

Arel was diving back towards Kerz, screeching madly at the wolf that had suddenly leapt on to the platform in front of him.

Go, Starburn, Jon thought, not even knowing if it was him, not caring, just wanting Kerz dead. Go, go.

Kerz took an instinctive step backwards towards the new, truncated edge of the platform. Jon held his breath. Two more steps and Kerz would fall. He'd fall far enough to be dead and it would be over.

Kerz stared from Jon to the wolf running towards him and then up to the great bird, and took another uncertain step back. The bird was almost above the wolf, and suddenly it was plunging down and slashing the wolf with its talons, bowling it over towards Kerz.

Kerz hesitated, then took another half pace back. Rising up hard on hammering wings, the bird screeched loudly and Kerz froze. He looked back and hurled himself sideways to the ground. The tumbling wolf vanished over the platform. Arel pulled in its wings and dropped out of sight after it.

The voice was in Jon's head again, fainter than a whisper, and this time the wind seemed to interfere with it.

Starburn had such feelings for you, Jon. I understand so much about you and so little . . . You humans . . . communicate . . . everything . . . gone.

The wind swelled, drowning the voice, and then it became a harsh digital crunch and immediately a screech that was neither animal nor anything else. It was simply triumph.

Jon watched Kerz pick himself up, the slack cape starting to punch and thrash again.

'Very good, Sciler. Very good indeed. I didn't expect that at all.'

The bird rose behind him, the wolf quite limp in its talons. Kerz pointed at the ground in front of him and the bird rose with the body as Jon remembered it rising before, but this time it dropped the wolf on to the stone in front of Kerz. The body thumped on to the platform and Kerz knelt beside it, taking a long knife from his belt. Hovering in the air above Kerz, Arel opened the hooked yellow blades of its beak and its screech came again, longer this time, echoing in the wind.

Kerz yanked back the wolf's limp head and steadily, deeply, slit its throat, then stood up to look at Jon.

'Success beyond expectations, I think, Sciler. Now, what to do with you?'

Jon felt lost and empty. Starburn was dead. The beast was dead too, and in his mind he couldn't separate them. He thought of them together, knowing each other. Such closeness. He found himself thinking of Chrye, and then of Starburn's, the beast's, last words. He found himself unable to separate them in his mind, the beast and Starburn.

His teeth were chattering. He was stretched out against the curved tower, running out of handholds. 'You said I'd live if you killed the beast.'

'I said if you helped me, Sciler, and you didn't do that. I'm afraid you're too dangerous now. You've been developed.'

The wind eased and Jon smelt it this time as the last of his handholds broke away. It was like mould and putrefaction. It was like death.

Chrye, he thought. Chrye.

He shouted it out, again and again. That was it, but it wasn't working. Kerz was sinking beneath him, the tower rising higher and higher. The wolf was a mess of red at Kerz's feet and the bird was circling up towards Jon.

What was it then? It *was* Chrye, it . . . 'Chrysanthemum,' he yelled. He closed his eyes, relaxing at last.

Nothing changed. The wind beat harder at him. He shouted it again, and still nothing.

The exitline's been disabled, he thought with a sudden emptiness. The stone slab under his right foot broke away as the eagle shrieked past his head. His foot slipped and he was holding on by a couple of toes and the

314

tips of his hooked fingers. He held his cheek hard against the slick, damp stone wall and the stone under his fingers crumbled like wet sand.

He choked off a scream and was falling.

It's not real, he told himself, but he knew it was. It had to be. He remembered falling before, only this time it took longer. The sky and the sea were oscillating, blue-grey-blue-grey-blue-grey, the rocks closing in on him, and he knew exactly how it would feel to be smashed into them and to remember every bLinkered instant of it, the bones of his arms and legs wrenching and breaking, his neck cracking, ribs spearing his lungs, his nose, jaws and cheekbones shattering, his eyeballs blowing out.

He tried to block it again, but the memory was flooding back and he was feeling the agony of it already, every bone about to be smashed without loss of consciousness. Faster now, blue-grey-blue-greyblue-grey . . .

It happened.

TWENTY-NINE

She was in his room waiting for him as he came stumbling through the door, and she knew immediately that he was dead. His eyes seemed to scan the walls without taking anything in. He just sat down on the edge of the bed and stared into space.

'Jon? Are you okay?'

She didn't expect an answer and there wasn't one. She wanted to hit him with her fists and scream at him, I *told* you so! I *knew* I'd lose you. But she cut it all off, cut herself away from it. Breathing deep, she switched off everything except logical thought.

'What happened? Try and tell me what happened. Can you do that?'

He didn't respond at all. Not good, she thought. There must have been a phobia after all, only it was locked away again. Kerz had used it to shut him down and now it was inaccessible once more, blocked off behind a wall of silence.

She took his hand and stroked it, watching his eyes carefully. There was something there when she did that. 'Don't you go catatonic on me now, Jon. You can hear me, I know you can.' You'd better be hearing me, she thought, or we're in real trouble.

'You wanted to save the world, Jon, didn't you?' she murmured. 'And look where it's got you. It's got you killing yourself here.'

There was pressure on her hand, not much but something. That's it, Jon, help me. Help me to help you. 'I want to help you, Jon. I was your exitline, wasn't I? And I'm not giving up on you. You understand me? I'm staying here. I'm not giving up on you.'

But what the hell can I do?

He was falling again. It kept coming and going. End over end, blue-grey-

316

blue-green. Chrye was somewhere nearby now, he sensed, but he was falling and it was too late. The ground was coming again. The wind was hissing past him, filling his ears with noise, and maybe the illusion of words too. Was the wind talking to him?

'You wanted to save the Earth, didn't you? And you thought you'd failed. So there was guilt, all that guilt, wasn't there? So much guilt. What did you do with it, Jon?'

Did his fingers squeeze hers then? What was it?

'Father Fury, was that it? You were punishing yourself for your failure. But you were stronger than that, a lot stronger. I don't believe it was Father Fury, Jon.'

Nothing. She took his other hand as well, holding them both and using them as gauges to wherever he was, trying hard not to squeeze them, not to let her panic through.

'Good. Okay, we'll go back. You did something with the guilt, you got a job as a spider, knitting the Earth back together. But you still had the guilt, so the job wasn't just trying to fix the planet.'

Both hands now. Definitely. She was getting somewhere.

'The job was self-punishment too, wasn't it?'

Yes. Yes. Good.

'Spiders, insects. Was that it?'

Nothing. No, of course not, that's too abstract. It would have to be something concrete, something direct. His eyes were looking odd, eyelids fluttering. His hands were starting to tremble too. It was accelerating, whatever the hell it was.

'Jon, I'm trying. Can you feel me trying? Can you still hear me?'

Maybe something. Only maybe.

'Okay, spider, you're down there, hanging there, what is it?' She closed her eyes and tried to imagine it. 'It isn't claustrophobia. There's space there. And it isn't agoraphobia, there isn't that much of it. You're hanging there. You're hanging over . . . height? Is it height?'

Close, so close. She could feel it.

'No, it's not quite vertigo because you cope with that and you wouldn't. But you're risking it down there, aren't you? It's . . .' The birds in the tunnel, the sensation of . . . Of course! He hadn't even known it, but he'd shown her. 'Christ, it's falling.'

She squeezed his hands now. They shook, but he resisted her. Thank God.

317

'Are you falling now, Jon?'

Squeezing.

'Close your eyes for me. I want you to close your eyes. That's it, that's just great. Okay, Jon, the ground's a long way off yet. A long way. There's plenty of time. You're falling, but there's plenty of time.' Making it hypnotic, trying to break what was happening in there.

He shook his head.

Shit.

'I'm here, and I've got your exitline.' Urgently now. 'I am your exitline, remember? I'm Chrye, Jon. Just say my name. Say it, Jon, and you'll stop falling and open your eyes. Say Chrye. That's all you need to do.'

His mouth was moving, lips jerking. His body seemed actually to be shifting before her as if he was passing through air at tremendous speed. She could feel it in his grasp, as if he was about to be yanked away from her. Her hands were losing their grip on him.

She held tight. It was taking all her strength to do it. 'I'm here, Jon. I'm not letting you go. Say my name.'

His body seemed almost to be blurring before her. It was crazy. There was a smell of something pungent in the air as she held on. Iodine? She was shouting at him.

'You know I won't let you go, don't you, Jon? Tell me. Communicate, Jon.'

It was just a whisper. The wind nearly swallowed it. 'I know.'

'You know because I told you, and I'm telling you that if you say my name, you will open your eyes and stop falling. Say my name, Jon. Say it.'

His hands were tearing away from her. She could hardly hold him. She leaned right into him and air seemed to whip at her.

'Say it,' she yelled.

'Chrye.'

'Again, Jon. Say it again.'

'*Chrye.*'

His eyes opened. There was complete silence. Everything was still except for a scrap of paper floating to the floor in a fading breath of air.

She stared at him.

'Chrye,' he whispered.

Jon said, 'It died for me, Chrye, it was telling the truth. The beasts were never killing us. We were doing it and Kerz knew that but he didn't care.

318

He just wanted to develop Arel to kill them back on Dirangesept. He used me and then he sent me back here to die. Just like all the others.'

He flexed his fingers, turning his hand around, making a fist and opening it again. The terrible kaleidoscope of the fall was receding. 'I know it all now, Chrye. Our brain's like a great landscape. Unimaginably great. We populate it with our small towns and villages, constructing our little roads and motorways, but we never even see most of it. But the beasts, they roam around inside us not needing our roads, running in vast strides. Sometimes we glimpse them in the distance or see them flashing across our path. In Cathar and here too. The sense that Starburn and I had of being followed outside the zone as well, and all the strange memories surfacing – all of that was our beasts exploring us.'

His head was bursting with it. He reached out and took Chrye's hand as if all the knowledge inside him could flow to her through the contact of their palms.

'They never meant to come back to Earth with us at all, Chrye. On Dirangesept they could enter us, but the autoids confused them. They didn't fully understand what the machines were. And they found that they couldn't use their magic once they were inside us, and they couldn't communicate with us either, though they still could between themselves. And they couldn't leave. They were trapped in our heads.'

Chrye frowned. 'I don't see why they couldn't leave you.'

'To transfer themselves, they need to *know* themselves, and they found that once they were inside us there was a bond, they were part of us. And as they couldn't yet communicate with us, they were trapped. Cathar helped them, and the process of knowing us could begin. Those of us into whom they could most easily transfer in the first place were the easiest to know. Like Starburn and me.'

Chrye nodded, everything starting to make sense at last. 'Low PI. Can they talk to you now, Jon?'

He was getting tired. The adrenaline rush was ebbing away, leaving him drained. 'No, not yet. Not outside Cathar.' He tried to rub the exhaustion from his eyes.

She held back again. How *could* it make sense? It was crazy. Magic? She looked around the solid walls of the room, the memory of his body ripping away from her a few minutes ago seeming no longer real. She didn't want this at all. What she wanted was Jon and some certainty. It didn't even matter if the certainty was of a dying Earth. She didn't care.

She said, 'Jon, it could *all* be in Cathar. Your . . . power might have been triggered by what happened in the zone, but the rest of it . . . there's no proof. It could be Kerz, the zone. You don't know what's real any longer.'

Jon had no energy to argue with her. He knew he was right. He was pulling her towards him, needing to hold the reality of her, when the door buzzer sang round the room.

The harsh noise was like a crowbar forced between them. Jon froze at the sound and Chrye jerked her hand away in surprise, then laughed at herself, standing up. 'We're paranoid,' she said.

But the buzzer went on shivering the air. As if someone was just checking no one was in, Jon thought lethargically. Chrye was moving towards the door and he started to tell her to leave it, knowing something wasn't right, but she was moving faster than the words came out. The buzzer stopped.

She was looking through the lens and turning back to him. 'It's two guys, Jon. I don't recognise them.'

It went through his head at the same time as he managed to say, 'Get back from the door, Chrye.'

But by then she'd already said through the doorcom, 'Who is it?' Telling them she was there. Kerz wanted him dead, expected him dead, and they were the clean-up team. Their instructions would be . . .

She was moving back, her head turning towards him, the expression on her face softening as she started to say something he never heard. The door seemed to explode at her, throwing her back. Jon saw a stream of light flow through the door and into her body, and then there was a man in the doorway, the doorframe an aura of light around him. The echo of Chrye's brief scream faded in the room but carried on keening through Jon's head as though she was falling away from him, the diminishing scream like an outstretched hand hopelessly and for ever beyond his reach.

The man in the doorway lowered the gun from Chrye and turned it towards Jon, and as he did so Jon saw what he thought was the man's shadow moving behind him. The shadow stepped to his side and it was another man, shorter and armed with some other weapon. He started to raise it at Jon.

'Christ, Maxie, he's still alive,' the second man said in an oddly deep and slow voice.

Jon had time to register a look of panic in the faces of them both as they stared at him, their fingers fumbling with their weapons, and everything was accelerating again.

Their reaction confused him for a moment, and then he thought, They know. Kerz told them. And they've shot Chrye.

He didn't know what he did or how he did it, but he knew it was him. It welled up in him like an irresistible fury. There were no pictograms for it, no words and no wind.

Too late to panic, he thought savagely. It's too late for you.

As the weapons came up towards him the doorframe erupted inwards, roaring, a rectangle of fire burning there like a furnace door slammed open. He squinted into it then had to shield his eyes against the brilliant heat. The men turned into silhouettes and then crumbled and vanished against the blinding doorway. They didn't even have time to scream.

The flames started to die as the smoke alarms went off. They were going off all around him as he knelt by Chrye's body. The sharplight had been set on broad beam and it had caught her just above the hip. He thought the heat had cauterised the wound. It didn't look too bad for a second, like a neat chunk had been cut out of her side, but then blood started to blur the wound's perimeter.

'Chrye?' he said. He checked her pulse. It was there but it was weak and uneven. She was in shock and unconscious. He smoothed her soft black hair away from her cheek. Here eyes were wide and dull.

Okay, do it again, he thought. I did it once without even thinking, I must be able to do it again.

He tried putting pictograms together, but nothing held still and after a few moments he knew why. It had to be raw, immediate emotion for the magic to work. It was there, but he didn't have conscious control of it yet. It wasn't the same as in Cathar. That was why he'd nearly killed himself, that lack of control, and that was how he'd killed the two men.

He thought of Kerz saying to him just before he fell from the tower, 'You've been developed now, you're too dangerous.'

'Chrye,' he whispered again, hopelessly, holding her hand. He pulled gently at her shirt but it wouldn't come away from the wound, and when he tugged a bit harder her skin started to come with it.

In desperation he tried the pictograms again but still nothing would happen. Even the wind wouldn't come. Now when it mattered more than anything had ever mattered, he couldn't play the game. He couldn't save

Chrye's life. She was going to die and there was nothing he could do about it.

He glanced at the scorched doorway. Nothing organic was left. The weapons were a couple of hard shining pools of metal lying in a nest of ashes. Beyond them was a slightly charred black nylon bag. Jon jumped over the glistening metal and yanked the bag open. He emptied cutters and a roll of clear bags on to the floor, and a camera. There was nothing else. Nothing traceable. They were from Maze, though.

Behind him Chrye moaned and he went back to pick her up, cradling her like a baby. She seemed to weigh nothing. There was a hole stamped in the wall behind her, a perfect circle interrupted by the bite taken out of Chrye's side.

He called Mira's face up on the screen, not knowing what else to do, Chrye still cradled in his arms.

'Jon, how are you? I saw Irf . . .'

Her voice trailed away. 'Oh, Jon. What happened there?'

'She was shot with a sharplight. She's lost a lot of blood. Mira, I don't know . . .'

'Is she conscious?'

'I don't think so. No.' He wanted to say more, but there was nothing else to be said.

'Stand back so I can see her.'

It didn't seem so bad as he showed Mira the wound. There was a lot of blood but it appeared to be slowing now. 'Mira?' he said.

She shook her head. 'That much blood loss. Sharplight trauma's hard to deal with and that's a bad one. It looks like a battlefield weapon on broad beam, full power. All the wrong things get fused, Jon. Her clothing will be part of the wound too. It's very, very bad. It looks like the beam penetrated her gut and took out most of a kidney too, spleen damage, and there's multi-sourced arterial bleeding on top of everything else.'

He tried to hold his voice down, almost pleading with her. 'You can't see it properly, Mira. The bleeding's almost stopped. Look.' Her clothes were sodden but there seemed to be nothing more welling out.

'Underneath, Jon. She's bleeding all over you.'

'I've got to do something, Mira. She can't die. She can't.'

'Well, I can tell you how to stabilise her temporarily, but you'll need something like a mains electrical source to keep her heart going. And get her to a CrySis unit as fast as possible. But she's lost too much blood already and the organ damage is quite beyond . . .' Mira stopped and pulled in a breath. 'Either way she's going to die, Jon. I'm sorry. I'm so sorry.'

Jon didn't have to wait long for Madsen to arrive. The microflite set down in the street with its lights flashing like the final embers of a dying fire. For some reason it reminded Jon of the last rocket of Starburn's scattering. So we will be.

Madsen said nothing at all to Jon as they laid her in the cramped back of the two-seater; he just launched the 'flite almost vertically and headed for Maze.

Maybe if her body could be stabilised in CrySis fast enough, she could function in a zone. Mira had said there was no hope, but Jon wasn't ready to accept that. Mira didn't know everything. She didn't know Jon had a beast inside him. Nor did Kerz. Maybe if he could get himself and Chrye to Cathar his beast would come out and be able to do something for her. It was the only chance there was.

He kept glancing back at her. Her face was growing paler and the blankets cocooning her were glossy with blood.

Over Stoke Newington Madsen said, 'We'll hit Maze in three minutes. Tell me what we're doing Jon. Tell me I'm not part of some grand suicide you've set up. I know all about them and they always end up the same. I'm not ready to see the other side of my job just now.'

'Okay,' Jon said. 'Listen to me. Just don't expect to understand anything.'

As Madsen shot the 'flite round in a descent towards Maze, the speaker on the dashboard shivered into life. 'You are making an unauthorised entry into military air space. Turn back immediately. Over.'

Madsen continued spiralling down. He leaned forward and snapped, 'This air space is not repeat not currently registered as restricted. I am a Pacifist officer landing with a passenger in extreme distress requiring urgent assistance. This message is being simultaneously broadcast on all repeat all wavelengths. Out.' He snapped the comm unit off, muttering to Jon, 'They might be thinking of shooting us down, but with the open 'cast they'll want authority and by the time they've got it we'll be down.'

Jon stared down at Maze. The complex was expanding in all directions, the great central building its black core with a soft indefinable blur at the

323

epicentre where the MagNet protected Kerz's private swimming pool. At the perimeter mobile visgel pumps were operating, their broad-ribbed drills and tubes cavitating the earth and substituting orange gel for London's mud and clay. The whole operation had changed gear. Inside the compound longloaders were drawing up to unship crates the shape of coffins at the doorway of a huge new prefabricated building that reminded Jon of Cathar's hall of wakers. CrySis pods. Hundreds of them.

'What the hell is this?' Madsen muttered. There were 'copters in the air all around them, shepherding them towards a landing circle beside the dark heart of the complex.

Madsen dropped the 'flite softly down and opened the door. Dust lifted in clouds and scuffed instantly into the cabin, forcing Jon and Madsen out. There was still a 'copter above them, its rotors bombarding them with air, dust and noise. Jon started to lift Chrye out of the 'flite, feeling the anger start to well up inside him again and trying desperately to keep it down. It wouldn't do any good here. He didn't know how powerful it was, but even if it destroyed everything around them, Chrye would die too. He stood straight with her in his arms, and the wind and dust subsided around him. For a second he wondered if he'd done it himself, but he knew he still didn't have the control. He felt the swelling power ebb away as he steadied Chrye's blanket-wrapped body in his arms. She was barely breathing. He brushed the hair from her eyes.

Aware of silence, he turned round.

Kerz was facing them, flanked by two soldiers. His hand was levelled at Jon, the entire fist cased in a snug metal sleeve that extended halfway up his forearm. Above his fist the metal flared into a slender barrel. The soldiers weren't armed, but one of them held a hand-scanner, directing it at Jon and Chrye, swinging it through the air. Madsen was kneeling on the ground, placing his gun at his feet. He pushed it towards the soldiers. The metal grated harshly over the ground.

Jon didn't recognise the gun Kerz was holding on them, but Madsen had. 'What can we do to you that you need that?' he said to Kerz, standing up again. 'Why don't you just take it easy and slide it off so we can all relax? None of us is armed.'

'I'm not worried about you, Captain Madsen. This is for Sciler here.' He gave Jon a thin smile. 'You know what I mean, Sciler, don't you? I expect it gave you as much of a surprise as it gave poor Maxie and Bly.'

'Easy, Jon,' Madsen said softly. 'That's a deadman's gun. It goes off if his physiological status is disturbed. If his pulse rate rises . . .'

'. . . If I start to get angry, or anxious,' Kerz said, still smiling. 'Boom. So you and I, Sciler, we're deadlocked. I know what you might do, and you know what I could do. So let's both of us just keep calm.'

The soldier with the scanner said, 'The men are clean, sir, but the woman isn't. There's something . . .' He pointed the scanner at her side.

'It's an electrical pacemaking device,' Jon said. 'Her heart's weak. She's bleeding to death. If you hadn't noticed.'

'I'm sorry, sir but that's not what my scanner's telling me. You'll have to remove it.'

Jon could feel it beginning to well up inside him again, but Madsen said calmly, 'Here, take a look at her.' He lifted the blanket to expose her bandaging. 'It's giving out now, she's started to bleed again. We need to get her into CrySis immediately. Feel that, see if it's a weapon.'

The soldier squinted at the wound, at the blood oozing through the bandages and into the blanket, and glanced at Kerz. 'I suppose it could be, sir. I can't tell.'

Jon said, 'She's dying, Kerz. This isn't a stalemate. Like you said, I can't control . . .'

Kerz looked at Jon, then said quickly, 'Okay. You can take her in. Mr Sciler looks anxious enough. She can die inside.' He waved the soldiers away, including Madsen in the gesture of dismissal.

'I'm coming too,' Madsen said.

Kerz hesitated, then laughed. 'Why not? You're dead already.'

Kerz jerked the barrel of the gun and the metal glinted in the stark light of the CrySis chamber. 'Put her in, Sciler.'

'Not just her. I'm going too, Kerz. You're going to send us both back to Cathar.'

A grin blossomed on Kerz's face. 'You think it's real? After all I told you?' He shrugged. 'Fine. Go back.' He waved at the pods. 'Get in, then.'

'You, too, Kerz. I don't trust you. I want you safe in CrySis as long as we're in Cathar. I want you out of the way.'

Jon watched Kerz trying to find a trick in that. 'Okay,' he said smoothly. 'In that case we'll need Dr Locke.'

'Go ahead,' Jon said. 'But I'm putting Chrye into a pod right now.' He carried her around the nearest pod so that he was facing Kerz across it.

'Madsen, can you give me a hand here?' he said. He pulled the blankets from her body and let them fall on to the floor. The wound was still bandaged, but the bandages would have to remain. Otherwise Chrye was naked except for the cut ruff of clothing he'd been forced to leave fused to the edges of the wound.

Kerz was hunched over a wallcom and whispering into it.

'Speak up,' Madsen told him. 'Let's all hear it. We don't want any misunderstandings.'

'I'm done,' Kerz said smoothly, cutting the connection. 'She's on her way.'

Madsen helped Jon lower Chrye's body gently into the pod cavity, Jon watching the gel rise slowly around her, coming to meet like a kiss at her lips. There was no airline for her. The gel would fill her up and stabilise everything. He could still see her through the translucent gel, but she could have been a universe away. The gel was cooling fast as he eased his hand down to push through the bandages and deactivate and then remove the palm stop. A delicate trail of blood began to follow his hand out of the gel, freezing there like a ruptured umbilical cord. He shook the gel from the palm stop and passed it quickly over to Madsen, Madsen's body shielding the transfer from Kerz. Madsen closed his hand loosely around it as Jon dropped the lid down over Chrye. Jon just hoped there was still some power left in the weapon.

Dr Locke pushed the door open and came into the room. She didn't look at all surprised to see Jon and Madsen there, didn't even glance at the closed pod.

'Ah, good,' said Kerz. 'Dr Locke, you're to put these two into Cathar, and my pod into CrySis for as long as they remain in the zone. Is that clear?'

Jon wondered whether there was a look passed between them. It didn't matter any more. At least he hoped not. Madsen knew what to do.

'Get into the pod, Kerz,' Jon said. 'Now.'

'You too, Sciler,' Kerz said, beginning to take off his clothes. He pulled his shirt carefully over the deadman's gun, keeping the barrel pointed at Jon. 'Dr Locke, you understand your instructions?' he said as he stepped into the pod, watching Jon do the same.

Madsen said, 'Don't worry about her, Kerz. Jon?'

'I'm fine.' Jon bit on the airline and started to lay himself back in the pod.

Kerz began to lie back too, watching Jon down, then made to sit up again, lifting the gun. Madsen brought the palm stop up to cover him. Kerz raised his eyebrows at the weapon.

'Stay right there in the pod and ease the gun off, Kerz,' Madsen told him. 'Jon's down and you're deep enough in the gel for your metabolism to be slowing down. Everything's square now and I promise you my reactions are better than yours.'

Kerz hung his hand over the side of the pod. The gun slid from his wrist and dropped on to the floor.

'That's good,' Madsen said, picking up the gun and sliding it into his pocket.

'I know you,' Kerz said softly, holding the airline at his lips. 'You're the CMS investigator. You have no idea what you're getting into here. Best thing you can do, Captain, is shoot yourself right now and save your pain and my time later.'

'And you can save your breath, Kerz,' Madsen muttered, watching the pod close over him.

In the congealing silence of the room, Madsen turned to Dr Locke. 'Now what?'

She turned to the door. 'We just have to go to my office and activate the program there.'

THIRTY

Mach Null. This was Mach Null. This wasn't the smooth bLink into Cathar.

Feeling sick, sick in his body and sick in his head, Jon opened his eyes on Dirangesept again. Kerz, he thought. Christ. He switched on his comms. That came without thinking, like a memory of breathing.

'Chrye? Are you there?'

'Jon? What's happening? I don't understand.'

In his head, her voice coming from darkness. She was still alive. She could have been whispering in his ear. Mach Null was still the same, but everything else was improved. The comms were perfect. The system was overwhelming. This was more than a zone, this was how it was going to be next time.

He walked forward and the foliage brushed damply against his skin. It felt perfect, as if he were standing there in flesh. Proprioception was unbelievably good, weapon systems readied with the flexing of his fingers, targeted and locked on with a glance. Weapons they'd never had. He checked his options, then set the range for the PlasMortar by bLink and squeezed off a round, realising that range-finding and weapon guidance were based on Cathar's spell-casting protocols. He followed the round through its high arc and then sight-guided it in. The boom from eight point three k's away came along slightly faster than it would have done on Earth. The training zone was perfect too. Earth wasn't going to get thrown back a third time. Jon thought of the wolf-beast hurling itself towards Kerz, trying to save Jon, and remembered that voice in his head on Dirangesept all those years ago, and felt uneasy.

Where are you? he said in his head. Are you there? I need you.

There was no response. Maybe his beast couldn't manifest itself in this zone. His heart thudded. He hadn't even considered that.

'Jon?'

'It's okay, Chrye. It's a game. I think . . . it's a game. You were hit by a sharplight, do you remember? I brought you to Maze, you're in CrySis . . .' Moving through the undergrowth, talking to her as he tried to locate her. And there she was, beyond his field of view, her machine a crimson blip on the ir display. 'Don't move, I'm coming.'

'How do I work . . . ?'

He had to collapse as the dets arced towards him to land metres away in a red flash and spray of earth and greenery, pulling in his arms and legs and drawing in his skull to let the riff of shrapnel crack off his armour. It was like being sluiced with ice water, almost invigorating. As he stood up she looked at him again and this time it was the sharplights screeching past his metal hull and burning the foliage to bitter smoke around him.

'Jon?' she said, panic in her voice, 'I don't know what to do.'

She was close now. 'It's okay. The controls are subtle. Most of the weaponry operates with movements of your eyebrows and your lips.' Words, he was thinking. Spells. He moved on, drawing nearer to her, saying, 'I'm certain Kerz is here somewhere too. We have to find him before he finds us.'

There she was. Identical to him, of course. These were new machines, different from the autoids he remembered from the Project. No attempt at camouflage, like before – nothing had made the slightest difference. You were never invisible. But the shape of the machine was slightly different. Lines were more angular, the legs less squat, the thorax with an extra joint. Jon remembered how hard it had been to twist round at speed. Balance mechanisms were improved, the hardware more compact. The arms were thicker to house more weaponry, the lower spine stiff with the new PlasMortar housing. He began to show her how to work the functions, checking all the time for beasts, for other autoids, for anything.

'This is hopeless, Jon. I can't do this.'

'Don't worry, Chrye. We'll just use what you can do.'

There he was. The blip moving closer, tacking, fading, using the cover of a magnetic rock formation. Jon moved Chrye away, keeping the rock between Kerz and them, moving towards the jungled area he could make out to the north.

It was a perfect training zone, but it wasn't complete. There were no

329

beasts. Kerz must have had Dr Locke nil the zone's beast option, probably to clear the ground for the battle with Chrye and Jon, and maybe that was also blocking Jon's own beast.

And something else was different, he realised, moving forward with Chrye. The zone didn't quite sound right. It was nearly there but it still didn't sound like Dirangesept, and that was a curious thing when everything else in the zone was so perfect. There were no beasts, but the sound wasn't so easy to work out. Something else was absent.

He moved briskly, keeping the scanners open but low, nining his ears and counting off the sounds, editing them out of the mix as he recognised and identified them. So far Kerz was staying back, probably trying to work out whether Jon was moving in a specific direction or just running, playing for time. Chrye was checking out her weapon systems and controls, throwing all her experiments towards Kerz, leaving a wake of fire and smoke behind them. Kerz was a constant blip, moving effortlessly through the destruction. That worried Jon slightly. While the machines were resistant to anything except direct hits, Kerz wasn't even being cautious.

After half an hour and about twenty kilometres Chrye was happy with her armoury and was conserving power, and Jon had dealt with most of the louder sound sources. The remaining sounds were thinner and fainter. Kerz was still hanging back for some reason.

Jon took the risk of subbing some of his visual range to channel more power to his ears and realised that it wasn't ever going to be enough, he'd never get there like this. There was just too much input to trawl through. He tried to conjure up in his head the dense sound of Dirangesept, then cut down the wavelength and frequency parameters of the search and went on with it, all the time keeping up the pace.

There was another blip on the display at the same time that Chrye said, 'Jon, there's something else here.'

Jon put the search on hold and nined his eyes again, looking up and scanning the sky until he saw what he was looking for. 'Arel,' he said. He checked Kerz's position. Kerz was accelerating slowly, starting to pull up with them. That's what he'd been waiting for, Jon thought. Or else he's worked out what I'm doing.

He could see Kerz now, his machine covered with mud and greenery, keeping low, almost invisible against the foliage. It was hard to be sure but the machine looked slightly different from his and Chrye's.

Arel was coming fast and high. Jon turned and threw a bunch of dets in Kerz's general direction, then carried on. He checked the bird, searching for its intent. It seemed to be plotting a mapping course, sweeping over them until it was way ahead and then crisscrossing the sky, left to right, descending and rising again, working into a pattern that Jon had no time to make sense of, other than guessing it was some sort of distraction from Kerz. Arel was a beast-killer, after all. The great bird had to be capable of attacking autoids but it wasn't dedicated to that. In this zone Kerz had to be the greater danger. Especially if Dr Locke had bLinkered him into a higher specification machine.

'Where are we going, Jon?'

'We have to . . .' he stopped. This wasn't Dirangesept. The zone was likely to be as fixed as Cathar. Kerz could probably hear every word they were saying. Jon was scrolling quickly through the maps in his head, searching. 'Concentrate on keeping up with me, Chrye. We have to keep ahead of him.'

There it was at last. 'This way, Chrye.'

He veered west towards the jungle.

After another half-hour he slowed down. The blip that was Kerz had dropped back again. Good. Maybe they were getting there. Arel was just hanging up there almost lazily, endlessly cutting the sky into squares. Time seemed to lose its meaning. The sound search went on.

'Chrye?'

'Yes.'

'Checking you're there. Keep up with me.' He couldn't tell her anything else in case Kerz heard. He wanted to touch her. He could do that, it would even feel like he was touching her, but there wasn't time for it now. Maybe there would never be time again.

'Keep your eye on Kerz, Chrye. Just tell me if anything changes.'

The foliage was rising around them and the ambient noise was changing subtly. That was fine, shift of microsystem. He could take that into account. There was a dense stand of trees to the left, and beyond it more sparse woodland, while ahead and to the right was the wall of jungle. Jon started to veer in a gentle sweep towards the stand of trees, hoping Kerz would think his only concern was cover from Arel. The crimson blip headed sharply towards the trees, Kerz heading to cut them off. Good. Jon increased his pace but remained on the slow feinting curve. Half his attention was still on the sound search. He noticed Chrye lagging behind and called to her to catch up. Arel was still soaring above just as before, monotonously swinging to and fro.

Okay. Now.

He shouted, 'Follow me,' to Chrye, and went hard right, accelerating, running straight for the edge of the jungle. He noticed as he did so that Arel's flight pattern had brought it directly overhead.

Then he registered Arel's altitude. Christ. He'd been so concerned about the pattern maintenance that he hadn't spotted that Arel was diving. He'd been looking for the wrong distraction.

Chrye was behind him, too far. There was a spurt of flame from Kerz's position and then a low thud. He could see the rising curve of the PlasMortar shell for a moment but lost it against the sky at the same time that he saw Arel coming down like a bolt straight at Chrye.

He threw a det behind her and followed it with a smoke shell to stop Kerz from guiding the mortar straight down by either scanner or sightline. Arel shot through the det blast and the smoke as if they didn't exist, arrowing towards Chrye, at the last moment pulling its head into its body and drawing in its wings to strike her on the back of the head. She hadn't seen it coming.

The shell came down between himself and Chrye, the impact throwing him to the ground. He stood up dizzily and checked his functions. His comms and scanners were fuzzy and vision was coming and going. Somehow the sound search was still ongoing in the background. It sounded like tinnitus.

'Chrye,' he called, not liking the echo he was getting. He tried to retune, searching for her among the interference. Arel would have been hit too, he thought. Maybe stunned, maybe killed. That was something.

She came back to him faintly, her voice weak and the channel fading. 'I'm okay, Jon. I just can't . . .' He lost her.

After a few moments his sight and scanners came back. There was Chrye, moving erratically away from him, and there was Kerz too. And another blip, rising fast. Arel.

Of course. He was stupid. Magic works here. Arel was magic-augmented software. It was a beast-killer. It would only exist for its target.

He started to move towards Chrye, but Arel had turned and was coming down towards him this time, claws out, like a missile. He had a feeling that those claws would shear through his armour like it wasn't there. Chrye was moving away from him in the confusion, towards Kerz.

The smoke from the mortar was clearing and there was something coming through the last grey swirls of it, materialising out of the mist. Arel's wings adjusted at the same time that Jon saw it, and the bird swerved away from Jon towards the fabulous cat that was emerging from the blast site.

Jon had a fraction of time to meet the eyes of the cat before Arel was upon it. He felt something electric pass between the beast and himself, and then Arel was there. The cat seemed to duck almost lethargically and Arel's talons missed it, the bird pulling up in a crack of wings and shearing away into the sky.

'Sciler.'

Kerz's voice over the comms. Panic there, too, but quickly under control.

'It's your beast, Sciler, isn't it? I wondered in Cathar, when we never found the body of Starburn's and then yours was a wolf too. No matter. The cat wouldn't come out to save you then, and it isn't going to save you now. Or the girl. Arel can handle both of them.'

You must deal with that one, Jon. The one like you. I'll take care of Chrye.

After all those years, he still remembered the voice. There was nothing else he could do, anyway. Kerz was between him and Chrye and closing in. As Jon made for the emerald wall of trees, the sound search completed itself. He nilled his ears and activated the missing component in the total silence.

It was a faint sawing of wings. Nothing more than that. He tried to remember what it was that had made that sound, and then he was in the cool deep green shadow of the trees.

Chrye felt groggy. She called out to Jon but he wasn't there.

I must be dying, she thought. She remembered the doorway full of light, then someone's voice saying, 'I'm so sorry, Jon,' and then she was here with him and it was all fine again for a short while. And now Jon was gone and she knew that outside the zone she had to be dying.

Something came from nowhere and hit her in the back with incredible force and she fell forward on to her face. The pain seemed to give her a jolt of energy. She didn't want to die yet. She didn't want to die in some zone either, and she wasn't going to die without Jon.

She pushed herself to her feet and saw the bird fuzzily, its wings beating the air as it pulled away again. Everything came slowly back into focus but the bird had swung round and was coming down again, claws out to rake her. She stared at it and sent a hard controlled spear of light straight into its chest. It came right on as if it was riding towards her along the beam.

The bird's eyes were locked on hers and growing bigger, mesmerising her, when something warm and solid slammed into her side, a soft warm animal's body that tumbled her over. As she rolled she saw the cat twist and strike at the passing bird, pulling out a small cloud of feathers. The bird rose strongly, wings beating as it regained height.

Keep down. Conserve your strength.

Chrye heard it clearly. It didn't seem to be coming through the comms unit. She didn't feel like disagreeing with it. There was something of Jon in its voice, but it wasn't Jon.

The bird turned high and swooped again, this time coming down in the distance so low that Chrye lost it in the blur of thick grass. Maybe it had been wounded. It wasn't on any of the scanners.

She looked at the cat. It was the size of a leopard, its coat somehow silver and black at the same time, the light shimmering off it like the sun on dark water. It stared back at her, then crouched back on its haunches and sniffed the air, tilting its head uncertainly. She thought she'd seen it before somewhere.

The long grass flared outwards and flattened an instant before the bird appeared directly behind the cat. The cat reacted late and one of the bird's talons ripped across its face as it turned. A red plume of blood spun in the air. The cat rolled and staggered to its feet, shaking its head, throwing blood on to the crushed grass.

The bird was gone again.

Jon went straight through the trees, sharplight set on broad beam to clear his way, throwing a pattern of dets behind to confuse the trail and laying mines after the dets. He just wanted to get some time. He wasn't going to fool Kerz or lose him. Kerz's scanners would be able to pick through the sparkle Jon was leaving, but it would take time and slow Kerz down.

After five minutes he set the rearguard process on auto/random repeat and nined the ambient audio, letting himself drift back to his memories of

Dirangesept. The sound in his ears still lacked that dissonant sawing, and he tried to visualise the insects that had produced it.

Stepping over the thick tailfin roots of a vast tree, it came to him. There had been clouds of them buzzing around the autoids most of the time in the jungles.

Yes, he thought with a sudden hard thrill. Buzzing around the joints. They couldn't get in because of the repellent gel flooded into the joints, but that's what they wanted, the combination of warmth, darkness and protection offered by the autoid joints. At night there were always thousands of them. Jon had found their presence almost comforting, the tiny black flies with their slender bodies and silvery wings, like midget dragonflies. He remembered their bulbous purple eyes, silicon bright. They'd rest on the armour and crawl over it, preening themselves, sawing their wings, searching for a way in. Every now and then one would work its way through the gel and there would be an irritating itch, but the scratch function would always clear it before it became a problem.

Kerz wouldn't have been able to scratch, though.

Jon checked his scanners. Kerz was at the very edge of the display, staying just in range. Jon stopped dead and remembered Dirangesept. He nilled the audio entirely and let the sounds of the jungle come directly to his mind, gazing up at the vast tiered canopies of the trees and down at the pads of great leaves underfoot with more constantly falling through the branches above. He conjured it all up in his head. Huge dry leaves clattered through the high canopy as if the leaves were shattering branches as they fell, pushing ripples of muffled echoes into the green distance. There were soft strange bird calls like the sounds of stones dropped into faraway pools of calm, deep water, and the snuffling of small animals searching for insects in the rich earth. All the familiar, forgotten noises came back to him and suddenly he realised how much Dirangesept had meant to him, its raw beauty and infinite peace. All the words he'd written had been the products of Dirangesept. They were its hymn, but he had never understood it until now.

The sounds of Dirangesept came to him, building, layer over layer, interweaving like the life of the planet interwove, like it was interwoven by the beasts who loved it.

They thought at first that we wanted to share it with them. They were trying to help us, to show us what they had. To break our tools and show us we didn't need them, not to kill us. And then it was too late.

335

Did Kerz know this? Had he known it all along?

The sounds were building around him. He was vaguely aware of the advancing machine to his rear but he slowly stretched out his arm and watched the metal carapace reflect the glorious colours, the greens and browns of the jungle, as if they were all emanating from him, rippling out from his arm, his fingertips.

At last the sounds were as he remembered them, and there on the fluted gun pods of his hand was a small insect, its wings a soft blur that came gently to rest, its eyes a pair of brilliant multifaceted purple orbs.

The insect took flight as he turned around to see Kerz standing beside the trunk of a vast tree.

Chrye crawled over to the cat's side. The beast was panting unevenly and bleeding from ragged wounds, and the fur on its flanks and haunches was red and matted. It turned its great head to her. One eye was covered with a thick red film.

I can't sense it. I don't understand it. But it senses me and attacks. It reacts as fast as I do. It will kill me.

'Then don't fight it,' Chrye said. She stroked her hand through its bloody fur, feeling the beast's life flickering there. When its eyes met hers she felt something else, something that she recognised from Jon. It's his beast, she thought, that's why. And then she thought, Jon is its human. It isn't doing this for me because it belongs to him, or to stay alive. It cares for Jon and it knows Jon loves me.

'The bird is there to kill us both,' she said. 'It's going for the greater danger. It still thinks that's you.'

Her scanners weren't registering the bird at all. It was agony but she made herself stand up to see it. Arel was there already, pulling out of its dive and hurtling towards them like a scythe through the grass. Chrye took a long breath then pointed at the bird and hit the sharplight. The beam cleared a burning path through the grass that Arel came down like a missile, keening, talons splayed.

She screamed as the cat leapt at her, hitting her and the bird simultaneously. The pain knocked her out for a moment and then she saw the two animals tumbling over in the grass. Arel's talons were deep in the cat's flank while the cat tried to rake its claws into the bird's belly. Chrye tried to stand up again but was too dizzy. The animals disengaged and the bird began to pull away into the air, its wings beating heavily down. One of the cat's flailing claws snagged a wing and dragged the bird down again. Chrye couldn't make out what was happening. She was falling in and out of consciousness. A piercing cry slammed her awake and the bird was rising unsteadily into the air from the cat's body, the cat not moving any longer.

'Are you alive?' Chrye said weakly.

There was nothing.

Kerz stood there, his sharplight trained on Jon. He's checking his scanners, checking everything, Jon thought.

Kerz's machine was different from his and Chrye's. Its body was thick with armour and the weapon pods on its arms and spine were longer and fatter. The sharplight barrel that Jon was staring into was as wide as a fist.

'What have you done, Sciler?'

'I've changed the program, Kerz.'

There was a moment of silence while Jon listened to the comforting background hum of the insects.

'What is it?' Kerz said eventually. 'Lile? Lile's going to turn up again? You think he's going to save you?'

He doesn't know, Jon thought. He hasn't spotted it. He's too involved with everything else.

Chrye, he thought. What happened to her? And the beast?

A bolt of light punched from Kerz's arm, the beam catching Jon across the hip, shooting a lance of terrible searing pain through his side. He smelt burning flesh and saw the swift red flash of function-error alerts at the edge of his vision. The sharplight beam carried on to shear through the trunk of a great tree behind him. The tree creaked and leaned to rest heavily against a pair of others in a long shiver of foliage.

Kerz followed up the sharplight with a det that landed wide as Jon rolled away behind the fallen tree and broke into a fractured run through the jungle. The pain eased slightly as auto-repair functions pulled in. Kerz wasn't immediately behind him, so he slowed down. Kerz would be trying to work out what was changed. Jon had to make his move before he did that, before he could try to reverse it.

He doubled back cautiously until he could see Kerz through the foliage, then he drew together the pictograms and began the spell. Kerz turned to locate him and raised his sharplight, firing through the foliage. The beam hit Jon agonisingly on the arm but he couldn't run again. He had to go through with it now.

Sinking to his knees, he carried on working through the pictograms, then realised it was happening anyway. They had been a focus while he was learning in Cathar, but they weren't necessary any more. He had the power now.

The foliage all around him was smoking, charred and licked with fire from Kerz's sharplight. The beam was still firing, but for some reason Kerz's aim was failing and the spears of light had shifted off to the left and were far too low, deeply studding the ground a few metres clear of Jon. After a while the sharplight fire ceased and a succession of PlasMortar shells surged up randomly through the canopy.

The spell was done. Jon stood up. Ten metres away Kerz was still firing, but reeling slightly. PlasMortar fire was continuing to puncture the high canopy and the freed beams of sunlight cascaded down to fix Kerz as if he were on a spotlit stage.

From Jon's distance Kerz's metal skull was looking faintly blurred. Jon nined and zoomed his eyes until he saw the fluid helmet of flies around Kerz's head. More were gathering around his torso, and a small cloud had already settled there. Kerz was still moving, the sharplight spasmodically throwing out tight jets of light, but his metal carapace seemed alive with flies. Jon watched them begin to filter into the joints at his neck and hips.

Kerz saw them at last. Or maybe he felt them. He stumbled heavily, then locked solid before he could regain his balance, slowly toppling over. The sharplight beam remained discharging into the sky, a blinding tube of light vanishing through the canopy.

Jon stepped over the smoking foliage and stood by the rigid machine. Kerz was saying something faintly over the comms. Jon nined his receive but still couldn't make it out. A single soft syllable repeated over and over.

The insects would be consuming Kerz's wiring now, methodically reconstituting it into a medium for their eggs. Kerz would know all about the process, would be recalling it in all its detail. Now it was terror that paralysed him, but in a few minutes it would be system failure. Later the eggs would hatch to carry on eating away at him. The pain would be unbearable and without release. Kerz was still repeating the same syllable. A mantra, or perhaps it was the start of a spell.

Jon stared into the empty lenses that were Kerz's eyes, wondering what

Kerz was seeing. 'This isn't Cathar. You can't do magic in this zone, can you, Kerz? Your beast never developed you.'

He finally caught the word coming over his comms. Over and over again Kerz was whispering, 'Love.'

For a moment Jon thought he must have heard wrong. It made no sense at all. Then at last, understanding, he shook his head. 'It won't work, Kerz. I told Madsen what to expect. I told him to make Dr Locke disable your exitline, just like you told her to disable mine and Starburn's in Cathar.'

There was silence. Not quite silence, but the silence of Dirangesept. Jon let it wash through him.

'Please,' Kerz murmured once in a voice of pain. Then his voice failed.

Jon stood back and raised his arm. Even Kerz didn't deserve to die like that again. He sent the PlasMortar shell straight into Kerz's skull, but when the smoke cleared the sharplight was still there, slashing up through the foliage. Kerz was still alive in his machine. Even a direct hit with a PlasMortar shell couldn't penetrate that armour.

There was nothing more Jon could do. He was about to turn away when the beam suddenly failed and his head filled with a scream of pain and terror that echoed into silence without him ever hearing it end. Jon began to run, feeling a swelling heat behind him, then like a thump on his spine the explosion of Kerz's autoid and all its ammunition.

The sound was an instant of deafening noise that he nilled instinctively. The thump on his back was still there and increasing, tumbling him forward and off his feet. Trees were vaporising around him. The wave of flame overtook him before the building shockwave punch finally picked him up and carried him with it in the firetide's wake. He nilled everything, pulled in every limb, and flew.

Fire was still all around him when he finally landed. He stood up, running the checks.

Everything still seemed to work. He looked back towards the source and saw something that seemed astonishingly to emerge from the fire, some sort of animal. It moved with incredible speed, untouched by the flames. For a moment it resembled an ape, but it was past him and gone before he could get a full view of it. He was left with the image of a cat vaguely similar to his own beast, but coloured a deep bronze.

He turned around. Love, he was thinking. Kerz's exitline. The word he would never use, never forget.

Jon started back to Chrye at a run.

Chrye felt the ground rumble beneath her and a faraway flare of light and fire briefly silhouetted the bird as it came down towards her again. Its flight was slow and awkward, its wings unable to draw up fully any longer. One of its legs dangled beneath it. It couldn't control its approach and fell on her in a thrashing flurry of wings, using its beak to drag itself up her chest. Pain lanced into her with every step it took until it was staring into her eyes. It was as if she were naked. Its beak closed into a hard yellow dart aimed at her throat.

Behind the bird there was a distant flash of colour and movement. She thought of Jon but it wasn't him, it was another animal, another cat. Not Jon's beast, though, the coat of this one was a tawny bronze. It was too far away.

She swept her hardhand desperately at the bird. The powered metal club began to move without contact straight through its body as its beak came down, and then something seemed to flow into her and flood through her head. She was filled with thoughts and memories until she felt she was going to explode with them. A terrible bolt of fury and desire coursed through her and into the swinging hardhand.

The bird's beak opened in a sudden shrill squawk. Chrye channelled everything inside her into the hardhand, not knowing what she was doing or how it was happening. She had a vision of the tawny cat and she was thinking and remembering everything that had ever happened to her. This is death, she thought. Death is everything.

But somehow the hardhand had become solid to the bird and as she swung it through its curve it locked and took the bird with it. She heard the crunch of bone as the bird's body smashed against the earth.

Chrye lay there and stared at the beast far away, still running towards her, its head bobbing up and down and its legs devouring the distance between them.

I did it, she thought. I did magic.

All of her energy was gone with it, though. She was dimly aware of the bird rising to its feet again, and then just as she knew that there was no more she could do there was a movement behind it, the flash of a silver claw sheathed in soft dark fur. The bird fell for the last time, a tattered heap of blood and feathers, and Jon's cat was lying next to her, warm, wet, just alive, as Chrye was just alive.

340

Thank you, Chrye said, or heard. Or maybe both.

'Shit,' Dr Locke said, punching at consoles. She gave up and hit the screen in front of her with the flat of her hand. 'Shit.'

'What was that?' Madsen said.

'Arel – ah, the machine blew. And Kerz . . . Shit.' She made to stand up.

Madsen put a hand on her shoulder. 'Sit down,' he told her. 'Wait.'

Holding the machine was like holding her body. If Jon closed his eyes he could imagine they were together again in flesh. It was a crazy thought, as crazy as what he saw when he opened his eyes, the machine beside his machine and the two beasts, the great cats staring at them. Her cat and his cat.

She was floating in and out of consciousness. Jon stroked her forehead, whispering to her. 'Chrye, it's nearly over. Kerz's beast showed you how to do magic, but you're still dying. It can't stop that. Nothing can stop that.'

He closed his eyes, not wanting to see her through tears. He imagined her with him back in his room before any of this, as if he could take them there with magic.

'There is a chance for us,' he whispered. 'We can go back with them, Chrye. They can take us. They know us just like Starburn's beast knew him, and they can take us back. On Dirangesept we can be whatever we want to be. We can be ourselves again. You can live, Chrye.'

Her hand was over his and he opened his eyes to stare at her. She said weakly, 'Jon, this is crazy. It isn't real, it's just Kerz trying to take us down one more level. It's Maze.'

'Chrye, I know it's real. I know what happened. I did magic. Not just in the zone. After they shot you I killed them with magic.'

'Those men worked for Maze, Jon. It could all have been fixed, just like that first game you played. Holos, hydraulic rams . . .'

'Chrye, what does it matter now? If you come out of CrySis you'll die. Let them take us with them. Please. I don't want to lose you.'

'How do we know they'll take us with them? How do I know they exist?' She stared at the cats. They seemed so peaceful, grooming each other after the battle. Her beast was patiently licking blood from the flanks of Jon's, while his was washing its face with wetted paws.

The bronze cat had been Kei's. She remembered it as a kitten, dancing in sunlight as if the world had been made for it to play in. She remembered thinking that the world could never end while the cat was still alive, while there was all that energy and life. And she remembered its limp body in the road a few months later. She looked at the cat and said to Jon, 'How do I know anything?'

'You know I want us to be together, don't you?' He was sounding fainter, as if he was moving away. Her arms and legs were growing heavy and starting to lose their feeling. 'You know I love you.'

'Yes, Jon.'

'Do you want to be with me?'

'Yes. I do.'

'Then take the risk, Chrye.'

She barely had the strength to shake her head. 'Kerz never told you he had a Dirangesept zone prepared, did he?'

'So what?'

'There might be more than one. We might never know, Jon. We might be part of Kerz's training program.'

'We won't be. Chrye, your comms are failing. I can hardly hear you. You must decide.'

She sighed. She didn't have the strength to argue with him any more. No strength for anything. She was feeling cold. 'All right, Jon.'

The cats stood up and stretched themselves. Everything else began to fade.

'Christ, what the hell's that?' Madsen yelled.

Dr Locke punched at switches until the alarm snapped off and silence bounced around the room. She was staring at the screens as if they were suddenly as meaningless to her as they were to him.

Madsen said, 'Doctor?'

'Life functions off,' she muttered. 'They're dead. I don't understand it. The woman was dying anyway, but both of them, both pods, that shouldn't, it just can't happen.'

'Well, goddamn fix it.'

She sat back, swivelling her chair around to face Madsen. 'There's nothing wrong with the pods,' she said. 'They are both dead. There's nothing we can do.'

'What about Kerz? Is he alive?'

'His pod still seems to be functioning.'

'Lucky, eh?' Madsen stood up, nudging her cheek with the palm stop in his fist. 'We're going down there again. I want to see them. I want to see for myself.'

The door was open and Kerz was weaving out of the CrySis chamber, half-clothed. His eyes were glazed, focussed elsewhere. Madsen raised the palm stop and then lowered it again. Kerz hadn't even seen him. He was scratching ferociously at his neck and muttering to himself. Madsen stood by as Kerz brushed past. He thought he heard a faint noise like a trans-former hum.

'Kerz?' Dr Locke said, but he stumbled right past her too, muttering, 'They won't . . . stop . . .'

'Let him go,' Madsen told her. 'You'd be wasting your time. Nothing's going to help him, is it?'

She watched Kerz wander down the corridor towards his office. 'No,' she said tonelessly.

Madsen pushed her into the CrySis chamber. Kerz's pod was open, the floor around it wet with gel. Madsen lifted the lids of the other two pods. The gel in Chrye's was at room temperature. Her body looked as if it was bathing in blood. The bandaging had drifted away from her wound and was floating around her like waterweed. Madsen reached into the gel of Jon's pod and checked for a carotid pulse. There was none. The body felt cool. They were both dead. He gestured at Dr Locke anyway. 'Drain them. I want to be certain.'

'There's no point. They're dead. I told you.'

He brought the palm stop up. 'They might not know that, Dr Locke,' he said. 'This project is over now. Soon Kerz will be dead, and everything's going to end with him. No more zones, no more doubt.'

Dr Locke still didn't move.

'Drain them, Doctor. If they're dead, what does it matter? Maze will be shrivelling in the heat tomorrow. There won't be any more Dirangesept projects once it gets out what's been going on here. No more cover-ups. The ministries will deny any involvement but I don't give a damn about that.' He gestured towards her with the palm stop. 'Kerz will be the last suicide, Doctor, and I can easily fix it that his last conscious act was to kill you. Or else you can live and let Kerz take all the responsibility.'

Dr Locke went to the console at the head of Chrye's pod and activated the evacuation function. Madsen stood beside her and added, 'But if you were lying, Doctor, if either of them so much as twitches, I swear I'll kill you.'

The gel in Chrye's pod began to sink away. Madsen watched the level fall, a red margin of blood staining the rim of the emptying tank. When the gel was halfway down, Chrye's body started to beach on the tank's base. The skin on her face was pale and waxy. Her head nodded to the side and her mouth opened as if to take a last breath of the ebbing gel. After another moment a slow stream of fat bubbles burst on the gel's surface. The process halted and a warning light started to flash red on the console.

Madsen felt his hand start to shake, squeezing the palm stop.

Dr Locke held a hand up, saying quickly, 'It's okay, Madsen. It's okay. Back off. The fibres of the bandaging are clogging the valves, that's all. She's dead like I told you. The pods are delicate, they aren't designed for contamination. I can flush the valves and carry on. You'll see.'

Madsen breathed out slowly, then nodded at her. 'Do it.'

When Chrye's body was at rest in the empty pod, he reached down and touched her cheek with the palm of his hand. He held the contact for a while before straightening again.

'Okay,' he said softly. 'Next one.'

The gel fled evenly from the other pod until Jon's head lolled back on the hard ceramic base. Madsen gazed at the body, but nothing moved. He whispered, 'So long, both of you. Luck, wherever.'

'As I told you,' Dr Locke said tersely. 'Dead.'

An air pocket hissed and cleared beneath the pod and Madsen rubbed his neck for a moment. He carried his hand on up to his hair, then dropped it back to his side again. 'Okay,' he said wearily. He raised the palm stop and pointed it at Dr Locke's head, his arm stiff. The vanes slid out between his knuckles. 'Tell me, Doctor, do you believe in an afterlife?'

She stepped back. 'You said . . .'

The corner of his mouth twitched. He said, 'You of all people, you believe what anyone tells you?'

He squinted at her for a long moment, then let the palm stop fall away. The vanes retracted and he slipped it into his pocket. 'I'm leaving. I need some coffee.'

Chrye opened her eyes and smiled. Almost as far as she could see, the plain was a vast field of yellow flowers. Everywhere there were cats sleeping and sunning themselves. In the distance was the green jungle.

She looked at Jon, then looked down at herself.

'Oh, Jon,' she said. 'Chrysanthemums.' She bent down and picked one. It looked so real.